Ensure Plausible Deniability

A Novel

by

D.M. Ulmer

Ensure Plausible Deniability

First Edition
Copyright © 2012 by D.M. Ulmer
All rights reserved.
First Printing 2012

ISBN-13: 978-0-9846638-4-2

Technical Review Editor: Nelson O. Ottenhausen
Managing Editor: Dari Bradley
Sr. Editor: Doris Littlefield
Cover Art: Hal Tatlow and Phillip Todesco

This is a fictional story: Use or mention of historical events, places, names of anyone or any similarity of the story line to actual persons, places or events is purely coincidental.

Published by Patriot Media, Inc.
Publishing America's Patriots

P.O. Box 5414
Niceville, FL 32578
United States of America
www.patriotmediainc.com

Special Thanks To

My wife Carol for encouragement and affording me time to feed this writing passion.

Doris Littlefield, editor extraordinaire, for keeping the train on the tracks.

Kris and Hal Tatlow for sharing their honeymoon story and to Hal and his son-in-law Phillip (Skip) Todesco for the superb jacket art.

Phil Giambri for editing help and authoring *Tears for Little Rico.*

George Bass for sharing his endless repertoire of after battery tales. George, you know I believe every word of them to be true.

Captain Jim Patton, USN (Ret), for his on-target advice in Submarine tactics of the mid-sixties.

Richard Raymond III, USNA '54 Class Poet for *The Pig Boat and the Crazy Ivan.*

Joan Walsh and Cindy McLane for advice on how characters should be dressed in period clothing styles.

Las Plumas Literary Critique Group of King County, WA for invaluable advice and counsel.

Nelson Ottenhausen, Dari and Ed Bradley for firm hands on the rudder and endless patience.

Dedication

For John Spear, diesel boat executive officer second to none.

To the memory of Brad Pace, Quartermaster Seaman. Every skipper should have such an exceptional periscope assistant.

DOWN, DOWN UNDERNEATH THE OCEAN

"... So rig for dive and take her down
Go Down, Down Underneath the Ocean,
Fearless men will find renown
In the deep blue underneath the sea."

*U.S. Navy Submariners' song, Lyrics and music
by Captain William J. Ruhe, USN and R. M. Wall*

The Pigboat and the *Crazy Ivan*
A Ballad of the Fleet
(Tune: *The Midshipmite* by Charles Dibden)

'Twas in sixty-five on a summer's day,
Cheerily, my lads, yo-ho!
We'd left the pier and were underway,
Round toe of "Boot", bound for Naples Bay,
Cheerily, my lads, yo-ho!

Chorus:
With an "Oogah! Oogah!" to clear the bridge,
We fight our battles below,
For the submarine is a threat unseen,
Sing cheerily, lads, yo-ho!

The sea was calm and the sun was bright,
Cheerily, my lads, yo-ho!
When a stranger warship hove in sight,
With a look that said she wished to fight,
Cheerily, my lads, yo-ho!
Chorus:

Now here we sailed, all alone at sea,
Cheerily, my lads, yo-ho!
On a mission as peaceful as could be,
But the Roosky bristled with guns, did she,
Cheerily, my lads, yo-ho!
Chorus:

Coming up astern, and a bone in her teeth,
Cheerily, my lads, yo-ho!
We could not dive, to attack beneath,
She seemed to bear us a funeral wreath,
Cheerily, my lads, yo-ho!
Chorus:

We were bound by the sacred Nautical Rules,
Cheerily, my lads, yo-ho!
To hold our course, like a pack of fools,
But the Roosky sailors, they grinned like ghouls,
Cheerily, my lads, yo-ho!
Chorus:

She passed us close, on the starboard side,
Cheerily, my lads, yo-ho!
The margin only a whisker-wide,
Just daring and hoping that we'd collide,
Cheerily, my lads, yo-ho!
Chorus:

But *our* skipper, cool as a keg of beer,
Cheerily, my lads, yo-ho!
Neatly dodged, and repaid their sneer,
With a thumb to the nose and one in the ear,
Cheerily, my lads, yo-ho!
Chorus:

Then away we sailed, never fired a shot,
Cheerily, my lads, yo-ho!
But the Rooskies knew–and what fool did not–
We'd been ready to sink 'em on the spot!
Cheerily, my lads, yo-ho!
Chorus:

So the Cold War warmed, by a mere degree,
And we had the photos to show,
Being in the right, would have won that fight,
Sing *Cheerily, my lads, yo-ho!*
Chorus:

Richard Raymond III 10-5-11

Introduction

By mid-1960, the Soviet Navy grew concerned over escalating NATO domination of the Mediterranean Sea. NATO forces, composed mainly of U.S. carrier battle groups, had free run of what they termed *our private swimming pool.* NATO ports bordering the northern *Med* welcomed the warships. Their limitless needs inflated economies of the host nations.

No NATO nations edged the southern Mediterranean coast. Of those that did, most had aversions to this new *presumptuous* organization. However, none wished to jeopardize sovereignty by accommodating Soviet forces.

To establish a presence in the *Med,* Soviets had to base naval units at anchorages in international waters south of the Greek Peloponnese peninsula at Kythira and on Hurd Bank east of Malta. Only cargo-oiler ships traveling over long distances to the Med from Sevastopol on the Black Sea supplied logistic support. This path led through the Dardanelles under watchful eyes of NATO member Turkey at Istanbul. Consequently, 1965 found only eleven Soviet warships operating openly in the *Med*, nine of these auxiliaries.

Soviet units flexed their muscles by harassing NATO diesel-electric submarines. Soft and vulnerable, these warships made easy targets. Risk of collision with submerged U.S. ballistic missile submarines deployed in the Mediterranean Sea required them to move about on the surface—diving to evade not an option.

The Soviet Navy embarked upon an aggressive agenda throughout the world's oceans provoking head-to-head confrontations with U.S. Navy warships on the surface and beneath the seas. Ensuing games of *chicken* between vessels armed with nuclear weapons portended disaster. It would take only one hotheaded skipper on either side to go off half-cocked and plunge mankind into World War III.

Diesel submarines, regarded somewhat as poor cousins in the U.S. Sixth Fleet, deployed to the *Med* mainly to provide target services for surface and air ASW forces. Blind eyes turned to diesel submarine superb performance in NATO exercises left their achievements largely ignored.

A U.S. diesel-boat once conducted twelve successful simulated attacks, four against aircraft carriers—this achieved in a two-week period. Nonetheless, a loud death knell sounded for the U.S. diesel submarine community.

The advent of nuclear power permitted indefinite submerged endurance, thus eliminating need for exposure above the surface, long the Achilles' heel of diesel boats. Congress withheld authorization for new diesel submarines. Touting tactical ability of these warships might well have overturned this decision much to the despair of Navy decision makers. In ten years, the last diesel-electric submarine would be stricken from the registry of U.S. warships, ending an era spanning three quarters of a century.

The nuclear power broom swept clean. Selection criteria would in ten years produce a submarine force manned only by officers with demonstrated academic excellence. Top of the class standings pushed aside tactical fitness. Demonstrated competence in the field had no bearing on an officer's fitness to serve aboard nuclear powered ships. And so skills that drastically reduced Japan's ability to conduct a maritime war, achieved with less than two percent of all Allied assets assigned to the Southwest Pacific, no longer mattered. Demise of U.S. diesel-electric submarines to make room for nuclear propulsion, a necessary event to maintain tactical superiority at sea, raised other issues. Might rejection of demonstrated submariner excellence have later exacted grave consequences?

Many characters in *Ensure Plausible Deniability* appear in *prequel* novels, *Shadows of Heroes* and *The Cold War Beneath*. These include a U.S. submarine penetration of Soviet waters the winter of 1949, then a *favor* returned when Russian submariners penetrated waters about New England on a mid-fifties clandestine mission of their own.

Thus are spawned the multi-conflicts of *Ensure Plausible Deniability.*

Cast of Characters

AMERICANS:

Baker, Chris, 28, Radioman First Class, *Pershing*
Beyers, Frank, 32, Radioman Chief, COB, *Clamagore*, wife Helen
Bondi, Benito (Ben), 42, Captain, PR Officer, Chairman JCS
Bradley, Ed, 58, Admiral, Chairman JCS, wife Dari
Bryan, William (Bill), 38, Captain, Aide to Chairman JCS
Center, Morrie, 32, Engineering Officer, *Pershing*
Dunn, Joseph (Joe), 30, Navigation school, assigned to *Pershing*
Epworth, Raymond, 62, Vice Admiral, Director of Naval Reactors
Ferranti, Lorraine, 32 (maiden name: Horner)
Ferranti, Rick, 45, Captain, DNI Agent
Ford, Dorothy, 33, CPO, CNO
Giambri, Phillip (Phil), 21, Sonarman, *Clamagore*
Gilliam, Frank, 82, Grandfather of Lorraine Ferranti
Harkins, Cliff, 39, Captain, Commander NATO Submarines,
    Mediterranean, wife Ruth 39, eight children
Hayes, Jamie, 37, CPO, missile fire control, *Pershing*
Howell, John, 19, Quartermaster Seaman, *Clamagore*
Junin, Jacqueline, 32, French Doctor, Palma Majorca
Keating, Bridget, 23, cousin to Tim Keating, Teacher, Naples,
    Soprano Songstress
Keating, Tim, 25, LTJG, *Clamagore*
Kolb, Denny, 29, Lieutenant, *Clamagore*
Martin, Terry, 57, Admiral, CNO, wife Brenda, children Emily 25,
    Paul 22
Meli, Ricardo, 18, Radio Seaman, RMSN, *Pershing*
Omensen, Ken, 25, Radioman 3rd Class, *Clamagore*
Owens, Buddy, 19, Seaman, *Clamagore*
Pace, Brad, 19, Quartermaster Seaman, *Clamagore*
Poulus, Greg, (Yeo), 38, MCPO, CNO, wife Joy

Rapinian, Emilio, 45, Stewardsman 2nd Class, *Clamagore*
Redmond, Phil, 35, Commander, CO, *Clamagore*, wife Katherine,
 children David 14, Vera 9, Theresa 6
Roberts, Adrian, 29, CPO
Roman, Benson, 27, LTJG, *Clamagore*
Scott, Paul, 29, LT, *Clamagore/Pershing*, wife Jean Ann 26, sons
 Benjamin 6, David 4
Tatlow, Hal, 28, Interior Communications Electrician 2nd Class,
 Clamagore, wife Kris
Wilcox, Harold (Doc), 24, Hospital Corpsman 1st Class,
 Clamagore
Williams, Peter (Pete), 39, CO, *Pershing*
Zane, David B., (Dave), 35, LCDR, Exec Officer, *Clamagore*, wife
 Dale, daughter Bea 9

RUSSIANS:

Denisov, Piotr, 33, *Kapitan* 2nd Rank, *Mayakovsky*, wife Irene,
 sons Pasha 5, Andrushka 3
Foster, Reginald, (Rege), 50, Soviet spy portraying an Englishman
 tracking Earl Adams
Knyazev, Evgenij, 34, *Kapitan* 2nd Rank, *Zampolit, Mayakovsky*
Kurinnyj, Maksim, 37, *Kapitan* 1st Rank, Commanding Officer,
 Soviet destroyer, *Spokoinyy*
Martinov, Pasha, 38, Soviet Agent returned persona non grata,
 married, two sons, godfather to Denisov's sons
Norovsky, Vasiliy, 51, (aka Earl Adams), U.S. Intel Agent
Smirnov, Andrej, 31, *Kapitan* 3rd Rank, Exec Officer, *Mayakovsky*
Sokolv, Oleg, 29, *Kapitan* 3rd Rank, Navigation Officer,
 Mayakovsky
Zhadan, Aleksandr, 33, Warrant Officer, *Mayakovsky*

Ensure Plausible Deniability

Chapter 1

USS *Clamagore*, a Guppy III diesel-electric submarine, plied the eastern Mediterranean Sea on a cloudless late summer afternoon in 1965. Westbound from Athens to Naples, Italy, she passed south of the Greek Island, Kythira. Uneventful thus far, *Clamagore*'s voyage stood on the brink of an abrupt change.

"Exec up," shouted Lieutenant Commander (LCDR) Dave Zane.

Lieutenant Paul Scott, Officer of the Deck (OOD), responded, "Come up, XO."

Scott passed his binoculars to Zane and gestured toward the starboard quarter. A Soviet Kotlin class destroyer sat in Kythira anchorage, black smoke billowing from her stack a signal she would soon be underway.

Zane studied the Russian, thumbs pressed firmly against his temples to steady the optics. "It's a Kotlin all right." *Wasp-head fire control director and slim net radar—dead give aways.* "Call the captain, Paul."

Russians had begun harassing U.S. submarines running on the surface. This served notice to NATO allies they no longer dominated the Mediterranean waters. The Soviets knew submarines in transit on the surface did not dive to evade. They perhaps knew or did not know the reason; U.S. nuclear powered Ballistic Missile Submarines patrolled the Med, presenting a hazard to submerged navigation.

Clamagore moved ahead on four engines through a flat calm sea at seventeen knots. The Kotlin weighed anchor and began racing toward *Clamagore* with the bone in her teeth—a white bow wave caused by the ship's high-speed.

"Captain up!" Commander (CDR) Phil Redmond mounted the tiny bridge. "What've we got, Paul?"

"Kotlin at one-six-zero, closing, Captain."

Redmond needed no binoculars to verify this. "I see him," he declared then ordered the lookouts, "Stay alert, lads ... don't get so hung up on the Kotlin that you miss something else."

"Aye, Captain," the men chorused continuing to scan the horizon but frequently looking aft toward the closing Soviet—their hearts pounding. *Russians are the bad guys* went through their minds. They knew at the Kotlin's current speed, its prow could slice through *Clamagore*'s three-quarter inch pressure hull like a messcook's cleaver opening a tin of fresh milk. Visions of floating helplessly in the sea dried their mouths.

"Okay, Paul, I have the conn." Redmond took charge of maneuvering the ship.

Scott acknowledged, "Stand relieved, Captain. Ahead standard on four, heading two-six-three."

Nodding, Redmond turned to Zane. "Lay below and hang the MK-four on number one." *Clamagore* carried a camera adaptable to periscope optics. "Get a shot every thirty seconds. Have the quartermaster log times. Get a good record."

"Aye, sir," said Zane as he hastened below.

International rules of the road require burdened vessels to maneuver and avoid privileged ships. Approaching from *Clamagore*'s stern burdened the Russian. A catch-22 in this rule put *Clamagore* between the devil and the deep blue sea. Privileged vessels must maintain course and speed until well clear—2,000 yards.

The Kotlin approached from dead astern then veered left, overtaking *Clamagore* to port one hundred yards. She pulled ahead, her huge bow waves tumbling over *Clamagore*'s low forward deck. Five hundred yards ahead, the Russian stopped and made a slow right turn bringing her to rest squarely on *Clamagore*'s track.

International rules define the condition *in extremis* when both vessels must maneuver to avoid collision. *Clamagore* and the Russian reached this and both became burdened vessels.

Redmond initiated evasive action. "All stop, left full rudder."

Clamagore barely missed the marauding Kotlin.

When clear, the captain ordered, "All ahead standard, come right to two-six-three," and then, "Conn ... Exec to the bridge."

A moment later, Redmond asked Zane, "Did you get the shots? What do you think?"

"I did, Captain ... is that dumb SOB completely out of his gourd?"

"Doubt he acted on his own ... likely some new asinine Soviet policy he hates as much as us."

The starboard lookout yelled, "Here she comes again!"

Contradicting Redmond's notion, the Kotlin raced by to starboard, her rail manned by sailors sneering at the beleaguered submarine. The Russian moved ahead again swinging across *Clamagore*'s bow, dousing the forward deck a second time. Satisfied with her mischief, the marauder returned to her anchorage.

Dave Zane said, "I admire your cool, Captain."

Redmond replied, "I learned at PCO (Prospective Commanding Officer) school ... never do anything dumb."

Zane grinned. "I'll remember that, Captain."

Master Chief Petty Officer Greg Poulus knocked at the Chief of Naval Operations office door.

Admiral Terry Martin called out, "Come in, Yeo."

Poulus entered the spacious office on the Pentagon E-ring, the outermost offices of the building—only rooms with an outside view. The admiral, a tall, slender man, his once brown curly hair mostly gray, sat at his desk, flanked by three flags, the American, the U.S. Navy and a dark blue one with four white stars indicating the admiral's rank. A window facing northwest admitted a final sliver of late afternoon sun.

As a writer, Poulus worked for the admiral from the time Martin made flag rank twelve years earlier. Proper Navy form of address for Poulus would normally be Chief, but they had been together so long and old habits tend to die hard. Martin addressed him as Yeo, Poulus's rating specialty at the onset of their association.

Martin said, "Have a seat." He poured two cups of coffee from a carafe. "Here, Yeo. Ran the numbers yesterday and figure you've served me at least twenty-one thousand black and bitters. About time I poured one for you."

"Thank you, Admiral."

An awkward silence prevailed, despite the genuine friendship between them. Poulus, technically still in the Navy, observed protocol.

Poulus had just completed twenty-one years of Navy service, his retirement ceremony occurred earlier in the day. He stayed on to help his replacement, a WAVE CPO Dorothy Ford, find her way about and to familiarize her with the admiral's idiosyncrasies.

At his ceremony, Poulus declared, "I'm on the payroll till midnight so I'll stick around till the job's done."

In 1945, at age eighteen, Poulus served aboard USS *Opaleye* on her final war patrol in the southwest Pacific commanded by Terry Martin. They lost contact until Martin's selection to flag rank nine years later.

They reminisced, Poulus wanting to hear most about the last Japanese ship sunk in World War II. Then Lieutenant Commander Martin attacked a hapless coastal patrol vessel. Though victory not significant, Terry returned from the war with at least one scalp under his belt.

CPO Ford's knock on the office door ended their discussion.

She announced, "Captain Bryan on the line for you, Admiral."

Bryan worked for Admiral Ed Bradley at the Chairman of the Joint Chiefs of Staff (CJCS) office.

Martin said, "I wonder what Admiral Bradley has for me today?"

Both men rose as if on cue and shook hands; Poulus knew their final meeting had ended.

With a choked voice, Poulus said, "Admiral, it's been an honor and a pleasure to work for you."

Martin smiled. "That's a two-way street, Yeo." He recognized Poulus to be on the verge of tears and resorted to levity. "But I have at times wondered who worked for whom."

With a grin, Poulus responded, "I'll bet you did, Admiral."

He turned to leave, but Martin stopped him. "Greg."

Poulus replied, "Yes, Admiral?"

"I'd really like to hear you say my name."

"Thank you for everything you've done for me, Terry," the words rolling off easily as Martin knew they would.

"And thank you for saying that."

When Poulus departed, Martin returned to his desk and picked up the phone. "Admiral Martin here."

"Captain Bryan, Admiral. Please don't lop off the messenger's head. Admiral Bradley instructed me to tell you to put on your steel-toed shoes, asbestos britches, hardhat, and get your sorry submariner butt up to his office right now."

Martin knew Admiral Ed Bradley like the back of his hand. "I'll bet the admiral didn't say butt, did he?"

"No, Admiral."

"Can you give me a subject, please?"

"Russian Naval Attaché asked for a meeting. Claims our diesel boats harass his warships in the Mediterranean. The situation is serious and requires immediate attention. He threatens a press conference if we don't cease and desist immediately."

Phil Redmond gloated. A full street ahead of Dave Zane, he stood on the verge of soundly defeating his exec in their cribbage game. They sat behind half empty coffee cups, unwinding after their incident with the Soviet Kotlin. *Clamagore*'s Operations Officer, Lieutenant (LT) Denny Kolb, looked on. A knock on the panel by the wardroom entrance interrupted.

Radioman Omensen handed Kolb a clipboard. "This just in, sir."

Denny's eyes widened. "I think your game just ended, Captain," then handed Redmond the operational immediate message.

The message read:

```
FROM CTF 69 TO USS CLAMAGORE.
REF: YOUR REPORT OF ENCOUNTER WITH
SOVIET KOTLIN DD.
   HELICOPTER FROM CARRIER USS
BRANDYWINE EN ROUTE YOUR MOVREP
POSITION, ETA 11750ZAUG65.
   COMMENCE TRANSMIT INTERMEDIATE VHF
150.6 MHZ SIGNAL THIRTY MINUTES PRIOR
```

```
FIVE SECONDS EACH MINUTE FOR HELO
HOMING.
     ASSEMBLE DATA RELATING TO INCIDENT.
CO LCDR PHILIP REDMOND USN DIRECTED
REPORT NAPLES VIA HELO WITH DATA.
     LCDR DAVID B. ZANE USN ORDERED
TEMPORARY CO DURATION CLAMAGORE
TRANSIT NAPLES.
```

Kolb said, "It's almost time. I'll have the VHF signal lighted off," and departed for the radio shack only to find the astute Omensen had beaten him to it.

Redmond said, "Dave, you're getting some stick time. Up for it?"

The captain knew the answer but wanted to hear it from Zane.

Dave said, "Any officer with a command opportunity is an idiot not to jump on it. I'll have Tim assemble the data along with the pics."

LTJG Tim Keating, as Weapons Officer, had collateral duty as ship's photographer.

Redmond hid the fact his pulse quickened on learning how he would travel. Though unconcerned over Dave Zane's ability to command, getting picked off *Clamagore* by helo did not set well. He'd done this on his first submarine assignment; a terrifying experience he vowed would never happen again.

Zane added, "We'll take stills of the Quartermaster's Notebook to cover the incident."

"Dave," Redmond said, "audit the data inventory. Be sure we got all bases covered. It's important, so I'll go re-audit when you're done."

"Aye, Captain. We'll put everything in a waterproof sack in case the *zoomies* (Navy flyers) drop you in the drink."

With a grin, Redmond said, "Damn, I wish you hadn't said that. But just in case, keep copies of everything here. And pack three sets of skivvies (underwear) and my toilet kit."

"Will do, Captain."

Officer of the Deck (OOD) LTJG Benson Roman's voice blurted over the 21MC tactical intercom system, "Wardroom … Bridge, notify the captain we have a Navy helicopter approaching."

Redmond answered, "Captain has the word, Bridge. Slow speed to one third on two engines. Have the anchor detail lay on deck to assist with helo transfer."

"Bridge, aye," Roman replied.

Moments later, Phil Redmond stood on the forward main deck wearing a life vest and foul weather jacket, the waterproof sack slung securely over his shoulder and tied about his waist.

Relieving Roman of the conn, Zane maneuvered *Clamagore* to let the helo make an upwind approach to starboard. Prop wash engulfed the main deck and engine noise required hand signals for coordination.

A cable from the helo boom had a loop to slip over Redmond's shoulders and beneath his arms. Radioman Chief Frank Beyers, Chief of the Boat (COB), checked with the captain and signaled the helo crewman to haul away. Prop wash put Redmond in a wild swing about *Clamagore*'s superstructure as the helo crew hauled him up.

Dave Zane ordered periscopes and radio antenna lowered immediately, but not before Redmond swung dangerously close. *So much for my first command decision.*

A moment later, Redmond tumbled into the helo and it soon disappeared over the horizon.

Dave Zane turned the conn back to Benson Roman. "Resume standard speed on four engines. Have the navigator make sure we're within the MOVREP box."

Submarines resubmit MOVREPS if they move beyond ten nautical miles from their reported positions of intended movement (PIM).

"Aye, Captain."

Hearing the title surprised Zane, but only for an instant. He commanded now. *Don't think I'll move into the skipper's stateroom just yet,* Zane thought as he went below. *He'll likely want it back when we hit Naples. It'll take three days and I'll savor every minute.*

A pair of Marine guards in dress blue uniforms stood before the Joint Chiefs of Staff (JCS) vault entrance. Terry and Captain Bill Bryan approached; the Marines snapped to attention, delivered crisp salutes then diligently checked the officers' IDs.

Bryan conducted Terry into the vault and said, "Have a seat, sir.

Admiral Bradley will be with you shortly."

"Thank you, Bill. Is he armed? Didn't have time to get my helmet and flak jacket."

"Hopefully, you won't need them, sir. Preliminary reports from CTF sixty-nine indicate the Soviets are doing the provoking. So the admiral has pulled in his horns—slightly."

"I know the officer in command at Naples personally. Captain Cliff Harkins. He's a charge-taker who gets things right."

The officers rose as Admiral Bradley entered the vault accompanied by Captain Benito Bondi, JCS Public Relations Officer (PRO).

Bradley, a small man, extended his hand to Martin. "Good to see you, Terry. This is Ben Bondi, my PR guy."

They exchanged handshakes.

Bondi asked, "Do you remember me, Admiral? It's been a while. Ten years ago at Norfolk when you had a Soviet Whiskey poking around New London."

"I do, Ben, also the incident. You did a helluva job preventing leaks from blowing our operation."

Looking irritated, Admiral Bradley said, "Let's get down to business. The CNO is a busy guy and we shouldn't waste his time. Is that so, Terry?"

Martin replied, "When your boss asks that question, there's only one answer, Admiral—Yes."

"Terry, the Russian embassy says your damn bubbleheads are provoking their ships in the Mediterranean. Your guy in Naples says not." Bradley minced no words. "I'm surprised you don't know all about this already."

Responding, Martin said, "I'm aware our units occasionally stare each other down over there, but so far nothing to get excited about. I've had no word of this latest event. Captain Cliff Harkins commands NATO submarines in the Med. He's a sharp officer. He likely reasons no blood, no foul and saw no urgency in making an immediate report."

"The Soviets claim otherwise, Terry. I preempted you and directed your guy to get the facts here ASAP. Didn't take him long. He's faxed a myriad of photos and has hard copy on the way. In the meantime, I thought you could make some sense of what we have."

Captain Bondi spread the material over a large table.

Seconds later, Bradley inquired, "So what do you think, Terry?"

Martin answered, "We've got enough to recreate the entire incident … pics, time they were taken, quartermaster log entries. I believe it's not our fault. The Kotlin is overtaking and the burdened vessel."

Bradley asked, "Kotlin?"

Martin said, "A destroyer … three thousand tons, four hundred feet length and a forty-two foot beam. Not too effective … they only made twenty-eight of them. CO's likely not the sharpest knife in the drawer, which may account in part for what happened. Kotlins make thirty-eight knots, about twenty more than our diesel boats on the surface. They've got the required mobility, but no big loss if they get damaged in the process."

Bondi asked, "Why do they focus on submarines?"

Martin replied, "We operate alone, so no witnesses. Rest of the Sixth Fleet runs in battle group formations."

Bradley asked, "So how certain are you this was not our fault?"

Martin replied, "Quite, Admiral. *Clamagore* maintained course and speed and maneuvered only to avoid collision after the Russian created the extremis situation. Our guy complied with the rules perfectly."

Heaving a sigh, Bradley said, "I see. If it's so open and shut, why do you think the Soviet Attaché wants to schedule a press conference?"

Bondi answered. "Notice they want to talk to us first, likely to see what we have. They won't make an assertion if we can blow their story out of the water."

Bradley asked, "Ben, what do the Soviets hope to gain from this?"

Bondi replied, "They use our constitution as a weapon against us, our free press in particular that likes nothing better than beating up on the military. The Russians know our media influences public opinion. Unlike in the Soviet Union, what the people think matters here. Riling up the American public could get us pulled out of the Med. That would leave only the balance of NATO forces to maintain stability there."

Next, Bradley asked for recommendations.

Martin said, "I suggest we give the Russians a meeting, but take the initiative. *Clamagore*'s materials give us a strong argument. Point out dangers and recommend both navies end this practice."

Then Bradley asked, "Comments?"

Hearing none, he directed Bondi to schedule the Soviet Attaché meeting immediately upon enactment of Martin's suggestion.

Later, Terry Martin phoned his old friend, Captain Rick Ferranti. "Rick, how would you and Lorraine like an all expense tour to romantic Capri and neighboring Naples?"

Chapter 2

Mooring space in the Mediterranean is scarce. Ships tie up stern to the dock permitting four ships to use space required by one moored lengthwise. The Med-moor involves dropping the anchor three hundred yards from the dock then back to the dock while paying out anchor chain. The stern is moored fast and anchor chain tightened to hold the bow seaward.

Clamagore rounded the Molo San Vincenzo at Naples and maneuvered for her Med-moor, a novel operation for U.S. warships.

Dave Zane stood supervising Conning Officer Paul Scott through the maneuver, though Paul needed little help. Best ship handler aboard, he'd done this often.

LCDR Phil Redmond came aboard and greeted Zane.

"You didn't break my boat, did you?"

"Not so's you'd notice, Captain."

Zane went on, "But transiting the Strait of Messina ... are rules of the road repealed there?"

Redmond answered, "A bit snug, but a piece of cake for an old salt like you.

"Let's go below, Dave. Got lots to tell you. For openers, we're losing Paul Scott. They want him at the Polaris Weapons School. SSBNs (ballistic missile submarines) are turned out faster than we can man 'em."

"Means an officer short and our most experienced one."

They wore tropical white long uniforms, short sleeve shirts, full-length trousers, white shoes and Navy blue shoulder boards with a gold star and striped to match their ranks. Like outfits worn by Good Humor ice cream salesmen, they were called ice cream suits.

Tim Keating, OOD, secured the maneuvering watch and set the regular in port watch. *Clamagore* crewmen crowded the limited toilet facilities and prepared to visit *bella Napoli*.

In the wardroom, Redmond related the CNO's concern over escalating interactions between U.S. and Soviet warships. "Until something's worked out, we'll comply with international rules." Then said to Tim Keating, "You got high grades on the pics. They got us off the hook for Russian allegations that *we* harassed *them*." Redmond grinned. "But a new ship reg, gentlemen. The captain may not be picked off this pipe in a helo."

Redmond broke the news on Paul Scott's transfer back to the states.

Denny Kolb spoke up. "Does that mean we gotta have a party, even here in the Med?"

"Right," the captain affirmed. "And Benson being *George* (most junior officer aboard) gets the honor. Paul leaves tomorrow so it'll have to be tonight."

Roman answered, "You got it, Captain."

His triumphal look didn't make Redmond suspicious.

"We've got to check in at CTF sixty-nine Headquarters. Benson … you, Denny and Tim go." He tossed the rental car keys to Paul. "I need at least one competent officer to keep these guys out of trouble."

The *Clamagore* fearsome foursome—Denny Kolb, Tim Keating, Benson Roman and Paul Scott—sped along the Naples waterfront in a tiny Fiat rented for ship's official business. The likelihood of business by the foursome being completely official rarely occurred, although motoring to Naval Headquarters in Naples gave a semblance of it. There they'd perform a bureaucratic rain dance deemed necessary to help newcomers fit quickly into the local scene.

Paul Scott, twenty-nine, the duty driver kept himself in superb physical shape. Five eleven, dark straight hair, tipping the scales at one-seventy-five, he appeared a good-looking man, though not particularly handsome.

Uncertainty of the route affected Paul's driving, earning frequent horn blasts and gestures raising questions about his family lineage.

Tim Keating said, "Scrub Paul for the beer mug farewell gift. Let's get him some wool socks."

Each officer departing *Clamagore* received a traditional wardroom gift: a pewter beer mug engraved with his name, submariner dolphin badge and bracketed dates denoting his period of service.

Tim, newest officer aboard *Clamagore*, a soft-spoken, quick-witted Boston Irish-American had earned a special niche in Paul's esteem.

WHOOSH.

Another near traffic miss and a flurry of audible and visual signals. Paul, his first drive in Naples, looked about for a landmark to confirm their progress toward Naval Headquarters.

"Tim, can you tell from that map if we're going the right way?"

"No, but I see a sidewalk café where we can stop to take bearings … and a few other things."

Officiality of the foursome's business approached a new threshold none wished to breach. Conspicuous in their ice cream suits, the four officers seated themselves behind large glasses of dark red Chianti at a table with an umbrella. American tourists among the café patrons cast glances at the young men.

Benson Roman complained, "We never should've worn uniforms. People will write their Congressmen and complain about using tax money to let us play here."

Denny Kolb, stocky with a sharp-nose and sleepy-eyed countenance inherited from his Bavarian forebears added, "Too bad we can't speak Italian. Maybe they'd think we're in a different Navy."

Paul countered, "Not a chance. These haircuts. No self-respecting Italian would permit themselves to look like us."

Suddenly Benson's eyeballs threatened to pop from their sockets. "*Mama mia!* I think I'm in love!"

A striking Italian woman walked along the *strada* by their table. Her sensuous gait and self-confidence bespoke a woman fully aware of her beauty. A brief white sundress accentuated near perfect proportions and each graceful step stressed her sensuality better than had she been totally nude.

Tim asked, "Did you say love or lust, Benson?"

Four pairs of eyes made no effort to hide their stares.

Benson said longingly, "Maybe she likes uniforms. If she does … to hell with the Congressmen."

"Not likely," said Tim. "She knows the pay's not good enough and has bigger game in mind."

A balding, overweight, middle-aged man in a handsome silk suit validated the assertion. He greeted the object of Benson's sudden infatuation with a warm embrace and ushered her into a cherry-red Lamborghini parked nearby.

Benson said, "Why doesn't she let me take her away from all that?"

Tim consoled his friend. "She's got too much sense, Benson ... too much sense, and you gotta learn to live with that."

The Lamborghini disappeared and for a time the four sat silent, able only to focus on the point where it had vanished.

Silence for a moment, then a precedent breaking subject change by the bulldog himself.

Denny asked, "Where do we stand on Paul's farewell party?"

Benson Roman's legendary resourcefulness glowed like a two hundred watt lightbulb.

"Marsalli's at seven. We begin with hors d'oeuvres and cocktails, live traditional Neapolitan music, including a pretty fair tenor, then dinner on the patio featuring selections of the best seafood in all of southern Italy. This is followed by liqueurs and dancing under the stars till the wee smalls."

Benson conveyed his message in a manner that would turn a world-class maître d' green with envy. Denny, Paul and Tim sat with astonished looks frozen on their faces.

From beneath a furrowed brow, Denny said, "There's no finer restaurant in all of Naples, Benson."

Paul interjected, "Hey guys, I'm touched, but the cost'll put you out of business for a year."

Benson shook his head. "Not to worry. It's not costing us a dime."

"I'd go along with a dime," came Denny's alarmed reply, "but you're talking our homes and life-savings."

"No," Benson insisted. "NATO regs say billings for trash removal are screened at Naval Headquarters to verify billing periods match up with dates a ship is actually in port. Nobody looks at the total."

Impatient, Denny asked, "What's that got to do with the party?"

A blasé Benson responded, "Marsalli might have the best restaurant in Naples, but he also has a Navy contract for trash removal at Molo San Vincenzo. You might say his bookkeepers concern themselves only with the bottom line and don't look too hard at where figures appear in the ledger. Restaurant tab or trash removal makes no difference as long as the payment is green."

Paul looked at the young officer through an expression of pure admiration. "Benson, stay this course and your future in submarines will find you ranked with the great ones."

Benson's grin would make the Cheshire Cat appear to scowl.

The fearsome foursome feigned their customary moment of serious contemplation in the same low-key, matter-of-fact manner as those who judged predecessor concoctions. They often held bogus courts on such matters, faces fixed in somber expressions, exchanging glances, heads nodding—a style that would set well in the Supreme Court.

"Hmmm?" Tim Keating mumbled, "Sounds like a plan."

Denny said, "You said dancing. With who? Each other?"

Tim replied, "My cousin Bridget teaches at the American school in the Navy complex. Her cohorts are always ready for action and jumped at the chance."

Again low-key nodding and expressions of approval were made.

No cost to *Clamagore*'s officers spurred Denny's eager agreement. "Well done, Benson, you got my vote."

The sun fell low and cast a magnificent red-gold hue on the ridge of Isla d'Ischia, guardian of the northern approaches to Golfo di Napoli. The Golfo itself formed an azure carpet spread out before the Isla that challenged the fabled *blue Italian skies* line in the Isle of Capri ballad.

It made Paul think of his wife Jean Ann back in Connecticut, but then what didn't? Thoughts of their impending reunion warmed him.

Another issue remained for resolution by the court. A second glass of wine would delay their arrival at Naval Headquarters and cause the foursome to be late for Paul's farewell party.

Benson offered, "What the hell, tomorrow is another day and likely a better one for official business. I say another glass of wine; this is *bella Napoli*, so why the rush?"

Kapitan 2nd Rank Piotr Denisov, slender blue-eyed, thirty-three-year-old Commanding Officer of the Soviet nuclear powered attack submarine *Mayakovsky*, peered through number one periscope and observed fading daylight. He searched in vain for a Russian destroyer lying in Kythira anchorage.

Piotr brushed back a strand of brown hair and with exasperation evident in his voice, he said, "Destroyer nowhere in sight."

It had been a long and slow run from the arctic Barents Sea to the Mediterranean. His crew restive, rumors abounded over possibilities of radiation sickness despite dosimetry specialist Warrant Officer Aleksandr Zhadan finding radiation levels normal.

Mayakovsky, named for the celebrated Russian revolutionary poet Vladimir Mayakovsky, 1893–1930, had been dubbed November class by NATO. Hastily thrown together with thirteen sister ships in an effort to keep pace with the Americans, even the Soviets now knew the effort to be futile, but declined to acknowledge this.

She displaced 4,380 tons submerged, measured 110 meters (361 ft) in length with a 9.3 meter (31 ft) beam. Two water cooled reactors pushed her along at 30 knots submerged, but at that speed made noise enough to make her sound, as described by U.S. sonarmen with occasion to track her, like a seabag full of broken dishes. And so *Mayakovsky* moved slowly to maintain stealth. Much equipment had failed during their long transit and only a destroyer would be at hand in the Kythira anchorage to assist with repairs.

Worse, Denisov wished to take his navigation officer *Kapitan* 3rd Rank Oleg Sokolv to task but knew well the problem confronting him. Electronic navigational aids nonexistent in the Med, a ship's position could be recovered only with astronomical observations. This could be done only while surfaced and in danger of being spotted by NATO warships and aircraft that plied the region. Denisov had strict orders to remain undetected.

Only early morning and evening skies accommodated celestial observations. Overcast ruled out celestial navigation for the past two days and so *Mayakovsky* relied only on dead reckoning. Denisov estimated a navigation error of at least thirty miles. They'd have to wait for their rendezvous.

Piotr Denisov pondered the question that troubled him most, *Why are we being sent secretly into the Mediterranean where no Soviet submarine has ever gone before?*

Chapter 3

Admiral Terry Martin and Captain Rick Ferranti lingered alone in the CNO dining room after lunch. Upon making flag rank, Martin made it a point to assemble top performers he had previously served with into his personal staff. One of these, a black Chief Stewardsman Milton Arter had accompanied Martin on USS *Kokanee*'s ill-fated mission into the Soviet Union White Sea sixteen years earlier. Arter brought the officers coffee.

"Will that be all, Admiral?"

"Chief, I meant to ask earlier. Do you remember Captain Ferranti? He was the spook on *Kokanee* with us on her final run."

Arter grinned as he recalled how he nearly lost his life transferring from *Kokanee* to the rescue submarine. "I'm not cleared to know that, Admiral. But I do remember … good to see you again, Captain."

"You too, Chief. Once in a while turn up the air-conditioning to remind the admiral how cold it got on that run."

"I'll do that, Captain."

Martin inquired about Arter's son. "How's Milton Jr. doing?" and then to Ferranti, "He's my son Paul's classmate at Annapolis."

"Just fine, Admiral."

"He's going to be a submariner, I hope?"

From beneath a furrowed brow, Arter replied, "Milton talks about being an aviator, Admiral."

"Paul already told me that, Chief. Just wanted to yank your chain."

"Your son will go into submarines?"

Martin smiled. "He doesn't want to be disinherited, Chief."

Arter laughed. "He'll do just fine, Admiral."

"So, Milton will beat Army single-handedly this year?"

Smiling, the chief said, "I know Milton believes he will, sir."

"His numbers put him on track for being the best running back the Academy ever had."

A proud grin threatened to engulf Arter's face. "Milton's a team player, Admiral. First comes winning. If he helps them do that, it'll make the Mrs. and me happy."

"Let's keep our fingers crossed for him."

"We'll sure do that, Admiral."

"Next time you see Milton, give him my best. I know he wants my job, but he should let me keep it a few more years."

"I'll tell him that. Will that be all, Admiral?"

"Yes and thank you, Chief."

Ferranti broached his purpose for requesting to meet: Martin's offer to Ferranti of temporary duty in Naples accompanied by his wife. He said, "Let me say right up front, Admiral, the answer is *no*."

The CNO unaccustomed to being turned down for anything, raised his eyebrows.

"I'll explain, Admiral. You'll need some background. When Lorraine and I married eight years ago, I couldn't imagine any man being happier than me."

Martin looked at him with concern. "Is everything okay with Lorraine and you?"

"It is now. And was for the first eighteen months. I fell apart after that. You know what I was involved in, Admiral."

Captain Ferranti operated as a field agent for Naval Intelligence. Exceptionally good at what he did, he got the tough assignments and being fluent in Russian, DNI exploited this.

"Specifically, only one," Martin replied. "When we put you and Dan Bennett ashore at Severodvinsk. I know it got pretty rough, but you came out with what we needed."

Rick looked older than his forty-five years. Dark hair heavily streaked with gray had begun to recede. His face became drawn and tired, but Ferranti's dark eyes remained sharp and clear.

Self-reproach tinged Rick's reply. "Taking out four souls in the process. This runs against my Catholic upbringing, so I had to develop emotional immunity. I got good at it ... too good. You can keep that stuff bottled up for only so long. Then it explodes. Staying in the business forced me to sustain the immunity, but when I met Lorraine, I also got my ticket out and I jumped on it."

Martin felt uncomfortable with what he anticipated Ferranti wished to tell him. "You don't owe me an explanation. If your decision is no, that's good enough for me. I know you have good reasons."

"Thanks for understanding, Admiral, but it's good for me to talk about this, if you don't mind. I'd rather you hear it from me than through the backdoor."

Already late for an appointment, Martin felt obligated to hear his old friend out.

"I want to hear about it if you want to tell me."

"I do, Admiral. I came in from the cold shortly before the wedding. The *cold turkey* approach proved a big mistake. The director figured I'd paid my dues and let me come in. But he cautioned the stuff I'd been through could haunt me and suggested counseling. But tough old Rick needed no help. He'd handle it on his own."

Martin interjected occasionally to assure Rick he listened. "I hope the Navy provides this. We should've had it back in forty-five, but didn't. Most troops home from the war did okay, but a lot of them needed help."

"Today, it is on the Navy, Admiral. It's taken serious now. But a career officer who asks for help better be ready to finish up in an innocuous desk job. Things deteriorated quickly between Lorraine and me. I became verbally abusive and once, damn near physically. It tears my gut out just thinking about it. She put up with a year of this. On seeing I made no effort to turn things around, she left and moved to her grandfather's farm on Maryland's eastern shore."

Martin pushed back in his chair. He saw his own hand in this, but knew they did what had to be done.

"I'm sorry, Rick. Truly sorry. It had to be terrible for you."

"It was. Without Lorraine, I started taking things out on my guys at the office. The director called me in for a private session. He suggested counseling again, but I refused."

Martin watched Ferranti's shoulders slump, completely out of character for him.

"Next came drinking. You would not believe how much I could put away. Weekends became blurs, and I'd show up at the office so badly hungover, I could scarcely function. Lorraine called often, but I didn't answer when her voice sounded on the answering machine. I was too ashamed."

Martin did not respond but maintained reassuring eye contact.

"One day, I tried to draw a service pistol from the armory. Fortunately, being taken off field work removed me from the weapons access list, or we wouldn't be having this conversation."

This time Martin did respond. "That wouldn't have happened, You're the man you've always been. Your instincts would block that."

"I'm not sure, Admiral."

Martin did not push the point. "But things are good with Lorraine now? You implied as much when you showed up today. What happened? How did you fix it?"

"Ever heard of intervention, Admiral?"

"I know of it."

"One night after work, Lorraine, her grandfather Frank, and Dan and Mimi Bennett showed up at my apartment. All the people in my life I really cared about. I was three sheets to the wind when they arrived, so Dan pumped coffee in me till I could function. It tore me apart for them to see me like that."

"They told me how my behavior affected them and pulled no punches. One by one, each let me know how much I mean to them and how painful it is to watch me go down the tubes. Dan first. He made me realize the great depth of his friendship. Lorraine went last. I heard her, but was so disconsolate over having hurt her—words did not register. I convinced myself there was nothing I wouldn't do to regain Lorraine's love, get her back and fill the void she left—she is my life."

Seldom at a loss for words, Martin offered, "Rick … I'm happy things worked out."

"It was tough. Lorraine moved back in knowing how far I had to go. Stood by me though she had plenty of reasons not to. No one waved a magic wand and it did not happen overnight, but I trended in the right direction, so Lorraine stayed on. I couldn't have done it without her."

"I've met Lorraine only a few times, Rick, but there's winner written all over her."

"I don't know how she toughed it out. Lorraine ..." Ferranti paused and wiped a tear as he spoke her name, "told me she never lost sight of the man she fell in love with. He was always there, but his pained mind held him prisoner."

"She knew what she had, Rick."

"We talk about children now and hope this is in the cards."

Believing Rick had talked the subject out, Martin smiled and lightened their conversation. "You recall Cliff Harkins on *Kokanee*?"

"I do, Admiral. Wasn't he the engineer officer?"

"Right. You should contact him for advice. At last count, I believe Ruth and he have eight."

Ferranti laughed. "I guess if Cliff doesn't know how to do it, nobody does. Going to Naples to do what I suspect you have in mind could pull the wrong trigger."

"I understand completely, Rick."

A full hour before dawn, *Kapitan* 2nd Rank Piotr Denisov stood on the bridge of *Mayakovsky* with his navigator and two lookouts. The past hour had been spent submerged at dead slow speed scanning all quadrants for contacts. In late summer, a layer of warm water extends down eighty feet from the surface to form a sound tunnel. Machinery noises of ships operating there can be heard over great distances, but the *Michman* (sonar operator) reported no contacts. The *kapitan* followed with a periscope scan. *Eyes verify ears* he'd often been told.

Denisov had to surface his ship to recover navigational position and locate the Kythira anchorage. A Kotlin class destroyer awaited them with further orders.

Navigation stars Fomalhaut, Altair and Deneb hung in the east, first measureable at the earliest trace of daylight. Intersecting distance arcs from two stars make a position. Three arcs passing through or near the same point validate a *fix*.

Oleg Sokolv took an early and quick shot at Fomalhaut. "Horizon not too clear, but I'm close," then read the elevation to Denisov to be recorded then set his sextant on Deneb.

A lookout cried, "Aircraft! Approaching to starboard."

Denisov ordered the bridge cleared then looked to verify the contact. A plane closed rapidly.

The *kapitan* ordered, "Dive!"

Mayakovsky slipped beneath the waves, passed through the thermal layer and descended to fifty meters (164 feet).

Oleg asked, "Could we have been spotted, *Kapitan?*"

"Not likely."

Denisov wished this to be true more than he believed it. NATO airmen, aware that submarines had to surface at predawn to navigate, surely exploited this opportunity.

"Were the observations good ones, Oleg?"

"Close enough to get us where we want to go, *Kapitan.*"

Sokolv also wished this to be true more than he believed it.

Hours later, *Mayakovsky*'s periscope broke the surface. Sokolv's hip shots were good. Denisov spotted a Soviet destroyer at anchor. He thought, *Maybe now we'll learn why we've been ordered to come to the Mediterranean.* He hoped the explanation warranted the trials and tribulations his crew endured to get here.

Botticelli could not have painted a better late summer evening sky in southern Italy than the real thing. Above Marsalli's rooftop patio, a setting sun adorned the underside of a scattered altostratus cloud deck with breathtaking gold and red hues. An ancient seaman admonition goes, *Red sky at night, sailors' delight,* hopefully a good omen for the *Clamagore* officers.

A magnificent vista over Golfo di Napoli stunned *Clamagore*'s partygoers to silence. Impending darkness ended this but left a dazzling necklace of lights about the Golfo's eastern reaches.

Violins, an accordion, and a mandolin roamed through a medley of Neapolitan street songs. Every other number featured a rich tenor.

A grateful Tim Keating reckoned the vocalist worked preliminaries attendant to hitting on one of Cousin Bridget's fellow teachers. Benson Roman had indeed called it right.

Some thirty patrons included *Clamagore*'s wardroom officers, naval staff, their wives, and teacher friends Tim's cousin had lined up. Conversation levels rose as night fell and dissolution of inhibitions by various libations of choice. Musicians matched decibel for decibel, partly from necessity, but also effects of *vino* provided by the proprietor. He reasoned, *How can good Neapolitan music be made from dry throats?*

Likes of the Italian beauty seen earlier on the *strada,* clearly not evident among the teachers, did not suppress the foursome's heretofore unseen social skills. Posing no threat to Cary Grant or Mr. Universe did not deter them in the least. Four weeks in the confines of *Clamagore* deprived of female companionship had honed company manners to a fine edge. Brilliance of emerging stars in the inky skies of a magnificent Mediterranean evening paled in comparison.

Bridget showed the Keating wit did not accrue exclusively to her cousin. She fielded each jest of the foursome gracefully and responded in kind.

A beautiful soprano voice augmented Bridget's quick wit and she convinced the musicians to accompany her in a solo rendition of *Danny Boy.* Not knowing the tune, they faked it, but faded quickly to silence as Cousin Bridget flooded the patio with clear notes of the mournful Irish ballad. Conversation hushed and vigorous sustained applause and several *bravissimos* followed her offering.

Bridget's blue eyes, pug nose, round face, all topped with a wealth of curly, disheveled red hair—hardly Italian traits—quickly became non-factors. In Italy, when a woman sings soprano well, nothing else matters. The tenor put on a charm clinic that held the foursome in awe.

"That's what I call technique," said Tim. "I can't wait to tell grandmother about this. In her day, respectable Irish girls were disinherited just for riding through Italian neighborhoods in south Boston."

Denny asked, "No mellowing since then?"

"The name Keating, translated from ancient Gaelic means *hardness of head.* If grandmother is an example of that, we come by the name honestly."

Cocktails ended, all seated for Benson's promise number one: '*dinner on the patio featuring selections of the best seafood in all of southern Italy.*'

Dinner nearly over, Philip Redmond struck a spoon against his glass to get everyone's attention. He cared for the people who worked for him and acknowledged their efforts at every opportunity. Paul Scott wielded a heavy hand in *Clamagore*'s many successes. Redmond cut Paul slack enough to do his best. The captain opened with his favorite joke, mouthed concurrently word for word by Tim Keating to those sitting nearby.

Redmond said, "You're probably wondering why I had you all come by tonight."

Polite, forced laughter followed, but genuine from Tim's audience.

"I checked the calendar this morning and found it's time to make Paul Scott somebody else's problem."

Again laughter, this time sincere.

"I'm told the *pucker factor* gets pretty high on ballistic missile submarines, so Paul's going out there to provide a little comic relief."

More laughter as Redmond's audience warmed up.

The skipper enjoyed being on a roll. "From now on, we'll all sleep a little better, secure in the knowledge that Paul Scott is sleeping too."

Tim's comment, buried in the laughter following Redmond's punch line went, "Makes you wonder how guys like Bob Newhart make a living."

"Come up here please, Paul."

The young officer ambled self-consciously to the head table and stood beside his captain.

"*Clamagore* custom is to present pewter mugs to departing officers, but these are available only back home. Paul will have to take an IOU. He won't leave here empty handed, though. I brought a present for him." The captain handed him a folded piece of paper and asked, "Would you read it please, Paul?"

Paul unfolded the paper, read it to himself and broke into a grin.

Redmond asked, "Well, what does it say?"

"Do I have to?"

"Only if you want to get out of here tomorrow."

"Okay, Captain. It says ... I, Paul Scott, acknowledge further corrupting *Clamagore*'s already errant fearsome foursome this date by diverting them from their appointed meeting at Naval Headquarters.

Likewise, I am guilty of leading these otherwise diligent rules obeyers further astray, if that's possible."

Another roar of laughter. The misdeed of the day had not slipped by the old man.

"Now, if you'll just sign these in triplicate, I won't cancel your orders."

Paul shook his head. "You're tough, Captain. Really tough."

Redmond went on. "If I could be serious for just a moment ... although serious and Paul Scott are mutually exclusive terms ... it is never a totally happy time when we must say good night to a fellow officer. Especially one who has served his ship as well as Paul. His strong hand is obvious in our successes and he was first to arrive with band aids when things went not so well." Redmond avoided the term *went wrong* which implies a mistake had been made. Submarines are compact warships, *there's room enough aboard for anything but a mistake*. Allusions to them are avoided in submarine-related communications, verbal and written.

"The youngsters among us," he nodded toward Benson and Tim, "are better officers for having come under Paul's good influence. He made my life easier as commanding officer ... loyal, dependable and makes the right things happen. I envy his future commanding officer and send Paul off with appreciation and best wishes from all aboard *Clamagore*. We'll miss his lovely and talented Jean Ann. She's been an asset to our wardroom and the Navy community back in New London. Please convey these sentiments when you see her in a couple of days—lucky rascal."

"I'll do that, Captain."

"Paul, would you care to give us a few words?"

A blend of applause from most and catcalls from his foursome mates stated approval for the captain's remarks and a greeting for Paul.

Paul grinned a sheepish but appreciative acknowledgement. "Thank you, Captain. I have a *Clamagore* first for you ... a speechless Paul Scott. Be grateful for that. Thanks to all of you for everything. Each of you know what that is better than I. It's been great having you as shipmates. I'm sure I'll be seeing you around."

A loud round of applause rang out. Formality did not suit Paul and his friends knew this.

Redmond took Paul's hand and held it firmly for a moment. Looking into his subordinate's eyes, he said in a low voice, "I'm very indebted to you, Paul. I do hope the future holds many re-crossings of our paths."

The festivities over, senior officers abandoned the party and left it for fulfillment of Benson Roman's promise number two: *'liqueurs and dancing under the stars till the wee smalls.'*

Another solo by Bridget Keating, this time *O Mio Babbino Caro*, a melody from Puccini's opera *Gianni Schicchi*, well known to the musicians. The couples, American and Italian swaying in dance on the patio, one by one stopped to listen. Resounding applause and more *bravissimos* followed, most from the Neapolitan patrons of Marsalli's who had arrived stylishly late for dinner.

Mario, the Italian tenor declared he'd be Bridget's slave forever and by morning all Naples would be at her feet.

Tim droned, "When grandmother Keating hears about this, all Naples will be repelling a Boston-Irish invasion."

Paul congratulated Bridget when she returned to the table. "That was beautiful, Bridget."

Admiral Terry Martin and Rick Ferranti sat behind the last of their coffees in the empty CNO dining room.

Rick said, "Thanks for listening, Admiral. It meant a lot to me."

Martin replied, "You do me a great honor by taking me into your confidence," knowing an officer requiring psychiatric help got it at the risk of serious damage to his career.

Ferranti smiled, his shoulders squared. The world had been lifted from them.

"Thank you for understanding why I cannot accept the assignment. But I do have a replacement, Admiral. It was a tough job getting this guy to shape up, but we got him turned around and he's damn good. Perfect for the job. Speaks fluent Russian and excellent English. Do you recall the guy who tried to shoot you after the *Kokanee* investigation back in forty-nine?"

Chapter 4

Kapitan 2nd Rank Piotr Denisov had to be on guard continuously. He served aboard a submarine that had been sunk near the American coast in the mid-fifties. A U.S. submarine rescued the survivors, Denisov among them. Under normal circumstances in the Soviet Navy, this would have been a career-ending event. His possible gratitude to the Americans would keep him ever under suspicion, but Denisov's superb innovative tactical skills offset this. U.S. submarine superiority over the Russians spawned a great need for Soviet officers best able to exploit capabilities of their ships.

A Soviet Project 56 *Spokoinyy* class destroyer (NATO term: Kotlin) appeared outwardly a warship, though in reality served as a covered up submarine tender. Each square inch of space below decks had been converted to workshops. Ammunition magazines had become spare parts bins. None of her four 130mm or sixteen 45mm guns could fire a shot. Nor could the ten 533mm torpedo tubes—all for show only.

Denisov sat uncomfortably with *Spokoinyy*'s commanding officer, *Kapitan* 1st Rank Maksim Kurinnyj, in the latter's stateroom. A gut feeling told Piotr his *Mayakovsky*'s assignment would be stressful.

"So, the voyage from Severodvinsk was uneventful, *Komrade* Denisov?"

Piotr took a breath to say what he really thought, but knew it would do far more harm than good. His *ship* had been rushed into production and her inadequate performance reflected this.

The previous year, a sister ship sank returning from patrol after participating in the large-scale Okean-64 naval exercise. Electrical short circuits in III and VII compartments simultaneously precipitated the disaster at a depth of 120 meters (394 ft). A subsequent fire in the air-conditioning system sealed the doom of that nuclear-powered submarine. Fifty-two crewmen including the commanding officer died from CO_2 poisoning and flooding of the surfaced submarine during eighty hours of damage control efforts in stormy conditions. A rescue vessel recovered thirty-seven survivors.

The ship sank in the Bay of Biscay on the west coast of France with her two reactors and four nuclear-tipped torpedoes to a depth of 4,680 meters (15,350 ft).

Much ran through Denisov's mind before answering and he wondered, *Why do we continue to get assignments beyond our capability? This ship has far too many issues to be in the fleet. Unfit for deployment, she should have remained in experimental status.*

His reply thoroughly debated, Piotr said, "The transit taught us many things." *Should be safe enough.*

"Before going on," said Kurinnyj, "let me read this recent statement by our Fleet Admiral Gorshkov. 'Further growth of power in our Navy will be by an intensification of its international mission. While appearing within our armed forces as an imposing factor to restrain imperialists' aggression and ventures, at the same time the Soviet Navy will consolidate international relations.' The admiral's words are guidance. It is for us to initiate actions that fulfill this guidance."

Densinov thought, *Here it comes.*

Kurinnyj's title, commanding officer, like his ship's exterior, covered up his true assignment. As the senior Soviet officer in the Mediterranean, he actually commanded a number of diverse warships stationed at various locations from Kythira anchorage in Greece to the approaches of Rota Harbor on the Spanish Atlantic Coast.

"We have a most demanding and hazardous assignment for you *Komrade* Denisov, but one critical to Mother Russia. I am told you have a wife and two children living in Stalingrad, is that not so?"

Piotr smiled. "I do sir. Irene and two sons, Pasha and Andrushka." He wisely did not mention they were named in honor of two fellow officers who served with him on the ill-fated submarine.

"Your great pride in them is apparent, *Komrade*." Kurinnyj's smile faded to a frown as he said, "You are aware, *Komrade*, that American submarines patrolling nearby have ballistic missiles programmed to destroy your city and home?"

"I have suspected that, *Komrade Kapitan*."

"Your suspicions are well-grounded. Soviet intelligence gathering ships observe these submarines exiting the American base at Rota, Spain. We are told their missiles reach out fifteen hundred nautical miles, enabling them to attack the infrastructure of our beloved homeland from many places in the Mediterranean Sea."

Denisov wished Kurinnyj would get to the point. It had been a long hard voyage and he wished to rest. Perhaps he could bring the meeting to a head.

"This is most serious, *Komrade*. Am I to assume *Mayakovsky*'s assignment will be to counter this threat?"

"You may, *Komrade* Denisov. As of now, Americans operate unhampered. We must change this." His voice tone and intensity made Denisov cringe. Kurinnyj continued, "Our intelligence gatherers have learned from observing test firings off America's Florida coast that they patrol at forty meters (131 ft), well clear of commercial shipping. Until now they have performed so unimpeded. *Mayakovsky* will make rapid transits throughout the area at that depth and give them much to worry about."

Denisov's heart flipped over. "But what if we collide, *Komrade*?"

"Our submarines are hard like rocks," Kurinnyj replied, "theirs are fragile like clay pitchers. Whether the pitcher hits the rock, or the rock hits the pitcher, it's going to be bad for the pitcher."

Kurinnyj went on to explain more harrowing details of his plan to a dismayed Denisov.

The morning following Paul's farewell party found him wishing he could get away sooner. A Paul *roast* erupted at breakfast and lingered until nearly ten. Each officer poked back at his nemesis of past years.

To Paul, eons passed before he heard the deck watch's merciful words over the 1MC, "Lieutenant Scott's ride is here."

Before taking final leave, Paul chatted with Redmond a few moments in the captain's stateroom.

"Paul, we're going to miss you."

"Thank you, Captain. I'll sure miss being here."

"I guess the foursome is a threesome now."

"That's less chance of getting you in trouble. I'll miss those guys most of all. Look, Captain, I'm grateful to you. Thanks for letting me run with the ball. And also for the mistakes you let me make so I could learn from them."

"Paul, do you think you'll reconsider and apply for the nuclear power program? Maybe on that BN, some of it will rub off on you. Diesel power is a dead end. We're gasping our last. Another ten years and we'll be gone."

"Don't worry about me, Captain. I'll find a place to land. It's just that it won't be with the nukes. Can't really put a finger on it, but I sense a growing attitude that will ultimately be trouble."

"Me too, Paul, but you didn't hear that here."

"Not a word, Captain."

The skipper extended his hand. "Everything I said at the party last night was genuine, Paul. You should feel good about what you've accomplished for us. Now get your sorry ass moving before I cancel your orders and keep you here."

Paul nodded. Graceful acceptance of a compliment evaded him. He recalled what Jean Ann often said, '*You really are the poor man's Sir Galahad.*' Where was Jean Ann at these stupid moments when he really needed her? By this reckoning, all Paul's moments are stupid. He ached for just a couple of days with her in Italy. They'd not go to Rome, but Venice and loll through long, warm days wandering about the city and its canals. They'd fill sleepless nights with lovemaking and then go to Florence where they'd visit Piazza Del Gran Duca. There Robert Browning and his bride Elizabeth passed fifteen happy years of marriage before death took her from him.

Conscience pangs overtook Paul.

"Uh, reminds me, Captain." Paul opened his wallet and removed two twenties. "Here's the forty you gave me last night. Tim's girls enjoyed the party so much, they insisted on paying for everything."

"Well, that's very generous. I'll have Denny pass along my thanks." Then Redmond handed the young officer his orders from the Navy Bureau of Personnel. "Here you go, Lieutenant."

Paul read the opening line aloud. "Report to the Commanding Officer, US Fleet Anti-Air Warfare Training Center, Dam Neck, Virginia for instruction as a ballistic-missile submarine Polaris Weapons Officer. Upon completion, report to Commanding Officer, USS *John J. Pershing* for duty as Weapons Officer."

"The thought scares the hell out of me, Paul. You know it'll be a lot different from our cozy existence in *Clamagore*."

It scared the hell out of Paul too, but he covered it well. "Like you always tell us, Captain, eat the elephant one bite at a time."

After they exchanged a final handshake, Paul turned to leave.

"Oh Paul. One more thing. When you go topside make sure our trash is picked up? The contractor soaks us for collecting it."

Paul thought, *Nothing gets by the old man.*

They exchanged knowing smiles.

Paul climbed onto the main deck into a bright, crisp morning. *Maybe fall arrived a bit early,* he thought as he gave a crisp salute to the topside watch.

"Permission to leave the ship, sir."

Denisov, clearly disturbed over his new assignment, returned to *Mayakovsky*. Two hours remained until dawn when it would be necessary to be submerged and out of sight. His executive officer, *Kapitan* 3rd rank Andrej Smirnov, assembled all officers in the mess to hear the orders given Denisov. Faces folded into grim expressions as their *kapitan* related *Mayakovsky*'s mission.

Piotr explained the U.S. SSBN mode of operation. "We will make high-speed runs through probable launch sites at the precise depth we believe them to patrol."

He spoke in steady and positive tones, certain that *Zampolit*, *Kapitan* 2nd Rank Evgenij Knyazev, kept an eye on him for signs of disloyalty growing from once having been rescued by Americans.

Smirnov asked, "But *Komrade Kapitan*. Can this be legal? I know of no provision in the international rules of the road."

"Submerged submarines are by definition the burdened vessels and responsible for their own safety. This applies equally to Americans as to us," said Denisov, but the lack of conviction did not match his tone.

"But with both vessels submerged, how do the rules affect that?"

"Nothing specific is included for this circumstance."

For the *zampolit's* benefit, the *kapitan* continued to sound positive and stern. In his heart, Piotr felt differently. He knew the general prudential rule to apply both on and below the surface.

In construing and complying with these rules, due regard shall be applied to all dangers of navigation and collision, and to any special circumstances, including the limitations of the vessels involved, which may make a departure from the above rules necessary to avoid immediate danger.

Denisov concluded, "We submerge in less than two hours. Those of us not on watch must get some sleep."

Pleased with how Denisov handled the matter—*forceful and no-nonsense*—the *zampolit* added, "You heard what the *kapitan* said."

Piotr stretched out as much as his five and a half foot bunk permitted, but sleep would not come. Appalled by this assignment, his stomach churned. *Think of something pleasant. Yes—Irene. No other thoughts make me happier than those of my wife.* He recalled when they first met five years ago at a funeral. Her father, Vladimir Selenski, lay in an open wooden coffin at his home in Stalingrad. Selenski served in the Great Patriotic War, a *komrade* of Denisov's own father.

No event in Russia is more somber than a funeral. Tradition mandates only staid eulogies. Smiling or laughing is considered rude and inappropriate. Women wear black dresses and must cover their heads with black babushkas.

Igor Denisov, Piotr's father, had spoken frequently of Vladimir's bravery during the defense of Stalingrad during the winter of 1943. Russians have a penchant to exaggerate, especially when speaking of *komrades* in arms and it left Piotr to wonder whether one man could have achieved and endured so much.

Piotr looked about a sea of mournful faces then came upon Irene's. Seated amongst the deceased man's family, her light-blue eyes looked serene from beneath a tuft of golden hair that protruded from beneath her black babushka. He guessed her to be the daughter. A whispered question to his father earned Piotr a sharp elbow in the rib cage.

Her peaceful expression showed she alone appeared to celebrate the life of her beloved father. Thoughts of him brightened her expression.

Piotr thought, *This man surely brought great happiness to his family. I am more impressed by this than the endless list of accolades given me by Father.*

He cast frequent sidelong glances at Irene throughout the Russian traditional all-night corpse vigil. Her peaceful serene countenance contradicted mournful expressions worn by those seated around her.

After interment the following morning, Piotr approached Irene. "I know this is hardly the time or place to ask, but might I see you again?"

Piotr's father owned a Zaporozhets automobile, named for the Cossacks of Zaporizhian Sich who lived in Ukrainian militarized communities between the 16th and 18th centuries. The cheapest auto in the Soviet Union made it affordable for most common people like Piotr's family. The elder Denisov objected when he learned Piotr's purpose for wishing to borrow the car, but loved his only son and could refuse him nothing.

"Piotr, it is improper to call upon Irene Selenski only a day following her father's burial. We gather again in nine days, then again after forty when family and friends will have dinner in memory of *Komrade* Vladimir Selinski. You must have patience and wait till these events have passed." Igor's thought comforted him. *Irene will honor her father's memory and refuse to see Piotr.*

Piotr had no quarrel with convention, but in two days he must report back to his ship, likely not to return for several months, too long a wait. Irene shared his feelings and accepted his offer to see the ballet.

At Stalingrad's Regional Philharmonic Theater the Kirov's prima dancers, husband and wife team of Yuri and Ekaterina Baknov, performed an elegant dance in a festival dedicated to the memory of the war. They danced lead roles in a play entitled *The Art of Town Heroes* involving only performers from hero towns that actively participated in the war and contributed to the Soviet victory.

Following the show, they sat quietly over dinner at a restaurant nearby the theater. Piotr enjoyed looking at her from across the table. For a time, they spoke little. He attempted to learn about Irene, but she disclosed a penchant for listening rather than going on about herself.

As they sat together, Piotr felt compelled to reveal pent-up thoughts held close for many years. He told her of his misadventure in the submarine lost off the American coast. She absorbed his pain with a compassion and understanding he had not known to exist. He found her ability to do this pleasantly heartwarming. By evening's end, though neither conveyed this thought, both knew it to be the first day of a life they would spend together.

Commander Phil Redmond sat in the COMSIXFLT (Commander U.S. Sixth Fleet headquartered at Naples, Italy) briefing auditorium where commanding officers of all ships in the area convened to be briefed on an upcoming operation change.

A lieutenant commander stood before an overhead projector that presented an eastern Mediterranean Sea chart on the wall behind him. The young officer wore gold wings of a naval aviator over his left breast. He spoke in clear sharp tones. "Gentlemen, early this morning, a P-3 patrol aircraft spotted a Soviet submarine here," setting a pencil on the projector to indicate its reported position in the Ionian Sea, "two hundred nautical miles northwest of the Soviet anchorage Kythira."

Anticipating the usual cynicism over target classification validity, the officer projected a series of three photographs and pointed out salient features of the contact.

"The light is not good, but it's clearly a Soviet November Class nuclear powered submarine."

The first slide showed a fully surfaced ship, the second partially dived and the third, a lingering wake after the November disappeared beneath the waves.

"That shot is not the clearest," a voice spoke up. "Have we checked to be sure none of our submarines were in the area?"

The briefer anticipated the question. "CTF sixty-nine confirms no NATO submarines within five-hundred nautical miles. Our spooks have enhanced the image and conclude a ninety-five percent probability it's a November. The first Soviet nuke in the Med."

The briefer took a moment to let this settle in. Much of his audience had been frustrated over chasing down false leads. Their cynicism had been come by honestly.

Another voice asked, "So where do we go from here?"

The briefer replied, "We have a game plan. Captain Davidson will overview it for you."

The aviator then surrendered the podium to Captain Davidson who began, "A Soviet nuclear-powered submarine in the Mediterranean is of great concern. We've seen the problems their reckless antics on the surface make for us. The most recent incident occurred with USS *Clamagore* running on the surface near the Russian anchorage at Kythira. But the greatest threat is to our ballistic missile submarines operating in the Med and we must expect Soviet intentions to be the same beneath the waves." He paused and looked about the room then continued. "We are going to nip this in the bud. Effective immediately, all Sixth Fleet operations are on hold while we show the Russians there's no way they can conduct undetected submarine operations in our pond."

He went through a series of overhead projector slides presenting a plan to divert all Sixth Fleet surface and air assets from normal operations to intense antisubmarine warfare (ASW) searches. He went on to detail what he expected of each surface and aviation unit.

Ending with an afterthought, he said, "We have not forgotten about you, Commander Redmond. We can't afford for *Clamagore* to run around creating false contacts for us. So you will remain out of the area. Look at it this way, skipper. Somebody has to play left field. And when we chase the Russki out, he may just come your way."

Redmond knew the Sixth Fleet tended to be an exclusive aviator and surface-skimmer club. *Clamagore*'s assignments in fleet warfare exercises validated this—provide target services.

Time and time again the summer thermal layer prevented surface ships' active sonar from detecting submarines operating below eighty feet. Redmond considered the plan to be *head-in-the-sand*. *Do something to give the appearance that something is being done even though it isn't.*

But Redmond did not reiterate this point to such a top-heavy crowd. If he did, he would probably receive a concurrent fitness report (a performance of duty assessment while assigned to COMSIXFLT), likely written by Captain Davidson, for *Clamagore*'s Mediterranean deployment. Redmond knew no good accumulated to burning bridges. *Why tell them what they already know and ruffle their feathers?*

A week later, *Clamagore* patrolled at periscope depth two hundred nautical miles south of the Sixth Fleet main search area, about as *far left* as *left field* can get. Provisions in the patrol order required visual observation to confirm detection and identification. Redmond thought, *Getting a nuke to surface without using a weapon on him? Good luck.*

Diesel-electric submarines have limited endurance submerged. When batteries become depleted, the ship must either surface or come to shallow snorkel depths in order to run diesel engines and recharge batteries. They can be driven to the surface if contact is maintained long enough, but nukes didn't have this problem.

Denny Kolb had the conning watch with Tim Keating, diving officer in the control room. To minimize prospects of acquiring bad cases of *periscope eye,* Denny and quartermaster of the watch, Quartermaster Seaman John Howell, alternated *dances with the one-eyed lady.* Conducting continuous visual surface and air searches meant draping an arm about the handle, plastering one's face against the optics and rotating the shaft in a sort of continuous dance. A bright, clear day above a glassy surface accommodated unlimited visibility. The remote station assigned to *Clamagore* found them devoid of contacts, hence boredom became the greatest threat.

Tim Keating yelled up through the control room hatch, "Denny, the main hydraulic accumulator dumped all its oil into the pump room bilges. I'm shifting to normal power."

Denny called down, "Hold up on that, Tim. Too noisy." Then with sarcasm clear in his voice, "Don't want to risk getting detected by all these contacts up here. Make your depth one-zero-zero feet. Trim so we'll float up against the thermal layer and I'll order all stop till the accumulator's fixed. How long?"

"Auxiliaryman of the watch says thirty minutes, Conn. One-zero-zero feet, trim to float under the layer, aye."

"Down scope," Denny ordered and keyed the 27MC to report their situation to the captain.

As *Clamagore* broke through the thermal layer, sonarman of the watch Seaman Phillip Giambri's excited voice blurted over the 21MC, "Conn … Sonar. Contact! I don't know what we got here, but it's loud as hell and headed right for us."

Chapter 5

Phil Redmond mounted the conning tower ladder in response to Denny Kolb's urgent summons with a speed that surprised even him. "What've we got?"

A panicked Denny replied, "Don't know, Captain. Loud as hell and heading right at us. Sonar's trying to get a fix."

Redmond knew his ship had just punched down through the thermal layer. *Has to be a submarine.* A lot flashed through his mind. Well honed instincts kept him from *hipshooting* a bad decision.

"Get a bearing drift."

Denny keyed the 21MC and passed the order, an edge in his voice.

An apprehensive Giambri reported, "Bearing three-four-three drawing left slowly, getting louder, Conn."

Rising noise from the closing contact erupted from the underwater telephone receiver (Gertrude).

Redmond thought, *Gotta be damn close to hear it on Gertrude.* "Good. He'll miss us but not by much." *A worried skipper's not good for troop morale.* He masked his anxiety then ordered calmly, "Don't sound the collision alarm. Use the one-MC. Set condition Baker (secure watertight doors and bulkhead flappers)."

Denny carried out the order and regarded the captain through a concerned expression.

Redmond anticipated the conning officer's question. "Stay where we are, Denny. Don't alert him to our presence. Trust me, he'll miss us. Not by much, but he'll miss us."

Redmond pressed the 21MC button. "Bearing, Sonar?"

"Three-three-two, Conn."

This confirmed the captain's assumption. The contact passed close enough aboard to rattle *Clamagore*'s hull, alerting all onboard.

Redmond thought, *Gotta be developing a lot of power to shake us like this.* He'd talk to his crew later, but for the present, milk the incident for every drop.

"Come left at dead slow, Denny. Stop when he's on our port beam." Redmond ordered fresh tapes installed in the recording devices. "Sonar, lock on with *PUFFS* (passive ranging sonar) quick as you can. We're maneuvering for best aspect."

Exact range is needed to measure a target's absolute sound pressure level (contact's noise level plotted against range), an exceptional intelligence find.

"Has to be a November, Denny. Nothing else makes that much noise."

Denny calmed as contact noises faded rapidly from Gertrude. He drew a deep breath and let it escape. *The skipper was right. The son of a bitch missed us, but not by a helluva lot.*

"Can't argue, Captain. Never heard one before."

"Me neither. But unless the Reds have pulled a new rabbit out of the hat, what else can it be?"

"Got me, Captain."

"Sonar, get me a course and speed. Check and recheck." Redmond then ordered Denny, "Soon as you can, give me coordinates of where this guy will be in exactly one hour."

Denny asked, "An hour from now, Captain?"

"Right. Ground rules require visual confirmation. We'll call for a patrol plane to drop sonobuoys and verify our find. Maybe separate audio contacts will equal a visual."

Redmond thought, *Damn. The whole Sixth Fleet whips the Med to a boiling froth with active sonar and comes up dry. The golden apple falls right into our laps. We gotta be doing something right.*

The captain believed that those sharing a common danger have a right to know what happens. He described the near miss over the 1MC. His crew understood *silent service* and would discuss nothing outside the ship.

Expressions of confidence and approval from his crew greeted Redmond as he walked through the ship. *This is what being skipper is all about.* An old syndrome revisited as he sat in the wardroom behind a cup of coffee. A vision of the prettiest girl he knew in high school flashed through his mind. This happened after each near crisis for a good reason: each time he'd approach her, a voice whispered, *Don't do anything dumb.* He heeded the advice well this day and his ship will continue to live and fight on.

Lieutenant Paul Scott liked everything about his new Duty Station except being without his family. Dam Neck, Virginia sits on the Atlantic coast near the community of Sandbridge comprised of summer beach residences. In two weeks, the post Labor Day rental rates would tumble then he'd rent a place so his family could join him.

Paul walked between the Polaris Weapons and Navigation buildings and encountered a Radioman Chief Petty Officer, head down, deep in thought.

Noticing Paul's shadow, the CPO looked up and snapped a crisp salute. "Good afternoon sir."

Paul returned the salute then stopped, peered at the CPO and then he asked, "Roberts?"

"Why, yes sir, Oh my God. It's you! Paul ... er, Lieutenant Scott."

Paul thrust out his hand and the chief took it. Ten years earlier they served together aboard USS *Piratefish* as seamen.

Roberts grinned. "Look at you. I heard you made it. Congratulations. Just goes to show. Never give the messcook any grief. Tomorrow he might be your division officer."

They shared a laugh.

"Really, Mr. Scott. It's great to see you. Everyone aboard *Piratefish* knew Annapolis would be no problem for you. You sure made us proud."

"Thanks, Chief. Looks like you didn't do too bad. Bilge rat to chief in ten years."

"Couldn't have been that long ago, sir."

Protocol made Paul uncomfortable, but it had to be maintained. "Do you know what happened to our buddy Sylvester Goins?"

Goins, the first black electrician to operate propulsion equipment on a diesel-electric submarine, gained for himself a measure of renown.

"Lost touch with him, but a year ago he was Chief Electrician teaching at Sub School."

Paul replied, "Good for him. Jim Dandy, remember? Does he still go by that?"

"I doubt it. Doesn't track with his goal of making Chief of the Boat. He's married with three kids."

"That's great, Chief. I report to *Pershing* this November in New London. I'll look him up."

"He'll be glad to see you, sir. Oh ... remember that girl you talked about so much? What was her name ... Shirley?"

Paul nodded. "Shirley Bintliff. You got a good memory, Chief."

"So what happened?"

"Gave it my best shot. My midshipman uniform didn't exactly blow her away. We dated once my plebe year. That's a freshman at Annapolis. We went to the Penn-Navy game in Philadelphia and dinner afterward. She was cordial."

"Cordial, Scott ... er, sir?"

Paul grinned at his old friend. How easy to fall back to their days aboard *Piratefish.*

"Means she had bigger fish than me in mind."

"That's too bad, Mr. Scott. Guess nothing stays the same."

"I wouldn't say that. The girl I married ... Jean Ann, she stayed the same. Just took me a long time to realize the kind of same I wanted."

Home during Christmas holidays in Moline, Illinois, Paul's first leave as a midshipman, he attended mass at Saint Mary's Catholic Church on Tenth Street. Here his parents exchanged wedding vows thirty years earlier. Baptized at St. Mary's, Paul remained a parishioner. Serving as an altar boy piqued his penchant for language and he easily followed the Latin liturgy. Paul's nonstop mind tended to race a mile a minute, so it took great effort for him to remain focused on sermons. Yet mass at St. Mary's church would be a joyful occasion. Comforting surroundings, statuaries of the Sacred Heart of Jesus, Blessed Virgin Mary at Fatima and a stained glass window depicting the gospel of Jesus and the Woman at the Well reinvigorated him.

Consecration of the Blessed Sacrament moved Paul deeply. Father Harris raised the Eucharist in an offertory gesture to his Lord. An altar server struck the side of a domelike bell with his hammer then dampened the sound by seizing it with a gloved hand.

Paul lowered his head, struck his breast and whispered, "My Lord and my God."

Continuing to smart from recent rejection by a young woman he'd been infatuated with during carefree days at Moline High School, Paul sought diversion. He'd passed the previous evening with old buddies hence did not make confession. Pre-Vatican II protocol prevented him from filing to the altar to receive the Eucharist so he recited the spiritual communion prayer.

Kneeling with head bowed, deeply moved, he whispered, "My Jesus, I believe that you are present in the Blessed Sacrament. I love You above all things and I long for You in my soul. Since I cannot now receive You sacramentally, come at least spiritually into my heart. As though You have already come, I embrace You and unite myself entirely to You; never permit me to be separated from You."

At prayer conclusion, Paul raised his eyes. The sight of a lovely young lady abruptly pulled him from deep reverie. *Good Lord, it can't be.* Jean Ann Peters, a parishioner he'd not seen in years walked by, eyes lowered, hands folded, and a serene expression on her face after having received Holy Communion. Her younger brother Tommy walked behind, a full head taller than Jean Ann.

Paul recalled a young child, giving mother-like oversight and supervision to a considerably shorter Tommy of those days. Three years difference in school, an eon in the perception of young children, made sixth grader Paul appear godlike to third grader Jean Ann. Paul assumed this accounted for frequent smile exchanges initiated by her. He liked those smiles and enjoyed seeing her at mass, though they rarely conversed.

Paul decided to seek her out after mass. When the final recessional note sounded, he bolted from the church and caught up with her.

"This can't be the Jean Ann Peters that dragged her little brother to mass. Maybe her big sister?"

He last saw her his senior year when she was a freshman.

She smiled the same smile she'd given him over the years.

"Paul Scott! Don't you look nice in that uniform. We knew you made it to Annapolis. Father Harris announced it last June."

Paul liked compliments but did a good job of shaking them off. Abrupt change of subject worked best.

"So how are things at Moline High? You're a senior now, right?"

"Everything's great with the maroon and white. I didn't repeat any grades, so you guessed right."

He struggled for a clever rejoinder, but came up empty. Best he could muster, "It's really nice to see you Jean Ann."

"You too, Paul."

An awkward silence portended an end to their conversation. Paul picked up on an ever so slight trace of disappointment in her face—all that he needed.

"Jean Ann, we've been looking each other over since we were little kids. Don't you think it's time we got some answers?"

Piotr Denisov grimaced on receiving a damage control report from executive officer Andrej Smirnov.

"It's the main packing, *Kapitan*. Our port shaft has seized."

Zampolit Evgenij Knyazev looked on ready to leap at and denounce the slightest hint of defeatism.

Denisov's belief that *Mayakovsky* fell woefully short of being ready for deployment often showed through to Knyazev.

Addressing the *zampolit*, Denisov said, "*Komrade*, we need a dry dock to repair this damage. We do not have one in the Mediterranean."

"Then, *Komrade Kapitan*, we must continue our mission with just the starboard propeller."

Almost too quickly, Piotr replied, "I agree." *How shall I deal with this asshole?* "At one-quarter of our maximum speed, we're unable to cover the full area assigned us, but we can pose a measure of threat."

"One-quarter? We've lost only half of our propulsion power. I don't understand."

"That is true, *Komrade*, but the shaft is locked and the propeller will not spin as we move along. It creates a great deal of drag. But this is actually a blessing. A spinning shaft could cause packing to fail completely and flood the motor room."

Exec Andrej Smirnov read his *kapitan's* mind like a book; *keep the jackass zampolit on his round heels.*

Smirnov warned, "I once experienced a shaft seal failure at sea. Disaster, *Komrades*. The after room flooded and we had to surface. It took full drain pump capacity just to hold our own. This absolutely could not have been done while submerged. We'd have ended up on the bottom."

Denisov knew *the learned zampolit* would opt for his skin over mission every time. He correctly sensed Smirnov and he were on the same page. *Let's make some hay of this.*

"But *Komrade* Smirnov, surely there is some way we can loosen the propeller shaft?"

"Exactly how our accident happened. We attempted to loosen it. Precisely why we flooded. I urge you not to try this, *Kapitan!*"

Facing away so the *zampolit* could not see Denisov's face, he winked at his executive officer then snapped, "Damn you, Smirnov. You think only of your cowardly skin. What value is a handful of lives measured against the needs of Mother Russia?"

Smirnov played his role to the hilt. A sidelong glance at the *zampolit* showed clear panic in his expression.

"As you say, *Kapitan*. I will assemble the engineers and get to it immediately."

Zampolit Kapitan 2nd Rank Knyazev intervened, unable to keep fear from his voice. He tried to project reason while the other two officers played their roles to perfection: Denisov angry, Smirnov meek.

The *zampolit* said, "*Komrade Kapitan*, your zeal and determination are applauded. This shall be noted. But our attack class nuclear powered submarines number far too few to risk losing one, even on a mission as important as ours. I suggest we contact naval headquarters for instructions."

Denisov scowled. "I will do that *Komrade Zampolit*. But I have made my feelings clear in this matter. Record this in the ship's log, *Kapitan* Third Rank Smirnov."

Zampolit Knyazev left the mess and disappeared into his stateroom.

Knowing the sound would carry far in the confines of *Mayakovsky*, Denisov and Smirnov restrained their laughter.

An hour later, a radioman handed the *kapitan* a message board. The directive read in part:

```
SURFACE IMMEDIATELY.  PROCEED AT
BEST SAFE SPEED TO GIBRALTAR.  THERE
RENDEZVOUS WITH FLEET TUG FOR TOW TO
SEVERODVINSK.
```

Alone in his stateroom, Denisov smiled. *Three weeks time and I shall be with Irene and our children.*

Phil Redmond awakened to a knock at 0230 (two thirty a.m.). He pulled back the curtain and saw Sonarman Giambri standing outside.

Giambri reported, "We have a contact, Captain. It's the same submarine that passed us yesterday. He's on the surface, and he has a problem."

Redmond rubbed sleep from his eyes and looked at Giambri intently. "How can you tell? What makes you think that?"

Seaman Giambri gulped. A strong sense of self-confidence earned on the streets of south Philadelphia sustained him well, but troops seldom address their captain. Giambri explained he'd reported this contact to the conning officer, Lieutenant Benson Roman. Owing to the complexity of the circumstance, Roman ordered Giambri to report the event directly to the captain. Protocol is observed in submarines, but not permitted to obstruct necessity.

Redmond put the young seaman at ease. "Okay, son. Tell me about it."

Giambri began, "I don't know quite how to explain it, Captain."

The terms sir or mister are forms of address for officers other than the commanding officer. The captain is always Captain. Redmond noted stress in the young man's expression and put him at ease.

"Give it your best shot. Pretend you're explaining it to your wife."

"I don't have a wife, Captain."

"Well, to that girl you were cozying up to at the pre-deployment ship's party."

A grin spread across Giambri's face.

Good, thought Redmond.

"A sound is the hardest thing to explain, Captain. When you hear something and hear the same thing again … well … do you think you could just trust me on this one?"

Redmond gave Giambri a stern, but reassuring look and said, "Trust you enough to run up the flag and get the whole Sixth Fleet over here?"

Giambri gulped again and responded in the best voice he could muster, "Sure enough, Captain."

"Good. How can you tell he has a problem?"

"Hearing the same noises he made yesterday but a few more. He's only using one propeller at low speed … cavitating, so he has to be on the surface."

"Thank you, Giambri. Get as much info as you can." Redmond got up and dressed. He entered the sonar shack and had Giambri turn up the speaker gain. "Still sure, Giambri?"

"Still sure, Captain."

Redmond made his way to the conning tower and ordered Benson, "Lead him thirty degrees at five knots. Adjust to his bearing changes."

This tactic would keep *Clamagore* close as possible to her target over the next few hours.

"Thirty lead and maintain it. Aye, Captain."

Next issue, what to do? Redmond headed for the wardroom where a cup of coffee would finish clearing his head. He found Denny Kolb there and asked if he'd seen the exec up and about.

"No, Captain. Dave just turned in. He's been up since the November encounter twenty hours ago."

Redmond thought a second. He had a tough nut to crack and treasured Dave Zane's advice. But a burned out exec might leave too big a chink in *Clamagore*'s armor.

Redmond related what he received from Sonar Seaman Giambri. "Pretty straightforward, Denny. Let the exec get some well-deserved shut-eye. Get our best position and a search vector for the zoomies (aviators). It's an hour till daylight. Draft a message to CTF sixty-seven and ask for one of their birds to confirm our finding."

"Aye, Captain."

Ten minutes later Kolb reappeared with the draft.

```
OPERATIONAL IMMEDIATE-USS CLAMAGORE
TO CTF 67.  CONTACT WITH SURFACED
NOVEMBER CLASS SUBMARINE
160530ZAUG65.  RECOMMEND PATROL
AIRCRAFT SEARCH BEARING ARC 065-075
FROM POSIT LAT 33-15N, LONG 24-37E.
```

Redmond thought an instant. *Simple as this is, I'd still like Dave to look it over. C'mon man. Don't be a wimp. He needs sleep more than rubber-stamping a no-brainer.* He signed the release and handed it back to Denny.

"Crypto machine's set up, Captain. We'll have this out in ten minutes."

"Good, Denny."

Redmond knew another cup of coffee'd keep him awake, but his elation would do that anyway. *Why not?*

So far, the entire Sixth Fleet had come up with nothing and *Clamagore* would lay a prize right in their laps. *If you want to find a submarine, send a submarine.* How much better could life get?

But, Redmond understood Navy politics. *Don't show up the king in his own court. When I get called into Sixth Fleet Headquarters, I'll be humble ... say it's a team operation. Clamagore could only point in the right direction. It took an airplane to make the find.*

Redmond turned in for a fitful sleep but finally fell off. At breakfast he explained their early morning success to his officers.

"Maybe this'll make the Sixth Fleet take us serious. We play the bad guy so often in exercises ... they must believe that's what we are."

A blinking, tired Dave Zane entered the wardroom and ordered his customary crisp bacon and eggs up while the captain related details of the November detection and his reasons for not having Zane review the outgoing message.

"Here, Dave. Here's what went out."

Zane looked and shook his head. "Captain, we misstated our position by a full degree in longitude. It'd be a miracle for the zoomie to find November from where we told him to start."

Redmond saw the error immediately. "Damn it!" He knew the data to be too old and correcting the message pointless. "Dave, write a new ship's regulation. The exec must be up and about at all times."

Radioman Ken Omensen's timing could not have been more perfect. "Message, Mr. Zane, a hot one from COM-SIX-FLEET," he said, handing a clipboard to the XO who signed and returned a receipt copy.

The width of Dave Zane's grin spread from bulkhead to bulkhead. He read:

```
COMSIXFLT TO ALLSIXFLT.  CTF 67
PATRON UNIT SIGHTED SURFACED NOVEMBER
160615ZAUG65 LAT 33-20N, LONG 23-25E
HEADING TOWARD STRAIT OF GIBRALTAR
PROBABLY TO EXIT MED.  SUSPECT SOVIET
UNIT LIKELY ACKNOWLEDGES FUTILITY TO
REMAIN UNDETECTED IN FACE OF SIXFLT
ASW PROWESS.  CONGRATULATIONS AND
BRAVO ZULU (naval term for 'Well
done.').  CEASE ASW SEARCH.  RETURN
LAST FLTEX POSIT ASAP.  RESUME
TRAINING-OP EAGER BEAVER
172300ZAUG65.
```

Zane said, "Good news, Captain. The longitude error was east of our actual position. The patrol plane overflew November in the darkness while outbound. And when he couldn't find it at the location we gave him, he returned to base after dawn then spotted it while flying back to Sigonella (U.S. Naval Air Station on Sicily)."

Redmond believed to learn from mistakes is better than fretting over them. "Ya wanna know what the bad news is, Dave? That zoomie will get a Legion of Merit and me an ass-chewing for sending him on a wild-goose chase."

The officers wanted to laugh but unsure remained silent.

Redmond added, "The exec's bunk is up for grabs 'cause he won't need it anymore."

Denny Kolb sensed the mood lightening. "How 'bout yours, Captain? Now there's a bunk I could get used to sleeping in."

"No, Denny, you can't use mine. But there's a CO bunk on a fleet tug in Nome, Alaska I can arrange for you to have."

"Captain. You have no idea how good it is to sleep in the four man bunk room."

Clamagore surfaced and raced through a warm, cloudless, late August afternoon en route her assigned position in the Aegean Sea.

Shortly after the forenoon watch was relieved, Benson Roman called the wardroom on the 21MC to summon Redmond. "Captain, I have what looks like a Soviet warship in tow."

Moments later, Redmond mounted the bridge. He raised his binoculars and focused on the contact.

"Well, what do you know? Same damned Kotlin that gave us the bad time. He's under tow and can't maneuver. What goes around comes around. Get the exec up here, Benson."

Chapter 6

Paul rented a cottage so Jean Ann and the boys could join him the remaining two months of Polaris Weapons Officer school. Summer lingered well beyond its September expiration date.

Paul bummed space available on a flight from nearby Oceana Naval Air Station to Quonset Point, Rhode Island, and got the pilot to put down at Groton, Connecticut.

Jean Ann met him at the airport. The top of her head came barely above Paul's chin and he continued a practice begun during their courtship, nuzzling her light-brown hair. Paul escaped Jean Ann's infrequent irritations by singing Stephan Foster's *I Dream of Jeannie with the Light Brown Hair.* She could not keep a straight face when he did that.

He asked, "Sleepy, Honey?"

Jean Ann looked at Paul through dark-brown eyes. Her happy expression bore traces of dimples of childhood smiles.

"You and your one track mind. I got a sitter. You get a few hours with the boys then you're taking me out to dinner. Maybe I'll be tired after that."

They passed the weekend packing up and shutting their home in the village of Gales Ferry.

The Scotts departed Connecticut early Monday in a dilapidated secondhand station wagon they'd acquired at the birth of Benjamin four years earlier. On the road at first light, the Scotts arrived at Sandbridge mid-afternoon. Jean Ann had an agenda and needed no hindrance from her *three* children, Paul recently added to that category for his rising excitement as they neared the beach.

Paul waded in the tepid surf with Benjamin and David. Jean Ann believed it easier to unload the *wagon* herself.

After dinner Jean Ann and Paul enjoyed a glass of wine on a deck atop the one level rambler and basked in remains of an afternoon sun.

Jean Ann asked, "How do we top this, Paul?"

"Dunno. We'll come up with something. Maybe when the boys get waterlogged, we'll move inland."

Benjamin and David attempted to wade in the surf but got herded away each time by Pumpkin, a big Newfoundland retriever from three houses up the beach.

Paul said, "Look how easily Pumpkin does what the boys won't let me do." The litter-less female worked out frustration by mothering the Scott children.

Jean Ann nonetheless kept a wary eye on her brood. *The ocean is so big and my boys are so small.*

"Yeah, Babe, it is great here." Paul used this pet name in private conversations. "But much as I love sitting here with you, freedom of the entire western world hangs in the balance, so I better hit the books." He rose and kissed her.

"Bring you another glass, Babe?"

"No, I better get started on the dishes."

"Just want to liquor you up for later."

"Sailors! Think all you got to do is give a girl a glass of wine. Then wham, bam without even a thank you ma'am."

"Worry about it when I stop?"

"Not very likely."

"You won't worry or I won't stop trying?"

"The latter of course, now get downstairs and hit those books."

He bent over, kissed her again, long and passionately. "That sure tasted like a promise to me."

Paul went down to a family room turned study.

A beautiful afternoon gave reluctantly away to twilight then yielded to inky black of a moonless star-studded night. After bedding down the boys, Paul took a break and stared out over a softly whispering surf. Star reflections danced on gentle billows of a glassy sea. He listened to Jean Ann move about and put final touches on her kitchen for their short stay. Softly, she sang a song from the Broadway Musical *Guys and Dolls.*

Paul thought, *Ummm ... sounds like maybe I'm gonna get lucky.*

Their cottage sat upon a terrazzo slab and the master bedroom faced the ocean through sliding doors that stood wide open.

Shortly after one a.m. they lay bathed in perspiration from their lovemaking. A breeze floated over them but gave only mild relief.

"It's hot as blazes, Babe. C'mon. Let's go in bare-ass!"

"You're crazy Paul. Not on your life!"

Paul raced across the sand and plunged into the waves. He swam underwater several yards stroking away from shore. Fluorescence traced movements of his arms and legs through the water. A hundred yards out, he stopped, rolled over onto his back and regarded the stars, never so clear and bright as when viewed above the sea. *What a magnificent life.*

Jean Ann's shout announced she'd followed him. "Paul, Paul, where are you?"

So much for 'not on your life'. "Over here, Babe. Glad you came."

She swam to him and they fell into a tight embrace and sunk immediately beneath the waves then they resurfaced, sputtering and coughing,

"It was the hug, Babe. We held each other too tight. Our muscles contract when we exert them and body volume is reduced. This reduces buoyancy and we sink."

"Thanks, Mr. Know-it-all. Do we have to worry about sharks?"

"No. We don't look like anything they like to eat."

Her closeness aroused Paul.

"No chance a shark will mistake your pecker for a minnow and bite it off?"

"Worry about yourself. Sharks sense a woman in heat for miles. You know they perform the sex act same as humans. Be careful."

"Likely story."

"Come here, Jean Ann. Ever make it in the ocean? How 'bout a new first for us tonight?"

"For *us*? Been there already, Sailor?"

"Not in this ocean."

"It's the only ocean you've been in so you're a virgin too."

Later, they stood in an outdoor shower to wash away sand and saltwater. They toweled each other off and climbed back into bed.

"Need a beer, Babe?"

"I think you should go to sleep. It's three a.m. How will you keep your eyes open in class tomorrow?"

"The eyes may shut, but the smile will remain."

Her head found its special place beneath his chin and they slept.

Paul awoke when first light peeked through the sliding doors. He sat up and regarded the splendor of her nakedness while she slept. Paul could not see stretch marks, nor the sag in her breasts from childbirth—only her beauty. *The poet John Keats got it right; Beauty is truth, truth beauty—that is all ye know on earth, and all ye need to know.* Jean Ann is truth. He reflected on the good fortune that made his eyes rise to see her at mass that glorious Sunday morning in St. Mary's church.

Phil Redmond, Dave Zane and Benson Roman crowded onto *Clamagore*'s tiny bridge. Seventeen knots through the water created a stiff breeze.

Soviet ships don't refuel at sea side by side like NATO navies, but are taken in tow by the tanker. The range closed to five thousand yards and Redmond used Roman's binoculars to confirm this.

"See. There's a slack fuel hose bowed beneath the towline. Up for a little fun XO?"

Dave Zane knew devil's advocating to be an important role for the exec, though he could think of nothing more satisfying than making the Kotlin squirm.

He scanned the Soviet ships through his binoculars. "Captain, the tanker is flying a tango flag. Per international rules, *Keep clear.*"

"I'll adhere to the rules as the bastard did for us. Have the stewardsman put a white cover on my cap and send it to the bridge."

"Aye, Captain."

"Benson. I have the conn. Tell maneuvering to answer bells on two main engines."

"Stand relieved, Captain. Bells on two, Aye."

Redmond replayed the Kotlin's antics of several weeks ago. Using seaman's eye, he estimated the second bow wave fifty feet aft of the Soviet warship's bow, indicating she made about nine knots. He put *Clamagore* four hundred yards dead astern and came to the Kotlin's heading.

"Maneuvering … Bridge. Make turns for eleven knots." Turning to Roman, he said, "Get Tim Keating in the conning tower to snap some pics."

"Tim has the word, Captain. He's already set up."

Crewmen anticipation of needed actions reflects well on a captain, but Redmond did not dwell on this. He made a quick mental calculation, *By the three-minute rule* (a hundred yards in three minutes equals one knot) *with a two-knot differential we'll be abeam in six minutes.* Two hundred yards astern of the target, the captain ordered a ten degree turn to port. Upon reaching a position two hundred yards off the Kotlin's track, he resumed base course.

"Dave, call all officers not on watch to the bridge. Ivan hates to be looked at. Point out every topside feature as we pass."

Redmond's cap would show all on the Soviet warship that he was the commanding officer. He thought, *No need telling Tim to keep the shutter snapping. He's already doing that.*

Clamagore slowed to nine knots as she pulled alongside the Kotlin's bridge. Redmond noted the Soviet CO bore no trademarks of a happy camper.

Dave Zane said, "Captain, we're close enough to communicate by bullhorn. What shall I say if he hails us?"

Redmond grinned at his exec. "Tell him it's not too early to panic."

"Not sure I know how to say that in Russian, Captain."

"Say it with a Russian accent, then."

"Captain, maybe he's panicking. They've manned the forward quad forty-millimeter guns."

"I'm betting his bark is worse than his bite, but advise me immediately if he trains them on us. We'll pull the plug (submerge) and get the hell out of here."

Satisfied he'd made his point; Redmond pulled ahead and defying the tango flag, crossed ahead of the tanker. Pirouetting like a prima ballerina about the two Russian ships, *Clamagore* completed a three hundred sixty degree photographic essay then headed off again for her fleet exercise rendezvous point.

As the Russians faded behind, Redmond said, "You know, Dave, someday this will fade to memory. I'd love to meet that skipper over a coupla vodkas and share what went through our minds this afternoon."

The Gangplank restaurant sat upon a barge moored on the east side of the Potomac River south of the 14th Street Bridge. It appealed to Captain Rick Ferranti with its spotless, white clothed tables positioned to give diners a good view of the river. *Something about the ambiance. A guy can set down a lot of baggage here.* Ferranti came often to unwind following many strenuous days at work. But always alone. Sharing pent-up feelings embarrassed him. He knew *spooking* to be a young man's field, and he grew less young with each passing day.

Rick particularly enjoyed the lingering daylight of summer evenings. Something about sitting at a riverside table watching pleasure boats pass and across the river, hustle and bustle of commuters heading home on George Washington Parkway. *What is it about Washington that makes everyone believe they have to work late? How much gets done seems less important than how long it takes to do it.* A stiff jolt of bourbon combined with watching the sunset through spotless glass windows worked better than a sedative.

These memories revisited Ferranti as he took Lorraine's arm and guided her up the gangway between a spacious glassed-in dining area and the dock. He quickly dismissed them and focused on his wife, delighted with how she'd turned herself out for their luncheon with Admiral and Mrs. Martin.

Lorraine said, "It's not every day a woman has lunch with the CNO and his wife. I hope I measure up."

She wore a black silk shantung A-line sleeveless dress over her tanned, trim body. The knee length skirt skimmed shapely legs clad in sheer black nylons in black silk pumps.

A narrow diamond bracelet about Lorraine's wrist matched her earrings. A cream-colored wool crepe Columbian shawl with a ribbon fringe would fend off chills from air-conditioning.

Rick's pride beamed in his smile. "You'll do just fine." He cringed at the thought of how close he came to losing Lorraine.

A handsome maître d', tall with graying hair, greeted them; his dusky skin tones offset by an immaculate white jacket enhanced his appearance. Politeness did not mask his absolute control over the staff and everything else in the restaurant.

"Captain, Ferranti. Good to see you, sir. And Mrs. Ferranti. Captain, you are indeed a fortunate man."

"Right, Markham. But you don't say this for a big tip, do you?"

"Of course not, Captain. And may I say we are honored to have the Chief of Naval Operations at our restaurant. I understand he and Mrs. Martin will be joining us."

"Thank you, Markham. I'll tell him that. He'll be in civilian clothes like me. We'd like this to be low-key, if you get my meaning?"

"I do and will see to that, sir. I'm glad you mentioned it. I was about to call the Navy Yard and arrange for eight side boys."

"You were in the Navy, Markham? You never told me that."

"You never asked, Captain." Markham grinned and then conducted Lorraine and Rick to a prime table overlooking the river.

"Policy of the Gangplank is all guests are special. It's just that some are a bit more special than others."

After Markham left, Lorraine asked, "Side boys?"

Rick answered, "An old custom inherited from the British Navy. Depending upon the officer's rank, two to eight side boys assisted during ceremonies. Change of command mostly, but for other ceremonial events as well: ship launchings, commissions and the like. They form a passage for the officer to walk through. A boatswain's mate *pipes the officer aboard* with a shrill whistle. Side boys salute on the first note and cut away on the last."

"This really goes on, or are you just taking advantage of your personal landlubber again?"

"Gospel, Lorraine. In sailing ship days, visitors to a ship were hauled aboard in a boatswain's chair. Heavier officers needed more side boys to lift them. Their weight was remarkably proportional to their rank, so the more senior officers rated more side boys. Admiral Martin is the top officer in the Navy, so he gets eight, just like Markham said."

"And this still happens?"

"Ceremony and tradition are the glue holding the Navy together. Helps to make sense of the weird things we do."

Lorraine used a surmising tone, "So that's what you've been up to all these years?"

Rick smiled at his wife. "You don't cut a lot of slack, do you? Let's just say guys are different. You gotta admit it can be a good thing."

She smiled through a cynical expression, liking nothing better than causing her husband to talk himself into a corner.

"Depends on the kind of difference you're talking about."

Markham came to Rick's rescue. "Captain, Mrs. Ferranti. We had a call from Admiral Martin's office. He's on his way. Mrs. Martin will likely be here before the admiral."

Ferranti replied, "Thank you, Markham," then looked at his watch and said to Lorraine, "Admirals are always three minutes late. Everybody else damn well better be ten minutes early. The admiral is pushing this a bit. Keeping us waiting is okay, but getting across the breakers with Brenda gives him a whole new set of problems."

As though on cue, Brenda Martin approached the table. Her trim, mature figure moved easily in a classic silk and linen Chanel of burnt-coral, rivaling midday splashes of sun on the river. She greeted the Ferrantis and made a silent request for Rick to help slip on her jacket against the arctic blast of the omnipresent air-conditioning.

Ferranti rose to assist then greeted her with a warm hug. "So good to see you again, Mrs. Martin."

"Brenda, please."

"It's been a while, but you remember Lorraine."

"Of course ... I remember you, Lorraine." She extended her hand. "Those days are far too exciting to forget. But despite all, we pulled through, didn't we? Where's Terry?"

Rick answered, "On the way, according to his office."

"He better not pull that late admiral bit with the Martin family long-haired messcook."

A submarine crew's meals are served by messcooks, hence submariners referred jokingly but affectionately to their wives as long-haired messcooks.

"How are things with you two?"

"A lot better. I'm sure your husband shared the story of Lorraine's and my ordeal. We make no secret of it."

"He did. I'm proud of you for toughing it out. I can think of nothing worse than waking up one day and regretting what you let slip through your fingers."

Admiral Martin arrived with as little fanfare as Markham would let him get away with. He bent over and bussed his wife's cheek then apologized for being tardy.

"I'd like to blame my secretary, Chief Ford, but she's in too close touch with Brenda."

Brenda added, "Between Dorothy and me, we keep Terry well-grounded."

Terry smiled while being introduced to Ferranti's wife. "Lorraine. So nice to see you again. What is it they say about good wines?"

Lorraine met the admiral only twice before, at a cocktail party the Martins hosted and at her wedding nine years ago. "And you, Admiral. Chief of Naval Operations. You've certainly done well."

"I'm Terry to all the beautiful women I know. Please. And let's just say I had a lot of help and luck along the way."

Lorraine replied, "You're far too humble."

Not one to miss so beautiful an opportunity, Brenda remarked, "Yes, and he has a lot to be humble about."

Ferranti winced, but Martin's smile put him quickly at ease.

Lorraine considered the men's attire. *Nothing more obvious than Naval officers in civilian clothing,* but she kept this thought to herself. They wore conservative suits and outlandish ties that did little to offset temperatures and humidity of late August in the Capital.

Martin glanced around. "Our guest of honor hasn't arrived yet?"

Ferranti replied, "I thought it best we first prepare the ladies. Brenda, Lorraine, a Mr. Vasiliy Norovsky will be joining us. He's cleaned up his act in the last sixteen years, but in forty-nine, he attempted to assassinate Admiral Martin."

Chapter 7

Clamagore resumed her *bad guy* role (Red Force) in NATO operation *Eager Beaver*. A combined carrier task group (Blue Force) per plan would *fight* its way up the Aegean Sea to clear the way for attack transports (APA—Auxiliary Personnel Attack) to enter the Bosporus and land four marine battalions on the Gallipoli Peninsula. *Clamagore*'s job: intercept and attack the *Blues*.

Commander Phil Redmond knew this to be like shooting fish in a barrel. Summer Aegean bathythermographic conditions combined with shallow water over a rocky bottom make submerged submarines all but impossible to detect. Surface warfare units further complicated their own vulnerability. Non-stop radio transmissions from the Blue Force warships enabled *Clamagore*'s electronic countermeasures suite to detect and locate the carrier task group. Next, banging of long-range active sonars from escort ships flowed through the thermal channel over great distances to submarine listening equipment. *Clamagore*, having received both of these clues, positioned herself directly on the Blue Force track.

Redmond ordered conning officer Lt. Denny Kolb to maneuver to keep their targets on a steady bearing.

"Don't show the scope longer than ten seconds every two minutes. Call me when you make visual contact. Plan is to slip beneath the escort ships and attack the bird farm (aircraft carrier). I'll be in the wardroom beating the exec's ass in cribbage."

"Aye, Captain. But take it easy on him, please. He get's ornery after back-to-back losses and takes it out on us."

Redmond grinned and said, "I thought that's what junior officers are for," then disappeared into the control room below.

Several men lingered over coffee in the crew's mess following the noon meal third and final setting, including Sonarman Seaman Phil Giambri, Electrician's Mate Second Class Hal Tatlow, Radioman Seaman Ken Omensen and Radioman Chief Petty Officer Frank Beyers, Chief of the Boat.

Otto Preminger's film *The Man with the Golden Arm* released ten years earlier tracked perfectly with having reached *Clamagore* at this late date. Submarines stood low on the feeding chain for getting new releases. After watching the flick, the crew created another of its analogies, this one for Giambri's brilliant act of sorting out the errant Soviet November from an overabundance of ocean noises. He became *The Man with the Golden Ears*.

Tatlow spoke up. "So Giambri. Does this mean we gotta store you at Fort Knox when we're in port?"

Omensen asked with an almost perfect straight face, "You mean we haven't been at sea continuously since I reported aboard eighteen months ago? How come nobody told me?"

The COB jumped in. "All those times when the ship wasn't rocking and you didn't stand watches, well that was it. We were in port. You gotta get out of the crew's mess and look around once in a while, Omensen."

A sailor returned to poking at Giambri. "Fort Knox? Isn't that where they send big time offenders?"

Another answered, "That's Fort Leavenworth. It's in Kansas. Fort Knox is in Kentucky."

The sailor replied, "Ya mean those are different places?"

Tatlow, arms tossed in surrender, shook his head.

Giambri, the most laid-back man aboard, marched to a different drum than his shipmates and easily fended off ribbing. His tactic of choice: take the initiative. He opened referring to *Clamagore*'s recent run-in with the Soviet Kotlin.

"You were on the bridge, Omensen. How hairy did it get up there?"

The lanky Texan looked at Chief Beyers. *Silence is golden* ruled in the radio shack owing to large volumes of classified material that passed through there.

Beyers, a New Englander, nodded in response to the implied question and through a nasal squeaky voice said, "Don't tell us about anything the Russians didn't see."

Jumping back in, Giambri said, "Gimme a break, COB. It was broad daylight. They saw everything."

Omensen gave a blow-by-blow of all that transpired the previous afternoon, particularly the frustration of the Kotlin CO and his bridge watch. "He was caught in a mousetrap and couldn't get out."

After a cautious glance at the COB, Omensen explained how the Soviets manned their quad forty-millimeter guns, and getting no frown from Beyers, went on to an attentive audience.

Giambri, self-designated ship's poet, had written a *Canterbury Tales*-like narrative blank verse poem on *Clamagore*, giving a stanza to each crewmember. In these, he plays the COB and Omensen off each other.

> The COB laughs loud and says,
> "Son, on the surface
> they all look a little different,
> but take my word for it;
> down below they're all built the same.
> Snorkle for a bit until you get a full charge up,
> Then, take 'er down to test depth.
> Getting married doesn't change the plumbing."

> Omensen passes by catching only the conversation's tail end.
> He nods at the COB and says,
> "Maybe you should stick to cribbage, BOY."

Abrupt clanging of the general alarm ended the discussion. The 1MC blared, "Now man battle-stations torpedo!"

The COB declared, "Showtime," and the men moved quickly to their stations.

Jean Ann drove Benjamin to his first day at Princess Anne School. A bus passed through Sandbridge, but she'd do the honors for this outing. A genuine mother, she wanted a good look at the new teacher.

She gave Paul a lift to Dam Neck, her first visit to the base that began life as an ocean side anti-aircraft gunnery range. Suburban sprawl of the late fifties engulfed it, making live firing too dangerous. It now housed school buildings equipped to instruct Naval personnel in rapidly evolving technology. Much of the area's rural character remained, however nearby truck farms gave way to private residences and disappeared.

Paul said to his son through a prideful look, "Okay, mister big time first grader, you behave. Got that?"

Benjamin replied, a grin engulfing his face, "I'll behave, Daddy."

"What about you, Paul?" Jean Ann asked, "Are you going to behave in school today?"

"Don't I always do what I'm told?"

"Only when what you're told is what you want to do."

"Then how 'bout lunch today at the O-club?"

"Rain check, Paul. Pantry's bare. I'm off to the Oceana commissary for some grocery shopping."

"Wouldn't be you'll spend some time checking out the teachers at Princess Anne?"

"I might. For a moment or two maybe."

"Sure, Babe," he said. "Pick me up right here at four thirty."

"See you then."

They kissed and she drove off.

Brenda's face fell. "Terry, why are we doing this?" Her voice low contradicted inner feelings.

Terry replied, "Bren, he had good reason to come after me." He looked about. "You must make certain this goes no further than here."

Lorraine looked on, eyes wide.

Terry continued. "I torpedoed and sank Norovsky's ship. Certainly a number of his friends went down with her. How could any of us not react as he did? We were sixteen years younger then. He has come to terms with American policies being more toward what he wants for his country than his former government. He's one of us, now."

Brenda persisted. "You've always told me it's not personal between opposing warriors."

"Ideally, yes, but assassination is not unique to only foreigners. Japanese Admiral Yamamoto didn't die as a victim of casual combat. His death came from specifically targeting him for who he was. That's not supposed to happen."

Brenda wouldn't let it go. "But why us? Why here? You're my husband, Terry. He tried to murder you."

"We have important work for him that requires personal interfaces with me. Any remaining apprehensions must be set aside. What better reinforcement for him than to be received by my wife and our friends?"

Brenda didn't show any signs of being convinced as she asked, "But why Lorraine and Rick?"

"Before Rick came into Lorraine's life, a Soviet agent befriended her. She knew neither his nationality nor purpose. Norovsky, working for DNI, tracked this man down and caused him to be deported. Bren, you recall fretting over the thought of having to tell Lorraine her friend was an enemy agent. Norovsky knew of the affection between them and this still troubles him."

"So what do we do, Terry? Have it out right here and now?"

"We do nothing. He knows you and Lorraine are aware of his past. A little congeniality will do much for a man who does a great deal for our country. I understand completely if you'd rather not do this, so there is time for you to leave before Norovsky arrives."

Lorraine, unnerved somewhat by Brenda's discomposure, recalled the circumstance alluded to by Terry Martin. Though not a threat to her own life, ten years ago a Russian Naval Officer, Pasha Martinov, set out to use Lorraine in conjunction with efforts to conduct espionage against the United States. Initially calloused, Martinov pretended interest in Lorraine to cultivate her. However, despite best efforts, affection for this remarkable young woman inevitably evolved and became an instrument in his capture by Norovsky, under his cover name Earl Adams. This resulted in Martinov's deportation to the Soviet Union.

Her feelings had grown for Pasha also, but limited time together precluded more serious involvement. A bittersweet parting concluded their relationship. She recalled her final words to Martinov before he boarded a plane that would take him back to the Soviet Union, *Live long and be happy, Pasha.*

Lorraine said, "I'm okay if Brenda is."

Brenda cooled down. "I'll stay, Terry, but I'm still simmering over not hearing about this before driving all the way down here."

"You're right, Bren. But this came together so fast, I didn't have time. Norovsky leaves for Naples tonight. I had not met him till this morning. Seems to be a sensitive guy, and nobody was more surprised than me to learn about this baggage he carries. I assured him we've all put this behind us. That's why I invited him to have lunch with us."

Brenda replied, "Okay, but we don't do this anymore. Right?"

"Right, sweetheart."

At that instant Markham greeted an aging Vasiliy Norovsky; the wear of fifty-five years under hard conditions made him appear more a benevolent grandfather than a DNI agent.

Brenda's glance at Norovsky dissolved any remaining animosity.

Phil Redmond mounted the conning tower ladder and asked the predictable, "What've we got, Denny?"

"Would you believe the whole Sixth Fleet, Captain?"

"No."

"Then how 'bout a bird farm and six escorts?"

"A little more like it."

A seven-man attack party jammed into the eight by eleven foot cylindrical conning tower and began lighting off equipment, donning headsets and manning their stations. This included the CO as approach officer, who would begin taking three-second periscope looks to direct the attack.

The soft burble of ventilation outlets and whirring of analog gears in the torpedo data computer (TDC) could be heard but nothing else. Battle stations rule: no one speaks except the CO, and he only to give orders and report what he sees through the scope. A compulsive joker, Redmond occasionally bent this rule to alleviate tension.

The XO, attack coordinator (AC), may initiate comments, but only to bring the captain's attention to items that might be overlooked. The AC directs the choir, but his most important job: prevent rapid accumulation of data from obscuring the big picture. He mentally keeps track of the escorts to ensure *Clamagore* does not get into a collision course situation. Dave Zane does what all good execs do: run the show quietly from the background.

Excitement hung heavy. Though their target is a fellow U.S. warship, the attack party thrills to the chase. All performed roles essential to breaching a screen of six destroyers, reach attack position and place an exercise torpedo beneath a U.S. aircraft carrier.

The exercise for surface units, equally important win or lose, permits learning hard lessons in a non-combat environment.

Denny reckoned, *We help the bird farmers by knocking them off, so why not do it often?*

Submariners are a competitive lot.

Battle stations quartermaster of the watch assignment went to the biggest and strongest man in the quartermaster gang to assist the captain with hefting the attack periscope about. Quartermaster Seaman Brad Pace filled this requirement with his powerful six-foot two athletic frame. On the captain's order, Pace activates a control rod to raise and lower the scope. The handles rigged out, he places his hands over the captain's. Pace must sense the CO's intentions by touch and assist him to train the heavy, manually controlled scope shaft to the ordered bearing.

At Redmond's command of "Bearing ... mark!" Pace ensures the optics are in high power by forcing the skipper's right hand firmly in a backward circular motion.

Quartermaster third class John Howell operated the dead reckoning tracer (DRT), moving a tracer that automatically indicated the ship's position across a bottom lighted table. Howell records times, target range and at periscope observation and reads target bearings from a gyro compass repeater mounted above the table. Here the exec keeps track of other contacts. He frequently nags the skipper to check bearings lest he become mesmerized by the closing bird farm and lose the big picture. Zane had confidence Redmond would not let this happen, but the lives of eighty crewmen hung in the balance, so the two most competent sets of eyes on the ship checked each other throughout the exercise. A destroyer's bow crashing through *Clamagore*'s fragile hull would ruin the entire day.

TDC operator Denny Kolb entered target ranges and bearings announced by the captain at each periscope observation. Differences between observed and indicated ranges and bearings, spoken aloud by the operator in response, are entered on the ensuing look to refine target course and speed. Data is computed and transmitted directly to the torpedo in a launcher. This includes gyro deflection angle that sends the torpedo in the direction it must travel to ensure target intercept.

An MK-14 exercise round waited for launch on the captain's command. The warhead was replaced with a tank of seawater. At end of run, compressed air ejects ballast to make the unit positively buoyant to float up for recovery. Exercise torpedoes run at sixty feet to ensure they pass well below the target. The ton and a half vehicle at forty-five knots would penetrate the hulls of most U.S. warships if struck.

Redmond recalled during his junior officer days seeing a patrol craft returning to port with an impaled MK-14 dangling from its side. The overzealous submarine attack party erred and set the torpedo at impact depth instead of the deep run. Heads rolled accordingly.

Redmond, on receiving report that battle stations had been manned throughout the ship, briefed the attack party. "We're six thousand yards off the target's track. We'll drop below the layer and close target at series batteries (enables ship to run up to nineteen knots for short periods) for fifteen minutes. That'll close the range to two grand." He scanned each face, particularly Zane's, to ensure no one had a problem with that then continued. "Sonar estimates formation speed to be fourteen knots based on escort propeller turn count. Denny, I'll give you a bearing and range to the lead escort. Enter them into the TDC for tracking. Check yours with sonar bearings continuously and let me know if they start to deviate."

"Aye, Captain."

Redmond nodded. "Okay, up number two for an observation to the lead escort."

The hydraulic lifters hissed as the scope rose from its well. Pace snapped down the handles and trained to the target's relative bearing. Redmond looked through the optics and said, "Bearing ... mark!"

He felt Pace's hand pressure to ensure high power.

"Three-two-five true," announced the DRT operator.

Ducking from beneath the yoke in time to clear his head from its downward path, Redmond said, "Sherman class destroyer, angle-on-the-bow, starboard thirty. Use masthead height one-twenty feet, two and a half in high power (he referred to the number of telemetry marks subtended between the target's highest point to its waterline). Second bow wave two hundred feet back tracks with target speed fourteen knots from sonar. Got it in, Denny?"

Kolb replied, "Entered."

Dave Zane said, "Telemetry range checks with initial estimate, Captain. Six grand."

Redmond replied, "Make your depth one-five-zero feet and kick'er in the ass (make best speed)."

Clamagore went to ordered depth and maximum speed, settling out slightly above eighteen knots causing the superstructure to rattle. Below the thermal layer, coupled with the escorts' continual banging away with active sonar, *Clamagore*'s generated high-speed noise could not be detected.

Fifteen silent minutes passed.

Redmond ordered, "All ahead two thirds, parallel batteries. Set condition Baker and come to periscope depth. Denny, do sonar and generated bearings continue to match?"

"They do, Captain."

"Good," and to Quartermaster Seaman Pace he said, "Raise number two at nine-zero feet."

Redmond pressed his eye to the optics well before they broke surface and swung the scope continuously to spot a possible escort that might have slipped through the mix. When the upper optics broached above the surface, Redmond swung the scope through three hundred sixty degrees. Noting the bird farm approached optimum attack position, he signaled for the scope to be lowered.

He grinned at his attack party and announced, "Gentlemen. We are in the hen house. Now let's interrupt the bird farmer's afternoon nap."

Chapter 8

Jean Ann asked her husband, "Why is it when you sail off and I ask you where you're going, all you tell me is *out*. And when I ask what you did, I always get the same answer, *nothing*. Are you trying to keep me from knowing something scary happens out there?"

"Babe, if I told you, I'd have to kill you. Bad thing on such a beautiful day. But how 'bout if I tell you how scary submarine training can get?"

The Submarine Base escape training tower stands beside the Thames River at New London, Connecticut. Ensign Paul Scott sat beneath it in an after torpedo room mock up with five Officer Submarine School classmates. Most compared the simulated compartment to an oversized septic tank.

One hundred ten feet of water inside the tank exerted forty-four pounds of pressure per square inch on a hatch atop the compartment identical to those on submarines.

An enlisted torpedoman, six feet three, arms resembling an Arm and Hammer Baking Soda label, snarled from a head that would fit easily into a size six hat, but sat atop an eighteen inch neck. Enlisted men rarely had control over commissioned officers and *size six* relished the opportunity.

"Do the math. A thirty-inch diameter hatch cover has over a thousand square inches. Forty-four psi makes twenty-two tons holding it shut. Anybody who doesn't believe this, try shoving it open."

Nearly oblivious to *size six*'s haranguing, a knotted stomach kept reminding Paul of his rising stress level. He wondered why in hell he'd volunteered for this in the first place. Married barely eighteen months, realization set in that decisions no longer affected only him. Jean Ann and eight-month-old Benjamin must also bear the brunt of Paul's errors. Thoughts of his wife, a favorite composure-regaining device, always worked its magic, but under these circumstances, the elixir barely kept pace.

Paul said to the officer seated beside him, "We're going to swim up a hundred ten feet with nothing, no Momsen lung breathing apparatus, no life jacket. Just us."

"Look at it this way," came the reply. "We at least get to wear swimsuits. They could make us do it bare-ass."

Size six snapped, "Listen up. You've been through this in class, but one more time for anybody who didn't take notes. You! Pay attention," gesturing toward an officer who raised his head in response but said nothing.

The instructor went over everything, point by point. "At forty-four psi, one breath equals four on the surface, so after I pressurize the compartment, breathe sparingly or your head will start spinning like a top. Good part is a single breath here has as much oxygen as four on the surface. This gives you plenty of time to make your way to the top.

"Don't worry about getting the bends. You won't be exposed to high pressure long enough for nitrogen to dissolve in your blood."

He scanned the officers a final time through his sternest look. "Form a line … we leave one by one, me last. Got that?

"So hear me good. Not paying attention will give you more trouble than you want. Come to the edge of the skirt, take a deep breath, duck under then climb up and out. Don't swim! Arch your back; hands at your sides and you'll float up on your own. Everybody got that?"

A chorus of tentative yeses followed.

"Good," *size six* acknowledged. "Now as you float up, whistle. That's right, whistle. It'll make bubbles and be damn sure you watch them. They rise at two feet per second, and you want to keep up. Not ahead, not behind, but keep up. Got that?"

More yeses.

"So watch the bubbles. If they go up faster than you, whistle softer. Slower than you means you're not whistling hard enough. Remember. Two feet a second. You got a hundred and ten feet of water above so you'll be at the surface in a minute. Do what I tell you and everything will be okay. Otherwise—" *Size six* interrupted himself then ordered the officer who had been perceived inattentive, "You. Get over here and give me a hand pulling this skirt down."

An overhead deck access hatch doubled as an escape route. A steel skirt is lowered to waist level of the occupants. Water is admitted, but stopped at the skirt bottom by bleeding air into the compartment. Equal pressure on both sides of the hatch eliminates the twenty-two-ton differential permitting it to be opened.

With obvious glee, *size six* admitted water into the compartment at maximum rate. A roar deafened occupants and mist limited visibility to a few feet. Air bled in so rapidly that the officers' hands flew to their ears in vain efforts to limit the searing pain.

That jackass loves this. A pragmatist, Paul believed too many had gone through this before him and emerged unscathed, so it can't be dangerous. The Navy had too much invested to let anything bad happen. *Logic, damn it, logic.*

Size six disappeared under the skirt, rose to the hatch, opened it and returned to the compartment. "Okay, let's get going. Remember everything I told you."

Three preceded Paul before he took a deep breath and ducked beneath the hatch skirt. Making his way up slowly, he arched his back and began the ascent. His biggest concern, bursting his lungs from excessive air pressure when he reached the surface.

Bubbles going up faster than me. Going up too slow, dammit. Blow softer, but not too soft. Ah that's it. Staying right with the little devils. Wonder if someone really painted a mermaid on the tank wall like they told us at school? Yep. There it is. What a pair of knockers. If the artist knew the woman who inspired them, I sure envy him. Better not mention that to Jean Ann. How long since I went through that damn hatch? Seems a helluva lot longer than a minute.

Paul caught sight of ripples above and kicking feet of those who went ahead of him. *The surface, dammit. Almost there.* Elation. His stomach now completely unknotted.

An instant later, Paul broached the surface and made his way to the edge of the tank.

He shouted triumphantly, "Graduation!"

Phil Redmond wore what could be the happiest expression of his entire life as the scope hissed down into the well. Every submarine CO's dream: put an exercise torpedo under a bird farm.

"Angle on the bow, starboard fifteen. Dave, I need a heading for a thirty degree target lead with the bow tubes. Come to a course thirty degrees ahead of target true bearing."

He asked for the optimum course to close target intended track.

"Zero-zero-five, Captain."

"Make it so, Dave. All ahead standard. Use masthead height one-four-eight, three point three divisions in high power. *Range?*"

"Three-five hundred."

The trigonometric relationship between observed angular measurement derived from periscope division marks and distance between the target masthead and water surface comprises target range.

Zane made a quick estimate. *Sine of an angle below thirty degrees is roughly that angle divided by sixty. For fifteen degrees, one quarter. That times range equals distance to target track. In this case, eight hundred seventy-five yards.*

"We're under nine hundred yards approaching optimum firing range. Recommend slowing to one-third, Captain."

Redmond ordered the slower speed, and then, "Confirm the exercise fish in tube one."

Zane had the phone talker verify this with the forward torpedo room.

Redmond looked at his exec for affirmation as he ordered, "Make tube one ready in all respects except opening the outer door. Set speed high, running depth six-zero feet. Verify settings."

Zane nodded as the phone talker relayed the order.

"Dave, I want to fire with a ninety degree torpedo track ... torpedo to pass under target at best angle to use maximum length for offsetting errors."

"Use formation speed fourteen knots. Okay, Captain?"

"Use it."

Zane used his sine of the angle thumb rule again for torpedo intercept. *Target speed fourteen divided by torpedo speed forty-five knots equals decimal point three one, sine of eighteen degrees.*

"Firing bearing three-four-two relative, Captain."

"Good," Redmond said, and then to Denny Kolb, "Give me a mark at target bearing three-four-zero."

"Three-three-nine now, Captain. Recommend final bearing and shoot."

Redmond ordered the torpedo outer door opened and hand signaled Quartermaster Seaman Pace to raise the scope. "Final bearing and shoot, but give me a range check before launching."

Clear of the well, Pace rotated the scope to the reported bearing.

Redmond plastered his face against the optics. "Bearing ... mark!"

He snapped up the handles, Pace's signal to lower the scope.

The DRT operator Petty Officer Howell replied, "Three-four-seven true."

Denny Kolb acknowledged, "Checks," indicating the bearing matched by the TDC. They had a good solution.

Keeping the excitement from his voice, Redmond said, "Twelve divisions in high power."

Zane responded, "Nine hundred eighty yards, Captain."

Kolb said, "Check," indicating the TDC solution had reached perfection.

"Fire one!"

The firing panel operator reported, "One fired electrically, Captain." A shudder registered throughout the ship signaling a ton and a half torpedo ejected from its launcher.

Sonar reported, "Hear torpedo running hot, straight and normal, Conn."

With six destroyers screening ahead, lookouts on the aircraft carrier USS *Monmouth* felt no need to scan their sectors carefully, but a newly assigned sailor persisted in holding binoculars continuously to his head.

"Officer of the deck, I see something."

Indifference clear in the OOD's voice, he asked, "What? Where?"

"There, sir. Broad on the starboard bow," said the sailor lookout, using a hand gesture to accompany his report.

Through his binoculars, the OOD sighted a bubble trail racing directly toward *Monmouth.* Too late! Bubbles rise at two feet per second.   At sixty feet and forty-five knots, a torpedo runs seven hundred fifty yards ahead of its bubble trail on the surface.

Sailors below decks in the engine rooms heard a loud *whumpf* as the torpedo passed directly beneath them.

Redmond picked up the UQC (underwater telephone) mike. "Oscar Sierra, oscar sierra, oscar sierra," the NATO code for having launched a practice weapon.

Then on the 21MC, "After Torpedo Room ... Conn. Load, flood and release one green flare."

The signal to show submarine position and validate it is within effective torpedo attack range of the target. The fantail lookout on the screen commander's destroyer spotted a green flare parachuting down close aboard *Monmouth* and reported this to the OOD.

Both the screen commander and destroyer CO went immediately to the bridge on receipt of the bad news. Looking aft in time to see a green flare hit the surface, a grim thought overtook both simultaneously. *Monmouth*'s skipper, an officer on the fast track for flag rank by virtue of his assignment would not be pleased that a lone diesel-electric submarine successfully evaded the destroyer screen and attacked his ship. This would not improve his promotion chances. The post-operation conference portended to be an uncomfortable one.

Oblivious to all this, the victorious *Clamagore* raced to recover her exercise torpedo that floated beyond the bird farm, its conical, international orange warhead protruding above the surface.   It resembled a nun buoy, marking the eastside of the Thames River channel at *Clamagore*'s far away New London, Connecticut homeport.

Chapter 9

Phil Redmond and Dave Zane sat behind cups of hot coffee in the wardroom as the triumphant *Clamagore* crew went about recovering an exercise torpedo, a complex task, but well within the crew's abilities. Redmond understood free reining. Nothing enhances morale quite like standing aside and letting the crew do its job.

"So Dave, where do you go from here, now that Epworth turned you down?" Redmond knew his exec did not take the rejection personally and said, "That guy fulfills an Abraham Lincoln prophecy ... 'Nearly all men can stand adversity, but if you want to test a man's character, give him power'."

Zane stood in company with a great number of competent submariners rejected by Epworth, while many who could not lead a goat out of a closet made the cut.

Redmond went on, "You know I'll punch your prospective CO. But do you really want to hang around and be a diesel boat pallbearer?"

Grinning, Zane said, "Since we're tossing quotations around, do you recall this one by Churchill? 'Now this is not the end. It is not even the beginning of the end. But it is, perhaps, the end of the beginning'."

"Yep. He said that right after the Nazis were kicked out of North Africa. What's that got to do with anything, Dave?"

"A lot, Captain. The submarine force cut its teeth on diesel power. We were the beginning, so ending it also ends us."

"Leave it to the exec to clear away fog."

"That's our job, isn't it? I've given thought to EDO (Engineering Duty Only) officer. Engineering always appealed to me."

"You thinking about PG (Post Graduate) school? Dale and Bea will love Monterey."

"You're a mind reader, Captain. There's a problem, though. Your tour in *Clamagore* ends a year before mine. I'm not sure the new CO will want to cut me loose till my tour's up."

"I don't think that'll matter. As diesel boats fall off the line, there'll be more qualified officers than billets. Pickings will be very good. Do you have a problem with getting booted off before I leave?"

"I was hoping you'd say that, Captain."

"Consider it done."

At six p.m. sharp, Joe Dunn made a grand entrance, his dog-eared banjo in one hand and two bottles of Merlot in the other. Handing his banjo to Paul, they shook hands and Jean Ann relieved him of the wine.

Paul introduced his former BOQ roommate to Jean Ann. A New Englander, Joe stood tall and muscular. Piercing blue eyes looked out from beneath light-brown curly hair cut military style.

Joe Dunn, his own stand-up comic, used feigned outrage as his *shtick*. No one did it better. He opened by clowning indignation for not having private time with Jean Ann.

"Can't you find something else to do but leer at us, Paul?"

Paul shook his head, "We're in for it tonight."

"In for what? Why does everybody treat me so bad? Give me my banjo, dammit. The hell with you, Scott. Have your damn beach party without music" then stomped toward the door like an upset five-year-old who didn't get his way.

Joe kept Jean Ann and Paul in stitches while they prepared the barbecue. Next came full up roughhouse with the boys on the family room floor. David and Benjamin shrieked their excitement as Joe demonstrated outrageously named wrestling holds. With exaggerated animation, he declared no one could possibly escape from them.

"Ha, the dirty rotten little kid squeezin' chicken wing hold. Nobody gets out of that! Nobody, I tell you!"

Once in the hold, Joe looked away from his *victim* and continued to extol the hold's virtues while David and Benjamin escaped. They'd then tap him on the shoulder as Joe did a perfect job of pretending astonishment on discovering they had freed themselves. The boys would have kept the game going all night.

They enjoyed a perfect barbecue—steaks, corn on the cob and garden salad, all beneath a clear, star-studded sky.

Paul declared, "Shades of Illinois."

Joe exclaimed in outraged tones, "This meat from there? Ptui!" He pretended to spit a mouthful of food on the beach. "Nobody told me I was eating Illinois food. You tryin' to make me sick? I'm going in the house and brush my teeth," he said, followed by a few steps of his hilarious walk.

Paul asked, "How much wine did you give him, Jean Ann?"

Joe abruptly changed his tone and pretended to weep bitterly. "See how I get treated? God knows how hard I try. A little compassion from my friends is asking too much?"

Another shift of character and Joe presented a TV commercial. He mimicked a staid physician delivering somber words on the importance of laughter to the proper digestion of food.

Paul complained, "Problem with the Navy is we don't have enough straight men."

The boys stayed up but vied for the most comfortable position beside their mother as Joe began to strum his banjo. His pleasant tenor voice gave a nice rendition of *Yellow Bird.*

"C'mon, let's hear it second time through."

Paul had not heard Jean Ann sing to accompaniment since her choir days. The blend of her voice with Joe's came across quite well.

Joe played songs everyone knew and all joined in, tentative at first, but prompted by David and Benjamin's unabashed enthusiasm, voices grew stronger. Selections included *Michael Row the Boat Ashore, Do-Re-Mi* from the Broadway show *The Sound of Music,* and for the boys, Stephen Foster's *Camptown Races* and *Oh Susannah.*

Many songs later, they closed with a lively version of *Those Were the Days,* popularized by the talented Mary Hopkin. Empty wine bottles resulted in proportionately elevated volumes. Joe sang each stanza and the others joined in on the chorus.

Jean Ann blinked back a tear in the darkness. The lyrics implied *days* would end and be inevitably spoken of as having passed. *Dear God please don't ever let these days end, for I am so very happy in them,* she prayed silently.

Later, at the good night sayings, Joe drew Jean Ann into an exaggerated sensual embrace then screwing up his face in a disgusted look, he turned to Paul, "Can we have a little privacy here? Do you have to hound everything I do?"

Joe stomped off in his trademark angry walk back to the car. He opened the door, threw his banjo into the backseat with a resounding *bong,* slammed the door and peeled rubber in a mimicked angry departure.

Kapitan 2nd Rank Piotr Denisov quietly oversaw his executive officer maneuver *Mayakovsky* alongside her berth at the port of Severodvinsk. *Kapitan* 3rd Rank Andrej Smirnov needed no supervision. Well qualified and overdue for command, his *kapitan* performed only a perfunctory task.

The city had a dubious claim to fame. Marina Prusakova, widow of Lee Harvey Oswald, assassin of President John F. Kennedy, had been born there.

Zampolit, Kapitan 2nd Rank Evgenij Knyazev remained below decks, excusing himself to complete reports. Actually, mooring a ship the size of *Mayakovsky* can be risky. In the event of a problem Knyazev distanced himself sufficiently so as not to be implicated.

Denisov knew the *zampolit* to be a fence rider. He recalled Knyazev's advice when Piotr feigned a desire to remain on station despite a major equipment failure. '*Komrade Kapitan, your zeal and determination are applauded. This shall be noted. But our attack class nuclear powered submarines number far too few to risk losing one, even on a mission as important as ours. I suggest we contact naval headquarters for instruction.*'

Denisov knew also the *zampolit* would abandon this advice like rats leaving a sinking ship if he learned the party saw otherwise.

Piotr put binoculars to his eyes and scanned the dock for Irene. How he had missed her. He spotted her with their sons Pasha and Andrushka at her side. He hoped she'd be alone and boys at school. Piotr's father, Igor, veteran of the Great Patriotic War, after half a vodka bottle once told Piotr of a ski soldier who returned home to his wife after a long campaign. '*Second thing he did was take off his skis.*'

Beside Irene stood a row of officers whose stern expressions told him his greeting with his wife and sons would be a short one. Likely several hours would pass before he could join her and return to their home in Severodvinsk.

Before long, Piotr stood beside Irene and looked into the same light-blues eyes that had stolen his heart at her father's funeral some years before.

Despite the unquestioned need for *Mayakovsky*'s return to port, a meeting in the officers' mess dragged on for three hours before a consensus validated Piotr's reasons. As the inevitable finding emerged, Knyazev maneuvered to take a lion's share of credit for the decision. He got no resistance from the assembled officers, who availed every opportunity to point out the wisdom of party views over those of Navy line officers.

Piotr pleaded with Irene to let him take her and the boys to a restaurant, but his wife insisted dinner would be at home. She would pull out all stops—Chicken Kiev, smoked fish, blini (pancakes topped with sour cream) and caviar. There would also be potatoes, pickled vegetables and Piotr's favorite borsch (beet soup).

Arriving home, Pasha and Andrushka vied for their father's attention, while Irene, the serene one, went about her chores as though it were any other day. Just a question of time before the boys tired and went off to bed as always. Irene knew passing time served only to whet Piotr's appetite for her. After dinner, they sat and fumbled their way through another glass of wine.

An hour and a half later, Piotr took off his skis.

Piotr had been given a fortnight ashore, the able Smirnov remaining aboard to oversee *Mayakovsky*'s repairs. He sat at breakfast with Irene and reviewed material she had gathered on Sochi—Russia's largest resort city in Krasnodar Krai on the Black Sea coast. They'd travel and stay there for a time to be joined by their sons' godfather, Pasha Martinov and his family.

Sochi sprawls along the shores of the Black Sea with snow-capped Caucasus Mountain peaks in the background. Ninety miles in length, greater Sochi claims to be the longest city in Europe. Its humid, subtropical climate, Mediterranean-like summers average seventy degrees Fahrenheit during the day to sixty-one degrees at night.

They traveled by train the next morning. None of Piotr's family had ever been there before so they looked forward to long days on Sochi's fabled beaches with palm trees and tropical climate—a respite from bleak Severodvinsk. Soviet families vacationed along the Black Sea to enjoy the beach, see waterfalls and visit Krasnaya Polyana, a conglomeration of small communities that feature a zoo, circus, and several wineries.

Pasha Martinov and Piotr Denisov sat on the balcony of the Denisov rental at Sochi. With pride, they watched their families enjoying the beach several stories below. Not quite mid-afternoon, they had already started on a vodka bottle.

Piotr said, "We Russians drink too much. Why do you suppose that is, Pasha?"

Martinov raised his glass and took a heavy swig. "I suppose because we have much to drink about."

Taking a generous swallow from his own glass, Piotr replied, "Why is that so, Pasha?"

"You surprise me *Komrade*," Martinov replied, using the term *Komrade* clearly sarcastic to make a point. "Since we arrived here, you've spoken of little else than of your disenchantment with the party's control over everything you do on *Mayakovsky*. Is that not so?"

"It's a sailor's right to gripe, my friend. You know that well."

"I do, Piotr. And talking about it with a good friend is what makes it bearable."

Pasha went on. "Piotr, do you sometimes think we live under bad conditions, but bear them only because we believe they will improve?"

"I never thought on that. Life is a heavy burden and all of us must bear it."

Pasha with eyebrows arched asked, "And then what happens?"

"Nothing. You just go on."

"No, Piotr. You bear up under it and then you die. Worse, it is the same legacy we leave our children." Pasha gestured toward the beach where their sons played happily in the water under the watchful eyes of their mothers. "Do you ever wish it could be better for them?"

"Of course I do, Pasha."

"May I ask why you hope that? What evidence of change do you see? We are given to believe these are but temporary conditions to be endured in order to reach a brighter tomorrow. The question is the duration of *temporary.* Forty-seven years have passed since the October Revolution. How much has the plight of common men improved since then? Little better than under the Czars, if at all."

Piotr had no wish to continue the discussion and attempted to lighten it. "Pasha! We have not yet had enough vodka to speak of such heavy topics."

"A wise observation ... it enables us to speak what is truly on our minds. It dissolves inhibition and with it our fear of being overheard."

Deciding he had no choice but to hear his friend out, Piotr yielded.

Pasha went on. "You know about the time I spent in America."

"It must have been a harrowing experience. I don't know how you could live under constant fear of being identified."

"It was anything but harrowing, my friend. Everything I saw in America contradicted what we have been told. People move about unfettered by national police. No one checks their comings and goings. Communities provide their own law enforcement that must report to elected officials."

"Are you certain of this, Pasha?"

"Absolutely. I needed to understand this to plan my movements about the country."

"How can a country exist that way? How can there be security?"

"Trust me, Piotr. There is. From what I saw, the crime rate is much lower than here."

Shrugging his shoulders, Piotr looked about and said, "Pasha, it is good we are not in earshot of anyone."

"My point exactly, Piotr. We must be concerned even while having private conversation. It is not so in America."

"But surely it is not permitted to openly criticize the government."

Pasha nodded at his friend. "It is. The American people would have it no other way. But if it makes you uncomfortable for me to say these things, I'll stop."

"Not in the least, Pasha. Can you tell me why it is as you say in America?"

Vodka loosened Pasha's inhibition and tongue so he said, "Because the population is made up of people like you and me. Except for descendants of Indian tribes that once roamed the land, everyone is either from someplace else or their forebears were. They have good genes inherited from people disenchanted with their homelands that had courage to pick up and move on. They have a legacy of initiative."

Piotr gestured toward the beach. "They are headed this way. We must talk about this another time, Pasha."

"We shall. Piotr, I cannot go back there. As you know I'm expelled as persona non grata. But you should think of going to America with Irene and the children. There you will find a far better life than is available in Mother Russia."

"Pasha my friend, you astound me."

"Do I? Did I not hear you'd like further discussion? What other possible reason could there be for this? Promise me you will think on it until we are next able to talk."

"I will, Pasha."

"Good. I know of one who could guide you out of Russia. He has done it before."

Chapter 10

Phil Redmond joked to Denny Kolb, "Don't get underway for home soon as I leave."

Kolb grinned at his skipper. "No, Captain. We'll wait till you're aboard *Monmouth*."

A Navy saying, 'The captain may go ashore, but the commanding officer is always aboard'. The responsibility went to the senior officer remaining behind so this went to LT Denny Kolb. Command at sea, even for only two hours thrilled Denny.

Dave Zane went over details with Kolb. Zane played his role perfectly—exec the worrywart—permits the skipper a cavalier image.

A destroyer CO in his gig (small powerboat for the CO's exclusive use) picked up the *Clamagore* officers for a ride to the flagship. Denny maneuvered *Clamagore* to put the wind on her starboard beam and make a lee (patch of calm water) to port for the pickup.

Redmond and Zane made small talk with the destroyer CO and his exec. No reference to the meeting agenda had been distributed, though surface officers expected it to be a butt chewing for letting *Clamagore* breach the screen and attack *Monmouth*.

Redmond and Zane climbed a ladder to the carrier then arriving at the quarterdeck, Redmond first saluted the colors flying from *Monmouth*'s truck then the officer of the deck. "Commanding Officer USS *Clamagore* requests permission to come aboard."

The OOD returned the salute. "Come aboard, sir."

The general announcing system blared, "*Clamagore* … arriving," as a seaman in dress white uniform led Redmond and Zane to the aviation briefing room.

They selected plush leather seats at the rear to await the admiral and as Zane settled into one of the chairs, he said, "Captain, this is more comfortable than my bunk on *Clamagore*. Don't make book on me staying awake."

The Task Group Commander entered the room. "Attention on deck!"

All officers rose and quickly reseated with the admiral's, "As you were, gentlemen." He went on, "I thought it well we summarize our eviction of Red submarines."

Zane said to Redmond in hushed tones, "Eviction? Did we participate?"

"Shhh," Redmond replied. "These seats might be bugged."

The admiral's chief staff officer (CSO) opened the first of several flip charts on an easel. The first depicted the operation area with positions of participating ships. The CSO went over the convening instructions, then went on to laud tactics overall. After much discussion of innovative actions but nothing on results (Redmond thought, *because there were none*), the briefer got down to the operation's piece de resistance—discovery of a surfaced November class submarine.

"Returning from searching a false contact report (clearly a slam at *Clamagore*), one of our aircraft conducted a careful search while returning to base." He flipped a chart page. "And there she is, top intelligence find of the entire cruise. The pilot who made this remarkable find is with us today. Commander Smith. Please stand up and take a bow."

A resounding standing ovation followed from all but Phil Redmond and Dave Zane.

The admiral remounted the stage and summoned Smith to join him. "Congratulations Commander."

They shook hands warmly.

"And now, on behalf of the Secretary of the Navy, I award you the Legion of Merit."

The admiral pinned the medal on Commander Smith to a second standing ovation. Redmond and Zane again remained seated.

An officer seated beside Redmond said, "I noticed you didn't stand."

Redmond replied, "If they pinned an LOM on the guy who really found the November, I'd have stood."

The officer regarded Redmond through a confused expression.

Clamagore's CO and exec expected the next meeting topic to bring redemption of sorts—how *Clamagore* slipped through the screen and sent a torpedo directly under *Monmouth*.

The admiral opted not. "This concludes our meeting. Dismissed gentlemen. Those who can, please join me for lunch in the Flag Mess (the admiral's personal dining room)."

The group rose to leave and the admiral asked the *Clamagore* officers to remain.

Redmond thought, *Crap. He noticed we didn't stand.*

The room cleared. Redmond and Zane approached the admiral.

Redmond said, "Yes, Admiral."

The flag officer looked sternly at Phil. "Captain, you surely know our flight deck is crowded with aircraft, some of them being refueled. It is dangerous for you to launch a flare close aboard like you did yesterday. I trust this won't happen again."

"It was stupid of me, Admiral. It will not happen again."

The admiral left.

Redmond turned to his exec. "Talk about head in the sand. We showed they're vulnerable to submarine attack, and the pompous ass chooses to ignore it."

Morose *Pershing* crew members formed a line before a coin-operated life insurance machine in the Quonset Point, RI Operations Building. The entire flight crew joined the line, doing little for the sailors' morale. Overage Super-Constellation airplanes chartered from newly established airlines to ferry Polaris crews across the North Atlantic rarely arrived Prestwick, Scotland completely intact. Landings never on all four engines and *Pershing* crew members routinely hand-cranked flaps and landing gear when hydraulic systems failed.

As the aircraft touched down safely, applause erupted from the grateful sailors.

Rain mixed with snow added to the gloom of a New England January night. Joe Dunn, perennial comedian, asked, "Is this anything like crossing the River Styx?"

The newcomers sat with other *Pershing* officers in a lounge. Only Paul acknowledged Joe's remark. No one else joined the conversation, so Paul and Joe spoke in low tones.

Joe said, "What a different atmosphere. In diesel boats, we could make light of any situation, regardless of how crappy. These nukes (nuclear power officers) act like having fun violates the rules."

Paul replied, "Do you notice there's a sharp line drawn between nukes and us? They're cordial but I think we're merely tolerated."

Joe nodded. "Most of these guys are former dieselers and know informality makes life bearable. Maybe your old skipper's right. Us unwashed are here to provide comic relief."

"Too bad you struck out with the Conn College chick. No surprise though."

"Easy for you to say … tucking in with Jean Ann every night. Where do I stand on the list if she gets fed up with you?"

"Don't mention it around her, Joe. If she knows you're interested, I'll get dropped like a hot rock."

"Give me her phone number and I promise not to mention it."

"Home wrecker."

"No, Paul. Liberator."

Vasiliy Norovsky became Earl Adams again, an undercover name used in a previous assignment. He went through his new cover story. On both sides, Cold War agencies were proficient at unmasking operative cover stories. Adams took no chances. On reaching Naples, if no one contacted him then all would be in vain. Adams liked the perks of his cover: an American tourist traveling to London, Paris, the Cote d'Azur, Venice and finally Naples, at DNI expense. He knew a Soviet agent would be assigned to follow him and enjoy the same agenda though likely anxious over costs. Adams spotted him in Paris. Soviet agents abroad stand out like hull numbers on a gray sail.

I'll show the dumb bastard how good things are outside the Soviet Union, Adams thought. Knowing he'd be followed, Adams dined in the finest restaurants and visited elaborate venues. *Maybe the SOB will see the light and defect.*

Adams stayed at the Grand Hotel Vesuvio Mantra, chuckling over thoughts of how this would set with his shadow's Soviet auditors. *America can outspend them. That's how we'll win.*

Adams dined at the Caruso Roof Garden Restaurant. Along with superb cuisine, he enjoyed a view of the Bay of Naples from Posillipo to Capri and Mount Vesuvius. Built in 1882, the Vesuvio had been the Neapolitan watering hole for kings, queens, celebrities and politicians. The hotel sits five minutes from Beverello Port for ferries that carry passengers to the Islands of Capri and Ischia.

Tomorrow Adams would take the one to Capri. In its confines, he'd approach his shadow as an oblivious fellow traveler and suggest they lunch together.

The Super-Connie touched down at Prestwick, Scotland with only two engines operating. *Pershing* crewmembers gathered their belongings and boarded buses for Gourock on the River Clyde. A barge would take them to Holy Loch and the submarine tender to await arrival of *Pershing,* their *boomer* (ballistic missile submarine). Per agreement with Great Britain, the entire installation had to be afloat. An anchored submarine tender with a supply barge moored alongside and a floating dry dock comprised the base. Somber moods at the Holy Loch base put Joe in mind of a Charles Dickens's nineteenth century London workhouse.

Dunn cast a look about the rural Scottish setting. Apart from the village of Dunoon on the Loch's northwest corner, he saw only cottages and farmhouses.

"Must really rip and roar around here after dark," said Joe. The Blue Crew watched *Pershing* slip into her berth. Two crews manned the boomers in order to maximize time spent on station. Two and a half days are budgeted for turnover, prior to the gold crew's return to the states for a month of standdown prior to two months of training before repeating the cycle.

Paul said, "I hear we should count on being aboard ship for the entire turnover. It's a twenty-four hour workday proposition."

"Nothing Fred Arnold and I can't handle over a few cool ones at the local pub," Joe replied. Fred had been Joe's roommate at Annapolis.

"Hell, I learned it all at Dam Neck. There's nothing Fred can teach me. What did you learn at Dam Neck, Paul?"

"Program used to be a noun, now it's a verb. That plus a little bit about missiles."

"What else do you need? Between the two of us we'll have enough time to make this a resort the Scots will thank us for. We'll improve international relations."

"Just don't leave too many international relatives here, Joe. The Scotts call 'em claymore weddings, not shotgun. Either you marry the girl or get your pecker hacked off."

"You have such a nice way of putting things, Paul."

Fred Arnold astounded Joe. Crisp, articulate Fred also projected the image of a man totally exhausted from demands of his new assignment. He spoke mainly in acronyms, implying he needed this to make it through their turnover agenda in two days.

To Joe, Fred appeared to hide his low confidence by tossing off Joe's suggestion of going ashore for a few cool ones, implying Dunn had no concept of turnover complexity. He detected the sham. Fred graduated *magna cum pelidentsium* (by the skin of his teeth).

The consummate joker, Joe began inventing acronyms. Fred pretended to understand fully lest voids in his knowledge reveal his insecurity. Terrified of his job, Fred attempted to smoke his way through the turnover.

Exasperated with the sham, Joe asked, "Do I get a look at the LKTCO log?"

"Sure. Eh, Chief," said Fred turning to the navigation gang's senior electronic technician. "Get the LKTCO log for Mister Dunn, please."

"LKTCO?" parroted the chief. "Must be a new term you picked up at Dam Neck."

"Yeah," said Joe, "Let's Knock This Crap Off and get on with it. Look Fred. Tell me what's wrong and I'll bail you out."

The navigation turnover abruptly improved.

Paul fared much better. His opposite number, Dick Olson, had resigned from the Navy, despite being selected for Lieutenant Commander two years early.

Olson joked, "What's the Navy coming to when they promote civilians?" He asked to know the specifics of what Paul had learned at Dam Neck.

After hearing Paul's account of the Dam Neck curriculum, Olson observed, "Figures. Instead of a simple overall approach, they plunge right into the mechanics of the inner workings and dazzle you with bullshit. It's really simple. The whole *bullet* sets in a launcher, just like a torpedo in the tube except it points upward. We tell the guidance system where we are and the direction and distance to the target. The guidance computer does the rest. There's a checkout of the missile just before launch, but what happens after it's on the way cannot be affected by us. Your job is to leave here with sixteen good birds and launchers, then keep them that way for the entire patrol. If what you do here has no traceability to that, then it doesn't need to be done."

"What you say makes sense, Dick. At Dam Neck we had hours on the guidance equation, binary math and Boolean algebra, but were never shown what to do with it."

Olson replied, "You'll have no use for that here. Makes you wonder how we ran diesel boats without being able to write the equation for fuel oxidation. We were too damn busy just making the damn things go to worry about unrelated nonsense."

The Navy rented a room at the Royal Marine Hotel on nearby Hunters Quay for use as an Officers' Club. It got little play from the submariners who had no wish to give the impression they had time for recreation. A defacto party was held on the eve of change of command, a formal transfer of *Pershing* from the Gold to Blue crew. Most *front-enders*—non-nuke former dieselers—attended.

After a quiet affair, the club emptied by 2000 (8:00 p.m.). The official change of command ritual would be held topside on the missile deck the following morning despite a cold, sluicing rain. The Scots had a term for this weather inherent in its very sound: *dreat*. The ceremony ended quickly and Paul found himself in charge of more explosive power than all the bombs dropped by both sides during World War Two, including the atomic bombs dropped at Hiroshima and Nagasaki.

Holy Loch, Scotland
Halloween 1965

Dear Jean Ann,

Hope this finds you and the boys coping well with the rigors of being engulfed with love and hospitality by Mom and Dad. Really tough life for you. I'd swap all the fun we have out here in a month for a day back there.

Joe and I went ashore Sunday and visited a Scottish pub at the head of Holy Loch called the Cot House. Don't ask me why. Not a single cot in sight. A three-piece combo: a piano, stool and a piano player of limited talent conducts sing-alongs that go well into the evenings. If the local constable fails to make his rounds (which he frequently does), it goes well into the next morning. Most clientele are retired people vacationing at a nearby resort for the aged. They like the Yanks very much, and with help from a good local whiskey, taught us lads more about Scottish folk songs than we ever cared to know. It was a fun evening. Our age group has no monopoly on having a good time. We missed your voice (I, other things). Joe did his usual shtick.

We got back to the ship to be cold-shouldered by the nuke officers. Most actually believe too much work needs to be done to permit recreation ashore, even for a few hours. It seems everyone works around the clock, or at least give that impression. It's not clear to me what really gets done.

My new commanding officer, Captain Pete Williams, also frowns on the notion we got time for the beach, but publishes no formal policy against it. I'm off to a bad start with him. I've been there before and it'll be okay.

We'll be shoving off soon. I'll get a letter in the mail before then. Remember our trip to New York when we heard Emil Gilels play Rachmaninoff's second piano concerto? I'm spinning it right now here in the wardroom and thinking about you. I know classical music is not your thing, and I appreciate you joining me for it every now and then. But I'm grateful for all the things you do for me. You're worth the chase, Jean Ann.

It's 0300 (three a.m.) and even the diehards have turned in. It's quiet.

I mailed a letter to Benjamin the other day. I hope he enjoyed it. Writing to him personally might help him over this hump. I hope he is dealing with being away from me better than I deal with being away from him.

I love you—seems I already said that, but what else is new?

Paul

Chapter11

USS *Clamagore* moored at Piraeus, Greece for a five-day visit prior to embarking on Phase II of Operation Eager Beaver. This phase, expanded to include NATO involvement, added three submarines to the mix, French, Greek and another U.S. ship reported to the Sixth Fleet.

Captain Cliff Harkins, Commander Task Force 69 (directs NATO submarine operations in the Mediterranean) waited on the dock, having traveled there to debrief Phil Redmond and his crew on the November encounter. Although Harkins's official grade is captain, he inherited the title commodore with his assignment.

Clamagore arrived October 28, a national holiday called Ohi Day (Day of *No*), celebrating Greek refusal to surrender to Axis Powers in 1940. Visiting warships fly the Greek National Ensign as a courtesy.

Prior to deployment, Denny Kolb procured national ensigns of each country to be visited. He did well except for the Greek flag that measured eight by twelve feet, too large to be flown from the pole mounted on the sail. This irritated Redmond considerably.

The resourceful Kolb, founding member of the fearsome foursome, had a plan. He knelt atop *Clamagore*'s fairwater and fastened the flag head to optics of a slightly raised number two periscope. Navy ceremony called for colors to be shifted when the first mooring line reached the dock, the national ensign struck from the mast, while another raised on a pole located on the stern. Simultaneously, the crew hoisted a Union Jack (blue field with fifty stars) on the bow jack staff. A shrill whistle from the bridge signaled initiation of this ritual. A quartermaster in the conning tower raised number two scope. Kolb fastened the flag foot to the huge shaft after it traveled eight feet. The quartermaster then raised the scope to full height. The smallest warship flew the largest Greek flag in the harbor, earning applause from onlookers standing dockside. Denny saved the day and his butt in the process.

Soon, Commodore Harkins with *Clamagore*'s officers sat behind ritual coffees in the wardroom. This included an uncomfortable Phil

Giambri, *man with the golden ears*, who detected and identified the Soviet November. Enlisted men normally entered the wardroom only for *Captain's Mast*, to be tried for a discipline infraction. Giambri later confided to his shipmates he felt like an Arab in a synagogue.

Harkins hung onto every syllable of the unfolding November incident. He asked frequent questions, surprising Giambri who believed officers concerned themselves only with results and not details. *Must have been a sonarman before he got commissioned.*

Harkins concluded, "Giambri, you did a superb job. I'm sure Captain Redmond told you your Legion of Merit for making the detection got hung on a naval aviator. I'm sorry about that. Maybe we can make it up to you. Your surname is Italian. Do you still have family in Italy?"

"My father's family is from Caccamo in the Province of Palermo."

"There's a vacant billet on my staff for a driver of a car that I never use. Maybe when *Clamagore* leaves the Med, your skipper can spare you for a month. Take the car and drive down to spend some time with your family. You can catch the ferry from Villa San Giovanni to Messina in Sicily."

"Thank you, Commodore. But there's a problem. My Sicilian cousins believe any Giambri in the Navy must be at least an admiral. I never told them I was, but then never said I wasn't. And all I brought with me are my uniforms."

Harkins smiled at the young petty officer. "Word goes around you're the ship's clown, Giambri. I can't let you impersonate an *officer*. However, will this work? The Naples Navy Drama Club recently produced Gilbert and Sullivan's *HMS Pinafore*. You can borrow the Rt. Hon. Sir Joseph Porter, KCB, First Lord of the Admiralty costume."

The grin on Giambri's face spread from ear to ear. "You're serious, Commodore?"

"Dead serious. What do you say?"

Giambri looked at Redmond, who nodded his approval.

"Why not?" Giambri replied, taking this remarkable turn of events in his usual easy stride.

Later, Harkins and Redmond remained in the wardroom while the crew scurried about preparing for visits to Piraeus and nearby Athens. Despite having only one shower for seventy-two crewmen, the men made it ashore in a remarkably short time.

Remnants of the fearsome foursome declared intentions to visit the Acropolis. They had only one shower to share, among eight officers.

The skipper confided to Commodore Harkins, "I think that's the Acropolis Bar and Grill."

"Taberna, Phil. Remember you're in Greece now. Too bad these guys aren't as straight-laced as we were at that age."

"Be careful what you wish for, Commodore."

Redmond went on. "I guess you heard about the meeting on *Monmouth*. Or should I say rhubarb?"

"You ruffled the Task Group Commander (TGC) I'm told."

"I ruffled him all right, but I'm not sure it's for the alleged reason … letting the flares go too near the bird farm. I suspect something else is bugging him."

"I know what you're thinking … uncovering the November when the rest of his force came up empty. That had to irritate him, but I believe your successful attack on *Monmouth* drove the problem."

"Then why did the zoomie get Giambri's LOM?"

"Do I think that was intentional? Yes. But it was the successful attack on *Monmouth* that pissed him off. Your job is simple, Phil. Find 'em and sink 'em. The TGC has to convince our NATO allies the US Navy controls the Med. Putting an MK-fourteen under *Monmouth* pricks that bubble. It's not his fault you can do that with impunity, but he's on the hook to explain it."

"Are you telling me to back off, Commodore? I sit too low on the totem pole to worry about that. My job is to get the most out of my ship. How can they fix it if they don't know what's wrong?"

Harkins knew Redmond smarted, but their discussion had run its course and he'd let it go at that. "So where do you want to go from here, Phil? I write your fitness report, not the TGC."

Making no effort to keep sarcasm from his voice, Redmond said, "With all due respect, Commodore, I'm not a nuke. I hear the New London real estate business is booming. Maybe I'll find a niche there."

Harkins shared the sense of injustice perpetrated on competent submariners simply because they didn't fulfill Rear Admiral Epworth's arbitrary requirement for high academic standing.

"A lot of your peers do well outside the submarine force."

"Like those who work for the TGC? I don't think I could live with covering up just to make me look good. I'm sorry, Commodore. I'm damn bitter about this class standing thing. I know I could get a helluva lot more out of Epworth's ships than some of the jackasses he took into his program." Redmond suddenly realized Epworth selected Harkins. "No offense intended, Commodore."

"None taken, Phil." For a moment he wondered why those selected did not take a stand on behalf of the superb officers being dropped by the wayside for no good reason. He knew the answer. It's Epworth's way or the highway, and no one has the courage to stand up to him. *Worse, nuclear power officers needed a reason to justify taking Epworth's inordinate abuse. They chose to acknowledge his insights to be better than their own and only Epworth's blatant rudeness can get officers to carry out the admiral's agenda. The fix for the admiral's distorted view of complacency in the submarine force would be to point out that error to him—career suicide for nuke officers. Edmund Burke got it right—the only thing necessary for the triumph of evil is for good men to do nothing.*

At 10:00 a.m., Earl Adams boarded the Aliscafo-Jet/Hydrofoil at the Beverello landing for a day trip to the Isle of Capri. As expected, his shadow boarded the crowded jetfoil a short time later.

Halfway through the crossing to Capri's Marina Grande, Adams approached the man, knowing it would make him uncomfortable, and extended his hand as he said in his well-trained New England accent, "How do you do, sir? I am Earl Adams. We have something in common. You were at the Lutetia Hotel, I believe ... a week ago in Paris."

Shadow attempted to mask the panic in his face. "It wasn't me," he said through a British accent. "I haven't visited Paris in ten years. I'm Reginald Foster." The man, mid-fifties, heavyset with receding black-gray hair, regarded Adams through pale blue eyes.

"I'm sorry, Mr. Foster. Or may I call you Reginald? I would say you have a twin brother in France," Adams said, not revealing the man he saw in Paris wore the same drab outfit, tweed coat, gray trousers and leather slouch hat.

Foster's confidence rose with the perception Adams did not recognize him, their meeting but a casual chance of luck. *This will be beneficial.* "Reginald is fine, but I prefer Rege."

Adams smiled. "Earl for me please. Such a beautiful place, do you agree?"

The magnificence of Sorrento Peninsula slipped by to the south, while ahead Capri began to rise out of Naples Bay.

"It is indeed. My first visit. I traveled here from London yesterday for a fortnight stay."

In a pig's ass, Adams thought. "Wonderful. I shall be here almost that long. It appears both of us are in need of a traveling companion."

Two middle-aged women, likely Americans, looked the men over, decided there are better opportunities and shrugged them off.

Adams asked, "So where do you visit today, Rege?" *This'll make the bastard squirm.*

With blatant concern in his voice and expression, Foster replied, "The Villa San Michele."

Adams continued to toy with his *shadow.* "Then we will part ways. I plan to visit the Blue Grotto."

Rege's face dropped.

Adams enjoyed yanking Foster about. "But tell me about the Villa. I might change my mind," he said and watched the shadow's relieved expression. *How did the KGB ever assign someone as transparent as this guy?*

Foster recited what he memorized from a tour guide. "The Villa San Michele was built around the turn of the 20th century by a Swede, Axel Munthe."

Adams detected a slight Russian accent in Foster's English.

"He built it on the ruins of Roman Emperor Tiberius's villa on Capri. The gardens have panoramic views of Capri, the Sorrentine Peninsula and Mount Vesuvius. It sits three hundred twenty-seven meters (1,073 ft) above sea level atop the Phoenician Steps, between the villages of Anacapri and Capri."

"That so, Rege? You might twist my arm."

"Twist your arm?"

"Yes. An American expression for getting one to change his mind." Adams had a bit more fun with his shadow. "I thought it a common expression in London."

"The first I've heard it."

"Well then, tell me more, Rege."

"San Michele's gardens have relics and works of art dating from ancient Egypt. They call it the Grandi Giardini Italiani."

"Good, Rege. I'm sold. May I join you? I'll visit the Grotto later during my stay. There's plenty of time."

Rege's face brightened. "Good. And I'll join you when you do."

Adams thought, *And perhaps I can pay the boatman to leave your sorry ass there with a chain and anchor bow tie.*

Paul Scott sat with *Pershing* officers at breakfast the morning of deployment on patrol number five. Blue crew had the odd numbered ones, Gold, the even. They'd depart Holy Loch, Scotland and return sixty days later. Paul had come to know breakfast in submarine wardrooms as a happy event, a time to socialize before attacking the day. Not so in *Pershing.* He'd learned that among nukes enjoying life ran counter to the mystique all tried to convey; time needed for work precluded everything else—frivolity considered akin to sin.

Fortunately, nuke officers applied this agenda to only themselves, not their troops. Had this happened, the impact on crew morale would be devastating.

Joe Dunn totally ignored what he termed the workhouse syndrome and made the best of his final evening ashore. Per lyrics of the song *Anchors Aweigh: O'er our last night ashore. Drink to the foam.* Apparently Joe expected a great deal of *foam* and he drank to it all. He looked like death warmed over, but this did not slow him down.

Pete Williams asked, "Will Dunoon ever be the same?"

"It'll survive, Captain. Problem is the Scots make whiskey faster than I can drink it."

If Williams had his wish, none of the officers would leave the ship during refit. He believed the likelihood of anything going wrong to be diminished substantially by the presence of officers, and Williams had his finger on his number—an officer on the fast track for promotion wishing to minimize the risk.

"Where did you go last night, Joe?"

"The usual. One of the tender officers has a pad called the hayloft. Lots of bachelor officers hang out there. It attracts babes like a magnet."

Williams said through a frown, hoping to deter Joe and keep him aboard, "I'm told by the intelligence officer it's under surveillance. Communist agents have been seen going in and out of there."

Dunn finished his eggs and looked at the CO. "Captain, if what goes on over there is communism, we're fighting on the wrong side."

Only Paul laughed in response to Joe's quip as the others looked at him through frowns.

Joe went on. "Captain, as long as everyone is here, I have a question. When I have the conn, do I represent you? When I give orders in that capacity should they be construed as coming from you?"

Williams looked about through an uncharacteristic concerned expression. "Why yes, Joe. Is there a problem?"

"When I had the conn during sea trials, it seemed maneuvering considered my orders to be suggestions."

"Joe, you must understand more is at stake with nuclear propulsion than with electric motors on the diesel boats. There are conditions we must meet. These are under the purview of the EOOW (Engineering Officer of the Watch)."

"Then priorities need revising. A conning officer's number one priority is keep the ocean outboard of the pressure hull."

"No. That remains in force."

"What happens when this priority conflicts with the EOOW's purview?"

Paul thought, *Joe just put a gun to his career's head.*

Dunn's Irish genes, egged on by a hangover apparently did the talking. "The way I see it, the function of every operation on this ship is to get Paul's missiles to where they can do their job. Everything is subordinate to that."

Williams said, "I see where this is going. Look. You non-nuke officers are not second-class citizens and won't be treated as such."

Dunn replied, "You already did, Captain. Paul Scott is a full lieutenant qualified for command in submarines. In the command succession list, he stands below a nuke JG (Lieutenant Junior Grade) who's never even been to sea."

Admiral Epworth stipulated this condition for non-nukes to serve on his submarines.

Bang, thought Paul.

Pershing cleared Ailsa Craig, an island in the Firth of Clyde off the Ayrshire coast. Locally known as *Paddy's Milestone*, it marks the halfway point between Belfast and Glasgow. Ailsa Craig is a spectacular landmark, rising steeply out of the sea up to 338.5 meters (1,110 ft). It can be seen from the Ayrshire coast, the Mull of Kintyre and from Northern Ireland.

Paul Scott, most experienced ship handler aboard, drew the OOD assignment for maneuvering watch—special setup for leaving and entering port or operating in restricted waters. He ordered the helmsman to new course two-seven-zero and reported this to the captain. *Pershing* complied like an obedient child heading into late afternoon beneath a foreboding gray overcast sky.

Paul ordered, "Secure the maneuvering watch, set the regular underway watch, section one. Rig ship for dive."

Forewarned, his assistant weapons officer, a non-nuke, came to the bridge dressed for heavy weather. A late autumn North Atlantic storm had abated, but swells continued, marching like soldiers in evenly spaced ranks above Belfast. *Pershing* headed directly into them and the relieving OOD had prepared himself, along with his two lookouts, to get a bit wet.

The watch relieved, Paul dropped below, made an inspection tour of the ship and reported his relief to Williams in the wardroom.

"Weapons Department ready for sea?"

"It is, Captain. We're prepared for any eventuality unless *Murphy* intervenes."

Williams replied, "There are no *Murphys* on the sailing list, Paul."

The young officer smiled, turned and went to his desk. *Joe would have told the old man Murphy has sailed and continues to sail on every ship in the Navy. He gives the most trouble to people who ignore his presence and don't anticipate untoward eventualities.* Paul envied his friend's verve, but new to the job, he'd leave things as they are.

Among several letters on Paul's desk, he noted one from Adrian Roberts, still at Dam Neck, Virginia. A Chief Navigation Electronic Technician—Chief Navette in emerging hi-tech jargon. Roberts remained at Dam Neck teaching at the Polaris Navigation School.

> Dear Paul,
>
> I know sailing dates are supposed to be classified, but arrival in port and the length of refit, 30 days, aren't. Armed with that information, it doesn't take a math PhD to figure out Pershing's just about to leave, so thought I'd get this in the mail to you.
>
> Please tell Lieutenant Dunn we are just now getting Officers' Navigation School back together. He went through it like a tornado. All kidding aside, he is far and above smarter than any officer student we've had. I'd love to measure his IQ.
>
> Paul, are you sitting down? Looks like 29 years of happy bachelorhood are coming to an end. You think the Jean Ann first date story was good. Wait until you hear this one.

Adrian Roberts loved to walk the beach at Dam Neck just before sunset. No matter what the day had brought, it helped him to unwind better than a stiff jolt of bourbon. Though not a teetotaler, Adrian took his teaching job seriously and refused to begin his day in class impaired. Imbibing kept till the weekend.

A brisk northeasterly breeze whipped up the surf, but thus far, more lullaby than roar. The usual seagulls zoomed and soared, screeching and squabbling, likely over some crumb of food one of them had gleaned from the beach.

He noticed a young woman tossing a ball into the waves for a Labrador retriever. As the distance closed, Adrian saw her to be attractive—classy but likely beyond his reach. Roberts, hardly an expert ice breaker, enjoyed the view from afar and kept moving.

Suddenly the woman yelled, "Skip! You come here."

Quick thinking Adrian saw opportunity. He turned toward the woman and said, "Yes, Ma'am?"

"Oh, I'm sorry. I was calling the dog. Time to load him in the station wagon for his ride home."

"Well, he's got a fine name. What a handsome guy. He yours?"

"No. My uncle's. I'm just walking him."

Roberts detected what he construed a softening in her voice. *She might like me.* "Come here often?"

"No. I live in Baltimore. Spending the week down here with my aunt and uncle. I'm Louise. I guess you're Skip."

They made small talk, their voice tones indicating increased mutual interest.

After a time, Louise said, "Well, I better get Skip loaded into the wagon. Don't want to worry Aunt and Uncle."

Adrian surprised himself. "Will you be here over the weekend, Louise?"

She gave him a smile that clearly green-lighted him to ask her out. "Yes. I actually go home next Tuesday."

"Do you think we could give Skip another romp on the beach on Saturday? Say about three?"

"I'd like that. Can you pick me up at Quarters A on the Base?"

Quarters A. My God. She's the base commanding officer's niece. Adrian's heart flipped. "I certainly can."

Louise looked quite pleased with his answer. "Well, very nice to meet you, Skip."

Roberts grinned sheepishly. "Adrian," he said.

Louise regarded him through arched eyebrows. "Adrian?"

"You'll have to forgive me, Louise. A beautiful lady was about to load a dog into her car and drive out of my life forever. I had to do something."

> *Paul, we've dated often since then. Maybe finding where Jean Ann and you are with the two boys and all primed my pump. If things keep going the way they are, I'll likely ask her to marry me. If this happens, will you be my best man?*
> *Will let you know the date.*
>
> *Adrian*

Chapter 12

Phil Redmond sat among the officers in *Clamagore*'s wardroom, his upbeat demeanor inconsistent with anger burning in his breast. He abhorred treatment received in the wake of what he knew to be *Clamagore*'s superb performance in Phase I of Operation Eager Beaver and the lesser-included witch hunt for Soviet submarines. He didn't reveal his frustration to the other officers, but did scratch his itch.

"Gentlemen, our job is to attack and sink ships ... nothing more. If there's an ASW deficiency in the Sixth Fleet, it's our job to illuminate it. Better to do it in a fleet exercise than have the Soviets do it in actual combat."

Denny Kolb added, "You mean kick a little skimmer ass?"

Redmond grinned at his subordinate. "Something like that. And look at it as an opportunity to hone our own sword. God forbid we could find ourselves shooting live rounds one of these days and we must be good at it. XO, anything to add?"

"Yes, Captain. The same goes for every man in the ship, and remember priority number two ... the sole purpose of everything between the torpedo rooms is to enable the launchers to reach attack position. Remind the crew of this also. Priority one remains ... keep the ocean outboard of the pressure hull. Everything helps ... even messcooks putting out good meals improves the crew's ability to do their jobs."

Redmond continued. "For daylight attacks, we'll use green smoke pots to mark attacks. Per Colonel Prescott on Bunker Hill, we won't shoot till we see the whites of their eyes, but don't want to drop a hot flare on the bird farm flight deck or a destroyer bridge. At night, green flares, but we'll attack from long-range. Questions or comments?"

None replied.

Zane said, "Okay then, get your troops thinking like this is a live war patrol. Someday, it might just come in handy."

Clamagore officers left the wardroom like the Green Bay Packers breaking huddle for a game-winning play—pumped.

They sat together at an outdoor café near the Villa San Michele over lunch. They marveled over the Bay of Naples vista spread out before them and then Adams began asking questions to make Foster squirm a little.

"So, you live in London?"

A nervous Rege replied, "Yes."

"Then you surely had dinner at the Cheshire Cheese on Fleet Street, right?"

Adams enjoyed his shadow's disconsolate expression.

"Of course."

"I'll bet you loved the roast potatoes and Yorkshire pudding. I certainly did."

"I did. Delicious to say the least."

Adams went on, citing bogus London haunts with Foster gobbling each bait and stating familiarity with these non-existent places.

Their lunch of a shared antipasti salad completed, Adams ordered a bottle of Chianti Classico.

Adams asked, "Did you know in 1932 the Chianti area was completely re-drawn and divided into seven sub-areas … Classico, Colli Aretini, Colli Fiorentini, Colline Pisane, Colli Senesi, Montalbano and Rùfina? Most of the villages added the new Chianti Classico. The wines labeled Chianti Classico come from the biggest sub-area of Chianti that includes the old Chianti area."

Foster, appearing overwhelmed, made no attempt to respond.

Adams went on, "This baffles you, Comrade?"

Foster gasped, "Comrade?"

"Yes. Comrade. Isn't that what you call each other in Russia these days?"

"I don't understand. I am from London."

"You are? Then how is it you are familiar with all the non-existent places we just discussed?"

Beads of perspiration appeared on Rege's forehead despite an umbrella shielding them from the sun and a cool breeze blowing across the café patio. "You are mistaken, Earl."

"I am? Then it will give you no problem if I advise the KGB that you are a transparent shadow? This condition, I believe, is known to cause nine millimeter headaches."

Foster sat silent a moment then asked, "What do you want of me?"

Adams knew he'd pushed the barb far enough. *Now cultivate the bastard and get him to give me what I need.* "Very little, Rege. Shall I continue calling you that?"

His discomfort obvious, Foster answered, "Yes. Now what do you want of me?"

"Do you know my mission here? Tell me, or you'll be sorry."

"No. Our DNI informant didn't—" Foster stopped short to prevent blowing his Soviet operative's cover.

Adams felt Foster's dilemma and bluffed. "Don't worry, Comrade Foster. We know your plant and feed him only what we wish to be passed on. Now that I have your cooperation, here's what I'm up to."

Foster feared Adams might reveal something he might not wish to know so he said, "We could end our discussion here and pretend this meeting never occurred."

"Then what would you report? I suspect, Comrade Rege, knowing nothing of me could bring you a great deal of trouble."

"Please don't address me as Comrade."

"As you wish, Rege. Now listen carefully. Soviet units and US submarines in the Mediterranean Sea are on a collision course that is dangerous for both sides. I am authorized to negotiate an end to this reckless nonsense and must meet with a Soviet agent similarly empowered. I'll remain at the Grand Hotel Vesuvio a fortnight and look forward to hearing from you. You will locate that agent for me. Understood?"

"Understood Mister Adams."

"Now. Those two American women at the table over there appear to have no one to settle for other than us. A proper Englishman would be accommodating under the circumstances."

Frank Gilliam bore his eighty-two years well. Disheveled thin gray-white hair tumbled about a head that came barely to his granddaughter Lorraine's nose. Pale blue eyes continued to sparkle, but less so than they once did, and the white moustache would ever sit atop a perpetual smile. The same scrawny legs hung below Frank's trademark short pants as did his arms from a tee shirt selected from a collection that always bore outrageous slogans. This one—*Unwed Mothers for Condoms.*

The farm, or what remained of it, belonged to Frank. Now a virtual resident caretaker, he moved to a remote corner of the former bed and breakfast once run by Frank and his wife Yvette. The master bedroom and rest of the house went to Lorraine and husband Rick Ferranti.

Frank and his wife Yvette once lived in St. Croix, U.S. Virgin Islands. She, separated five generations from French planter ancestors, adored their language, culture and décor of elegant plantation homes. She adorned her life with all three. When Yvette and Frank retired to an eight-acre farm on Maryland's eastern shore, she recaptured all this to perfection. Yvette passed away twenty years earlier leaving Frank unable to tear himself from this place of so many happy years shared with his beloved wife.

Lorraine said with a stern expression, "Okay, Grandpa, out with it."

Frank's face folded into its usual astounded expression on being caught dead in his tracks. "Out with what?"

Lorraine saw through him as she would a newly washed window. Whenever Frank wished to discuss a topic falsely alleged by him to be *none of his business* he stuck out like a sore thumb. She could never quite figure out why. Perhaps mental telepathy. Frank saw much of Yvette in Lorraine, so perhaps the deceased grandmother channeled her husband's thoughts.

"With whatever's on your mind."

Frank and Lorraine sat on the veranda and enjoyed a gorgeous October sunset while her husband Rick drove a grass-mowing tractor several hundred yards away.

She thought, *It's something he doesn't want Rick to hear.*

Frank quickly confirmed her suspicion. He began, "I know this is none of my business—"

She reached across, squeezed his hand and finished the sentence for him. "But—"

He grinned. "Your intuition terrifies me, Lorraine."

"You think flattery will work, Grandpa? You should know better by now."

"Okay. Let's talk about the opportunity that you and Rick have to visit Naples."

Lorraine made a mental note; *quit sharing things with Grandpa.* "I can't do that, Grandpa. As head of the Behavioral Science Department at Johns Hopkins Hospital, I couldn't get away that long."

"Did I ever explain the indispensible person test?"

"No, Grandpa, but I have a feeling you're about to."

"Quite simple. Fill a pail with water and stick your finger in. If the hole remains after you pull it out, you're indispensible."

"Grandpa, you're oversimplifying everything."

"A grandfather's job."

"What about the hell Rick's been through withdrawing from what they're asking him to do again. He must avoid triggers."

"Sometimes a hair of the dog that bit you can be the best cure. If I got it right, all he will be is a sounding board for the field operative. Nothing more. He can handle that. Otherwise, Rick shouldn't read the stack of spy stories he keeps in the study."

"You're a manipulator, Grandpa."

"That's a grandfather's job too. Actually, I do have an ulterior motive, Lorraine."

"Now that's something I'd have never expected."

"Your grandmother and I were married at the Palazzo Vecchio, the town hall in Florence, Italy. He produced a photo. "Here. Maybe you and Rick could have a picture taken at the exact place where Yvette and I stood that day."

At 0430 (4:30 a.m.) the messenger of the watch nudged Paul Scott and roused him from a sound sleep. "Mister Scott. Wake up sir. The captain wants you in the attack center."

Paul resisted the urge to ask why. He knew the messenger would not have the answer and had no wish for him to return to the captain with that question. Scott rubbed sleep from his eyes, got up and dressed in his poopie suit—dark blue coveralls with Velcro fasteners, a departure from the wash khaki uniform he wore on diesel boats. Paul slipped on another Polaris symbol—sandals—and padded his way into the Attack Center.

"You sent for me, Captain?"

"Yes, Joe needs help and I hear you're good at identifying stars."

"No more than what I learned at Annapolis, Captain. But I'll take a shot at whatever you want me to do."

"Good. We need to initialize the Type 11."

The captain referenced a special periscope used to enter navigation star elevation and azimuth into the Navigation Data Computer.

Polaris missiles flew ballistic trajectories. In order to strike targets hundreds of miles away with accuracy, *Pershing*'s precise geographic position had to be known. The Type 11 provided an option for doing this. Part of the test involved validating the scope's ability to spot navigation stars. These had to be above the horizon and visible—not obscured by overcast.

Paul's job: identify available navigation stars through the Type 8 scope—featuring wide optics to admit light sufficient for night use. He spotted constellation Ursa Major (big dipper) to the north. Its *pointer* stars Merak and Dubhe aligned to Polaris, the North Star. The constellation contained three other navigational stars—all visible. Paul spotted each one and coached the Type 11 optics into position.

He next searched out the constellation Orion that held two useable stars and formed a path to eight others.

The alignment completed, Paul asked, "Will that be all, Captain?"

"Yes, Paul, good job. Get some sleep. You've got the next watch."

Later, Paul discussed it with Joe Dunn. "Why did the captain pick me? His top of the class standers took the same course I did."

"Some guys get the grades, others learn the subject."

"I don't understand, Joe. Look at the complexity and mission enhancing contribution of Polaris. How come they let unwashed slobs like us run it?"

"The nukes argue disaster potential for nuclear propulsion and only the brightest can keep it safe."

Paul replied, "What has greater disaster potential than sixteen nuclear warheads atop giant roman candles squeezed into a submarine?

If a missile accidentally ignited at Holy Loch, chunks of the reactor would be spread all the way to Glasgow."

Joe's IQ likely exceeded that of everyone in *Pershing.* "I don't have that answer, Paul, and don't waste time fretting over it. I personally believe it's an ego trip for Admiral Epworth. He gets his kicks from making top people jump through hoops."

"You really think that?"

"Yes. But there's a lot more Scotch whiskey out there than I can handle, and I can't fix everything that's wrong in the Navy. I've made peace with both."

Joe hoped to erase the dejected look on Paul's face and knew exactly what to say. "Any final instructions from Jean Ann in the stack of letters on your desk?"

Paul's mood broke immediately. "Just the usual dos and don'ts. It's like she was talking to Benjamin and David. I think Jean Ann was a mother from the onset. When we were kids, my earliest recollections are of her at mass herding her little brother around."

"It's bred into 'em, Paul. Don't fight it. How did you ever corral a woman like her?"

"You'll never know how close I came to letting Jean Ann slip through my fingers. You know how it is … anything worth having had to be somewhere other than Moline. Yet she was there all along and I never realized what a catch she was. Like looking all over the place for your car keys and then there they are … right on the vestibule table where you left them."

"With such romantic comments, how could you not sweep Jean Ann off her feet?"

The remark went over Paul's head and he retold the story of Jean Ann and him as related a few months earlier to his friend Adrian Roberts. "Think it was a given we'd get married, but didn't start dating until I got into Annapolis. We never got intimate, but about as close as you can get. You know how it is with us Catholics. Holy Mother gets the final word. And if we don't go to communion Sunday morning, the whole damn congregation knows what we did the night before."

Joe answered, "You're a better Catholic than me, Paul. Can we leave it at that?"

"Sure, but do you want to hear the story of how I proposed?"

An exhausted Joe thought, *Oh crap, why the hell did I bring this up?* "Sure, Paul."

Paul Scott, first of the blue collar St. Mary's Parish to enter a college of any kind, basked in his friends' adulation. All watched the unfolding relationship between Jean Ann Peters and him, much as they would a favorite romantic film.

On the eve of Paul's return to Annapolis for first class year, friends and family gave a party for him in St. Mary's Parish Hall basement. Close to a hundred friends and well-wishers attended. Among the rules bent, men and women who normally provided refreshments following funeral services turned out a magnificent spread.

Paul arrived alone, not in uniform but wearing jeans and a plaid shirt. He became immediately inundated with friends and spoke with each who wished a moment with him. Paul occasionally looked about for Jean Ann. He planned what he hoped would be a surprise for her. Though confident of her love, he nonetheless wished to *seal the deal.* Jean Ann grew lovelier by the day, which in Paul's view made their long distance courtship risky under even the best circumstances.

After hearing the dozenth, *remember the time,* Paul spotted Jean Ann arriving with her mom and dad. He caught her eye, and they exchanged smiles. She wore a flowered cotton dress beneath a beige sweater, turning heads of every eligible young man present.

Paul considered taking her to the riverside bench where they sat on their first date. His dad's car in the shop as usual, they walked. Paul took her to a movie, *Around the World in Eighty Days* starring David Niven and Shirley MacLaine. He hoped to impress her with his memory. *Women go for guys who can remember that kind of stuff.*

However, the male attention Jean Ann received on entering the hall gave him second thoughts. *A clear public statement is needed here. Stake my claim so no one tries to move in after I leave. Should I really do this? Yes, dammit.*

Paul excused himself from a circle of friends, walked to the middle of the room and in his best command voice attempted to stifle the crowd noise. Third time a charm, everyone ceased talking to hear him.

He began, "I can't tell you how grateful I am that you've come this evening. Thank you so much. There's not enough time to chat with everyone, so please bear with me a moment. I am honored by your presence and proud to be a member of St. Mary's Parish—"

A voice shouted out, "We're proud of you, Paul," interrupting him, followed by loud applause.

"Thank you again. I can think of no place I'd rather be than among friends in the place where I grew up."

More applause.

"Now if you could gather 'round here I have a question for Jean Ann Peters. Jean Ann, would you step forward please?"

A chorus of aah, validated all knew what would follow.

Paul looked at her. *Damn, she grew up pretty.* "How to begin?"

A woman asked, "Why not at the beginning?"

"That's a long time back, but it's as good a place as any. Jean Ann, I'm sure I've loved you since the first time we saw each other at mass when we were just kids. I was too young to know it then, but I do now. You're the most beautiful and intelligent woman I've ever known." He fell to a knee. "Will you marry me, Jean Ann? Please say yes, or I'll feel like a darn fool."

The hall erupted with laughter.

A male voice asked, "Well, Jean Ann?"

Her expression showed how pleased Paul's proposal made her. Jean Ann knew this to be in the cards, but not sure of the timing.

"I've loved you since the beginning too, Paul, but I bet you don't remember the name of the first song we danced to in high school."

He looked up and smiled at her. "Joni James, *Why Don't You Believe Me?*"

Though touched, Jean Ann nonetheless decided to make Paul squirm a bit. "But how could I have been so smitten? You were skinny, gawky and had teacup ears. But you seemed to turn out okay."

Prolonged laughter.

When it subsided, she added, "And I could always tell when you showed up at mass even when you sat behind me. Your knee made that funny thumping sound when it hit the floor as you genuflected, like it did just now."

Another blast of laughter.

Jean Ann said, "Paul, you never had a chance."

His heart sank an instant, but Jean Ann lifted it. "I decided to marry you years before you asked. I don't want you to feel like a darn fool ... so yes, I will be your wife."

Cheers throughout the hall.

A male voiced shouted, "Somebody help the poor guy to his feet so he can kiss her."

Joe Dunn thought, *There's far too much missing in my life. I better get a move on.* "Great story, Paul." Joe surprised himself. He really meant it. "Now you better hit your bunk. Like the captain says, you've got the next watch."

Chapter 13

Earl Adams shook his shadow with such ease it embarrassed him. He and Rege Foster boarded a tour bus for a visit to Pompei. Minutes before departure, claiming he'd forgotten his wallet, Adams left the bus to retrieve it. Then hidden inside the lobby, Adams watched the bus pull away with Foster peering anxiously from a window.

Adams pondered, *maybe too easy*. He'd make certain Foster had not passed him off to another shadow. Plenty of time; three hours before a scheduled meeting with Rick Ferranti at *Certosa e Museo Nazionale di San Martino* (Carthusian Monastery and National Museum of St. Martin) near the center of town. Adams took a taxi to be sure Foster had no time to double back and resume shadowing. He had the driver stop near a small restaurant chosen for the limited clientele that could be seated. He drew a mental picture of each customer and then surveyed the street to ensure no one waited outside. Adams had become a superb spook. After a biscotti and coffee, he left the restaurant, walked a block, then abruptly turned about to ensure no patron followed him.

Good. Gives me a few hours to enjoy bella Napoli before the meeting. He wandered about downtown Naples savoring the hustle and bustle of Neapolitans going about daily chores. He'd never been to Italy. As he walked about, strands of Tchaikovsky's *Capriccio Italian* ran through his mind. Although Italian street songs and tarantellas weaved through the piece, it brought to Adams's mind a description of what Naples would be like had it been conquered and occupied by the Russians. He could always hear sounds of his beloved homeland in strands of the great composer's music. *Perhaps things will change, and I'll again be able to return there.*

An hour before the appointed time, Adams hailed another taxi, looking about carefully for a tail. He found none and gave the driver an address with a forty-five minute walk distance to the *Museo*. There, he'd meet with Rick Ferranti and his lovely wife Lorraine, whose presence would further distract suspicion. Prospects of seeing her lifted his spirits already elevated by a sunny Naples' morning. She more than the others sensed his discomfort at the luncheon meeting at Gangplank Restaurant in Washington, D.C. and made accommodations to alleviate his uneasiness. *Captain Ferranti is indeed a lucky man. But it is perhaps as he often says, 'The harder I work, the luckier I get.'*

Moments from the *Museo*, Adams ducked into an espresso shop and went immediately to the men's room. There he pulled a beret and silk scarf from his pocket. These added to a green shirt under his blue blazer over gray slacks presented the perfect image of an eccentric artist, exactly the effect he sought. He reentered the shop and assured himself none of the clientele resembled anyone he'd seen earlier. He left without ordering, earning him a frown and suitable hand gesture from the proprietor.

Rick and Lorraine arrived at the *Museo* just minutes after Adams. Ferranti's regulation haircut identified him as an American military officer. He dressed accordingly, conservative suit and outlandish tie.

Officers' wives felt obliged to offset local impressions possibly created by their husbands' lack of style, this to the pleasure of both European and American men alike. Lorraine outfitted herself in a soft tan, wool crepe, shirtwaist dress with slim leather belt at the waist, big pocketed for those ubiquitous acquisitions of the enthusiastic traveler.

A colorful, Mondrian patterned whisper of silk around her neck and shoulders added a vibrant splash of color. She chose tan loafers for comfort while museum crawling. Her only jewelry—hammered gold disc earrings.

Earl Adams did a double take. *When this is over, I must find myself a woman.* But reflecting on the recent Capri experience with two American ladies on the make, *Maybe just think about it.*

Lorraine checked a navy blue, lightly down-filled raincoat in the museum coatroom, useful for November in sunny southern Italy when the rain doesn't always stay in Spain.

They greeted each other like typical American tourists meeting for a day at the *Museo*, a warm handshake with Rick and a hug from Lorraine. Attire validated their American tourist cover with no agenda other than savoring *Museo* artifacts. These included an unparalleled collection of 8th century BC to 5th century AD ancient art forms and culture of the Mediterranean region from the second half of the 18th century, a period in which Europe experienced a feverish interest in ancient archaeology and art.

Rick and Earl stood before an enchanting Pompeian wall decoration and pretended to discuss it. Body language, including hand gestures in no way paralleled their actual discussion: a review of what Adams had gleaned from his Soviet shadow and Ferranti's instructions incident to further discussion with a Soviet operative.

Adams said, "I can't believe how easy he was to spot. Too easy. Made me suspicious, so I exercised great care while coming here. I'm certain we're clean as a whistle."

"Good," Ferranti replied.

He cast an eye about for his wife. He'd instructed her to wander through the *Museo* aimlessly but watching for anything unusual. Her signal: shift purse from left to right arm.

Lorraine enjoyed the assignment. *Makes me feel like a modern day Mata Hari.* She thought the need for secrecy more humorous than sinister. Ever the true humanist, she wondered, *How simple it would be if we could be honest with each other. All seeking the pursuit of happiness. Too bad differences in the manner we pursue it make such problems. If each listened, we actually might enjoy hearing what the other has to say.*

Adams reviewed all that transpired between Foster and him. "He promised to put me in touch with someone who can talk. It certainly isn't him," he said gesturing toward an aspect of a decoration, which he knew absolutely nothing about.

Ferranti, arms folded, said through an expression of intense interest, "Sure you're not being set up?"

"Sure as we can be of anything in this business."

"Here, let me return this to you," Ferranti said loudly as he handed Adams a catalogue of *Museo* artifacts, then in a barely audible whisper, "Be careful. You're only five years from retirement."

Adams accepted what he knew to be a list of concessions he could make as mutually agreed between the State and Navy Departments.

"Don't worry. My mother warned me not to do anything stupid."

"How come you never listened to her?"

As *Clamagore* sped out into the Aegean Sea for Phase II of Operation Eager Beaver, crewmen not actually on watch prepared for what they knew would be an arduous month. Vigorous visits ashore in Piraeus and Athens further added to their need for a breather, so most had turned into their bunks.

A few hung out in the crew's mess over coffee, among them Quartermaster Seaman (QMSN) Howell who intended to get married on return to the States and conducted himself accordingly ashore. Taking the advice of country and western singer Johnny Cash, Howell *walked the line.* He'd had an interesting visit to the Parthenon in Athens and related details to Interior Communications Electrician's Mate 2nd class (IC-2) Hal Tatlow and QMSN Brad Pace.

Howell told them of his encounter with two sailors from one of the destroyers during a visit to the Parthenon. He said, "You won't believe this. Ed the younger sailor said to Harry the oldest, 'Gee, Harry, this place must be awfully old.'

"Harry said, 'Very old, Ed. Very old.'

"Then Ed asked, 'How long did it take to build this?'

"Harry said, 'A very long time, Ed. A very long time.'

"Then Ed asked, 'How did they do it?'

"Harry said, 'Rock by rock, that's how they did it. Rock by rock.'

"And Ed said, 'It's really great to go ashore with you, Harry. You're such a fountain of knowledge.' Can you believe these guys?"

Pace answered, "What's unusual about that, Howell? Tatlow here told me it took a very long time to build *Clamagore.*"

"Yeah, sure, Pace."

Brad added, "I hear you're getting married when we get back. You should listen to Tatlow on that subject. Maybe you oughta get transferred before you do that. Tell him what happened to you, Tatlow."

Hal replied, "Why do I want to tell him about that? It would just worry him."

Howell took the bait. "What? What would I worry about?"

Pace sat back and grinned while Tatlow went on. "Oh I don't think you'll have my problem."

Howell said through a concerned expression, "C'mon, Tatlow. You gotta tell me."

Having stirred the pot, Pace settled behind a cup of coffee and grinned his satisfaction.

Tatlow said, "When we get back, we'll be in upkeep for two weeks, so this probably won't happen to you."

Howell wondered, *Two weeks? I've saved up a month's leave for my honeymoon.*

Tatlow began, "My wife Kris and I were married three weeks before *Clamagore* left for the Med. We headed off to Canada for a leisurely trip around Quebec Province. Kris took French in high school and was pretty good at it, so we thought it would make for a really fun time. We were gone just a day when my mother received a call from the boat. They told her they needed to get ahold of me. My stepfather was a retired chief petty officer, so Mom knew a lot about the Navy. She figured if the boat was looking for me it had to be important."

Howell appeared clearly uncomfortable.

"Well, Mom put out an all points bulletin to the State Police. She explained the circumstances and requested they look for us. They're good at what they do. Too good, dammit. They found me and I called home to find out what was up. Mom explained ... then I called *Clamagore* and learned they needed me for a trip to Norfolk for pre-deployment degaussing. I reported to the boat and found I was the only senior controllerman aboard."

Howell gasped. "You don't mean—"

"Yep. The honeymoon ended. Another controllerman was damn near qualified, but I'd be needed for the trip. Worst, I'd have to stay in maneuvering till the new guy got signed off. This lasted the whole trip. I never believed my honeymoon bed would be a Naugahyde covered bench in maneuvering."

Howell winced. "Oh crap!"

"Worse, the on-call senior controllerman in New London never responded to the ship's call, so they contacted me."

"Did you find out who he was?"

"No. Good thing because he'd have to be put in the witness protection program."

"Any chance you'll ever find out?"

"Well, actually I did. The morning *Clamagore* deployed to the Med, I came closer to missing a movement than I really cared to. As I came down the pier, the maneuvering watch was set, lines singled up with the skipper on the bridge."

Howell pressed, "But what's that got to do with finding the on-call guy who didn't show up?"

"Right after that, Kris came to terms with her great introduction to the Navy. She set off to find us a place to live. The old Ledyard motel had been changed over to apartments and Kris got what used to be the office area comprised of two rooms and a bath. There, she met a woman who claimed to be married to the on-call electrician for the day *Clamagore* departed for Norfolk. Having an agenda of her own, this woman took the phone call and said her husband was out of town and couldn't be reached. Actually, he was at the base Acey-Deucey (first and second-class petty officers' club at the submarine base) having a cool one. He didn't know, so how could I stay mad at him?"

Pace interjected, "Do you want me to have the yeoman type up your transfer request, Howell?"

Paul Scott had been warned to expect nothing but boredom on an SSBN patrol. For him this turned out to be a masterpiece of understatement. Once *Pershing* reached her Launch Reference Point (LRP—spot in the ocean from which missile trajectories had been pre-computed), nothing remained but to cruise back and forth over it every half hour. Joe Dunn's Navdac worked offsets from the LRP so Paul could accurately program the missile guidance systems in the event a launch message reached the ship. Above, a floating wire antenna trailed for a quarter mile behind *Pershing*, enabling Joe to update positions for three huge Submarine Inertial Navigation Systems (SINS) that occupied a lion's share of limited space in the Attack Center.

Lieutenant Scott would have to come to terms with not experiencing the thrill of the chase he'd enjoyed in diesel powered attack submarines. *Surely no one would be assigned permanently to 'BN duty. That'd be cruel and unusual punishment. And anyone who'd volunteer for this full time, well I just don't know about them.*

Paul's Weapons Department departed Holy Loch fully ready for patrol. Routine maintenance could be organized and accomplished by his troops whom he had no wish to micro-manage. Emergent problems, reported by them immediately, always included corrective action recommendations. *If you want the best from your guys, give them the opportunity to provide it.*

Joe and Paul sat at desks in a three-bunk stateroom shared with a nuke officer they seldom saw. He headed the Engineering Department Auxiliary Division, apparently requiring eight hours a day to oversee his men. This, plus two four hour watches, left him haggard and tired looking.

Paul suggested, "He must like that look. But what the hell does he do back there all day? He's got the most experienced chief petty officer on the boat."

Joe asked, "How can a system be truly ready for deployment if it needs that much attention?"

"I agree, Joe, but suggest you don't share that notion with the skipper."

Joe grinned at his friend. "You think he already knows it?"

"No. But I get the sense he knows he's not as smart as you and does not particularly like it."

"Maybe you should tell him?"

"I plan to get out of here with my hat, coat and ass. Hopefully get command of one of the few remaining diesel boats. You think our roommate might do that?"

"Couldn't be squeezed into his tight agenda."

Paul shifted the subject. "'BN patrolling is a little less exciting than watching grass grow. When I was a troop back on *Piratefish* we put together a newspaper. I know the radiomen copy press broadcasts. Maybe we can get Chief Baker (leading radioman) to put it together."

"One hell of an idea, Paul. Bounce it off the exec. Here's what to call it in honor of SSBN's everywhere—*Silent Service Breakfast News.* I'll even write the first story. Seems somebody swiped Chief Baker's pinup picture from the radio shack door. I'll do a parody on it that should light up the board."

Dave Zane finished losing another cribbage game to Phil Redmond. "I only let you win 'cause you're the Captain."

"Right. And I never get hydraulic oil in my hair from looking into number two periscope."

"Chief Engineer says he's going to fix that, Captain."

"And I'm gonna fix the Kentucky Derby next year and make a fortune."

"Ye of little faith. I know, first things first, Captain. We gotta kick a little skimmer ass in Phase II, but there's a few others I need decisions on to handle red tape lead time."

"For openers?"

"Letting Giambri go for a month okay with you?"

"I don't see why not." Redmond didn't want to interfere with his exec's agenda so gave him an out if he wanted one.

"I agree. When we wrap up 'Beaver, we're ordered directly to Palma Majorca for a few days, then on to Rota for turnover. We can wait till then, but it'd hack off a lot of time if we could stop at Sigonella. Giambri could get a flight to Naples and we could get Tatlow started on his way home."

"Tatlow?"

Zane explained the interrupted honeymoon.

"Why didn't I know about this?"

"Well, Captain, you just took command and we didn't want to send you a *can't do* message. And rumors floating in from your last boat had us running a bit scared."

Redmond thought a moment before responding. "Well, you know better now."

"Yes, we do, Captain. And we got some other bum dope."

"Like?"

"You're a lousy cribbage player."

Frank Gilliam walked the quarter mile from the house to his mailbox where a brightly colored envelope with an Italian stamp waited. He tucked several other pieces into his pocket and opened Lorraine's letter as he walked back to the house over a gravel driveway.

Naples, Italy
November 12, 1965

Dear Grandpa,

As usual, your advice is right on. Thank you. We are having a wonderful time. Rick is almost finished spooking and soon we're off to Florence and the Palazzo Vecchio (town hall of Florence, Italy where her Gilliam grandparents were married).

Would you believe I was an accomplice? Must leave it there. If I said more, I'd have to kill you. And then who'd run the farm?

Frank gasped a bit more than usual from the uphill walk. *Appears to me like you better think about lining someone else up to do the farm chores.* He read on.

I cannot believe the change in Rick. His apprehension incident prior to taking this on was dense enough to cut with a knife. Now it's like a great weight has been lifted from his shoulders. It became clear to me early in our marriage he'd been involved in some pretty terrible things. Before that, he'd developed an effective self-defense mechanism and functioned well. Perhaps it was because he had only himself to account to. When I came into the picture, he was no longer alone. You know the story. Turned to alcohol ... I don't want to go there. Quite happy to leave it where it is—in the past.

He had you, girl. What better incentive to turn his life around.

Are you old enough to be a great-grand? No, this is not an announcement. Tomorrow evening we'll have dinner with one of Rick's former shipmates, Cliff Harkins and his wife Ruth. Rick says Cliff is on the fast track and to look for him to make admiral. What has all this to do with being a great-grand? They have eight children and Rick is hoping some of it will rub off.

That combined with a visit to Palazzo Vecchio is surefire.

Grandpa, don't be surprised if in a year Rick pushes you out of your head of the farm seat. He openly expressed to me his intention, as he puts it, to come in permanently from the cold. Maybe you should buy him a straw hat.

Whew.

We will do a reenactment of Grandma's and your photo at the Palazzo Vecchio. First order of business when we reach Florence.
                                Love, Lorraine
P.S. If I sound happy, it's because I am.

The shortest list in the world is of those who deserve it more.

Earl Adams arrived at Alexandria, the second largest city in Egypt, on an early morning Al Italia flight from Naples with plans to return that evening. His appointed shadow, Rege Foster, told him a meeting had been arranged there to hopefully improve escalating friction between U.S. and Soviet warships in the Mediterranean. It would be aboard the Russian ship *Nmah*, moored at an inner harbor dock at the foot of Al Batash Road. He took a taxi there directly from the airport.

He wished to extend his visit to the city whose ambiance and cultural heritage distance it from the rest of the country, though only two hundred twenty-five kilometers (139.8 miles) from Cairo. However, circumstances of this visit warranted a quick return to Naples. Adams knew his neck stuck out a mile.

Alexander the Great founded the city in 331 BC, which became the capital of Greco-Roman Egypt; its status as a beacon of culture is symbolized by Pharos, the legendary lighthouse once one of the Seven Wonders of the World. Since the 19th century, Alexandria has played a new role as a focus for Egypt's commercial and maritime expansion.

Tempted to remain a few days, He thought, *Perhaps another time.*

The taxi pulled up beside *Nmah*. He paid and dismissed the driver and approached the gangplank, valise in hand. This contained written authorization for him to negotiate and a draft agreement with space for adding conditions. He studied and memorized concessions the American government agreed to negotiate and destroyed the document. Ferranti had taught him to play a good game of poker and Adams intended to do exactly that.

A Russian seaman greeted Adams in English and conducted him to a dark compartment. A pair of bright spotlights pointed directly in his face. He could make out a table and a figure seated behind it but no detail. Adams could not detect the presence of others in the room but sensed there were. He sat in silence for several minutes before a voice spoke to him in deep tones.

"You have asked for this meeting. Please give me your agenda."

Can it be he is someone I know and he wants to disguise his voice? It became clear why Adams had been called upon for this task. *Who better than me understands Soviet interrogation techniques? That's what the bastard wants. Scare me out of everything I'm authorized to concede. He'll get no picnic with me.*

"I am Earl Adams, authorized by the United States Government to discuss means of arresting the dangerous practices that emerge between our navies in the Mediterranean. May I ask who you are?"

Deep Voice replied, "Who I am is unimportant. So tell me of these dangerous practices. I know of none."

"First, you should see my credentials." Adams attempted to rise and deliver them, but a pair of powerful hands from behind pushed him back into his seat.

"I have no interest in your useless papers. Please explain these so-called dangerous practices."

That voice, dammit. No Russian accent. It's American. One I'm familiar with. "If I might proceed?"

"Please do."

Adams summarized the two incidents between USS *Clamagore* and the Soviet Kotlin class destroyer. He had been briefed on several others and presented them also.

He then concluded, "This conduct is reckless and dangerous. Both Soviet and US warships carry tactical nuclear weapons. We depend on our commanding officers to prevent anything untoward, but these are young men prone to let anger override good judgment. I am certain your country screens candidates vigorously as we do, but there is always the margin of error."

Believing he stated the case well, what followed astounded Adams.

Deep Voice dropped his disguise and completely disregarding Adams's summary of the problem, he said, "I am quite sure you remember who I am *Kapitan Leutnant* Vasiliy Norovsky. Ten years ago you captured me in America and said for me the Cold War is over. It apparently was not, but clearly it is for you."

Norovsky conceded his cover had been blown. *I'm in big trouble. Neither deny nor admit anything till I know what they have.*

The man stepped forward between the lights.

Norovsky's heart sunk. Before him stood Pasha Martinov.

Chapter 14

Relationships between officers and crew in a diesel-electric submarine could well be the most unique in the U.S. Navy. Mid-sixties protocols, established well prior to turn of the twentieth century, remained in place and continued to be observed—to a degree, that is.

Enlisted men addressed officers at and below the rank of lieutenant commander as mister followed by a surname. They addressed commanders and above by their rank, omitting the surname. The commanding officer is addressed as captain regardless of his actual military rank.

Officers addressed enlisted men below the grade of chief petty officer by only surnames and CPOs as Chief.

Larger surface ships have separate accommodations for officers and crew who exist in a sort of isolation, each from the other. Some claim the U.S. Navy established a Marine Corps to protect shipboard officers from the crew.

Confines of tight living spaces aboard diesel boats dealt a different hand than the one on large surface combatants. Submarine officers and crew, driven into daily close contact, had to adjust accordingly. There could be no secrets. Before long, each crewmember knew all about the other, enlisted and officer alike. No one fooled anyone. Even the captain had only a thin privacy screen. A strong sense of mutual respect and loyalty both ways grew from this, though on occasion manifested itself in unusual manners.

Emilio Rapinian, Stewardsman second class, created magnificent omelets which could grace menus of any upscale restaurant. People are prone to be good at what they like to do. Rapinian obviously loved to make omelets and then bask in subsequent adulation. He had a shtick, however. The mid-forties Guamanian loved to pretend demands on his time exceeded reasonable expectations. He'd put on a show and stomp angrily about while producing his epicurean delights.

Clamagore officers made the best of their last night ashore in Athens. They'd be underway in the morning for Eager Beaver Phase II and remain at sea five weeks. They made the most of their evening, including a modicum of imbibing the Greek liquorish flavored Ouzo. This is best drunk conservatively and the young officers had yet to learn this. Consequently, they had an 0300 (3:00 a.m.) boisterous return to *Clamagore*.

Rapinian waited until his officers sat comfortably behind head-clearing black coffees and then invented an excuse to walk through the forward battery passageway in plain view of the revelers.

"Rapinian!" they shouted in chorus.

The stewardsman stopped and faked a glower.

Denny Kolb said, "Save us! Only onion omelets can do that."

With an expression fierce enough to frighten the bravest of men, Rapinian stomped into the galley.

Before long, the wardroom fell silent as the officers attacked their delightful repasts, clearly not products of an angry man.

Rapinian averaged ten years older than the officers. It is likely he fancied himself to fill a sort of fatherly role. But then it may well be he reckoned the following morning these officers would be directing *Clamagore*'s movements and he wanted to ensure they did it safely.

So went day-to-day life in diesel-electric submarines.

Paul Scott shook his head and grinned at Joe Dunn's promised article for the initial issue of Silent Service Breakfast News (SSBN). It centered on a pinup *kidnapped* from the radio shack door. Shortly, a ransom note appeared in its place that read, 'If you ever expect to see Rita again, leave three jars of Peter Pan peanut butter in a plain unmarked package behind the oxygen generator.'

The crew circumvented boredom with imagination. They likened the submarine to a small nation, in this case, *Persha*—a play on *Pershing*. The 1955 film *Guys and Dolls* showed the first two nights underway, set the mood for this patrol. The plot is based on the activities of New York petty criminals and professional gamblers in the late 1940s.

Joe Dunn offered, "If it works in New York, it has to work in Persha. So let's go with it."

Gangs, already an established submarine term, (groups within divisions) known as the radio gang, sonar gang, torpedoes gang, and so on worked well in the imagined environment. Deck seamen used a different term—deck force, but that fit the postulated scenario also.

Invented crewmen names described them as characters in this marathon drama. Bad News Baker because he gathered press broadcasts for inclusion in SSBN. Radioman Seaman (RMSN) Ricardo Meli, 18 and a natural for Little Rico, worked under Baker and held forth in the radio shack. Leading Cook Sean Casey crew's mess became Casey's Greasy Spoon. Other names in Joe's vignette apply to crewmen in the same manner.

Joe Dunn's article, written under a pen name, the norm for all contributors, read:

TEARS FOR LITTLE RICO
By Seaman Synge

I'm hanging around Casey's Greasy Spoon this afternoon having a Pastrami sandwich when I get the word from Bad News Baker that Little Rico's girl Rita has been kidnapped. I figure for sure that it is the work of the Enforcer (Jamie Hayes, a huge missile fire control CPO), but Bad News says that the Enforcer and his entire mob and Big Greg Capone and his mob has pledged themselves to Aaron the Animal to help Rita. I immediately go over to the shack of the Animal to find out for myself. Upon entering, I see Little Rico holding the telephone in his hand and tears cascading down his greasy cheeks from eating too many burgers in the Spoon. The Animal tells me that Bad News was indeed telling the truth and then Guido Zacchi and the Mad Rabbi commence to work me over in the event I may be concealing important information.

After they finish working me over we get to discussing Little Rico's misfortune while he lies down beside the phone still bawling like he lost his last sawbuck on a Pamlico nag. The Animal says to me like this, "Seeing as how you are a writer for the daily scratch sheet, me and the boys would appreciate it greatly if you write a little warning to the effect that if Rico's girl is not returned within two days, unharmed, that an underworld war will be declared on all non-Italian gangs within a thousand miles."

So I tell him that I can't print that sort of stuff in the scratch sheet and ask why he doesn't take the case to the feds, to which he replies, "You will print that story if you wish to remain my friend and stay alive, and you will also ask around the *Pershing Club* for all the guys to throw in a jar of Peter Pan plain peanut butter for as you know there ain't nothin' but crunch within a hundred miles of the shack."

I ask him why all of a sudden he starts liking plain peanut butter and Masher Wood hands me a ransom note which says the kidnappers will not harm Rita if Rico shells out three jars of Peter Pan plain. I promise them that I will try to print the story. I'm ready to leave when the phone rings and Rico answers it. He immediately starts screaming and crying again so we hang up the phone and when Rico gets a little composed, he says it was Rita on the phone and she said that he better get the peanut butter fast or the kidnappers would turn her in to the feds for sneaking into the country on a banana boat. Just then Enforcer and Big Greg come busting in and tell us that so far there are no leads yet as to the whereabouts of the chick but that both of them were starting to raid every gang shack on the boat and the chick should turn up shortly.

As I leave the shack, I see Little Rico huddled in the corner crying and going over his peanut butter inventory for the hundredth time and I say to myself, *Is this the end of Little Rico?*

Thus *Pershing* crewmen, as do Navy men throughout the Navy, hold boredom at bay by taking their jobs seriously and not themselves.

Rick Ferranti and Cliff Harkins sat together in the latter's office at Naval Headquarters in Naples.

Ferranti thought, *This must be damned serious. He hasn't even called for coffee.*

Harkins asked, "Have you heard anything from Adams?"

"No, Cliff. He has no way of getting in touch. I've become too notorious over the years and must expect a Soviet pin in the map anytime I change locations. This means a phone tap. Kinda fun, actually. DNI makes phone calls about absolutely nothing and puts them in coded instructions. Has to drive 'em nuts. But a call from Egypt would raise hackles. These guys are not stupid. Except that Foster guy they assigned to shadow Adams. He's not playing with a full deck."

Harkins listened and then dropped his bomb. "The *Nmah* sailed yesterday from Alexandria, and Adams has not returned to Naples."

"You sure?"

"Our spooks are right on top of it. The guy in Alexandria watched him board *Nmah* and never saw him leave. Nothing has been heard of him since. What do you suggest?"

"Wow! Keep them under surveillance. Lot of possibilities. They could transfer him to another ship, possibly even a submarine."

"I doubt that, Rick. We've had no indication of Soviet submarine activity since the November incident."

"Yeah, but it took *Clamagore* to find him. Your ASW gurus came up empty."

Harkins smiled. "Remember, you said that, not me. I think the skimmers are upset because our boats make them look bad. I got hauled up before COM-SIXTH-FLEET's chief staff officers and reminded that submarines are here to provide target services."

"Seems I recall hearing Admiral Martin say there are only two kinds of ships in the Navy: submarines and targets. Maybe Redmond sees it like that's exactly what he's doing. Providing service to targets, which really is target service in reverse."

Harkins shifted to their original conversation. "So what do you think about Adams, Rick? Are they likely to toss him to the sharks?"

"Seriously doubt it. At least not before the KGB milks him for every drop. And Adams is about the most resourceful operative out there. I'm guessing no matter what, he'll land on his feet." Ferranti saw no value to expressing his concern. *What other choice do I have?* "They won't get much … if anything from him."

Harkins, surprised by the relative ease with which Ferranti took the news, knew the importance of not letting emotion interfere in Rick's line of work. *Otherwise, how can these guys keep from going nuts?*

"If *Nmah* returns to Russia via the Bosporus, we can have the Turks detain and inspect her. If Adams demands political asylum, they have to give it to him."

"I don't think *Nmah* will go there, but our surveillance will confirm that. And remember, the Reds know as much as we do. Adams is too hot for them to take that risk. I can't give you details, but ultimately they'll ship him to Severodvinsk. Simple logic makes it easier for them to do this by sea."

"Okay to pass this along? Our bird men claim to be busy and I may need ammunition to get them to keep an eye on *Nmah.*"

"Not a problem, Cliff. The Reds already know everything that's passed between us and likely more. Now, don't you think it's time to do coffee and discuss more important things?"

"Like?"

"How come Ruth and you have eight kids and Lorraine and I come up dry?"

"Coffees coming up." Harkins buzzed the pantry. "So Rick, are you telling me you're finally coming in from the cold? Permanently?"

"Meet the new Rick Ferranti, civilian farmer of the Maryland Eastern Shore. Come by it honestly; my Italian forbears kept a garlic patch and olive trees. But my New York City family and goombahs (Italian expression for macho male friends) will likely disown me."

Denny Kolb spread an Aegean Sea chart over the wardroom table while the rest of *Clamagore*'s officers sat about. Chief of the Boat Beyers had relieved to officer of the deck so he too could be present. *Clamagore* sped through a sunny afternoon on the surface at standard speed on four main engines. With no contacts in sight, Chief Beyers, finger through the pad-eye (coffee cup handle), settled back for a pleasant hour.

Redmond said to his officers, "Last time I spoke with you, I was a bit hot under the collar. Hanging Giambri's LOM on a zoomie got to me. Very unprofessional of me to let that happen."

Faces about the table looked on, wondering what would be the next shoe to drop.

"Put all that behind ... right here and now. We are all in the same Navy. Our greatest wish is to have the skimmers succeed. But the best way ... the only way for this to happen is for us to pull every possible rabbit from our hat."

He scanned expressions of his officers. One of Redmond's main strengths is an uncanny ability to read faces and body language. He liked what he saw. *Every skipper should have such a cadre of officers.*

"Insure every man recognizes the importance of his job to our success. Everyone has an assignment. The messcooks and I have different jobs but each is essential. Bottom line, I want every head in the game. Let's give the taxpayers full return on their investment. *Clamagore* turns twenty-eight this month. It's not the age of the ship that matters, but the skill of the men who operate her. In two years, she'll be decommissioned and likely a year later we'll be shaving with her remains. But in the meantime, let's milk the last drop. She deserves it. Proved her worth in World War II. Four patrols totaled over a hundred thousand tons including a Jap cruiser. Our main goal, we want the skimmers to win, but this can be valid only if we give it our best shot. Anything less is a disservice to the Navy. Questions?"

None. Only wide-eyed expressions of enthusiasm.

"Okay, Denny. Lay out the track that you expect the carrier task force to follow."

"Captain. How do I do that? I don't have a crystal ball."

"Then how can you expect me to get that answer? Did you hear a word of what I just said?"

Denny's grin spread from ear to ear. "Okay, here's the way I see it. We start from where they want to be at end of exercise and work backwards. Here." He backed up a pencil track from the Bosporus to the task force's current location and indicated several chokepoints. "Best chance is to hit 'em here. Downside … they know that too and will be expecting us."

Redmond sat back. *The skipper's not to have favorites. All officers are special. It's just some are more special than others.*

Pasha Martinov threw open the door to Norovsky's stateroom turned prison cell. "On your feet traitorous swine. The *kapitan* says you need a few minutes on deck. I don't know whether he's over compassionate or simply believes a sea breeze might blow away your disgusting stench."

Norovsky thought the worst. *The son of a bitch is taking me topside to blow my brains out and dump me into the sea.* Though terrified, Vasiliy remained his own man. *Don't give him the satisfaction of seeing me cringe. Show him that Russian-Americans may falter but don't break.*

"Shall I wear my coat, *Komrade* … or is this a one-way trip?"

"You shall be returned. I have no plans to deprive my countrymen of seeing what happens to traitorous scum."

They reached the main deck as a late fall Mediterranean bora (northwest storm) had begun to kick up waves. *Nmah* headed north putting the wind on her port bow.

In Russian, Martinov said, "We shall go to the stern on the starboard side where we can better converse, Vasiliy Ivanovich (the Russian manner of addressing a good friend—Vasiliy son of Ivan)."

Vasiliy Ivanovich? Does he believe there is something he can stroke from me?

They reached the ship's starboard quarter and Norovsky quickly huddled behind the deckhouse out of the wind.

"No," Martinov said then ordered, "Out here by the rail where the wind will carry our words out to sea so no one but us will hear them."

Norovsky's guard went up. *What is going on? If he believes anything can be gotten from me, he's sadly mistaken.*

Backs to the wind, the two men stood at the rail.

Martinov began, "I am sure you know I must return you to Russia."

Russia? Not the Soviet Union? What accounts for this change?

"Once there, you will face a list of charges as long as your arm. This comes as no surprise to you, Vasiliy?"

"It doesn't. I trust many former colleagues will attend and salivate over my fate."

"You certainly did not make a lot of friends in Severodvinsk. This is a known fact."

Norovsky responded, "But I have a sense there is more on your mind, Martinov."

"You may call me Pasha, but only when we speak privately. And we must not do that often. Suspicions will be aroused. You recall I spent three months among the Americans and have remained under tight scrutiny since then. When you are interrogated about this conversation, say you pleaded with me for clemency. Tell them I was totally disgusted and berated you for your betrayal of Mother Russia."

He did not react but this struck a nerve with Norovsky. *I am more Russian than any man on this planet. It is the people who run my country who are not true Russians.*

"Here's what will happen. Your trial will be long, humiliating, well-publicized and dragged out so that others who might be similarly disposed will take note. You'll be sentenced to death, of course."

Through a sarcastic voice, Norovsky said, "Wonderful! What do you expect of me after that?"

"Much, Vasiliy Ivanovich. Just as you did sixteen years ago, you will escape to America. However, this time, a man, his wife and two children will accompany you. The Americans rescued Piotr Denisov at the time you arrested me. He too has remained under suspicion. Now this conversation has already gone too long."

Martinov shook a finger at Norovsky, grabbed him by the shoulders and thrust him back toward the door through which they had emerged onto the main deck.

Chapter 15

Clamagore raced into the Aegean in peak form, each crewmember infected by Phil Redmond's high setting of the bar. They took ownership of their ship's assignment and would put heavy shoulders to that wheel. Redmond reasoned people do best at what they like. *It's a no-brainer, so why not get them to like it?*

Denny Kolb stood OOD bridge watch, the normal two lookouts augmented by two more. All held binoculars continuously to eyes and scanned from the horizon thirty degrees up to watch for aircraft. The exercise had begun an hour earlier and engagement rules prohibited search before the opening whistle. *Clamagore* immediately intercepted radar and radio signals from the Carrier Task Force.

Its position determined, Redmond needed continuous speed available only on the surface to make an effective intercept, and so elected to take the risk. Detection by patrol aircraft would enable the Task Force to take evasive action, putting a deep kink in *Clamagore's* game plan. However, lookouts are a competitive bunch and none wanted the stigma of letting a *zoomie* slip through.

Clamagore closed to within easy submerged reach of her intended dive point when one of the port lookouts reported, "Warship on the horizon bearing three-four-five. Heading right for us."

Denny pulled the diving alarm without checking. "Clear the bridge!"

Four lookouts preceded him down and disappeared into the conning tower hatch like a clutch of gophers jumping into their holes to avoid a marauding coyote.

A bad time to lose his footing, Denny missed the hatch lanyard and tumbled to the deck like a sack of potatoes. The alert Brad Pace snapped the hatch shut with one enormous hand and engaged the lugs with his other.

Denny, from an unceremonious heap of mankind declared through a grin, "Last man down, hatch secured, Captain!" As an afterthought he asked Pace, "Is it?"

"Hatch secured, Mr. Kolb."

Redmond looked down and asked, "Got an encore for that? When's the next performance? You okay, Denny?"

Kolb collected himself. "I'm fine, sir. Spotted a warship on the horizon headed this way."

"I'll check him out. Sure you're okay, Denny? Anything the Doc (ship's medic, Harold Wilcox, Hospital Corpsman 1st Class) should have a look at?"

"I'm good, Captain."

Kolb then dropped into the control room and took charge of the dive. A bit banged up, Denny reasoned, *Plenty of time to check that out later*, and went on with his duties.

Redmond ordered over the 21MC, "Sonar ... Captain. Search carefully two-seven-zero to three-zero-zero true—measured clockwise from true north. I expect you'll hear a lot of noise. We should be right on the Task Group track, but watch carefully for a bearing drift in the unlikely event that warship spotted us."

"Two seventy to three hundred watch the bearings," replied the unmistakable voice of Giambri.

Clamagore reached ordered depth of six-zero feet.

Redmond ordered, "All ahead one third," and then to Pace, "Give me a mark at three knots on the log." The captain wished to leave no telltale plume when he raised the scope. Though the contact was too far out to detect *Clamagore*, Redmond exercised caution.

Minutes passed before Pace announced, "Three knots, Captain."

"Very well. Up number two for a three-sixty in low power. We'll dip and I want you to put me on the last bearing to the contact."

Pace raised the scope, shifted to low power to provide a wider view and to permit the skipper to scan three-sixty in five seconds.

Redmond reported, "No contacts. Shifting to high power for a better look. Put me on the contact."

"Three-four-five relative ... measured clockwise from the bow ... by lookout observation." Pace raised and positioned the scope.

"Got 'im! He doesn't see us. Estimate range twenty thousand."

Redmond pulled his head clear and snapped the handles to the stowed position; Pace's signal to send the huge Monel shaft hissing into its well.

The skipper called down through the control room hatch, "Have Tim Keating relieve you, Denny, and come up here to take the conn."

In the interim, Giambri reported strong contact on a group of warships to the northwest closing on a steady bearing. Redmond passed this to Kolb as the latter took the watch.

"Keep an eye on the inbound warship. Have Giambri check him out. And let me know when you have a good visual on the *bird farm*. Looks like the fox is in the henhouse again, but there's just enough time to lay below and whip the exec in cribbage."

Redmond disappeared into the control room below.

Minutes later, Denny called the skipper in the wardroom. "Better get back up here, Captain. Giambri says the lone warship doesn't sound like anything he's ever heard. And I got a pretty good look at him. He's not one of ours."

On the eve of Lorraine and Rick Ferranti's departure for Florence, Rick met a final time with Cliff Harkins.

"So Rick, it looks like all the Soviets had in mind was to recapture Norovsky."

"That's just about it. Too bad we can't pick up this Foster guy, or whatever his real name is."

"Not a chance. The Italians would never sit still for that. So do you think this harassment at sea business was all about luring Norovsky into the trap? That seems farfetched to me."

"You're right, Cliff. Norovsky was a target of opportunity. But the harassment thing is a nut that has to be cracked one way or another before a skipper on one side or the other goes off half-cocked. And you know all the bad roads where that could lead."

"So how will this be pulled off?"

Ferranti replied, "Hopefully not above the Navy Department level. Drag State in and they'll give away the farm at the drop of a hat."

"Is there anything we should be doing?"

"SecNav (Secretary of the Navy) is fully briefed and concerned. Next move is his, but I doubt we'll have to wait long for that answer."

"Norovsky. What do you think will happen to him?"

Ferranti grimaced. "Lots of things, ranging from the worst to perhaps recruiting him as a double agent. Don't think that would work. Vasiliy loves his country with a passion and believes the current regime is leading it to disaster. My guess, they might try that. He's damn good and might convince them he bought in, but I know he won't."

"The spook business. Glad I never got involved."

"You oughta be, Cliff. It doesn't go along well with big families."

"On that subject, any plans by Lorraine and you. Or is that none of my business?"

Ferranti grinned. "Why do you think I've been taking notes on your diet? We'll likely not catch up with Ruth and you, but hope to make a start. Lorraine's grandparents got married in the Palacio Vecchio in Florence. We're hoping to do a reenactment of more than just a photo at the wedding site."

"How can you go wrong, Rick?"

Both officers rose as Ferranti prepared to take leave.

Shaking his friend's hand, Harkins said, "So great to see you, Rick. The submarine Navy is a small one so I'm sure our paths will cross again soon."

"I'm sure they will. Thanks for everything."

Harkins nodded and Ferranti left the office.

The Soviet supply ship *Nmah* exited the Mediterranean and headed northwest into the Atlantic. Though mid-November approached, seas remained remarkably calm and a late afternoon sun bathed Pasha Martinov and the commanding officer as they stood on the bridge.

A messenger arrived and handed a clipboard to the *kapitan* who scanned it quickly and said to Martinov, "The submarine has us in sight and wishes to remain submerged till after dark. Perhaps we'll be fortunate and our prisoner will disappear beneath the waves during his transfer."

"That would please me also, *Komrade Kapitan*, but we must do nothing to facilitate this. Every drop of information on his traitorous activities must be squeezed from the swine. When this has been done, I am certain that Norovsky will find drowning more preferable to what the KGB has planned for him."

Later, *Nmah* lookouts searched a darkened horizon carefully with radars secured. "They work both ways," Martinov observed, when the *kapitan* wished to activate them to augment the visual search. "Turn it around," Pasha suggested. "Use our passive ECM to determine whether anyone is looking for us."

Half an hour later, satisfied they had this part of the ocean to themselves, *Nmah* cycled her navigation lights on and off, a pre-arranged signal for the submarine to surface.

Martinov went below and ordered the prisoner, Vasiliy Norovsky, to prepare for transfer.

The unmistakable silhouette of a November class submarine pushed its way above the surface. After a brief flurry of flashing light exchanges, a line was fired to *Nmah*. Soon, an inflatable life raft, tethered between the ships made its way alongside and Norovsky climbed aboard.

Loud enough for all to hear, Martinov said, "Perhaps you will save Mother Russia the cost of a bullet and drown yourself during the transfer."

The men's eyes met through scowls that covered the true message that passed between them.

Phil Redmond raced to the conning tower, took a look at the approaching warship and ordered the scope lowered. "A Soviet Krupnyy class guided missile destroyer headed right toward us with the bone in her teeth. Estimate range ten thousand."

Dave Zane reached the conning tower just behind the captain. "Which means he's heading toward the Carrier Task Force also. I'm sure he has no idea we're here. Can I have a look, Captain?"

"Two pairs of eyes are better than one."

Brad Pace raised the scope.

Zane confirmed what Redmond had just seen.

"Think we should notify the task group, Dave?"

"And give away our position? The Krupnyy's radar is spinning like a top. I'm sure the carrier's got him and dispatched a plane by now.

"What do you think is going on, Captain?"

"My guess is the Soviets look to equalize our Med superiority the easy way. Put a guided missile cruiser in trail of our bird farms for instant response in the event the balloon goes up. Let's turn this into an advantage. The task group will be so focused on the new arrival, they won't even think about us."

"Isn't that cheating?"

"Hell no, Dave. Those guys have got to learn to multitask. It's the way it'll be in real combat, so they might as well get used to it. We'll follow the Krupnyy in. Denny, you got the conn. I think the exec wants to scissile out of our cribbage game. I'm ahead by almost a street. Got my priorities straight. First the exec, then the bird farm. Call me when you see the whites of their eyes, Denny."

"Aye, Captain."

SSBN patrols in no way approached the activity level Paul Scott had come to know in attack submarines where the object is to seek out enemy units and be prepared to engage and destroy them. 'BN's avoided any contact, friend or foe, at all costs. For sixty days they cruised slowly at a hundred thirty feet, taking the optimum escape course even from ships detected at great distances. A floating wire antenna trailed on the surface for half a mile, all but invisible in the restless North Atlantic. This enabled Chief Baker's radiomen to continuously listen for the dreaded launch signal. This would be initiated only by the President and in response to a Soviet nuclear weapons attack on the U.S. mainland, hence the main mission: deterrence. Initiation of such an attack by either side would be tantamount to putting a gun to the world's head. Ballistic missile submariners put all this from their heads lest they go mad.

Boredom loomed as the biggest obstacle to be overcome. The crew therefore put effort into maintenance to the extent the ship remained in mint condition. But they needed more.

The Silent Service Breakfast News took up some of the slack. As expected, a new writer emerged to do a follow-on for Seaman Synge's

(Joe Dunn) piece *Tears for Little Rico.* Under the pen name Chep, obviously a member of the sonar gang by the opening line, the article read:

> Sonar Shack – December 11, 1965.   Described as the most dastardly deed since the downtown Dodgers departed Brooklyn, scraggly Rita Cellini, gun moll for the infamous Little Rico, was filched from her perch on the door of the radio shack and seems to have vanished from the earth.
>
> The first news of her disappearance was flashed when Little Rico, returning from a hard day of qualifying, discovered Rita missing and found a second note that upped the ante from three to five cans of peanut butter.
>
> *To Little Rico:*
> *Rita is with us and unharmed. If you want to see her again, it will cost you five cans of Peter Pan creamy peanut butter … NOT crunchy but CREAMY, understand? Or else!!!*
> *Signed, Slinky Solly*
>
> Inquiries at the radio shack netted a simple "No comment" from an obviously lovesick and heartbroken Little Rico.

Though absurd and meaningless, these pseudo literary crutches enable 'BNers to endure monotony of arduous and seemingly endless submerged patrols.

Paul finished reading the paper and said to Joe Dunn, "Think some nuke officers are behind any of these pen names?"

"I doubt it, Paul. They're too busy studying."

"Studying what?"

"Nothing, probably. The culture likely regards having spare time as goofing off and nobody wants to send that signal. Ever notice at wardroom movies the average number of viewers is four; the number of non-nuke officers not on watch."

Paul thought carefully to be sure he'd state his views accurately and unbiased. "Is it just me, or do you get a sense non-nuke officers are *Pershing*'s second class citizens? In the wardroom, I feel more like a guest than shipmate."

Joe replied, "That doesn't bother me a bit. If these guys don't want a life, that's their problem. Mine is when I have the conn, my orders to maneuvering are regarded as suggestions. I believe that's downright dangerous."

"I suggest you don't share that view with the captain. You push him to the limit, Joe. He can make the rest of your career damn rocky."

"How can someone not in the Navy be damaged by someone who is? I'm resigning after this tour in *Pershing*. Face it; we have no future in submarines. Through no fault of our own, an admiral fraught with obsessive-compulsive disorder symptoms has the whole submarine navy jumping through his hoops and too scared to do anything about it. You should come with me, Paul."

"You make a good point, Joe. But before I leave the Navy, I want to command a submarine. The bug bit hard when I was a seaman aboard *Piratefish*. The captain was God! I need to be skipper to round out my life. There'll still be a few diesel-boats left when I'm eligible, so maybe I'll be lucky enough to get one. If it's all the same with you, I'll continue sucking up to Williams."

Aboard *Clamagore*, Brad Pace sat in the crew's mess, his grin spread from bulkhead to bulkhead. Submariners go about their jobs in tiny, windowless compartments with no view of how their ships go about conducting their missions. Pace, the crew's eyes and ears of what happens in the conning tower, waited while the crew assembled to get his straight scoop. Brad liked the idea of shipmates having to come to him for the scoop on *Clamagore* operations. He related the captain's strategy of following the Soviet Guided Missile Cruiser into the task group formation to take advantage of the ensuing confusion.

"Talk about excitement! The old man got us so close to the bird farm, he had to use green smokes instead of flares to signal the attack."

Ken Omensen added, "Word is he got his ass chewed by the task group commander for damn near dropping a flare on the flight deck last time we attacked her."

Pace went on. "You won't believe what happened next. Well this destroyer turns around and heads toward what he thinks is our position. No sonar. Nothing. He musta thought we were still under the smoke pots and simulated a depth charge attack there with hand grenades."

Radioman Omensen asked, "Did he get us?"

Pace replied smugly, "Hell no. He found out where we really were when a green flare marked our attack on him. He doesn't have a flight deck, so no danger of one falling on it."

Hal Tatlow jumped in. "How close did we get?"

"The skipper fired at five hundred yards, torpedo minimum enabling distance. And we had to let him open the range to get that far away. Talk about rubbing it in. The old man told the exec to say in the attack message he could see rust streaks on the destroyer's hull number and recommended someone paint over them."

The crew's mess resounded in the laughter of Phil Redmond's pumped up submariners. USS *Clamagore* pulled no punches for the balance of Operation Eager Beaver.

Captain Harkins picked up his phone and waited for COMSIXFLT Chief Staff Officer Marvin Davidson to come on the line.

"Cliff Harkins here, Captain."

"Cliff, put on your asbestos britches and hard-toed foundry boots, and get your sorry submariner butt up here."

"I guess this is a bad time to ask for two weeks leave."

"Right. I'm told they need a navy captain up in northern Canada on the Defense Early Warning (DEW) and the admiral thinks you're perfect for the job."

"Will he fit the family out with snowshoes? There's ten of us at last count. I must've done something really great to get selected for that one."

A while later, Cliff sat across from Captain Davidson at the latter's desk as Davidson said, "I don't have guts enough to take this into the admiral and thought maybe you might. He slid a message across his desk summarizing successful Orange Force submarine attacks. It read:

03090925Z/DEC/65
FROM: CTF 69
TO: USS CLAMAGORE
    USS JALLAO
    FNS L'AFRICAIN
    GNS TAXXOLI

EXERCISE EAGER BEAVER
SUBJECT: ORANGE SUBMARINE ATTACKS PHASE TWO
1. ORANGE SUBMARINE ATTACKS REPORTED ARE SUMMARIZED HEREWITH: READ IN FOUR COLUMNS

TIME	UNIT	POSITION	TARGET
140848Z	CLAMAGORE	3643N 1682E	1 CARRIER
			1 DESTROYER
141742Z	CLAMAGORE	3722N 1355E	1 CARRIER
141815Z	CLAMAGORE	3722N 1355E	1 CARRIER
150315Z	L'AFRICAIN	3833N 1708E	1 TANKER
161015Z	CLAMAGORE	3700N 1605E	1 CARRIER
			1 DESTROYER
161206Z	CLAMAGORE	3704N 1600E	1 DESTROYER
170844Z	L'AFRICAIN	3754N 1743E	1 TANKER
180130Z	JALLAO	3912N 1349E	1 DESTROYER

NO REPORTS RECEIVED TO INDICATE WHETHER TAXXOLI MADE ATTACKS DURING PHASE TWO.

2. BOX SCORE ON ATTACKS MADE TO DATE:
    CLAMAGORE   — 7
    L'AFRICAIN   — 2
    JALLAO   — 1
    TAXXOLI   — 0

Harkins managed to suppress a grin.

"Cliff, I thought we made it clear to Redmond he was supposed to low-key it during Phase Two."

"He did. If you think those numbers are bad, just imagine what they'd have been if he didn't."

"He's damn good, Cliff. I hope he's the exception. If not, we've got some serious rethinking to do about ASW in the Med. What do you think happened?"

"Maybe Redmond was irritated about something and took it out on the task group. Nothing was said to him during the interphase meeting, was there?"

Harkins knew Redmond smarted over his dressing down for launching green flares close to the carrier, and for the hanging of Sonarman Giambri's Legion of Merit on an aviator.

"I think if *Clamagore* can perform like that, we'd be putting our head in the sand to not pay attention. Bad side is we've got NATO convinced submarines are not a problem in the Med. And there's Greek and Italian addressees on the message."

Harkins answered, "Bear in mind, *Clamagore* is a diesel powered submarine. A nuke would be significantly better."

Davidson added, "And I understand the current setup prevents Redmond from getting command of one. The Russians have to be happy about that."

"Is there any follow-up you need from us, Captain Davidson?"

"Yeah. Make sure Redmond gets a suitable pat on the back when you write his ticket on how he performed here."

"I will, sir."

Harkins regretted that nothing he could write, do or say would get Redmond into the nuclear power program where they marched to a totally different drum.

Clamagore stopped at Sigonella long enough to offload Tatlow and Giambri and to refuel.

The commodore's personal car and driver arrived to pick up Giambri who donned his *HMS Pinafore* admiral's costume for photos. He looked quite genuine in white stockings and knee-length knickers topped with a navy blue jacket heavily brocaded in gold lace down the front. He wore a traditional nineteenth century fore and aft naval hat topped with a large white plume. White gloves and a ceremonial sword rounded out the effect. He'd ride to his tiny ancestral village in the Sicilian back country and there greet relatives he'd written to, but never actually met.

Redmond accompanied his top sonarman to the car, stopped, saluted smartly and asked, "By your leave, Admiral?"

A grinning Giambri returned the salute.

Redmond went on, "Captain Harkins will get you back to us one way or another. Don't worry about a thing. Have a good time and stay out of trouble."

He extended his hand and Giambri took it.

"Captain, you have no idea how much better than a Legion of Merit this trip is going to be."

Redmond said, "And Admiral?"

"Yes, Captain?"

"Would you mind giving one of my men a lift to the Naval Air Station?"

"Not at all, sir. Be glad to."

Redmond shook IC2 Hal Tatlow's hand. "Thank you for bailing us out for the Norfolk trip. Give Kris my thanks also, and tell her had I known you were on your honeymoon, there's no way I'd have permitted it to be interrupted."

"I will, Captain, and thank you."

"And don't worry about running out of leave. Got that?"

"I got it, Captain."

Tatlow loaded his gear in the trunk and the *Admiral*'s car drove off.

Phil Redmond returned to the ship where Dave Zane greeted him. "Captain, we have a Lieutenant Pierce in the wardroom. A naval aviator. The one they hung Giambri's LOM on."

Redmond greeted the young officer who expressed his regret over getting an award he really did not deserve.

"I appreciate what you say, Lieutenant. I'll pass that along to Sonarman Giambri."

Pierce replied, "If it's all the same to you, Captain, I'd like to tell him myself."

"Afraid that's impossible, Lieutenant. He's been dispatched on an important ... shall we call it ... a public relations mission. And to set your mind at ease, Giambri said, and I quote, 'You have no idea how much better than a Legion of Merit this trip is going to be'."

Redmond figured a five-day port visit at Palma on the Spanish Balearic Island of Majorca would not prevent getting back to New London in time for Christmas. Additionally, the port visit provided his crew with an opportunity to shop for gifts. *Clamagore* moored outboard of a U.S. destroyer in the port of Palma, fortunately not one of the ships *sunk* by *Clamagore* during NATO Operation Eager Beaver.

Denny Kolb surprised his skipper by asking for a private meeting. Under normal circumstances this request would be made via the exec, however Redmond sensed urgency in Denny's voice and agreed.

They sat in the CO stateroom with curtain drawn.

"So what's up, Denny? You want a raise?"

Denny minced no words and got right to the point, "Captain, I might have a bit of a problem. Chest pains."

"You're only twenty-nine. Isn't that early for cardiac symptoms if that's what you're implying?"

"When a Kolb baby is born, it gets two certificates ... birth and death. They leave the date off the second one, but fill in the cause ... heart disease."

"Have you talked to the Doc? What did he say?"

"Nothing good. He told me to put a pill under my tongue and asked if it made me feel better. It did and he said that wasn't a good sign."

"Shall I call for a chopper and send you to Rota for a check?"

"Captain, I'd like to find out if I really have a problem before you do that. Otherwise, if I'm okay they'll put me on the watch list. I've got a request in for post graduate school and that could jeopardize it."

Denny, too, saw the handwriting on the wall and would seek a career outside the submarine force.

"So what do you want to do?"

"Maybe Wilcox and I can find an infirmary in town and get it checked there. Shouldn't cost too much and it'll be on me."

"Okay, but if the news is not good, I call the chopper. Right?"

"Right, Captain."

An hour later, Denny stripped to his undershorts lay on a gurney in El Santo Theresa Infirmary in the outskirts of Palma. Attached electrodes on his bare chest wired him to an electrocardiograph machine. An English-speaking technician advised the Americans a Dr. Junin, who speaks only French, would soon be in to conduct and evaluate the gram. The tech said he would translate.

Denny, almost fluent in French, said that would not be necessary.

Doc Wilcox and Denny went back and forth while they waited.

"You gotta tell me everything the doctor says, Mister Kolb. You know the captain's gonna pump me when we get back."

As Doctor Junin walked into the room both men dropped their jaws in perfect unison. The most beautiful woman either of them had ever seen said, "*Bonne journée. Je suis le Docteur Junin. Pouvez-vous me dire qu'est-ce qui ne va pas, s'il vous plait* (Good day. I am Doctor Junin. Can you tell me what the problem is please)?"

Tall, creamy-skinned, shiny black hair secured behind her head in a bun, the doctor looked at Denny through eyes far bluer than any midday sky over the clearest day at sea. He pondered, *Such a beautiful woman and intelligent enough to be a doctor.*

Denny's French came back quickly as he got into conversation and explained his circumstance.

He'd been at sea in an all male conclave since leaving New London four months earlier with no contact with a woman since then. Dr. Junin approached and touched him to reposition some of the electrodes. This plus her scent had the expected effect. Lying on his back in only boxer undershorts, he struggled to prevent the obvious and toyed with asking whether an EKG could be measured while lying on his stomach.

Denny, glad a male had accompanied him, focused mentally on Wilcox in a vain attempt to alleviate the situation.

Before long, Denny noted Doctor Junin's French had slipped into the familiar form—used to address children and personal friends. *Perhaps this is a technique for making patients feel comfortable.* Yet Denny felt an abrupt connection to which he could not respond. The doctor had no problem when Denny responded in the familiar form. *What's going on here?* He wondered.

An uncle had married a French woman with whom Denny often practiced while studying the language. She once told him of the thunderbolt love—*coup de foudre*—a French term that means love at first sight. She claimed to have experienced this when she first met his uncle. *Quand je l'ai vu, ça a été le coup de foudre*—When I saw him, it was love at first sight.

To Denny's great relief, Doctor Junin announced she'd found nothing in his EKG to indicate cardiac disorder, then poked a bruise on his upper rib cage, nearly lifting him from the gurney.

Dammit. So that was it. That spill I took while dropping from the bridge into the conning tower.

The doctor added that she thought Denny suffered from fatigue and suggested he take some time away from work as she put it.

He mused, *A common submarine officer affliction*, but opted not to share that.

Their appointment concluded, Doctor Junin shook Denny's hand and looked at him with more than a cordial expression.

Denny's mind raced like a sport car. *It's clear neither of us want this to end here. She likely considers it unethical to date a patient, but what've I got to lose?* "The ships are giving a reception at the Palma Yacht Club tonight. Would you care to be my guest, Doctor Junin?"

She replied through a pleased expression directed at Denny, but with unsurprising aplomb kept her answer impersonal. "*Je serais honoré d'assister à la réception, de la Marine Américaine, le Lieutenant Kolb* (I would be honored to attend the US Navy reception, Lieutenant Kolb)."

Damn she's good, Denny thought, *improper for her to date a patient, but accepting an invitation for an official US Navy function is within the bounds of professional conduct.*

Much to Denny's relief, they would see each other again.

Chapter 16

Vasiliy Norovsky descended into the bowels of a Soviet November class nuclear powered submarine and the ship re-submerged almost immediately. He expected to be greeted with the same contempt he'd received on *Nmah,* but to Norovsky's surprise the crew treated him cordially. After being shown a bunk in the crew sleeping quarters, Vasiliy made his way to the crew's mess for a cup of tea. Several sailors sat about, and though none drew him into conversation he sensed no hostility.

A seaman approached. "*Komrade* Norovsky, I am to take you to our *zampolit, Kapitan* 2nd Rank Knyazev."

Soon, Norovsky sat opposite the *zampolit* in the latter's stateroom.

Knyazev spoke in low tones, even though the door was shut. He wished no one but Norovsky to hear what he had to say. "By the *Kapitan's* order, only he and I know the true circumstances of why you are aboard. He is concerned of what some overzealous crewman might do to you were the facts known."

Norovsky had nothing but contempt for *zampolits,* well earned during past experiences in the Soviet Navy. Knyazev contradicted Vasiliy's perception of a *zampolit's* physical appearance. A tall, blond, gray-eyed man, handsome by some standards; he nonetheless spoke through the characteristic snarl of his peers.

The *zampolit* explained a cover story set in place to protect Vasiliy Norovsky. "You are a civilian technician who reached retirement age while aboard *Nmah.* We are merely taking you home to Mother Russia for shall we call it … the retirement ceremony?"

Knyazev turned up Norovsky's anger for *zampolits* two notches.

The *zampolit* went on. "You must understand however, I shall watch your every move."

Norovsky thought, *What the hell do you suspect? Escape? To where? Sabotage? I'd try to sink a submarine with me in it?* He spoke with feigned remorse in his voice. "I understand, *Komrade Zampolit.* I will cooperate fully. And please thank the *kapitan* for me."

"You can do that for yourself," Knyazev replied. "The *kapitan* wishes to see you in his stateroom."

The *zampolit* took Norovsky to the adjoining room and knocked.

A slender blue-eyed officer raised his eyes in response to the *zampolit's* introduction and said through a scowl, "I am *Kapitan* 2nd Rank Piotr Denisov, commanding officer of this ship. Best you not forget that."

"I won't, *Komrade Kapitan.*" *Piotr Denisov?* Norovsky looked for the first time at the man he would lead to freedom from Russia.

Lorraine and Rick Ferranti stood before the Palazzo Vecchio—the old palace—now the town hall of Florence, Italy. The massive, Romanesque, crenellated fortress-palace is among the most impressive town halls of Tuscany. It overlooks the *Piazza della Signoria* with its copy of Michelangelo's David statue and a gallery of statues in the nearby *Loggia dei Lanzi* beside the River Arno. The Palazzo is said by some to be the most significant public place in Italy.

Lorraine looked at a clock on the simple tower atop the Palazzo's cubicle-shaped building. It indicated exactly 2:00 p.m.

"It's time," she said and took her place beside Rick.

She recognized one of the nine painted coats of arms of the Florentine republic in her grandparents' wedding photo so they would appear exactly where they stood that day so many years ago. The photographer hired for the occasion snapped away.

"I want at least ten," Lorraine said, "and we'll keep the one that comes closest."

They mimicked positions once taken by the elder Gilliams in their wedding photo.

Later, Lorraine and Rick sat over Chiantis at a table beside the Arno. The proprietor told them it would be far more comfortable inside, but they insisted. He recognized that special glow shown by people very much in love. *This is likely a ritual for them.* He'd expect this from younger couples, but figured Lorraine and Rick old enough to have more sense and would prefer to keep warm. The proprietor believed the American couple likely had a special agenda and he acquiesced with abundant grace.

"Antonio," he ordered a young Italian. "Set a table with two chairs on the patio by the river. Quickly!" For a moment, the man watched from the window. Not too far from Rick's age, the proprietor thought, *Perhaps I should set a table for mio sposa Alfreda beside the Arno. Maybe one more bambino.*

Italians hold amore in high esteem.

"Do you think Frank will like the photos?"

Lorraine replied, "How can he not? This place has always been so special to him. He loved grandmother so. They were married in Mussolini's time, but before he completely robbed Italy of her charm."

"The disaster Il Duce brought to his country. You'd think we would have learned by now, but we sure in hell don't."

Lorraine recognized traces of the expression she had come to know so well during the troubled days of their early-married years. She reached across the table and laid a comforting hand on Rick's.

He looked up. "Guess that's not a good place to go anymore."

"You've been there long enough, sweetheart. Granddad used to tell me, 'You don't have to beat up on yourself. There's plenty of people out there happy to do that for you'."

He acknowledged with a forced smile.

"Look, Rick. You did what you had to do. It's all in the past and can't be changed, only learned from."

He took his hand from beneath and laid it atop hers and gave it a gentle squeeze. "I can't think of a more appropriate time or place to ask you this. How do you think Frank would feel about me jumping in and taking over? On a full-time basis."

Lorraine's heart nearly leapt from her chest. Her happy expression gave Rick all the response he needed. She thought, *What a beautiful and loving God to give me two such happy things at the same time. First the photos and now this.*

Rick spoke of his recent conversation with Cliff Harkins on the subject of children. "Told him I emulated his diet. He agreed that plus a reenactment of the Gilliams's wedding photo in Florence had to be surefire. So what do you say we finish these Chiantis, go back to the room and lay the keel for Frank's great-grandson?"

"Great-granddaughter," Lorraine corrected.

Commanders Phil Redmond and Harold Lang, destroyer CO, headed a reception line that included their XOs and a destroyer junior officer's new bride. The delightful young woman had followed her husband from port to port in the Mediterranean as a sort of honeymoon. She added considerable class to the line but slowed the process as male guests tended to linger by her.

The American Consul at Palma had extended invitations to all local *counts and no-accounts.*

Lang, who once visited Palma as executive officer of his previous ship, confided, "Looks like he rounded up all the usual suspects."

A trio of guitar players wandered about strumming classic Spanish melodies in a large room well-appointed in a nautical theme. Junior officers held charm school on unaccompanied young ladies. All except Denny Kolb who spent ninety percent of his time looking hopefully at the entrance door. A half hour passed. He thought, *Shoulda known it was too good to be true.* Another half hour. *Scrub it,* he thought, and then spotted Doctor Junin. A coat check boy took her fur wrap while Denny made a beeline for her.

A well schooled model could not have shown off Doctor Junin's scooped neck, midnight blue, silk cocktail gown to better effect. The slightly fitted, knee-length dress ended in a flared skirt above black suede heels. She wore her raven black hair down and diamond earrings to round out the effect.

Denny thought, *Have I died and gone to heaven?*

She greeted him. "*Bonsoir, Lieutenant Kolb. Pardonnez-moi s'il vous plaît pour être en retard. Plus de patients qu'ordinaire. Je suis heureux ainsi à bientôt. Traduiriez-vous pour moi s'il vous plaît? Mon anglais est si pauvre, il m'embarrasse pour l'utiliser* (Good evening, Lieutenant Kolb. Please forgive me for being late. More patients than usual. I am so glad to see you. Would you translate for me please? My English is so poor, it embarrasses me to use it)."

"Of course I will. Please, Doctor. I am Denny."

"Yes, Dennis. And I am Jacqueline."

He'd prefer Jackie and Denny, but an inner voice told him that would not be so. "May I introduce you to my captain?"

Jacqueline melted Denny with a smile and slipped her arm into his then walked across the room, the heads of each male following as though on a common swivel. Even the guitar trio fell silent.

Dr. Junin looked to more properly belong on the arm of a handsome celebrity like popular movie star Ricardo Montalbán, but for whatever reason had chosen Dennis.

Redmond watched them approach. He knew earlier of Denny's encounter with Doctor Junin and initially considered his description of her to be exaggerations of a man who'd been too long at sea. With effort, he kept his jaw from dropping.

"Captain, may I present Doctor Junin?"

Her English good enough to hear omission of her first name. "Jacqueline," she corrected.

"Jacqueline, Captain." Denny's face beamed through an, *I told you so*, expression.

Redmond shook Jacqueline's offered hand and took a stab at his long forgotten high school French, but his "*Enchanté*" won him only a "Pleased to meet you," translated by Denny, who then introduced her to Dave Zane who spoke no French at all.

Tim Keating and Benson Roman quickly converged on Denny and his new friend, falling over themselves with offers to retrieve hors d'oeuvres and drinks. Jacqueline, continuing to hold Denny's arm, politely declined through an engaging smile.

Redmond said to his exec, "So what do you think, Dave?"

"What's there to think, Captain? Denny's a very happy camper and we'll only be here a few days."

"I'm not sure about that. Denny told me there was an instant connection between them," then repeated the French thunderbolt love concept given earlier by Denny.

"You really think something will come of this? Isn't it a bit early? He's only known her a coupla hours."

"I agree, Dave. But I've never seen him like this."

"He's a logical young man. Whatever happens, he'll handle it."

"I'm the proverbial cynic, Dave. If it looks too good to be true, it probably is." He reminded the exec of a recent contest among the *Clamagore* junior officers—who had been dumped the most times?

Denny won hands down. "Yet he seems to have something only the good doctor can see."

"What are you thinking, Captain? That she's got an angle?"

"I can't imagine what she'd want from Denny. Certainly there's nothing he has that she could possibly need. And look. Every guy in the room wants to hit on her, but she hangs onto Denny's arm like a life raft in a sea state six (severe weather)."

Dave Zane looked and agreed. "Captain, I'm not a lotta help here. Never was much good at matters of the heart. Bea (his daughter) is ten now and thoughts of what lies ahead terrify me."

The reception came to an end among a plethora of goodnights and thank-yous. Phil Redmond watched Denny disappear into the night with his beautiful friend and wondered, *Why in hell do I worry about things I can't control?* He knew the answer, but did not belly up to it; a commanding officer is always concerned with what happens to anyone on his ship.

Joe Dunn stood the midwatch at *Pershing*'s conning station. To give the crew a sense of night and day, standing orders required the attack center to be *rigged for red* between sunset and sunrise (all but dim red lights turned off).

Midway through a conversation between Joe and the COB who stood chief of the watch, the EOOW reported from maneuvering over the 21MC, "Conn, experiencing low lube oil pressure in the main thrust bearing and have stopped the engine."

Dammit, ran through Dunn's mind, *I have the conn. You request permission from me to do that.* But this is the new nuclear Navy and things are done differently; at least as established by the skipper, Captain Williams. "Conn, aye, Maneuvering. Get it back soon as possible. We need speed to hold depth."

"Maneuvering, aye," came the reply via an obviously bored tone. Newly certified, the EOOW had yet to become qualified in submarines.

Pershing's speed began to bleed off and Joe observed the ship to be settling. *A bit heavy overall.*

"Chief, pump auxiliaries to sea, two thousand pounds."

"Two thousand pounds auxiliary to sea, sir."

A minute later Dunn noted the ship to be settling faster and called maneuvering, "What's your estimate on when you can give me the bell. We need speed to hold depth."

"Will let you know, Conn."

The arrogant bastard is making this a test of wills. No time to ruminate.

"Messenger, notify the captain his presence is urgently needed in the attack center," and then to the COB, "Shut the vents and give me a fifteen second blow (air into the main ballast tanks)."

"Shut the vents and fifteen on the blow. Violates patrol quiet (reduced radiated noise to remain undetected)," the COB reminded.

The blow completed, Joe saw the ship descend even faster and approached test depth.

"Blow all main ballast. Cross connect missile service air (fifteen hundred pounds per square inch higher than the main air system)." This slowed the rate of descent, but *Pershing* continued downward."

At that instant, Williams entered the attack center and demanded, "What's going on here?"

With deliberate calmness in his voice, Joe replied, "We're sinking, Captain. We need a full bell, but maneuvering refuses to give us one. You've got to order it or we're going straight to the bottom."

Williams demanded, "Give me a full report."

"No time, Captain. We need that bell or we'll lose the ship."

The captain did not respond and seemed to choke.

As the ship passed test depth, Dunn seized the 21MC mike. "Captain is in the attack center. He orders all ahead full immediately," and then to the helmsman, "All ahead full." This backed up the order to maneuvering on the engine order telegraph.

Pershing shuddered as the huge propeller dug in and pushed the ship to safety.

As they approached patrol depth, Williams said to Joe, "Call your relief and see me in my stateroom immediately."

"Aye, Captain."

Williams did not hear the apprehension and fear in Dunn's voice that the captain expected. Normally, his officers quaked in their boots when he spoke in anger. Williams left the attack center and waited for

Joe who showed up shortly and knocked on the passageway door.

"Reporting as ordered."

Williams snapped, "Sit down, dammit. You learn this and learn quick. You do not defy my orders. Never!"

"I didn't defy your orders, Captain. You failed to give me one, so I did what I had to do to save the ship."

"The ship was in no danger, except in your opinion which I find to be increasingly not worth much. And don't you ever use the word fail when talking about me, or I'll bust your ass right out of this man's Navy," the Captain said, clearly seething.

Joe resisted the urge to grin. He replied in a calm voice, "That won't be necessary, Captain," then handed him a letter.

Williams looked quickly at it initially, but then on reading the subject: 'Resignation of my commission from the U.S. Navy'. He read further and caught the words, 'because I cannot carry out enforced policies clearly not in the best interest of the submarine force and the U.S. Navy'.

Mrs. Williams didn't raise any fools. The skipper set aside his anger and began to assess the impact this could have on his own career. A regular Navy officer resigning on his watch and citing enforced improper policies as his reason. *But he'll have to prove it. I'll make it damn difficult for him to do that when I endorse his letter. But still.*

Williams said in a calmer voice, "So what policies are being forced down your throat, Lieutenant?" A submarine CO addressing a junior officer by his rank instead of first name is a clear put-down.

Dunn said, "It's quite a list, but they all converge on a single issue. The shift of emphasis accompanying the changeover from diesel to nuclear power is fraught with danger and will likely result in disaster."

"Like what?"

"Like what just happened. The officer in charge of reactor operations permitted absolute compliance with prescribed procedure to hazard the ship. In diesel boats that would never happen. Priority one is keep the ocean outboard of the hull. And no officer would be assigned the responsibility of EOOW until he was a qualified submariner. I think we learned today that is something you would do well to take under advisement."

"Am I hearing sour grapes?"

"If I had even the slightest interest in becoming a nuke, I'd say you had a point. But I don't. Look, Captain. I suggest we not drag this out. My letter was written a week before today's debacle. I planned to hold it until we got back to Holy Loch. Nobody wants to be shipmates with a short timer. I believe it would be advantageous to both of us for you to honor that."

"You know with my endorsement, I can drag this out as long as I want. Like recommending disapproval pending disciplinary action."

"You won't do that, Captain. Seven witnesses and I just watched you choke while your ship was about to sink. And each one of them would be dead as hell now were it not for my action, so I'd look for a lot of anger in their testimonies. So why don't we both let sleeping dogs lie?"

A stanza from the poem *The Laws of the Navy,* by British Admiral R. A. Hopwood, the most famous and oft-quoted piece of naval literature ever penned, reads, "'Tis well if the court should acquit thee – But 'twere best had'st thou never been tried'.

Williams knew simply being tried regardless of the outcome would shatter any hopes he might have for promotion to flag rank and elected to make no reply.

Without requesting permission, Joe Dunn walked from the captain's stateroom and into his own. Despite the outward calmness shown during their heated session, Dunn had a great need to let off steam. He took a lined notepad from his desk. *It's time I got to doing better things than squabbling with the Old Man.* Joe picked up a ballpoint pen and began to write.

LOVE COMES TO LITTLE RICO; THE FINALE
By Seaman Synge

"I tell you, he must be nuts to fall for a broad like that," said Aaron the Animal, as the sinister foursome sat in a dark corner of the Pershing Club discussing the unfortunate plight that had befallen their partner in crime, Ricardo "Little Rico" Meli.

The foursome, composed of Aaron the Animal, The Masher, Guido Zacchi and The Mad Rabbi, argued until it became apparent to Guido that nothing was getting settled. He rose from the table pounding his fist saying, "Look here you guys, let us analyze the situation and then proceed to remedy it. Now first of all, this chick that Little Rico is hung up on lives way over in Navigation Gang territory, which means that if Rico kidnaps her back, our contract with Big Greg Capone is off. No more tuna fish, no more chocolate, and no more candy. Why he'll cut us off 'til we starve to death in the hideout. Do you think Little Rico is worth that?"

The guys stared up at Guido, their eyes moist with tears at the thought of having their tuna cut off and waited to hear what he would propose. "Look you guys," Guido said, his bellowing voice down to a near whisper, "Did any of you see this broad? She's a damned greaser. Yeah, and what's more, she's uglier than my cousin Annette; you know the one that plays the violin?" The boys all looked at each other trying to imagine how anyone could be uglier than Irish's cousin Annette. Guido continued to speak. "And what's more, she don't wear nothing at all except a towel all the time ... and she just hangs around the navigation center waiting for Rico to come around and gander at her and then she talks to him in broken Guinea English.

"Before we decide what to do, I would like you guys to know that if this chick is brought into the radio shack, I, personally, will see to it she gets a bath every day and don't go stinkin' up the place with her purple feet." Guido sat down leaving the smell of ripe provolone cheese hanging in the air.

Aaron the Animal, who during Guido's speech sat silently biting his toenails, now felt the need to say something profound. "Boys," he started, "I, myself, have been observing this chick and she is indeed uglier than Guido's cousin Annette who plays the violin. But I, being Little Rico's stepbrother, feel myself slightly obligated to look out for him. Not wanting to see him get snuffed out by Big Greg Capone and not wanting to see us lose our tuna fish, as well as the now gone Peter Pan crunchy, I have conceived of a plan which might merit a try."

A look of impending evil crept into Guido's eyes as The Animal unfolded his plan. "You guys all know that dumb blond, Judy, who goes with The Enforcer? Well, I got the scoop from White Rat Walters that she just lays around in a sailor hat in MMC headquarters and with some inside help from Mad Dog Pleau, we can kidnap her and swap her for this Rita Cellini that Little Rico is so hung up on. I think this will appeal to Big Greg because one of his boys has it bad for this Judy chick, who now belongs to The Enforcer."

The group sat silent, going over the plan in their small minds, and finally they all agreed to it. The Animal bent forward slightly and kissed first The Mad Rabbi and then The Masher, making it known that they were the ones chosen to carry out the plan.

Little Rico sat in the shack with headphones on listening for expected messages from the main headquarters in Palermo, totally unaware that at that very moment, Cupid, in the form of two unshaven mugs, was firing his first salvo of arrows, .38 caliber slugs, at the indigent Enforcer and his mob, while The Animal and Guido were closing the deal with Big Greg Capone.

Two hours later the boys stood in the shack unhappily watching Little Rico passionately embracing Rita.

And they lived "happily ever after", I think.

Joe put down his pen and smiled. *Damned if that doesn't make me feel a hundred percent better.*

Denny Kolb arrived back aboard *Clamagore* midway through breakfast doing his best to contain a smile. He took his place at the wardroom table and Benson Roman went immediately on the attack.

"So, c'mon, Denny. Out with it."

"Out with what?"

Tim Keating asked, "What did you do last night? And don't leave out the censored parts. I'm past twenty-one and cleared for X-rated."

Denny rolled with the punches. "You guys have no idea how much there is to see on this little Island. Take Valldemosa Monastery for example. Bet you don't know that Frederick Chopin didn't hang out with George Sand like he did in the movie, but at the monastery. And George Sand was no Merle Oberon. Had a face like a busted easy-out and smoked cigars."

"Nice try, Denny," Keating continued. "Where did you and the belle of the ball stay last night?"

"I came back here about one and you guys were all crashed. I went out and jogged this morning before you woke up."

"In dress blues?"

"That's the uniform of the day. What else would I wear?"

Benson Roman demanded, "Witnesses, I demand witnesses."

Phil Redmond and Dave Zane sat back, content to watch the unfolding drama, lamenting that their own junior officer days had slipped by so quickly.

Stonewall Denny did not budge and the others gave up; all but Tim who took one more shot. "Captain," he said. "I got an ingrown toenail and need to visit the Palma infirmary."

At that, Redmond declared breakfast over. The exec and all the JOs slipped out except Denny who quietly asked if he could speak to Redmond in his stateroom.

With the curtain drawn, Denny began in a quiet voice. "Captain, I know this sounds crazy, but can I take leave and meet the boat in Rota. Jacqueline wants me to go to Capri with her."

Redmond did a good job of masking his astonishment. "Are you sure you want to do this?"

"Never more certain of anything in my life. Set the thunderbolt love nonsense aside. From the instant we met, there was mutual attraction. Yeah, I know. I'm not the best looking or most suave man she ever met. And she ... well you saw for yourself, Captain. I guess we're the beauty and the beast, but damn well stuck on each other."

"Denny, the last thing I'd ever do is advise someone in affairs of the heart. Say the wrong thing and it'll come back to haunt you. But you've known her barely twenty-four hours."

"You're right, Captain, and both of us like what we've seen so far. The only way to find out the rest is with more time together. Do you think you can spring me until Rota?"

"Sure, Denny. But Capri in December? It's all but closed down. Katherine followed me to the Med on my first deployment. We spent a few days in Chamonix in southern France. Had a wonderful time skiing there. One of the best winter resorts ever. Does Jacqueline ski?"

"I don't know, Captain. She told me her life dream is to visit Capri with a special person. Can't for the life of me say why she picked me, but I'll go with it."

Redmond failed in his attempt to give Denny a stern look. "Okay, but have your sorry lovesick ass in Rota before we leave for the states."

"Count on it, Captain. And thank you."

"Have a wonderful time, Denny."

"I will, Captain."

Redmond added, "I wish you all the luck in the world and hope you find what you're looking for."

Chapter 17

An unwritten law of the Navy goes: if one officer brings an issue to the commanding officer, it's a good thing. If two or more collaborate on the same issue, it's a mutiny. Even though Joe Dunn and Paul Scott shared most everything, Dunn opted to discuss neither his tiff with the captain nor his resignation. However, the near sinking, an event from which lifesaving lessons can be learned, did not fall into this category.

Paul asked, "So what do you think happened?"

"Negative buoyancy overall resulted in speed being all that enabled us to maintain depth. And we were going too fast to read normal trim clues. When we stopped, the bottom fell out. Pumping two thousand pounds from auxiliaries didn't answer the mail. Matter of fact, it didn't make a dent."

"But the shot of air in the main ballast tanks. Shouldn't that've done it?"

"We're plowing new ground here, Paul. These ships are bigger which means a lot more inertia once it gets moving. And the deeper we are, the less air can expand in the ballast tanks to restore neutral buoyancy. We were moving down at a pretty fast clip when COB blew the tanks. My guess is simply increasing sea pressure as we went deeper exceeded our ability to counter with high-pressure air. But the experts will have to work that one out. All this is simply my theory."

"Sounds good to me, Joe. Somebody must be working on it."

"I wouldn't bet on it. Was totally new to me. I tried to maintain ordered depth and remain undetected. It took me too long to recognize the seriousness of our situation, but I'll tell you this. If it ever happens again on my watch, we're going to the surface. Damned if I'll let myself be lured into that trap again."

"So what happens now?"

Dunn answered, "My guess is we'll make a full report and toss it off to the Bureau of Ships. We exceeded test depth, so as a minimum COM-SUB-LANT will hear about it. And they're likely to ask questions. Just hope it's not left for some hardheaded nuke to decide."

"Ya know, Joe, most of the nuke guys are good heads. We lucked out and they know it. A few recognize the injustice meted out to us unwashed souls and don't gloat. But the others, like that idiot EOOW who damn near sunk us, looks on diesel-boaters as dirt underfoot."

Joe replied, "You're right. You ever get the feeling they believe diesel-boaters are a disease that has to be stomped out and they're the ones who have to lead the charge? But let's get off this. Too damned depressing. What have you got lined up for when we get home? Besides hitting on Jean Ann that is."

"No comment. But add to that, I'm to be best man at a good friend's wedding. Adrian Roberts, a chief now, but we served together on USS *Piratefish* ten years ago."

Denny looked out over the Gulf of Naples into a stiff northwest wind and said to Jacqueline, *"Va faire c'être trop rugueux pour vous? Nous pouvons passer la nuit à Naples et essayer la première chose de nouveau le matin* (Will this be too rough for you? We can spend the night in Naples and try again first thing in the morning)."

Both had gotten sufficiently grounded enough after *the thunderbolt love* to discover among other things their keen senses of humor.

She responded through a teasing tone, *"Est cela si brutalement il rendra ma mer de garçon marin mal de mare* (Is it so rough it will make my sailor boy seasick)?"

Hydrofoils unequal to the weather, they boarded a large ferry that would take them to Capri. Despite a chilling wind, Jacqueline and Dennis went forward and stood on the passenger deck below the wheelhouse. He felt a bit obvious in his *Clamagore* foul-weather jacket and woolen cap, not quite up to the Italian style standards, but quite comfortable.

Jacqueline's solvency revealed itself in her clothing. She wore stylish slacks and a hooded black wool greatcoat. A gray scarf fended off wind gusts and sea spray as the ferry plowed directly into the weather when it departed Naples.

Dennis stood behind her with arms wrapped about Jacqueline. "It's good that we share body heat."

She replied, "Is it an American custom for men to use their women to shield them from the weather?"

"I'm told it started out that way with the Native Americans, but the Europeans arrived and changed all that."

They reversed positions. "This better?"

Jacqueline found a bare spot below Dennis's left ear and kissed it. "That should warm you for our voyage."

She now encircled him with her arms and he gave her hand a squeeze. Though no words had been exchanged on the permanency of their relationship, Dennis perceived this likely had entered both minds. *No one can fake what this woman has shown me.*

Omensen, Howell, Pace and Stewardsman Rapinian sat about the crew's mess after a night on the town in Palma. Though Rapinian had to first learn Tagalog, he knew enough Spanish to make their visit ashore go better and the others appreciated this. The usual post liberty (shore leave) high spirits prevailed.

Pace declared, "*Fundador e siphon* (a Spanish brandy and seltzer) has to be the best bar drink in the world."

Omensen added, "Lucky for you they don't ask for ID cards here. Otherwise you'd have had Coke on the rocks."

The remark drew laughter from the others. Howell said, "Pace didn't do so bad … as long as we propped him up."

"Too bad Mister Scott isn't here," Omensen said, "he would love this place."

"I never got to know him," Pace said, "but I sure liked what I saw."

Having once been an enlisted submariner caused the crew to look upon Scott as one of their own.

"He's the best officer I ever served under," Omensen said.

Rapinian added, "He was less bother than anyone else in the wardroom."

Howell asked, "I wonder how he likes it on the boomer? And how the crew likes him?"

Omensen answered, "My guess, if the crew doesn't already, they'll like him before they finish a patrol with Mister Scott aboard."

Pace asked, "Anybody notice how the Fearsome Foursome quieted down after he left?"

"The Foursome has become the twosome now," Howell said. "Just Mister Roman and Keating since Lieutenant Kolb disappeared. By the way, did I ever tell you about the time when Mister Scott and Tatlow installed a new gyro singlehanded in just twelve hours?"

Rapinian exclaimed in broken English, "I remember! Tatlow and Mister Scott were gone all night. And we had much trouble with the submarine base repair people next morning."

With that remark, he piqued everyone's interest then like an excited child awaiting a bedtime story, Pace, baby of the group, said, "Well, c'mon, Howell. Tell us about it."

Howell needed little persuasion to get started on his favorite Paul Scott tale. "Our MK-eighteen gyro (master ship's gyro compass which keeps track of true north) was down and needed at least three days for repair. We were scheduled to get underway at 0800 the next morning for a hot two-week exercise. The skipper was ready to toss in the towel, but Mister Scott talked him out of it. There was a new MK-eighteen at Portsmouth, New Hampshire. The captain argued it would take all night to go up there and back with a base pickup. And then, how long to pull the old one out and install the new one?"

Omensen remarked, "That is a pretty damn big order."

"Not for Scott. He had a plan. He instructed the COB to get the old gyro hauled out with a crane while he and Tatlow drove to Portsmouth for the new one. A little fly in the ointment they didn't know about. Per regulation, the crane had to be returned to the base when the removal was completed."

Pace said, "So that was the end of that?"

Howell went on, "It well could have been. Here's the funny part. Mister Scott was furious when he returned and found the crane had been taken away. Never seen him so pissed."

One of the others said, "Pissed? Mister Scott? He wouldn't say crap if he had a mouthful."

"We must not be talking about the same officer," said Howell. "Well, old Scott storms into the base repair duty officer's bunk room and insists a crane operator be called in immediately."

"The base guy refuses, saying off hour crane operations can be performed only with written permission of the repair department head, a full captain."

Mister Scott tells him, "If you don't have someone here in twenty minutes, look out your window. You'll see that damn crane passing by with me driving."

Omensen said through an astonished look, "I don't believe it."

Howell replied, "You damn well better."

Rapinian finished the story. "By the time Tatlow and Mister Scott got the gyro aboard, down comes the Base CO and the repair officer. There was much angry talk. The captain said he would discipline Mister Scott. That satisfied the two officers and they left."

Howell said, "You'll never guess what the punishment was. For two weeks, Mister Scott had to be on call to play cribbage anytime the captain wanted."

Jacqueline and Dennis debarked the ferry at Capri Marina and spotted a lone taxi. The driver hoped to get a fare from an unlikely tourist among the passengers, mostly residents met by family or friends. They entered the cab and began their ride up a winding road to La Collina in Alto (hilltop) Bed & Breakfast.

Dennis thought, *And she suggested we hike uphill,* just following Jacqueline, carrying their bags exhausted him. She'd already shown herself to be athletic and her pace would likely break him

They drove by stores and restaurants near the marina, all closed for the season and he worried about where they might find a place to eat that evening. As they rode further from the marina, both began to wonder where in the world they might be staying.

The taxi stopped at a tiny garden gate before La Collina in Alto. The proprietor and his wife, an elderly but vigorous couple that spoke good but broken English with a delightful Italian accent, greeted Jacqueline and Dennis.

On learning they were not married, the proprietor explained Italian law required passports be left at the desk and double rooms can be let only to couples able to show proof of marriage. Dennis and Jacqueline would occupy separate rooms.

The proprietress easily read disappointment in Dennis's expression, correctly surmised the circumstance and saw his was not a case of raging hormones to be quelled in a one-night stand.

"I have just the rooms for you."

Knowing full well he would not use it, she assigned Dennis an inexpensive room that could easily double as a broom closet and then took Jacqueline to hers. Beautiful flowers and the fresh smell of jasmine and lemon trees greeted her. Blooming in Capri knows no season. An incredible panorama of hills and seascape unfolded before a private patio and viewed through a spotless picture window.

The proprietress smiled a knowing smile. "I hope it is all right that we don't make the room up until eleven."

This gave Jacqueline and Dennis needed escape from the double room requirement. Dennis arrived moments after the woman departed.

Pleased to be finished struggling with her host's broken English, Jacqueline said in French, "Don't you just love it here? The view, our own private patio. And look. It even has a stand-up shower."

Nodding his agreement, Dennis said, "In the submarine Navy we have a saying, 'Save water. Shower with a friend.' I understand there's a serious water shortage on Capri. Don't you think we should do our part?"

"Dennis! What am I going to do with you?"

His grin faded to a tender expression. He groped for a suitable response but came up dry.

"This," and he folded Jacqueline into his arms and kissed her.

She whispered, "It's been such a long day, Dennis. Perhaps we should have a nap before going off for the evening."

Vasiliy Norovsky stood on the bridge of *Mayakovsky* with *Kapitan* 3rd Rank Oleg Solkolv, ship's navigation officer, as the nuclear powered submarine approached Severodvinsk. The city sat above the Arctic Circle where in mid-winter night prevailed continuously. Despite the circumstances, it elated Norovsky to again see his home for the first time in sixteen years.

Solkolv, unaware of Norovsky's circumstance, said, "I am certain the port looks good to you, *Komrade*. How long have you been away?"

Norovsky smiled in the darkness unseen then said, "It's been longer than I expected."

"Does she still look the same to you?"

"Hard to tell in the dark."

He noted many more lights than what had been there last time he brought his ship, the former *Erich Steinbrinck*, a postwar reparations prize from the Nazi *Kriegsmarine*, to Severodvinsk. Norovsky ran his ship with a firmness bordering on tyranny. His officers and crew obeyed mostly through fear of repercussion rather than confidence in his leadership. Sixteen years left Norovsky with haunting regrets over his conduct. As with most former COs in the interim, he discovered much about himself that should've been applied while in command. Hindsight is 20/20. *The past cannot be recovered, only learned from. I have far too much on my plate now to dwell on such things.*

Norovsky doubted Pasha Martinov would be on hand to meet *Mayakovsky* and the good treatment he received would soon come to an end. He suspected the *kapitan's* hand to be strong in this. Piotr Denisov fabricated the returning retiree myth not because he feared his crew might harm Norovsky, but in appreciation for agreeing to lead the Denisov family to freedom.

As *Mayakovsky* moored, Norovsky noted one thing that had not been altered by time. Two pairs of NKVD boots awaited at the gangway foot to end Norovsky's respite.

Jacqueline and Dennis's precious few days together in Capri sped by, though they chose not to acknowledge this as it portended that which neither wished to think about—parting. And so they lived as though this time together would be without end. Though it made time go swifter, keeping a busy schedule deterred them from agonizing over how soon their time together would end.

After breakfasts of cappuccinos, croissants, fresh fruit salad and scrambled eggs prepared to their liking, they set off on robust hikes, oblivious to the bleak December weather. They visited Grotta di Matermania, a cavern on the islands south side and on this brisk day, its leeward side. Dennis knew the 30 by 20 meter (98 by 66 ft) cavern beside the sea with a median height of 10 meters (33 ft) to also be called by a different name—Grotta del Matrimonio—cave wedding.

Far too early for even remote thoughts of such things, Dennis pondered, though he knew no other woman he'd prefer more to share the rest of his life with. He said, "In Roman times, it is likely the cult of Mithras might have been practiced here." He explained the Mithraic initiation ceremony ended in a ritual bath. "Plenty of water nearby to do that before the initiate received a mark on his forehead. Or the cave could be that of Cibele, goddess of nature, of animals and wild places. That would be a good fit."

"Dennis. You amaze me with your knowledge."

He actually gleaned the information from a pamphlet before leaving La Collina, but chose to not let it interfere with her compliment.

Dennis learned that Jacqueline was three years his senior and he wondered how such a beautiful lady had gone unclaimed for so long; his good fortune he reckoned. That evening as they lay in bed together, he spoke of what he hoped would be their future.

"There is a US Submarine Base at Rota, Spain. I believe I can get assigned there. I'll apply when I get back. My tour of duty aboard *Clamagore* ends in four months. Would you like that, Jacqueline?"

In the darkened room he could not see her expression of despair.

"I would like that very much, Dennis," Jacqueline said and then went on. "I will remain here for a day after you leave. I want our parting to be in this place where I have been so happy. It will be much easier than in some bustling airport and give me another night in this bed we shared."

Later Dennis awakened and found Jacqueline gone. He got up and walked to their private patio where he found her crying. "*Qu'est-ce qui ne va pas, chéri* (What is wrong, sweetheart)?"

"Nothing, Dennis. It's just I am so happy here with you."

Several hours after USS *Clamagore* departed Palma, sailing past the Rock of Gibraltar, OOD Tim Keating reported to his watch relief Benson Roman. "Throughout the watch there's been a constant flow of troops with cameras up here. Seems they all want their personal Prudential Insurance Company logo."

Benson agreed and then went on, "Do you think Denny will hook up with us before we leave Rota?"

"Dunno ... but if he's with that French doctor lady, all I can say is if it were me, I'd desert."

"Did you ever wonder why she picked Denny when she could have had me?"

Keating said, "Let me think on that a bit ... no, haven't wondered."

Benson suggested, "Maybe her dad's a French fireman."

"Probably something like that," Keating replied then said, "Look, I'm hungry enough to eat the butt out of a skunk, so I'm going below."

"No skunks down there with Denny out of the picture."

Keating concluded the watch turnover formalities. "Okay, Benson. All ahead standard on four, heading two-seven-nine. The lookouts are relieved, no contacts and the ship is rigged for dive."

He took a breath to poke a little fun but Benson interrupted him.

"Yeah, I know. There's air in the banks, crap in the tanks, the boats afloat and I'm the goat, right?"

The morning of Jacqueline and Dennis's final day at Capri arrived. They continued to ignore their fleeting time together, now measured in hours and minutes instead of days. They visited Arco Naturale (Natural Arch) an extraordinary Paleolithic sculpture, all that remained of a deep and incredibly high cavity discovered in the aftermath of a landslide. The incoherent nature of the rock resulted in continuous corrosion of the stone leaving a 12 meter (39 ft) section of the vault suspended 18 meters (59 ft) above the ground to form a natural bridge between two pillars of rock. The Natural Arch is elevated high above sea level; its semicircular opening provides a perfect picture frame for the spectacular distant sea scenery.

Jacqueline said, "Now you know why I wanted to come here, Dennis. I have heard and read much of Capri's natural beauty and had to see it for myself. And I wanted to share it with someone special. If it had to be December, that was good with me."

"I promise to bring you back here in summer, Jacqueline. If I get assigned to Rota, it will be more sooner than later. But I promise to return to Capri with you, Jacqueline."

Later, they returned to La Collina to put the finishing touches on Denny's packing. Wrapping her arms about him, Jacqueline said, "My darling Dennis. Regardless of what lies ahead for us, you have given me the most happy days of my life."

A taxi arrived to take Dennis to the marina. The inevitable moment of parting and both grasped for things to say, their hearts heavy.

His bag packed and ready, Dennis thought Jacqueline would accompany him outside for their good-bye.

"No, Dennis. Let us say good-bye here."

They held each other close in a parting embrace. She whispered in his ear, "Please forgive me, Dennis, I beg you. *Mais nous ne pouvons jamais nous voir de nouvea* (But we can never see each other again)."

"Fifteen-two, fifteen-four and eight makes a dozen and I whip your ass for the twentieth time!" Joe Dunn gloated triumphantly and pegged off the cribbage board. "Maybe we should play for money, Paul."

"Why do you think I let you win? Been setting you up. Just watch how the old *Scotter* performs when there's cash on the table."

Having tossed the fat into the fire, Joe could afford to be indiscreet. He asked, "You know why you never see a nuke playing cribbage?"

Paul answered, "No, why?"

"Because they can't play cards and drink coffee at the same time."

The remark earned him a scowl from the young nuke seated nearby in the wardroom poring over a thick manual on the Oxygen Generator. Joe knew his remark would make its way to the captain, but he didn't give a rip.

"This is the captain speaking," boomed over the 1MC. "We have just received this bulletin over the press broadcast. A diesel-electric submarine on post-overhaul sea trials out of Portsmouth, New Hampshire is reported overdue and most likely sunk. This is all the information available at the moment. I expect a message from the force commander will soon arrive. Updates will be announced as they are received. That is all."

Paul and Joe looked at each other through astonished expressions. Soon afterward, the captain entered the wardroom, took his seat at the table head and ordered coffee.

Joe asked, "Captain, which diesel-electric submarine was cited in the news release?"

Pete Williams expected Dunn to press him for the patrol duration, shrugging, he said in a bored tone, "None, but what else could it be?"

Joe replied, "Diesel boats are no longer overhauled at Portsmouth, only nukes."

Williams's mouth fell open.

A radioman interrupted the skipper's intended response. "Message, Captain," and handed over a clipboard.

The CO's face fell into disbelief as he read the line, *Nuclear powered submarine USS Trenchant sank beyond the continental shelf off Portsmouth, New Hampshire. There are no survivors.* Williams thought, *How in hell does our best nuclear boat sink herself?* A thought he did not share with Joe and Paul.

Williams spoke with greater concern after this news than when he suspected a diesel boat had been lost.

Joe looked at his friend. "No big deal if we buy the farm, but it's a whole different story when it's nukes at the ocean bottom. Why the hell don't you get out with me, Paul?"

An hour before *Clamagore*'s departure from Rota for home, Phil Redmond looked at his watch. *Where the hell's Denny?* Forty-five minutes passed. Redmond's apprehension gave way to anger. *Even if he makes it, he's got no damn business cutting it so close.* At that instant Denny came down the forward torpedo room hatch and made his way to the forward battery, his face a mask of despair. The perceptive Redmond ushered the young officer into the relative privacy of the captain's stateroom.

Both seated, the captain began, "What's wrong, Denny?"

Tears streamed down Kolb's face. "She's married, Captain. How could I have been so stupid?"

Determined to maintain his composure, Redmond thought, *How come they didn't cover this at Prospective Commanding Officers' School?* "Tell me about it, Denny."

Kolb related all that passed between Jacqueline and him at Capri. "I was never happier in my life. And all along she was using me."

Redmond answered, "Denny, there's something that just doesn't add up here. Where's her husband?"

Denny recomposed himself, embarrassed at his emotional outburst. "She didn't drop this on me until a few minutes before I had to leave. I asked her, but she was bawling her eyes out and couldn't answer. Or maybe she refused to answer."

"Look, Denny, I sense a big piece of this story is missing. Just look at her. If all she needed was a roll in the hay, the queue would reach all the way around Majorca."

"I don't know, Captain. I hunt for explanations, but come up dry."

"Denny, trust me. There has to be an explanation. You're hurting pretty bad right now. Try to lean on belief in that. It'll help."

"A big order. Look, is it okay if I turn in? This has me wiped out."

"No, Denny. Get suited up and report to the bridge. You're getting *Clamagore* underway and after that take the first watch."

"Captain. Please. I can't do that."

"You can and will. You're the best ship handler aboard. Now get up there and do your job. It'll force you to take your mind off this."

"Are you sure, Captain?"

"Damn sure. Get your sorry ass into uniform and report to me on the bridge. We set the maneuvering watch in five minutes and I want you up there."

Redmond had been raised during the Great Depression by parents who were dirt poor. Home generated recreation involved, among other things, gathering about the kitchen table after dinner to sing. He recalled his mother's favorite song, *The Isle of Capri*. The final stanza seemed very appropriate, where the love-struck beau bent to kiss the hand of his heart's desire, saw the gold band on her finger and knew it meant good-bye to their Isle of Capri romance.

Chapter 18

Admiral Terry Martin, Chief of Naval Operations, sat behind his desk reviewing the latest SITREP (situation report) on the loss of *Trenchant.* Martin's Chief Stewardsman Milton Arter had just brought Martin a cup of coffee.

"Have a seat, Chief, and I'll tell you all I know about the disaster."

Both men had former shipmates aboard the stricken vessel.

"Thank you, Admiral. This for certain?"

Submariners worldwide are concerned when one of their own has fallen on bad times. Regardless of how often one goes down to the sea in a submarine, he is constantly aware that a mere three-quarters inch of steel hull is all that separates him from the relentless ocean. Such thoughts are set aside lest they deter performance of duty; a submarine disaster, however, raises these thoughts from dormancy.

"Afraid so, Chief. There's no other plausible scenario. She sits on the bottom well below her crush depth. Tragic as it is, we must not add to it by offering false hope to the victims' families. I'm going to the memorial service at New London on Monday, care to join me?"

"Of course, Admiral."

"Good. Can you bring the Mrs. along? I plan to bring Brenda. Perhaps they can do a bit of good there."

"Adelaide will come, Admiral."

Dorothy Ford, the admiral's writer, interrupted. "Admirals Sloan, Bailey and Turley are here, sir."

The heads of submarine, surface, and air warfare groups at CNO entered the room.

Martin invited them, "Please sit down, gentlemen."

Excusing himself, Arter scurried to get coffee.

After a perfunctory exchange of pleasantries, Admiral Sloan handed everyone a copy of *Hawkbill*'s UQC log. "Not enough here to even begin figuring out what happened to them."

Martin had already seen the log and agreed. However, it comforted him to have so much experience amassed about the table.

Sloan went on. "Task now is to look at options and develop a plan to determine the cause of *Trenchant*'s sinking. It's early, but so far we've lined up the bathyscaphe from Wood's Hole to see if the wreck can be located and surveyed. Might be some clues there."

Martin asked, "What about the overhaul work package? Could that tell us anything?"

Sloan replied, "Possibly, maybe even hopefully. BUSHIPs (Bureau of Ships) has a team at Portsmouth and will find what they can."

Martin added, "I'm sure nothing will happen fast ... nor should it."

Admiral Turley said, "Gentlemen, this is a delicate topic to bring up, but I think it needs to be. More often than not, naval aviation crashes are caused by pilot error. For a valid search, painful as this might be, it must be a consideration until it is dismissed."

Martin corrected his statement, but only in his thoughts. *Admiral Epworth will make sure that consideration is dismissed ... and he'll make it happen fast.*

Pershing's crew demeanor darkened when they read an article received over the press broadcast. Submariners are a thick lot, and many had former shipmates and friends aboard USS *Trenchant*. The captain vacillated over whether to release this to his crew, but in the end believed they had a right to what he knew of the tragic incident.

Diesel officers aboard saw *Trenchant*'s dilemma analogous to what they had recently experienced during *Pershing*'s near sinking. They held these feelings to themselves, again wishing to broach this individually to the captain rather than through consensus. The press release, though sketchy, had a ring of authenticity. It read in part:

> Submarines conducting new construction or post overhaul sea trials are accompanied by a submarine rescue surface vessel, USS *Hawkbill* in the case of the nuclear powered submarine *Trenchant* disaster. *Hawkbill*'s underwater telephone (UQC) log—the official record—recorded that at 9:12, a satisfactory UQC check was completed. Subsequently, it documented a report from *Trenchant*—"Have positive up angle, attempting to blow all main ballast." *Trenchant* was clearly experiencing difficulty.

The sound of air under pressure could be heard over *Hawkbill*'s UQC.

At 9:14, *Hawkbill* transmitted to *Trenchant* that contact appeared to be lost and asked for the submarine's course, speed, bearing and distance to *Hawkbill*. No response.

Hawkbill transmitted, "Are you in control?" No response. The question was repeated three times, but still no answer.

At 9:17, a garbled message was received from *Trenchant.* The radio operator said he distinctly heard the words "test depth." Seconds later, the operator, a World War II veteran, said he heard the sound of a ship breaking up, "like a compartment collapsing."

Paul Scott reviewed *Pershing*'s draft patrol report (official record of all that had transpired during patrol) and saw it contained no account of the incident that nearly destroyed the ship. This astounded him. He requested and got a meeting with the captain to discuss the matter.

"We simply made a mistake. Took a calculated risk to insure we reached our area on time and lost. Happens all the time. It makes no sense to put ourselves on report because our recommended action will be to follow submarine procedures, which is a common practice."

"I don't think we exercise common practice, Captain."

"Oh? Nothing's been reported to me."

Paul said, "The chief engineer and I discussed it and believed we could work it out at our level. If what happened with the near sinking is an example, we clearly can't."

"Near sinking? Loss of depth control, but certainly not as bad as you say."

"We exceeded test depth, Captain. SUB-LANT regulations require us to report that."

"That's the chief engineer's call. I haven't had a recommendation from Morrie yet."

And you won't get one, Paul thought.

"Captain, the problem is a tug-of-war between the nukes and front enders over who controls the ship when we're underway. I think what happened points out the danger in this. If this is only a local problem, let's correct it here."

"Nonsense. There's no tug-of-war. Lines of authority are clearly drawn. Haven't you read the Ship's Organization Manual?"

"It's not clear there either," Paul replied. "What happens when there is a conflict between protecting the reactor and saving the ship? I can't find anything in the Ship's Org that talks to that."

Exasperation evident in his voice, Williams exclaimed, "Common sense, of course!"

"My point exactly, Captain. I didn't see a lot of common sense in the event of last week. And you must admit the article on *Trenchant* shows much in common with what happened to us. We had a positive up angle and attempted to blow. And we exceeded test depth. Joe Dunn deviated from procedure and took us back up with the engine. Maybe there was no one on *Trenchant* who knew to do that."

"An unofficial offering by a newspaper. Nothing more. We cannot hang our hats on anything until the matter is investigated and reported."

"We should have reported our incident, Captain. It might have saved *Trenchant*'s bacon. Her skipper had barely a year in diesel boats. After that only nuke boats where he had no latitude to deviate from procedure. It was Joe Dunn's diesel boat experience that pulled our chestnuts out of the fire."

"Paul, you resent that you were not picked for the nuclear power program, don't you?"

"No, sir. I don't."

"You come across that way to more than just me."

Sounds like Morrie and the captain have talked. "I'm sorry I do. My problem is with new policies that appear to contradict what we've had to learn the hard way."

"Times are changing and you can't live in the past."

"*Live* is the key word, Captain," Paul countered. "I get the feeling we're losing sight of that."

"And you appear to be losing your value to this ship. I won't have officers aboard who won't line up with command policy."

"I can only line up with policies I believe to be in the best interest of the ship, Captain. I have problems with what I see here. A major example being the officer responsible for damn near killing us is eligible to succeed to command and the one who saved our bacon is not. That logic evades me."

"Then maybe you should ask for a transfer."

"I've never run away from a problem in my life. I don't intend to start here. If I'm convinced a dangerous situation exists, then I am obliged to find an unbiased audience to hear me out, and either prove me wrong or help correct it."

Williams said, "Be my guest, Lieutenant Scott," and concluded the meeting.

As Paul left the captain's stateroom, Williams thought, *Why in hell can't these guys accept the fact that they didn't make the grade?* But a note of concern visited him: logic in similarities between *Trenchant*'s disaster and *Pershing*'s event. *Dunn and Scott sing the same song. Could all this come back and bite me in the ass? Not if I can pass it off as a case of sour grapes.*

Williams knew exactly what to do. Admiral Epworth could not officially circumvent the Navy chain of command, so he'd generated an effective means of bypassing it. He instructed nuclear submarine COs to write personal letters directly to him. This ran contrary to a tried and true premise that served the Navy well since its inception in 1775. U.S. warship commanding officers reported to senior commands charged with combat effectiveness of the service.

Epworth had no such responsibility, but nonetheless tightly controlled the officers in his program. He literally ran a Navy of his own and could destroy a career with the flick of his wrist. Those in his program knew this well. Epworth expected to be kept informed of what transpired on *his ships*.

Williams withdrew a blank sheet of personal stationery from his desk and began to write:

Dear Admiral Epworth,

 I wish to bring a matter of concern to your attention; namely, assignment of officers not trained in nuclear power to ballistic missile submarines. These officers perform Polaris System Weapons and Navigation officers' duties. Not qualified to perform Engineering Officer of the Watch duties, they are relegated to Conning Officer and Officer of the Deck responsibilities.

I am aware of the shortfall in nuclear trained officers and the need to fill the aforementioned billets. However, I wish to bring your attention to certain adverse effects emerging from these circumstances. The Polaris officers resent not having been selected for the nuclear program and take out attendant frustrations on the nuclear trained officers, at least aboard Pershing. Most of this is in the form of unfounded complaints and bickering. They simply have not come to terms with realities of the shift from diesel to nuclear power. These officers are generally older and senior, hence their antics affect the morale of young nuclear trained officers.

This is a manageable situation, but in my view suggests the importance of sending SSBN's to sea with only officers from your program. I respectfully recommend you canvas other SSBN COs for their view and end current Polaris officer assignments in the nearest possible term.

Very respectfully,
P. M. Williams, CAPT, USN
Commanding

Williams thought, *This'll be a helluva good arrow to have in my quiver if Dunn and Scott get too noisy.*

USS *Clamagore* left New London Ledge Light to starboard and turned north up the Thames River to the Submarine Base. Blustery, chilly weather did not dampen heightened spirits, for they had made it by twenty-three December, much to the pleasure of crew and their families alike.

Phil Redmond would prefer for his ship to look perfect while entering in port, but *Clamagore* wore her accumulated rust streaks and patches devoid of paint as well earned battle scars. She had performed exceptionally well in the Mediterranean as attested by a stream of kudos flowing in from the many strata of submarine command levels above *Clamagore*. Recalling the paucity of SIXFLEET back-pats, Redmond thought, *It's good to be back in the bosom of the family.*

Denny Kolb stood OOD watch. Though an unspoken squadron policy mandated commanding officers to negotiate the intricate mooring process themselves, Redmond would let Denny do the honors. *He likely handles the ship better than me, but I'll never tell him that.*

Clamagore passed the Squadron Ten submarines nested beside a tender at State Pier, just south of the railroad bridge on the river's west side. Nuclear powered ships now outnumbered the diesel boats. *A sign of the times*, Redmond mused. *Our days fly by quickly. But there is much the new kids on the block can learn from us old guys, though I doubt they will.*

Denny brought the ship alongside a finger pier at the submarine base, a north wind and ebb tide combining to aid his maneuver. The submarine base band at the pier head blared away their rendition of *Anchors Aweigh* while enough gold braid to rival stocks at Fort Knox awaited setting of the brow (gangplank). Senior officers filed aboard and made perfunctory, but sincere welcome home pronouncements to skipper Phil Redmond. Crew families and friends crowded the pier, eager to greet their men, and the official welcoming committee had no wish to delay this.

Tatlow and Giambri stood on the dock also and assisted in making *Clamagore*'s mooring lines fast to cleats on the dock. The crew surged ashore to greet their loved ones. Wives turned themselves out in their best to greet spouses they had not seen in four months and embraced them, a signal for the band to play *Back in the Saddle Again* per submariner tradition. Most moving of all, the children, young tykes especially, clinging to their dads as though they'd never let go. And making it home in time for Christmas frosted the cake.

Denny Kolb volunteered to be duty officer first night in port. Normally, an officer from a different ship stood this watch for the new *homecomers*, but Denny had no plans for the evening and would drive to his home in Vermont the following morning.

Rapinian, duty steward stood by and resisted Denny's offer to send him home.

"I can make it one time in the crew's mess. So why don't you hit the road?"

Stewardsmen looked upon it as a point of honor not to let their officers eat in the crew's mess. "I can stay, Mister Kolb."

"Look, Rapinian. Why don't you put together a cold plate for me and leave it in the fridge? I'll be fine."

Rapinian frowned, but weakened. "I'll make a fresh pot of coffee."

Denny agreed, but when he had the in port watch, he drew his coffee from a big urn in the crew's mess.

"Thank you, Rapinian. Now finish up and be on your way."

The Stewardsman expressed his gratitude and left.

First night in port involved sifting through several sacks of mail, a task which Denny undertook in the wardroom.

Midway through the third sack, he came upon a letter to him from Jacqueline Junin. It created contradicting emotions for the young officer. Redmond had once joined him on the bridge on several evening watches during the recent ocean crossing. Between North Atlantic winter storms, they enjoyed a short spate of dry weather. The most significant of three discussions succeeded in setting Denny on the only path he had.

The captain advised, "You must put it all behind you, but don't lose sight of the positives. A brilliant and beautiful woman who can have just about any man she wants, chose you. You'll ultimately start looking around Denny, though it might not seem to be in the cards right now. Because of Jacqueline, you can set the bar high as you like. Something good will come of this. As my sainted mom used to say, 'everything happens for the best'."

Dennis fingered the letter a bit, and for a fleeting second, toyed with the idea of not opening it. Agonizing as a plethora of emotions raced through his mind, he knew in the end he'd neither the strength nor resolve to leave the letter unread.

Denny poured the last of Rapinian's coffee into his cup, opened the envelope and began to read.

Mon cher Dennis (My dear Dennis),

How do I begin? Please understand I believed it best to end our relationship as I did. I knew the remorse our parting would bring you and hoped to offset it by giving you cause to be angry with me for having led you on. But it pains me far too much to know the terrible things you must now think of me.

How could I ever feel anger toward you, Jacqueline?

I owe you a better explanation than the one given at Capri. Yes, I am married, but unable to live with my husband. He is a wonderful man, and like you will always have a place in my heart that only he can fill.

Three years ago, Eugene, that's his name, fractured his neck in a tragic auto accident. He is permanently paralyzed from the neck down and confined to a sanatorium. Each time I see Eugene, he pleads with me to have our marriage annulled and to get on with my life. He does this from deep love, for he has no wish for me to suffer consequences of his affliction.

When we exchanged wedding vows we promised God to stay together in sickness and in health. A devout Catholic, I honor that vow. You are a loving and understanding man and must see why I will remain with Eugene.

I permitted what happened between us out of loneliness and the need for affection Eugene can no longer give me. I knew you to be the right man when first I saw you in the infirmary. Since Eugene, you are the first and will be the only man to share my love.

You gave me the four most wonderful days of my life. I sensed and welcomed your love and knew if I told you of Eugene you'd have asked me to end my marriage. The strong feelings I had developed for you by then would have prevented me from resisting.

Darling Dennis, please be forgiving of whatever hurt I
have caused you. I pray to your patron Saint Dennis, he
was French you know, to watch over and protect you, and
to fill your life with the happiness you so richly deserve. I
love you Dennis. There is no way you could not know
that. I survive on the memory of our days in Capri where
we belonged only to each other. You are a very special
man and must never forget that. I never shall.
Writing to you lifts a great weight from my shoulders.

Always, your Jacqueline

Vasiliy Norovsky saw much that changed in Severodvinsk, but not
the prison. It remained cold, damp and dark. He sat in his cell and
wondered about the task remaining ahead, conducting Piotr Denisov
and his family to safety. He had not volunteered and it gave him great
concern. He thought, *So many questions. How old are the children?
Old enough to be brainwashed into believing the so-called Soviet
precepts? If they have, what problems that will make. His wife? What
will her attitude be? They surely have family here who will be subject
to severe reprisals. Can any of them speak Polish or German? We will
have to pass through those countries.*

Norovsky settled back and reflected. *But Martinov is not an
irresponsible dreamer. He must have thought all of this out. And he
has to be very good at what he does to have been given that assignment
in America.*

Vasiliy Norovsky had correctly figured Pasha Martinov. Months
earlier as Pasha Martinov and Piotr Denisov sat on the balcony of the
Denisov rental at Sochi on the Black Sea and concocted their plan, the
two men touched on all these items.

Martinov, perfect for the job owing to his high regard within
NKVD circles, had assembled a small cadre with the purpose of aiding
people to escape the Soviet Union. He'd developed a remarkable
ploy—assignment to uncover the exact activity he participated in. A
need for successes, he exposed party zealots, not worth the powder to
blow them to hell by his reckoning, on trumped up charges. The
NKVD, anxious to give evidence of their value to the Party, took

Martinov's findings at face value.

Pasha laid out the escape plan for the Denisov family to Piotr.

"Against everyone's cautions you will take your family on a kayak trip in the Black Sea. Being a sea *kapitan*, you will explain simply that weather is a problem only for landlubbers."

"And that will be believable, even to the NKVD skeptics?"

"Especially to those jackasses. Aren't they the ones who believe we surpass the West in every endeavor?"

"Go on, Pasha."

"You will gather all the materials for the trip, two kayaks, tents, sleeping bags and other camp utensils. Be sure the boys are with you when the items are purchased. Their enthusiasm and excitement will add to the credibility of our plan."

"I understand, and then what?"

"On the eve of your trip turn all this over to me. A colleague will drive you to Severodvinsk. There you will meet a Vasiliy Norovsky who will lead you to freedom."

"And what of you, Pasha?"

"I will take your materials to a remote place by the sea. There I will set up a camp, leaving ample evidence that your family has been there. And then some miles away, I'll leave the kayaks capsized and washed up on the shore. Tell everyone you plan to be there for a week. No one will search until you fail to return home."

"You truly believe this will work, Pasha?"

"As sure as I can be of anything."

"Then let us go on with it. Irene is in agreement, and the boys will find it all a great adventure. Thank you for this wonderful thing you do for us, Pasha."

Phil Redmond stopped by the ship on the morning following *Clamagore*'s return to port, but only long enough to determine whether Denny found anything of consequence in the mail.

Rapinian arrived bright and early to prepare special homecoming omelets for Denny and Tim Keating who would relieve the watch. The stewardsman went through his usual antics when the captain showed up unexpectedly, but nonetheless prepared him a magnificent omelet.

Redmond's wife Katherine had given him a superb breakfast, but he had no problem making room for Rapinian's omelet.

The captain extended sympathies to Tim for having the Christmas Eve watch. Both knew someone had to do the job, so they let it pass.

Breakfasts and coffees consumed, Redmond and Denny went over significant pieces of mail and saw nothing worth interrupting the holidays over. As the captain prepared to take his leave, Denny asked if he had a few minutes. They retired to the captain's stateroom and Denny handed him Jacqueline's letter.

Surprised, Redmond remarked, "Had a feeling there'd be more to this. If you want me to know the content, you'll need to interpret."

Denny read the letter, translating from French to English.

Redmond listened, then carefully considering his response, he opened by probing Kolb's feelings. "What do you think, Denny?"

"It clears up an awful lot, Captain."

"Does it really? I pretty much concluded from all you told me that Jackie didn't collar you just for a roll in the hay."

"Jacqueline, Captain. She made that clear from the onset."

"Jacqueline" said Redmond.

"I just want to be sure I handle this right. I was up half the night trying to write a reply and trashed all of them. I'd really like your advice, Captain."

"Denny, I can't advise you. I can only say what I'd do. Write her back and thank her for relieving you of a great burden. Say the feelings she expressed are reciprocated. Respect her determination to remain in marriage and wish her a good life."

The young officer's expression revealed the captain did not say what Denny wanted to hear.

"And then do you know what I'd do, Denny?"

"What, Captain?"

"This will never be resolved through letters. If I still felt the same a year from now, I'd go back to Palma and tell Jacqueline what she must do to make both of the men in her life happy."

Chapter 19

Aboard *Clamagore,* Giambri held court in the crew's mess to a captive audience of bachelor shipmates. Though voluntary, submarine sailors exchange watches to insure married crewmen are at home on Christmas Eve and Christmas Day. Pace, Omensen, Howell and others sat gorging themselves on the bounty of goodies sent them by grateful spouses of the marrieds.

Giambri began, "No kidding, guys, this is no crap."

Pace responded, "Giambri, why is it the crappiest stories you tell us always begin the same way ... this is no crap?"

The star sonarman ignored Pace's remark. "You would not believe the welcome I got in Caccamo! The whole town rolled out for me and my driver."

Omensen jumped in. "Caccamo? Where the hell is that? And *driver*? How do you get off having a driver?"

"It's a small town in the mountains about an hour outside of Palermo, in Sicily. Talk about the boonies, most of the cars and trucks in town are pulled by donkeys. We had to drive twenty miles to find gas." He explained how Captain Harkins set up the trip to offset a Legion of Merit going to an aviator who photographed Giambri's November. "We had more fun than the night I drank my dolphins in Glasgow ... food, booze, babes, you name it."

Howell asked, "Nobody got suspicious of that phony admiral's costume?"

"Phony! You shoulda seen the mayor's outfit ... top hat, sash, morning coat. You'd think he was going to a wedding."

Another sailor suggested, "Maybe he was ... yours."

"Don't think he didn't try. Every available gal in town turned out. I think the driver might've actually got hooked."

Pace asked, "Did you get a key to the city?"

"Don't think there was a lock in the whole damned town."

Omensen replied, "I bet they got 'em now."

"They'll likely put one on the town wine cellar. The driver and I gave it our best shot, but they turn out Sicilian red and grappa faster than we could drink it."

Howell asked Giambri when he planned to go back.

"That might not be a good idea. A few jealous husbands. Yeah, Italians can be vengeful. But Siggies, they're a whole other breed! What they would do, would make even Frank Sinatra think twice."

Omensen said, "I can't believe you, Giambri. All those new models and you hit on a used car."

Giambri replied, "I like to think I'm like George Washington. First in war, first in peace ... but who does he marry? A widow. But hey, guys. It's Christmas. I hope you all hung up your stockings ... 'cause I've got a story for the season."

Pace said, "Long as it doesn't start with 'This is no crap'."

"Hey, this is no crap, really! When I was a kid in south Philly, this nun worried about what we'd be having for Christmas dinner. Times were tough."

Howell, a Catholic boy, asked, "What do you know about nuns?"

"What do I know about nuns? I was eight-years-old before I knew a ruler was for measuring things." He showed Howell the scars on his knuckles. "I got my stripes the hard way. Can I go on now?"

Pace replied, "Why do I get the feeling there's nothing any of us can say that would stop you?"

The comment rolled off Giambri like water off the dive planes in an emergency surface. "Sister Irene? She measured two and a half ax handles across the shoulders and could do fifty one-arm push-ups without breaking a sweat."

Howell said, "You expect me to believe that?"

Giambri ignored the remark, sized up the crowd and convinced himself he still had the floor. "Well, the good sister had a connection at the Philly Navy yard ... must have been the chaplain. There were always ships in the yard for overhaul, so she sets us up for Christmas dinner on a big skimmer, a battleship, I think."

Omensen grinned. "You mean big target. Right?"

"You have no soul, Omensen. You know that? Here I am trying to relate a joyful yuletide saga and all you can come up with are trite clichés. Now can I finish, please?"

Pace said, "Okay, we're hooked. Get on with it."

"Well, we all have this fantastic dinner, but Sister Irene, God love her, took only enough to feed a non-qual on his first dive."

Howell jumped in again. "The old Catholic guilt thing?"

"Whatever. Well, next the crew takes us to the engine room and tells us Santa will come down through this big pipe that lets air into the boiler room. This sailor stands under the opening and says in a loud voice, 'I expect Santa will be coming down the chimney soon.'

"We hear shuffling in the pipes above us and the sailor gets an anxious look on his face. 'I expect Santa will be coming down the chimney soon,' he says again. And then we hear this voice echo through the pipes, 'Ho, ho, ho. I'm stuck. Get me the hell outta here'."

Almost on signal, a pair of black boots followed by red trousers, coat and tasseled hat descended through the after battery hatch. It's the COB in a Santa outfit, complete with sack.

"Have you all been good sailors?"

Two days after Christmas, after all had basked in the glow of the holiday spirit, Phil and Kathie Redmond had his wardroom come by for cocktails and dinner.

Dave Zane's wife Dale and the hostess combined to do what wives do best, persuade bachelors to set aside perceived happiness in exchange for sharing their lives at hearth and home with a dedicated spouse and children.

Denny Kolb, with his family in Vermont, would likely be a vulnerable target, but the jaws of Benson Roman and Tim Keating remained set.

In private, Benson said to Tim, "Can you believe it? Dale told me her cousin Jan is coming for a visit and suggested we meet. And when I asked, 'what's she like'... all Dale would say is she's nice to her mother."

"So how did you squirm out?"

"I asked when she'd be here. She gave me the dates and I said, 'My leave is scheduled for then so I'll be home on the west coast'."

Tim responded with, "You make me proud, Benson."

Roman showed the best of his classic Cheshire Cat grins.

Dave Zane gathered the junior officers in an attempt to lead them in song, but quickly found he dealt with an entirely new generation. His suggested song titles drew only confused expressions.

Despite all, spirits remained high and the officer cadre basked in the afterglow of their successful Mediterranean deployment. Phil Redmond made it a point to insure all knew the importance of each personal contribution. Three married junior officers attended with their wives. Redmond extended appreciation to the young women who, in his words, "kept the home fires burning."

At evening's end, Dale took a parting shot at the bachelor boys. "Good night, you two. I guess it's back to BOQ."

Tim returned Mrs. Exec's fire with, "Matter of fact, Benson and I are driving down to New York to see if we can find a little action."

Clamagore remained at New London and underwent a month of post deployment refit, commonly called the *wound licker*. Resourceful submariners provided mission sustaining bailing wire and chewing gum fixes, much to the chagrin of the submarine base repair force. They had not only to make permanent repairs, but also unscramble the crew's complex jury-rigs.

Toward the end of January, Redmond and Zane sat together in the Submarine Development Group 2 (SUBDEVGRU2) conference room. The well-deserved standdown approached its end and thoughts went to returning to work.

SUBDEVGRU2, established to develop and evaluate submarine tactics, claimed a lion's share of diesel-electric submarine time. The Development Group Operations (DEVGRUOps) officer put together a plan that focused mainly on the threat to U.S. Naval and maritime forces—Soviet submarine warfare. He developed a series of exercises to be conducted in the Gulf of Maine. Bordered on the west by Cape Cod and Boston; north by the west-east coastline from New Hampshire to Portland, Maine; and on the east by Nova Scotia, the Gulf presented a challenging area for conducting submarine warfare. Shallow depths attracted fishing boats of all types with resulting high background noise levels, a detriment to submarines trying to sort out the sound of bona fide targets.

The DEVGRUOps officer went over this background though most of it already well-known by his audience: four diesel-electric COs and execs and the lone nuke CO. He went on to explain a Permit class nuke, USS *Permit* would assume the role of hunter and attempt to intercept and *attack* the multiple transits of diesel-boats over L-shaped tracks running east-west and north-south in the Gulf. This hopefully would validate alleged U.S. submarine superiority over their Soviet counterparts, to whom they conceded a five to one numerical superiority.

Dave Zane said, "Talk about the deck being stacked against us. We gotta make a high SOA (speed of advance), while the nuke coasts around and picks us off at leisure."

Redmond reminded, "It's not us against them, Dave. The suggested scenario is a valid one. A mass Soviet submarine exodus through the Barents Sea will be opposed by a handful of our nukes. We gotta find out if this is doable."

"But to make a ten knot SOA, we'll be snorkeling half the time and be pretty easy to find."

"The SOA is pretty close to the one the Reds will have to make to get where they want to go. Look on the bright side, Dave. We'll learn a lot from this and maybe teach a little. I know the nuke CO. He's a good tactics guy. Unlike others in the program, he's not lost his perspective."

"Agree, Captain. Sometimes I let resentment get in the way. Another ten years and the last diesel boat will be replaced by a nuke. This is a good thing. Too bad they don't let us run them. We'd do a better job. But I guess the best we can do is try to teach 'em what they'll have to do when they take over."

Redmond grinned at his exec. "Something like that, Dave. Let me introduce you to the nuke CO. He's a good head. You'll like him."

No further words had been exchanged between the captain and Paul Scott since their recent heated discussion except in the line of duty. Both men did a good job of not letting their disagreement become the subject of ship's gossip. This would serve neither Paul nor Williams. Consequently, the captain's upbeat attitude surprised Paul on the morning of their arrival at Holy Loch.

"Had a message from the Squadron Commander, Paul. A nice surprise is in store for you when we reach the tender. I'm obliged not to tell, but you'll be the envy of every man on *Pershing*."

"Well, you really got my curiosity up," Paul replied. *Not some sort of backhanded pat on the back,* he hoped.

Paul, preoccupied with giving mooring directions, did not notice then he saw her. "My God, it's Jean Ann! Here in Scotland?"

"I said you'd be the envy of all of us, Paul. You have a beautiful wife. Now get down on deck so you can be first over on the tender to greet her."

"Aye, aye, sir." Paul saluted and left the bridge. He scampered up the ladder to the quarterdeck where he asked and received permission from the OOD to come aboard the tender.

Jean Ann and Paul stood with arms wrapped tightly about each other oblivious to men bustling about at the work of refitting SSBNs and noise of the final securing of *Pershing* alongside. They held each other a full minute, bathed in a rare mid-April sun before either spoke.

"I missed you so much, Jean Ann."

"Me too, Paul."

"Now tell me, how did you ever get over here?"

"I'll tell you all about it later. For now, I can't get enough of you."

Is that a quaver in her voice?

Suddenly, Captain Williams stood by their side.

"Jean Ann, this is my commanding officer, Captain Pete Williams."

"How do you do, Captain?"

"Pete, please, Jean Ann. How very nice to meet you. Now if you don't mind, I have an order for your husband. Paul, the Commodore's Barge awaits at the officers' gangway. I want you to take this lovely lady to the Royal Marine and get reacquainted. Don't worry about turnover. I've talked to Joe and he'll do the honors. With Jean Ann in town, your mind wouldn't be on ship's business anyway. Now get going. We'll send your gear over to you."

"Thank you, Captain. Sure this is okay?"

"It's okay, Paul. We'll see you later."

In a few moments, Jean Ann and Paul boarded the Commodore's Barge and sped over the mile and a quarter to Hunter's Quay by the Royal Marine.

For the second time, Paul asked, "How did you get here?"

"My parents said I need a break and sent me."

Paul sensed a lack of conviction in her voice. She had something to tell him, but Paul would leave it to Jean Ann to bring it up in her own good time. *Can't be anything wrong with the kids or she'd have blurted it right out.*

They reached the Quay and walked to the stately Royal Marine, an Elizabethan style hotel built in the nineteen twenties to accommodate vacationers during the gorgeous summers of western Scotland.

Jean Ann said nothing, content to listen to nervous talk by Paul who rambled through the monotonous events of his past three months.

They reached their room and Paul's arms encircled her. "What's wrong, Babe?"

She burst into tears and held him tight.

"Oh Paul, something dreadful happened. I'm here because you'll need someone when you hear this."

He held her at arm's length and looked into her teary eyes.

"Adrian's dead, Paul."

Paul fell to a knee. "Oh my God … no!"

She knelt with him and cradled his head against her bosom.

"How? Where?"

"He was aboard *Trenchant*."

"Oh God, he was supposed to go to a boomer. What happened?"

"*Trenchant* had a Submarine Inertial Navigation System installed at Portsmouth. Did I get that right?"

"That's right, Jean Ann, a SINS." Paul clung to each of her words.

"Adrian was at New London awaiting assignment. *Trenchant* needed someone with Adrian's rate for sea trials, so he volunteered."

"What a terrible waste! Brilliant Adrian! Such an asset to the world. Why him? He asked me to be best man at his wedding."

"Only God has that answer, Paul. Hopefully, He will share this with us, but in His own good time."

Paul sobbed, "Gentle Adrian, oh God, how can there be any sense in taking him from us? How did you find out, Jean Ann?"

"Adrian's fiancée Louise Kirschner knew we lived in Gales Ferry and got our number from directory service. She called and asked for you. She was terribly distressed as you can imagine. Louise never met you, but from all Adrian had told her, felt she knew you very well."

Paul lay face down on their bed and sobbed. Jean Ann rubbed his back gently. "I'm glad Louise asked me to come, Paul. She said you'd need someone when you got the news."

"When we get home, we visit her first thing. Right, Jean Ann?"

"Right, darling. *Trenchant*'s memorial service was held at the base movie theater, there was no other space available that was big enough. Submarine officers stood shoulder-to-shoulder surrounding the entire room when dependents and friends walked in. There was room enough for only them, so no one else attended. I'm not sure I could have handled it."

"I know I couldn't, knowing Adrian was aboard." Paul silently reflected on similarities between *Pershing*'s near disaster and what he knew of *Trenchant*'s final moments. For the rest of his life, he would wonder whether a report from *Pershing* might have prevented *Trenchant*'s sinking and saved his friend.

Jean Ann listened as Paul recited all he and Adrian did together. And then silence, often the best salve for circumstances like this one.

A while later, Joe Dunn called from the desk and asked if Paul would see him. A few moments later, Jean Ann responded to his knock at the door.

With tears in his eyes, Joe embraced her. "God, I'm sorry. I feel I know Adrian from all Paul has told me."

Joe then embraced his friend. "I'm so sorry, buddy. I know what Adrian meant to you. What a tragic loss!" And to Jean Ann, "It's tough for you to have to go through all this again. You've had time for mending, but Paul's wound is freshly opened."

The three talked for half an hour.

Joe said, "This might sound tough, but we're going to the bar."

Reluctantly, Paul followed as they proceeded to the hotel lounge.

Joe demanded of the barkeep, "Three whiskeys," without asking Paul or Jean Ann.

The barkeep set out the glasses. He correctly sensed the somber mood of his customers and filled each glass with Islay Mist, finest Scotch whiskey in the area.

Joe raised his glass, "To Adrian Roberts, sailor, gentleman, shipmate and good friend."

"And great submariner," Paul added.

"And great submariner," Joe repeated. They clinked glasses and downed their whiskeys in single gulps.

Joe then turned and dramatically dashed his glass into the fireplace, declaring, "This glass will never be raised in a less worthy toast!"

Paul and Jean Ann followed while the barman looked on, masking his astonishment. The Scots are class people.

Joe said, "I saw that in a movie once and always wanted to do it."

Jean Ann put her arms about his neck. "Joe, you're the right man at the right time."

He drew a breath to make a funny rejoinder, but thought better of it.

A bathyscaphe from the U.S. Naval Oceanographic Station at Woods Hole, Massachusetts, aboard a floating dry dock, deployed to the *Trenchant* sinking site. The bathyscaphe consisted of a solid vehicle able to be driven independently to depths well below *Trenchant*'s final resting place at 8,400 feet beneath the sea.

Neutrally buoyant and non-compressible gasoline permitted the sides of the bathyscaphe to be quite thin. A sphere mounted at the bottom held a crew of two and had sides measuring 12.7 centimeters (5.0 in) thick to withstand pressures of 1.25 metric tons per square centimeter. Observation of the sea outside can be conducted through a single, tapered, cone-shaped block of acrylic glass (Plexiglas), the only transparent substance identified to withstand the pressures needed, at the design hull thickness. Quartz arc-light bulbs, able to withstand over a thousand atmospheres of pressure, provided outside illumination.

Nine tons of magnetic iron pellets placed on the craft as ballast enables a speed descent and allows for a certain ascent. These had to be used as extreme sea pressures to be experienced exceeded ability of compressed air ballast-expulsion at great depths. This additional weight, held in place actively at the throats of two hopper-like ballast silos by electromagnets, would cause the bathyscaphe to automatically rise in the event of electrical failure.

After a four-hour descent, one of the crewmen on viewing the trail of *Trenchant* debris spread over a mile on the ocean floor exclaimed, "Good Lord!"

It defied his imagination as to how sea pressure alone could rip this mighty warship into so many tiny pieces. He later likened what he saw to a poorly maintained junkyard.

Once in NKVD hands, the kid gloves came off for Norovsky.

The sadistic bastards. It's the same cell they had me in last time.

He was taken to a prison inside the Severodvinsk shipyard where local guards, former labor camp prisoners, bought their freedom by betraying other labor camp inmates. The cold and filthy condition of Norovsky's cell caused even the rats to abandon it. His many foes wished his final days to be as miserable as possible.

I hope Martinov has a plan. After what happened last time, I am certain the watch will be doubled.

Two months passed and Norovsky heard nothing. *Has the plan fallen through?* This and many thoughts ran through his mind. *What will become of me if it has? But look at the good side. I've already lost thirteen pounds.* A passion for American fast food had taken its toll on Norovsky's waistline. His meager rations, diminished substantially by the doubled guard, provided barely enough to sustain life. The guards rationalized their prisoner's impending demise to not warrant full rations. It made sense that the nourishment is best used to sustain those who will live on. Only the requirement for Norovsky to be alive for his trial prevented the guards from taking all his rations.

One day the guard thrust a newspaper into the cell with Vasiliy's noon meal.

"Here," the guard snarled, *"Komrade Kapitan* 1st Rank Martinov wishes you to read of your coming trial and fate you can expect from Mother Russia whom you betrayed.

Norovsky set the paper down to first attack his food. He then unfolded it and the headline sent a thrill through the beleaguered prisoner.

> Ядерна командир підводного човна, дружина і двоє дітей побоювалися потонув у човнах аварії (Nuclear Submarine Commander, wife and two children feared drowned in boating accident).

Vasiliy read on to find what he expected. The article identified *Kapitan* 2nd Rank Piotr Denisov and his family as the victims. He thought, *The first shoe has fallen.*

Eric Danis completed a mandatory three-month tour of duty at Naval Reactors attendant to taking command of a Sturgeon class SSN based at Pearl Harbor. Submariners referred to the class as *charm school;* the final chance for Admiral Epworth to let Prospective Commanding Officers' (PCOs) know who they really work for.

Eric and wife Eve, quite pregnant with their first, visited the family Zane in New London prior to traveling west. Dave's ten-year-old daughter Bea couldn't get enough of the Danises, particularly Eve, the impending mother. Bea, exhibiting levels of enthusiasm well above the women, came up with a new question each time the adults thought they'd heard the last. Bea reflected the sense of family grown between the Zanes and Danises and likely looked upon the pending addition as a prospective sibling.

Dinner ended, the men retreated to the living room, drinks in hand, to discuss *charm school* before a warming fire.

Dave began, "So what did you guys do all day? Drink coffee?"

"Hardly." Eric explained his class held twelve, including several surface warfare officers and an aviator en route an aircraft carrier command. "We had classroom sessions on reactor design and operation taught by senior engineers on Admiral Epworth's staff. We studied how a system operates and then the actual designer spoke to us.

Lots of good stuff. The Reactor Plant Manual (RPM) specifies limitations but gives the commanding officer authority to exceed them in battle conditions. The experts told us what the real limitations are. There's design margin built into operating limits but only the commanding officer knows just how far they can be pushed."

"Hell of a concept, Eric. What do you do in a battle situation when the CO's incapacitated? Surrender?"

Eric grinned. "Hopefully we'll have enough diesel boat experience aboard to keep that from happening."

"So, what else did you do down there?"

"Routine stuff, mostly. Plant chemistry and the like. My favorite part was getting some pretty good heads together to work the 'what ifs.' Some pretty smart guys there." Eric regretted his words as soon as he spoke them. "I didn't mean to imply you aren't—"

"Forget it, Eric. I know where you're coming from. Sounds like some of what you got would be as useful as me being able to write the equation for burning diesel fuel. How much time did you spend on tactics and operations?"

"In a word ... none."

Dave went on. "Thing that worries me most is the amount of time that has to be spent on that damn teakettle. What will come out of it? You don't get something for nothing."

"Epworth also used us as inside men when he interviewed young officer candidates for the Nuclear Power Program. We sat in chairs behind the candidates and took notes. Epworth is abrasive and direct, which a frightened candidate could think was abuse."

"I thought the guys he selected were too smart to misconstrue things. Anything in particular ever bother you in the brave, new world?"

"Frankly, yes. When Epworth got his copies of the *Trenchant* report, he spread them out on a table and called in all the submarine PCOs. He gave us a disgusted look and said, 'The blood of these men is on your hands'. No one replied or objected, so Epworth walked out offering no further explanation."

"So what did you guys do, Eric?"

"Nothing really. We sat around to see if we could figure out the message embedded in the admiral's words."

"What did you conclude?"

"Probably that he wanted us to pay more attention to detail."

"Seems to me like he should have explained or apologized," said Dave. "Now I know why I never made it in. I'd have insisted he put up, shut up or join me in a press conference as the only man in the Navy who can affix cause and responsibility for the *Trenchant* disaster."

Chapter 20

Buddy Owens, leading seaman planning to strike for quartermaster, referred to himself as a bilge rat, a well-deserved title per the newly reported crew to *Clamagore* while the others called him ornery.

"Nah," he'd reply, "just a little mischievous."

Knowing newcomers to be anxious to prove themselves useful, he exploited this to the fullest. With *Clamagore* back from a six-month deployment, Owens had an abundance of new arrivals.

To one new crewman, he said, "The captain wants you to crawl into number one torpedo tube and get the serial number off the outside of the outer door."

The victim would take off to deliver with unbridled enthusiasm.

First, the outer door had no serial number; second, even if it did, opening the outer door to see the number would flood the tube and its occupant. The torpedo room watch would never let this happen, but did permit the unsuspecting newcomer to crawl through twelve feet of twenty-one inch diameter torpedo tube. End result: Owens's desired effect. It made the errand boy feel stupid.

Rubbing salt into the wound, Owens also ordered, "When you get in there, be sure to lubricate the outer door with relative bearing grease."

Relative bearing, a direction from the ship, existed only as a tool to report locations of objects and other ships, hence had no need for the non-existent grease making it a double Owens's barb.

Owens, a slender lad with brown hair and green eyes wore a continuous pixie-like expression, hence projecting sincerity and honesty. Who possibly would not believe him?

Buddy had other ruses, most of them sending unsuspecting newcomers to find non-existent materials. The victim would be passed from person to person, all in on the game, till the new guy finally realized he'd been had. Among these, pre-mixed camouflage paint borrowed from another ship always moored at the greatest distance from *Clamagore*, and Owens's favorite—ordering water slugs. He once had a newly reported torpedoman striker order ten water slugs. Submarines have ten launchers and exercise them by ejecting water slugs (torpedo tubes flooded with sea water, supplied of course from the sea, hence no need to order them). Oblivious to this, the new striker proceeded to order Owens's requested ten water slugs. He completed the paperwork only to be told by Buddy that the captain, complicit in the scheme, must sign this type of request. The victim brought the chit to Redmond who advised the new man he'd ordered the wrong size water slugs. After a few back and forths, the young torpedoman striker, suitably embarrassed, came to realize Owens had snookered him.

Owens rationalized, "It's my duty as leading seaman to insure these rights of passage are carried out. Essential to the training of new personnel. I don't envy the guy who'll follow me. He's got one helluva big pair of shoes to fill."

However, the lad sent on the wild water slug chase confided to his peers, "What goes around, comes around."

With sailors like Buddy Owens in the crew, life aboard a diesel-electric submarine was anything but dull.

Phil Redmond returned from the Gulf of Maine exercise highly frustrated and said to Dave Zane, "Now I know how it feels to be a metal duck in a shooting gallery."

Zane laughed, shook a finger and reminded his skipper of what he'd said in a benevolent mood prior to their deployment. "It's not us against them, Dave." But he knew Redmond to be a competitor and would not take anything lying down. Getting *killed* four times without a single counterattack did not measure up to the captain's sometimes overly ambitious agenda.

Redmond ordered his exec to transcribe each post attack UQC conversation he'd had with the nuke skipper who said after the final attack, "You're getting too quiet and I won't tell you more or I won't be able to find you."

Redmond went on, "We begin the next phase with those changes as a going in position."

"Denny's already started on it, Captain. Plus he's got the chief engineer and first lieutenant working up a list of everything we can squeeze to suppress radiated noise."

Redmond said, "Giambri made recordings of the fishermen that run around up there. Get an average blade rate (number of times per minute each propeller blade passes top position. A three-bladed propeller making fifty revolutions per minute has a blade rate of one hundred fifty). Then figure out what speed we can make on one shaft with a similar rate."

He planned to confuse his pursuer by sounding like a fisherman.

The men spoke as they walked to SUBDEVGRU2 headquarters to be briefed on the next phase.

"That might work for a while, but your nuke buddy CO will figure that out pretty quick."

"He might. But like I said before. We should pull every rabbit out of the hat we can. Soviet COs will do that for sure, and we need to project reality."

Later, they sat among the target ship skippers and listened to details on how the nuke had eaten their lunches ... a subtle but clear message ... a single U.S. nuke could easily handle attempted multiple diesel-electric transits.

Redmond comforted himself, *that's a good thing*, but nonetheless smarted over it.

The DEVGRU2 operations officer took the podium. "Some changes. Our *Permit* class ship has to go in for a sub-safe overhaul."

For whatever reason, the *Trenchant* disaster had been attributed to material failure, and Epworth demanded his submarines cease operations to be inspected.

Each nuclear powered ship made its way to a shipyard and underwent tests of all systems. Redmond wondered, *They're the same yards that built diesel-electrics. How come we're not being called back?* He knew the answer. Public concern had to be assuaged by action, so the route would be taken, but only for nukes.

The operations officer continued. "She will be replaced by a *Sturgeon* class, USS *Pike*, quieter and a lot faster, so you diesel boaters can expect a run for your money."

Redmond and the other COs smiled but said nothing.

"But this time, you'll have a nuke on your side, USS *Ling*. One of the older boats. Noisy, but fast. She'll add a new dimension to the exercise. Her noise levels are about equivalent to the new Soviet nukes so the scenario will be realistic."

Dave nudged his skipper. "If he's making high-speed transits at depth, we better warn him about that rocky shallow spot at the elbow of the transit lanes."

"Good thinking, Dave. We don't want him kissing the bottom going that fast. The rocks sit on the Loran baseline extension, so navigation is not too good there."

Later, they collared *Ling*'s CO and exec. Redmond laid out a careful explanation of what *Clamagore* had experienced.

Both nuke officers looked on over glazed expressions that all but declared, *You guys are too stupid to fit into our program and we should take advice from you?*

Redmond and Zane sensed the put-down. The nuke CO gave them an insincere thanks then left the meeting to attend to matters of perceived higher priority. Zane and Redmond looked at each other and shook their heads.

Zane said, "Some people sure are hard to help."

A muffled rumpf awakened Norovsky from a sound sleep. He looked from his cell and saw a huge man hovering over the guard who lay dead on the floor. The man dragged the guard to Norovsky's cell.

"Here," the man said. "Reach through the bars and remove the keys from the guard's belt. Then try to unlock the door from the inside. This must look believable."

Even the unflappable Norovsky needed time to get his mind around the saga unfolding before him.

"You are escaping, Norovsky. You knew the plan. We must make it appear you called the guard to your cell, grabbed his pistol from its holster and shot him. Then you removed the keys from his body and let yourself out. You'll don his clothes so it will not look suspicious as we walk from the building."

"Then what?"

"First things first!"

Norovsky donned the unfortunate guard's uniform. He'd not been a party to violent death since he left the Soviet Union sixteen years earlier. Americanization had softened him.

The man sensed this. "Don't worry about the bastard. He's the reason you lost so much weight. Look at the size of him. He took the best of your rations for himself. See how his uniform hangs on you."

Norovsky nodded then together the two men walked from the building drawing no suspicion from the sleep-deprived staff. Shortly, they entered a car and drove through the early morning darkness to a nest of fishing boats at a network of docks at the waterfront.

"Walk to the outboard boat. There you will receive further orders."

"*Spasiba, Tovarisch* (Thank you, Comrade)," Norovsky said and extended his hand.

The man did not take it. "Save your thanks for the Almighty if you make it through the rest of your journey."

He waited until Norovsky disappeared across the line of fishing boats then peeled a skintight disguise from his face. He thought, *If you make it through, you'll be thanking the Almighty for his greatest miracle since the virgin birth.*

Paul and Jean Ann Scott, Dave and Dale Zane, and Denny Kolb joined Phil and Katherine Redmond at the submarine base O-club for cocktails. Phil had broken confidence with Denny and discussed the young officer's dilemma with Katherine. He knew his wife would respect Kolb's confidentiality and Redmond had gotten in well over his head in a matter Katherine could handle much better. He needed her advice.

On noting Denny arrived alone, she whispered to her husband, "He remains smitten by the good doctor, I see. He came to our party by himself also."

"It'll take some time, Kate. And I'm seeing this side of him for the first time. I'm confident that whatever the end result, Denny will land on his feet."

Dave asked Paul Scott, "So how do you like the boomers?"

"Ask Jean Ann. She is recorder of all such matters and owns a share or two of stock herself."

Jean Ann added, "Ask when you have about three hours, Dave."

Dave then spoke to Paul in a more serious tone. "I'm very sorry about Adrian Roberts, Paul. I remember him from my brief stint in *Piratefish*. A nice lad."

"Thank you, Dave. Adrian was the best. Engaged as you might have heard and asked me to be his best man. They scheduled the wedding to fit in my post patrol standdown. Jean Ann and I drove to Baltimore and met his fiancée."

Jean Ann said, "Louise Kirshner. A lovely girl, naturally devastated over this. At our meeting, though she'd never seen Paul, she threw her arms about him as though she'd never let go and sobbed."

"I felt bad when Jean Ann gave me the news in Holy Loch and worse when I came face to face with Louise."

Katherine broke a moment of silence brought on by the new topic. "I think it's wonderful that Jean Ann and you went down there, Paul. That poor woman needed something to hold onto after so devastating a loss. And you gave it to her."

Paul's voice shook a bit. "She asked me why. Why would God take the life of this beautiful young man? I explained I had no answer, and then thought of what a priest said to the parents of a cousin who died of polio at age thirteen. 'God has a plan, and what happened somehow fits into it. It's hard for us to see this through the veil of our grief, but faith assures us it is there'."

Paul's eyes filled with tears. Both Jean Ann and Katherine put an arm across his shoulders.

Katherine said to him, "You and Jean Ann brought her the greatest consolation she could possibly receive, the gift of your presence."

Paul wished to relate similarities between the incident of *Pershing*'s near demise and what they knew of *Trenchant*'s final moments. And how a simple report might have spared his friend's life and all those aboard the stricken warship. It would be a topic for a later time.

Denny broke the mood. "Paul, you need to know the fearless foursome heritage continued despite the loss of our leader."

"You, Roman and Keating? Tell me they didn't do anything stupid after I left, Captain."

Paul's resilience showed through. He would not let the intended ambiance of this event be diminished by his personal grief.

Redmond replied, "Actually, I saw a distinct improvement when your hand let go of the throttle."

Spirits lifted and they exchanged outrageous stories of days past. Camaraderie evolved among diesel-electric submariners is likely unique in the world. And so the seven friends built upon a quality that would ultimately result in entire crews of retired submariners assembling from across the country each year just to pass a few days with each other.

Paul suggested they drink up. "Let's move on to Seven Lamperelli brothers. I'll show you the place where Adrian tried to hit on a monstrous second class torpedoman's girlfriend and got Killer Cadrain his nickname."

Phil Giambri spent most of his weekend at the base sonar school listening to tapes of *Sturgeon* class submarines at various speeds and ranges. He toyed with the idea of making a few bootleg copies of the highly classified material, but thoughts of the Portsmouth Naval Prison deterred him. Giambri did not like what happened during the first phase and took their non-response to the simulated attacks personally.

As *Clamagore* proceeded down the Thames for phase two of the exercise, Phil Redmond looked onto the main deck and grimaced. Benson Roman, First Lieutenant, had his deck force find every possible loose panel and tightened them with wedges.

Redmond wondered, *I hope Benson hasn't secured anything we might need to open.* He knew Roman to be a competent young officer who would take no action without first weighing all the consequences. Redmond believed the best way to get the most from his crew is to let them give it. Some of his colleagues, obviously less secure than him, chose to lead by fear, badgering officers with threats of what they could expect in the event of an error. Their ships did not wear battle efficiency E's on the fairwater.

Clamagore wore an E with a hash mark beneath signifying back-to-back wins of this award. Redmond thought, *I must be doing something right at least.*

The other three diesel boats entered the exercise by going deep and running on the battery.

Redmond figured the nuke CO would anticipate this and wait at a point down the intended track where the submarines would have to snorkel in order to maintain the ten knot SOA (speed of advance). He called his officers together for a council of war. Sonarman Giambri attended, as his sonar would be critical to success of their efforts.

First, Redmond addressed the enlisted sonarman to put him at ease in the company of so much *brass.* "Giambri, soon as you can, get us a blade rate on the nearest fisherman."

"Aye, Captain."

"Denny, take the first watch. Soon as we're submerged, secure one screw and duplicate Giambri's blade rate with the other."

"On the snorkel, Captain? It won't be very fast and snorkeling is the bread and butter of making our SOA."

"Here's how we'll fix it, Denny. We won't even need one engine to match the blade rate. We'll use the rest of it and one more to jam as much into the battery as possible (submarines use up to two engines on the snorkel). With a full can (fully charged battery) we can make up the SOA and cover most of the ground in our quietest condition."

Redmond looked about the wardroom. "Comments? Speak up. If I'm telling you to do something wrong, now's the time to tell me."

Giambri responded. "I think our attacker will be most vulnerable right after we secure snorkeling. His sonarmen are no fools. They'll bite on the blade rate scam for a while, but will hear enough to make them suspicious. I'm betting now that we've gotten quieter, he'll think we're farther away and be hustling to catch up. Right after we go quiet it'll be easy to hear him if he's headed this way. Bang! The hunter becomes the hunted and we bag him."

Redmond replied, "You've been working on this pretty hard."

"Have to, Captain. The nuke sonar jocks gave us such a bad hour last time ... well you can imagine the ribbing I took at the EM (Enlisted Men's) Club. No, Captain. No more of that."

Benson Roman suggested, "Let's keep track of the noisy nuke transiting with us. Maybe we can use him as a screen."

Redmond replied, "We'll do it! Everybody got that?"

A chorus followed of, "Aye, Captain."

Giambri broke the dam. Not wishing to be outshone by an enlisted sonarman, ideas from the officers flowed like water over Niagara Falls.

Later, Redmond's spirits soared. Three quarters through the first transit, they'd experienced no attacks and things just improved as they rode the learning curve.

Ending the final snorkel period as the ship quieted, Giambri's voice blurted over the conning tower 21MC, "Contact passing below making twelve knots. Recommend simulating an attack on the son of a bitch!"

Conning officer Benson Roman grinned from ear to ear.

Coarse language over the 21MC violated ship's regs, but he knew Giambri to be a Siciliano on a vendetta and let it pass. "Pace, sound the general alarm and pass the word: Man battle stations torpedo."

Vasiliy Norovsky reached the outboard fishing boat to be greeted by Pasha Martinov. "So we meet again. It seems like every time we do, one or the other of us leaves the country."

"You confuse me, Martinov. First, why are we here? I understood I was to lead your friends over the same escape route I took in 1949. Why am I on a boat?"

"Simple. The KGB is aware of how you escaped last time and will be looking for you there."

"So why did you not tell me this in the beginning?"

"You cannot reveal what you don't know. A well-known KGB tact you must have forgotten. Come below. There are some people I wish for you to meet."

Ladder treads creaked as Norovsky and Martinov descended into the fishing boat. Vasiliy saw enough to make him wonder, *Surely I am not expected to take this derelict to sea, especially this time of year.*

Huddled in the limited space below decks, the family Denisov waited in anticipation of their next move. Irene looked at Norovsky through an expression of concern, while her husband Piotr, no stranger to adversity, betrayed no emotion at all. Their sons—Pasha, five, and

Andrushka, three—had been well protected from knowing the dangers to be encountered during the family's flight from Russia and went about their play unperturbed.

Pasha made introductions to Piotr and Irene using a bit of levity. "Vasiliy is making his second escape from the Soviet Union and is well experienced at this sort of thing."

Irene remained tentative. She wished to escape, as Pasha put it, only because she believed it in the best interest of her children and husband. Like many Russians, she had come to expect not much from life and would have been content to remain in her circumstance.

Turning to his wife, Piotr said, "Irene, would you take Pasha and Andrushka up on deck for a while so the three of us can talk?"

This to the chagrin of Norovsky who had begun to get grandfather practice with the children.

When Irene left, Pasha said, "You must understand, I can give you only instructions on how to proceed."

Denisov and Norovsky nodded their assent. Should things go awry, they'd have nothing to reveal.

Piotr said to his friend in the same context, "I know the great personal risk you take by helping us, Pasha."

Norovsky had other concerns. "This boat, or should I say sieve, is not to venture far from the dock, I trust?"

Pasha regarded him through a forced look of surprise. "Soviet warship commanders can do everything with nothing."

Already privy to this, Piotr did not react, but Norovsky had his answer and he did not like it.

Continuing, Pasha said, "Here is the plan. You will depart at 0300 (three a.m.) tomorrow. Come to a heading of three-five-zero true with fishing nets down. You have been provided with suitable clothing so no suspicions are likely to be raised if you are spotted. Just a couple of Soviet fishermen going about making your livelihood."

Norovsky asked, "But what will happen when the owner of this decrepit tub returns and finds it has been stolen?"

Pasha began to enjoy dueling with the veteran. He knew deep inside that Norovsky loved the challenge, but would not admit it. "As I said before, it is impossible for you to reveal what you do not know."

Shaking his head, Norovsky said. "So go on with the plan."

"Depart here on a true heading of three-five-zero. As I said before, fishing nets down. Retrieve them in two days time. Then proceed north on the White Sea to this latitude and longitude. I will give to you only verbally for reasons you well know. Plan to arrive there two weeks from now. Lower your nets again and fish."

"What about provisions and water?"

"Plenty," Pasha said in a tone that suggested Norovsky should trust him with details at this level.

Remain within ten nautical miles of that position. On the twenty-first day, shut down your engine for five minutes, four times a day. Run it for two minutes, stop for five then run for two more. Wait an hour and repeat the sequence. When you've done this four times, wait another five minutes then resume fishing as normal."

Both men understood this to be a signal that a submarine could easily detect, but expressed no such opinion.

"Questions?" There being none, Pasha said, "Call Irene and the boys, for I must leave now."

Pasha hugged both boys and wished them a happy voyage. They responded to Uncle Pasha with unbridled enthusiasm. He next put his arms around Irene.

"You must take good care of my dear Piotr." Tears streamed down the faces of both. "And I have a message for you to deliver when you get to America. To a woman. Lorraine Horner Ferranti. Vasiliy Norovsky will help you find her. Say that her friend Pasha Martinov sends his kind regards and has carried out your parting expression when last he saw you. He has lived long and is happy. He sincerely wishes it has been the same for you."

"I will do that for you, Pasha. But you must promise to give up these dangerous pursuits. I too wish you happiness and long life."

"I promise," he lied.

The two men embraced, then stood back and surveyed each other.

"Till next time old friend," Pasha said.

Piotr responded with, "May God grant it be soon."

Pasha Martinov went topside and made his way across the moored fishing boats to shore.

Phil Redmond picked up the UQC mike. "Oscar Sierra, Oscar Sierra, Oscar Sierra," he announced while the rest of his attack party combined to simulate launching an MK-37-1 from an empty launcher.

"Roger attack," a voice boomed over the UQC speaker. The nuke CO went on to ask, "Have you seen or heard anything of *Ling*?"

"Nothing," Redmond replied. "Should we?"

"She was running around at top speed a few hours ago."

Redmond said, "Maybe she got tired and went home."

Chief Beyers's voice from radio interrupted over the 21MC, "Conn ... Radio. Intercepted a transmission from *Ling*. She's on the surface and has a problem."

Redmond passed this to *Pike* who replied, "Okay, won't look for her for a while. Resuming the exercise. Out."

Zane said, "Doesn't seem too worried about his buddy."

"Surprise, surprise. Dave, I got a hunch. Let's break off the exercise, surface and proceed at best speed to the spot we warned *Ling*'s CO and XO about."

Clamagore had been on the surface less than an hour when Beyers interrupted a CO, XO cribbage game in the wardroom and passed the message to Zane then said, "*Ling* hit bottom and is seriously damaged."

Redmond determined the nuke had struck the exact pile of rocks she had been warned about. A brisk northeast wind began to whip the sea to medium wave heights. *Clamagore* stood by close enough to permit communications via battery-powered bullhorns.

Ling's CO advised they had hit bottom at top speed and broke off the rear end of the ship, including the rudder. Having twin screws, the CO attempted to keep the ship pointing into the seaway by adjusting speed and direction of the propellers.

Redmond warned, "You only have a watertight bulkhead holding out the sea. Let me put a line over and I'll keep you pointed upwind till the oceangoing tug arrives."

Ling's CO refused, likely because of humiliation brought on by a nuke having to be towed by a lowly diesel-electric submarine.

Redmond called over, "I'll stand by astern as close as I can."

"Stand off no closer than five hundred yards," *Ling*'s CO replied.

"Don't think so, skipper. If that after bulkhead fails, there's gonna be a lot of people in the water that'll want to be pulled out."

Ling did not respond.

Dave Zane's voice came over the 21MC. "Soon as you can, Captain, I need to see you in the wardroom." Zane's tone meant he wished more than just to finish the cribbage game.

Redmond turned the watch over to Denny Kolb. "Use your best judgment, Denny, but stay as close as you can." He had no need to tell the young officer to call him in the event of a change.

The captain dropped below.

Zane suggested they retire to the CO's stateroom. There, he spread out a message from COMSUBLANT on Redmond's desk. It read:

> UPON ARRIVAL OF OCEANGOING TUG TO ASSIST
> LING, TERMINATE CURRENT OPERATIONS AND
> PROCEED AT BEST SPEED TO POLARIS BASE, HOLY
> LOCH, SCOTLAND.

"What do you make of this, Captain?"

"Your guess is as good as mine. Do we have enough fuel and groceries?"

"Enough and then some."

"Alert the chief engineer to get ready to show us what he's got."

Chapter 21

Fourteen-year-old David Redmond yelled, "I got it, Mom." He picked up and silenced the jangling phone hoping it would be the new girl in his freshman class. "Oh," he said with disappointment in his voice, and then shouted, "It's for you, Mom. Captain Bernard from the base."

Katherine had met Fred Bernard at several social functions. *Good Lord. He's the Development Group Commander.* For a rare instant, she thought the worst. *No. For that kind of news, the chaplains come calling in person.*

"Hello Captain Bernard. Katherine Redmond speaking."

"Fred please. Captain makes me feel so old."

Bernard's light tone further dissolved her initial apprehension.

The captain went on. "For openers, nothing is wrong, Katherine. I know things have been a bit tense around here since the *Trenchant* disaster and there is no need for you to be alarmed. I'm calling to let you know *Clamagore*'s return to port has been delayed. I'd rather not discuss details on the phone, so might I drop by on the way home, say about six?"

"Six works, Fred. See you then."

Gives me time to feed the kids. She would set out hors d'oeuvres for the captain and would snack on those for her dinner. Katherine took five minutes to straighten up the living room, which needed no straightening at all. But rearranging cushions and a few magazines burned up nervous energy. *Something big is up or he'd have told me on the phone.*

The hour and a half dragged by more like twice that time. At six, the doorbell rang and Katherine invited Captain Bernard into her home.

"May I get you a drink, Fred?"

Captain seemed more appropriate for an officer who sported the honorary title of Commodore as DEVGRU2 Commander, but she'd yield to his invitation.

"Scotch-rocks is my panacea for the day's turmoil," he answered.

"Coming up." Katherine poured their drinks, a Merlot for herself.

"I'll get right to the point, Katherine. There's a big NATO exercise underway in the north Atlantic, and one of the Brit diesel-boats had to drop out with material problems. Your guy got picked because he leads the pack in tactical know-how." *Saying nice things about a spouse will make the pill easier to swallow.*

Bernard's body language did not reflect his attempt at an upbeat demeanor. Katherine knew he had not leveled with her, but it made Bernard uncomfortable and this evoked her forgiveness.

"Can you tell me when we might expect them back?"

"No earlier than a month's time or maybe longer. I'll contact you when I have some answers."

"I'll activate the telephone tree we wives have with the good news."

As a diplomat, Katherine kept traces of sarcasm from her voice.

"I was hoping you'd do that. And the bachelors. Would you be kind enough to ask everyone to notify people who might be expecting them back Friday? The *Trechant* thing again. We don't want people waiting on the dock thinking the worst."

"I'll add that to the list too, Fred."

Bernard relaxed as he finished his scotch and the topic changed to small talk. Children, families, next duty station and the like.

When he rose to take his leave, Katherine took Bernard's hand. "Fred, thanks for letting me know," then added, "I really don't envy you your job."

Good. She understands and I didn't have to breach security. From time to time, he did not enjoy his job either. "Thank you," he said.

Walking to his car he thought, *Damn us submariners can really pick 'em.*

Dawn broke with lights of Severodvinsk fading astern of *Tanya*, the broken-down fishing boat provided by Pasha Martinov. She shuddered along making barely three knots with her nets down.

Norovsky'd heard better sounding diesel engines in worn-out tractors on his brother's collective farm in the Urals. "Tell me, Piotr. How much further do you think this bucket of bolts will take us? It sounds like it suffers serious asthma."

"She will go as far as she takes us. We must expend our energy on things we can control. My concern is navigation. Whoever runs this tub does it by the seat of his pants and likely stays within sight of his home port. We have a long journey but must stay in sight of land and use lighthouses and other visual aids to navigation. We have no tools for celestial or radio navigation."

"How will we identify the navaids, Piotr?"

"You have sailed these waters longer than I. We have a chart."

Norovsky replied, "I have seen it and believe the best service it can give is in the head (toilet). I can position enough landmarks on the chart, but are they accurate now? You must remember it has been sixteen years."

"I have great faith in you, Vasiliy. You must have the same in yourself. Legend has you as the best seaman to sail the White." Piotr went on, "Our magnetic compass seems to hold well, but the problem is in what direction?"

"Early this morning, skies were clear to the north. This is good news and bad news. The good ... I was able to determine the variation to be precisely twelve degrees west. The bad, a clear sky means entrance of a high-pressure cell, so look for high winds and rough seas. I hope our *Tanya* is equal to them."

"Ah Vasiliy, ever the pessimist. If anyone, it is I that should worry with my wife and sons aboard. How many times has this boat ventured into the White and always returned? Why do you think she will let us down on this voyage?"

"An old custom. Expect the worst and have a plan for it. Good fortune will take care of itself. You cannot know such things. I am told an old head cannot be fitted onto young shoulders."

"I won't argue that, Norovsky. But on the subject of fortune, my experience has been the better I plan, the greater my good fortune."

Vasiliy thought, *This young dog seems able to teach an old one new tricks.* "Have you given thought to how we'll observe bearings to these landmarks when we identify them?"

"My Irene is beautiful, don't you think, Norovsky?"

"A masterpiece of understatement. I often wonder why she settled for you."

"Irene's beauty is subordinate to her skill as an artist. When it is light, I will have her take a tin plate from the galley and copy the rose (direction markings) from the magnetic compass onto it. We'll nail it to the capstan head and align the zero bearing mark to the bow. The instant I mark the bearing to a landmark, you will record our exact heading. From the two we will compute a true bearing line from the landmark."

"Ah Piotr, you have thought of everything. But your Irene. Can she cook?"

"Come, Vasiliy. What respectable Russian would marry a woman who is not skilled in the kitchen? And have you looked at the provisions Pasha provided? I suggest, my friend, we put away our worries and think of the magnificent epicurean cruise into the White Sea that lies before us. Wealthy people pay many rubles for just this sort of thing."

By mutual agreement, no farewell party had been given Joe Dunn by the *Pershing* wardroom officers. He celebrated the event with his friends, Paul Scott and wife Jean Ann at their home. Good thing. Dunn, not pleased with the circumstances of his transfer from *Pershing*, had imbibed substantially, a common trait for *angry young men* of the mid-sixties. He needed to be off the road and Jean Ann would see to that. The evening started off well, Joe playing the clown for the Scott boys making them shriek with laughter. Throughout dinner, he did his usual shtick, raving about his hostess and demanding to know why she settled for Paul when she could have had him.

After dinner, the boys in bed, the three sat in the living room.

Paul said, "You don't deserve this Joe, but I do." He produced an unopened bottle of Remy Martin Cognac, VSOP.

Joe countered with, "You took out a second mortgage for this? See what I'm talking about, Jean Ann? This man has no sense of responsibility."

Paul made generous pours into Joe's and his snifters, but Jean Ann applied a restraining hand over her glass. "No more, thank you."

An old custom mandated no Navy talk with ladies present, but pre-dinner martinis, wine with the meal, and now the cognac loosened Joe's tongue and inhibitions.

"I can't say the *Pershing* will miss me, but they sure as hell won't forget me."

Jean Ann said, "I'd think not, Joe. All the laughs they'll be missing."

Paul said, "It's not laughs, Jean Ann. Boomer sailors belong to a different Navy. Enjoying life aboard is considered an indication you're not working hard enough."

Jean Ann regarded them through a puzzled expression. "Most of what I get from you two is levity."

Joe jumped from his chair and fell to a knee. "You're not telling me you consider my proposals of marriage a joke?"

"See what I mean?" she sighed with upturned palms.

Paul said, "Jean Ann, Joe and I found ourselves in a different Navy than the one we grew up in. It'd take hours to explain. And it's a story you really don't want to hear."

She made a mental note. *Joe has something to get off his chest and my being here will impair that.* She would finish her wine and leave them to sort it out, but only after gathering up Joe's car keys.

Later, the men sat alone and Joe blurted out, "Damn it, Paul, how in hell can we sit on our thumbs and let a near sinking go unreported. How many more submariners might buy the farm if we don't let this cat out of the bag?"

The fifth of Remy lingered at two-thirds full and effects of the missing third showed on the young officers. Paul recalled a remark once shared with him by Jean Ann's dad. *Vino et veritas* (from wine flows the truth). They would speak only what truly dwelled in their hearts, but would make no decisions that later might embarrass them when they had to be rescinded.

Paul said, "I know a former naval officer in the area. Trent Warden, a pretty good head, once my CO on *Piratefish*. I expect he's into the CNO for a big favor. But you can't ask me why."

"Been there, done that. I didn't just fall off a turnip truck, you know. Who is this guy?"

"Might be just the person to run with this ball for you if you really want to hand it off to him."

As the Remy dropped to half full, the conversation grew more animated. Determination to straighten out submarine force ills rose proportionately.

Joe asked, "Why'n hell can't we come up with solutions like this when we're sober?"

But the dust settled. Naval officers do not end run, and both had been too long inflicted with this condition. Frustration. Both realized paths open to them prevented scratching of their common itch.

Joe rose, went to the closet and donned his jacket. "Where'n hell are my car keys?" he demanded through a slurred voice.

"Steak and eggs for breakfast, Joe. Now get your sorry ass upstairs into the spare room."

"Aye, aye, sir."

Both men glanced at the other and for an instant savored the closeness of their camaraderie.

Katherine Redmond had apprehensions over using the *Clamagore* dependents' telephone tree for her announcement. They normally used it for good news ... time and place of the ship's arrival, scheduling of social events and the like.

She thought, *Bend the rules a little. They're not enlisted men. Just Navy dependents.* The O-club normally accommodated only officers, their guests and families. *I'm an officer's wife and these are my guests,* Katherine reasoned. She reserved a room and scheduled the meeting in full knowledge that Captain Bernard would clear any possible resulting logjams. Katherine knew the event would be well attended for most of the women had never seen the inside of the O-club.

The meeting morning dawned bright and sunny and *Clamagore* ladies, well turned out, sat about dining room tables. Coffee and pastries, all on Captain Bernard's tab elevated spirits. Katherine, accompanied by Dale Zane, moved about ensuring they passed some time at each table.

Finally the moment of truth arrived and Katherine garnered attention by the traditional rapping a spoon against a glass. Despite her own misgivings, she determined not to betray the slightest trace of concern while making her announcement.

"Ladies, there is good news and not so good news."

What little conversation continued fell immediately silent and Katherine beheld a sea of anxious faces. She thought, *Damn, wish I had Phil's gift for levity.*

"We all know the superb job our men did on the Mediterranean deployment ... too superb, hence the not so good news. *Clamagore* has been ordered to join a NATO exercise in the north Atlantic to replace a Royal Navy submarine that returned to port for repairs."

A voice asked, "How long will they be gone?"

"That's a good question. Captain Bernard of the development group works on that answer, but in the meantime, ladies, we've fallen back into our jobs of holding down the fort till our men return."

Chief of the Boat Frank Beyers's wife Helen rose. "Mrs. Redmond, many of us have been there before. We never really like it, but we'll do what we have to do."

"Thank you, Helen. My husband is Captain Redmond, but to all of you, I'm Katherine. With all that's been on the forefront lately, there is nothing sinister to be read into this. You have my absolute assurance. It's unfortunate timing with only just getting reacquainted with our husbands after the Med trip. But it's nothing more than that. Are there any questions?"

"Will paychecks be mailed to us like before?"

"Yes. But there are new wives among us. Please leave your addresses with me before you leave."

Helen Beyers offered, "Thank you very much for looking into this for us. You certainly make us feel like family. I think a round of applause is in order for Katherine."

The women responded with vigor.

"Thank you. You are very kind. We can't expect the ship home anytime soon, so for some of us, it might be a good time to visit family. I'm sure this would delight a great number of grandparents. And if there are any problems, please get in touch with me."

News assimilated, the *Clamagore* wives settled down to coffee and pastries, socializing and enjoying the rest of the morning.

Later, as Katherine left the club, she reflected on the situation. She expected the older women shared her trepidations. They'd been around too long not to suspect the obvious. *Hopefully, I unburdened the younger ladies. Worrying about a situation does not improve it.* Like Captain Bernard, there were times when Katherine did not like her job.

At dusk, a Kashin class destroyer approached *Tanya*.

"Irene. Get the boys below. The three of you must remain silent and stay out of sight."

Piotr and Vasiliy, consummate maritime warriors, knew panic to be the enemy of success and remained calm.

Kashins had been built for the Soviet Navy in the early sixties. This one bore RBU 6000 and 1000 ASW rocket launchers that identified her as BRK (large ASW ship). They were the first Soviet purpose-built anti-air warfare ships and the first to carry the RBU ASW launchers, but her intended design was not what concerned Piotr and Vasiliy.

The Kashin's signal light flashed. *The peoples' Soviet warship Опытный (Proficient) demands your identity.*

"Damn it," Piotr muttered. "If we had a signal lamp, we'd simply respond and she'd go on about her business. Now, she'll approach and investigate."

"So what is your plan, Piotr? You told me the better you plan, the greater your good fortune. How great will our fortune be?"

"Perhaps the best plan is to rely on an old man's experience. What do you suggest?"

"Play the role given us. An old fisherman trying to teach a new one how to fish. Appear stupid and humble. That should be easy for you."

Proficient repeated her message then turned toward *Tanya* and laid off a hundred meters (328 ft). A powered bullhorn blurted out, "Why do you not respond to my signal?"

Vasiliy yelled as loud as he could. "We have no signal lamp."

The bullhorn replied, "The law says you must carry one. Lie to and prepare to be boarded."

"Maintain your composure," Norovsky said. "I shall say something to convince them we have no hidden agenda." He shouted through cupped hands, "Can you bring two bottles of vodka? We have rubles."

No reply from *Proficient* as she lowered a small boat which proceeded toward *Tanya*.

Norovsky raised his binoculars then said to Piotr, "It worked. A seaman carries two bottles. This visit will be perfunctory. They are just fulfilling a requirement. You are a very intelligent man, Denisov. When they come aboard, you must not appear so."

The small boat puttered alongside and a young officer climbed aboard *Tanya*. "I am afraid I must write a citation for failing to carry a signal lamp." He looked about and perceived the austerity Martinov wished them to project. The officer said apologetically, "The Navy does not make these rules, only enforces them. Here, this might compensate." He passed the vodka bottles to Norovsky. "You may keep your rubles."

"I am told these fishing boats are comfortable. May I go below and see for myself?"

Denisov gasped, but Norovsky seized his arm and said, "Please do. May we go below with you and share a glass or two?"

"No, *Komrade*, I must be getting back."

The young officer disappeared below.

Piotr whispered, "He'll find Irene and the boys. Then what?"

"You underestimate the intelligence of your good wife."

Though it seemed hours to Piotr, the officer emerged after only a few minutes. "You do indeed have many comforts. Even a woman could not keep things more orderly."

He climbed aboard the small boat and headed off to *Proficient*.

As Piotr started to move toward the cabin, Norovsky stopped him. "I am sure they watch us. Be unperturbed like the good fishermen we are and wave good-bye."

The small boat hauled aboard, *Proficient* headed north.

Norovsky said, "I don't like the looks of this. Though Martinov didn't say, it has to be a submarine that will pick us up. And *Proficient* is well configured for anti-submarine warfare."

They went below, and to their surprise, Irene and the boys were nowhere to be seen.

Suddenly the cushions flew off a bench locker and the three emerged with great fanfare.

"Irene!" Piotr took his wife into his arms.

"I told Pasha and Andrushka we would hide and surprise you, but they had to remain absolutely quiet."

Norovsky thought, *Not only beautiful, a good mother and excellent cook, but also intelligent. I didn't think the Lord made women like that.*

Clamagore left Castle Levan on the lower Clyde estuary to starboard and began a slow left turn to the northeast into Holy Loch and the American Polaris base.

Excitement ran amuck in the crew's mess, fueled by Sonarman 3rd Class Phil Giambri. He'd made four patrols on a boomer out of Holy Loch before being transferred to *Clamagore*. The bachelor enlisted men hung onto each word.

"You would not believe the chicks over here. By day, they're anti-war demonstrators, but after dark they put away their signs and head downtown to the pubs with boomer sailors. Talk about a good time."

Omensen challenged, "Not another one of your 'this is no crappers,' is it?"

"Would I lie to you guys?"

Pace replied, "Does the sun rise in the east?"

"Station the maneuvering watch," boomed over the 1MC and ended their jesting.

Phil Redmond and Dave Zane confabbed on the bridge with OOD Tim Keating.

"Dave, do you think we'll be here long enough for the *threesome* to get us in any trouble?"

"If we're here half an hour, it'll be time enough for those guys."

"Is it the sound of envy I hear, or—" Keating abruptly changed subjects. "Flashing light from the tender, Captain." Then hitting the 21MC press-to-talk, he ordered, "Quartermaster up."

Seaman Howell mounted the bridge and manned the signal lamp while Pace recorded for him. Howell read aloud, "Proceed directly supply barge. Moor starboard side to."

Dave Zane frowned. Back in sixty-one, with his sidekick Eric Danis, he'd served a boomer tour at Holy Loch.

"Wonder what's going on, Captain? Supply barge is the leper colony. No one moors there."

"Guess we'll find out pretty quick."

Clamagore, engines secured, slipped quietly on the battery past first the huge floating dry dock then the tender and moored alongside the supply barge. Several line handlers assisted from the tender, but disappeared quickly with the mooring completed. A Navy captain flanked by two armed marines stood at the head of the brow when it had been set in place. Redmond went on deck to greet the captain who came aboard leaving the marines to control access to and from *Clamagore.*

The captain crossed the brow, first saluting the U.S. flag and then Redmond. "Permission to come aboard, sir."

Redmond returned the salute. "Granted, Captain. Welcome aboard. Let's get below and out of this weather."

A brisk wind blew down the Loch under a gray overcast, normal for this time of year in west Scotland.

The officers shook hands. "I'm Phil Redmond."

"I'm Rick Ferranti, Office of Naval Intelligence. Bad news for your troops, Phil. Have them lay below. They are to have absolutely no contact with anyone. You won't need a topside watch. The marine sentries will see to that."

"But loading stores and fuel?"

"It's been arranged. We'll talk about that, skipper."

The officers went below.

"We'll meet in the wardroom, Phil. I hate to be so melodramatic, but you must clear the forward battery, shut the watertight doors and post sentries in the forward torpedo and control rooms."

"That serious? Can I have my exec sit in?"

"Afraid not. When I lay out details, you'll understand."

Several crewmen sat about the after battery mess table.

In response to the crew being directed to lay below and secure the hatches, Omensen asked, "What the hell's going on?"

Brad Pace said, "No contact with anyone? So much for hitting on Giambri's Peaceniks over in Dunoon."

Howell added, "You can't believe what Giambri says."

Omensen replied, "It's gotta be gospel. He didn't say, 'No crap'."

Giambri addressed Chief Beyers, "What do you make of it, COB?"

Beyers looked at the men through a stern expression. "What's to make of anything? Anyone here got that in his rate description? The captain's job is to worry. Ours is to give him as little cause for that as possible."

Phil Redmond and Rick Ferranti sat together in the wardroom, having to pour their own coffee seeing stewardsman Rapinian had been ordered out of the compartment.

Redmond opened with an attempt to inject levity into the obvious stressful circumstances. "This has got to be the biggest *sock blower off'er* ever."

Ferranti replied, "Something like that. Here's your cover story." He opened a single page operation order and laid it before Redmond.

COMSUBLANT OP-ORD 3-66. USS CLAMAGORE PROCEED EARLIEST TO STATION FORTY NAUTICAL MILES NORTH OF KOLA PENINSULA. THERE GATHER ARCTIC HYDROGRAPHIC DATA AS SPECIFIED COMSUBLANT INST 7805.2C. DO NOT, REPEAT DO NOT ENTER SOVIET WATERS. REMAIN UNDETECTED. IF DETECTED TAKE ALL MEASURES TO ENSURE PLAUSIBLE DENIABILITY OF US SUBMARINE PRESENCE. REMAIN ON STATION UNTIL RECALLED.

"Plausible deniability. That's a new one, Rick."

"No one knows better than you about the rising number of close encounters between US and Soviet warships. The Navy doesn't want to fan that fire."

"Okay. Sounds pretty simple to me, so why all the hush-hush?"

"Here it comes skipper. Pay attention. You're only getting this verbally." He spoke latitude and longitude coordinates to Redmond twice. "You must remember those. Do *not* write them down. Understood?"

"Yes, if memory serves me, that puts us about sixty miles into the White Sea. What about 'Do not, repeat do not enter Soviet waters'?"

Ferranti grinned. "When did you guys ever pay attention to what the Op-Ord says? Now here's the meat. Remain at that location until you detect a fishing boat."

"Give me a break, Rick. There's gotta be a hundred fishing boats around there."

"Sounds like you've been there before. Good. This boat will distinguish itself by routine of running and stopping engines." Ferranti gave the same instructions Pasha Martinov had given Vasiliy Norovsky and Piotr Denisov. "Surface at night and pick up five occupants from the boat. Then get the hell out of there and head home."

Sarcasm clear in Redmond's voice, he said, "Maintaining plausible deniability, of course."

"Something like that."

"Look, Rick, why the hell not send an SSN in for that? It'd be a piece of cake. Do you realize how many times we'll have to snorkel to do this? It won't be all that hard for Ivan to find us."

"SSN's are all laid up for sub-safe overhauls."

"Can I make a little conjecture?"

"Shoot."

"Couldn't be the mission is too risky to send one in there?"

"Remember. You said that, Phil. Not me. Now repeat the latitude-longitude coordinates so I can be sure you got them."

Chapter 22

A high-pressure weather cell sat to the northwest and delivered a strong northeast wind that quickly whipped the sea to a state five. Neither Norovsky nor Denisov admitted to the other, but both believed a state three was as much as *Tanya* could handle. Being professional naval officers, they knew it far better to anticipate than react.

"Piotr, I am thinking it best for us to ride at slow speed with the weather on our port quarter."

"No question, Vasiliy Ivanovich, but this will diminish our speed of advance to the rendezvous."

Norovsky used a term he picked up in America. "Better late than never. Though we haven't been told, it can be nothing other than a NATO submarine that will meet us. From what I've learned of their mettle, they'll not cut and run simply because we're not there on time."

Tanya came left ninety degrees from their heading and slowed.

Yelling to be heard above the howling wind, Norovsky said, "Our greatest danger is taking on seawater faster than our one-lunged bilge pump can handle. It would be wise for one of us to go below and stuff whatever we can find into any cracks that might appear. First check the seal on the cabin door. Before long, seas will slap over the stern and right into it."

In prophetic fulfillment, a big wave crashed over, dousing both men with frigid water. A shriek from Irene confirmed the door leaked.

Piotr said, "I'll go below and toss you a blanket. Place it over the opening and slam the door shut. I'll dog it shut from inside … here." Piotr handed his friend a length of line. "Tie yourself down. I don't want to steer this tub to the rendezvous by myself."

Going below confirmed his suspicions; the door leaked like a sieve, but his blanket fix slowed it to a trickle. The boys screamed with laughter as *Tanya* pitched and rolled in the seaways. To them it seemed like a ride at the amusement park. Irene, however, had fallen victim to severe seasickness. Piotr comforted his wife and had her lie

down on a bunk while he stroked her back. He resisted the temptation
to ask her what she'd prepared for dinner.

He inspected the gasoline-powered bilge pump then fired it up and
checked for leaks lest the sealed compartment be filled with deadly
carbon monoxide gas. Although the exhaust tied into the main engine
exhaust stack, he found one and secured the engine immediately. Piotr
wrapped wet linen strips torn from a galley tablecloth about the exhaust
pipe and fired up the engine again. He tested the fix by placing a cheek
near where he'd discovered the leak—nothing. He periodically doused
the patch with bilge water to keep it from overheating and bursting into
flames. *Good! The pump is keeping up.* Piotr drew a sigh of relief so
he returned to Irene and stroked her back again, all to no avail.

He doused the exhaust patch again and determined the correct
interval to be five minutes. He strapped his watch on Pasha, his oldest
son. The young boy, delighted to be assigned this responsibility,
attacked his job with vigor. This freed Piotr for continual monitoring
of the aging hull for new leaks.

Then *Tanya*'s stern lifted high out of the water and seemed to free
fall into a trough with a resounding crack. Piotr became conscious of
rushing water sounds. An inspection confirmed his worst fears. The
seam between two main hull planks opened and seawater flowed into
their fragile boat at an alarming rate. Something had to be done and
quickly. If the water level reached the pump engine and it stopped,
their fate would be sealed.

Piotr grasped a crowbar and called to his wife, "Irene. Get up and
bring me your blanket."

His voice tone apprised Irene of their situation urgency. With a
surge of strength, she set aside her own misery and complied.

"Roll the blanket and start the end here." He pointed to the breach
end, now a foot underwater."

Irene paused long enough to subdue a spasm of gags and complied.

"I'll jam this end in with my crowbar and we'll move along the
seam until it's sealed."

When finished, water flow into the boat ceased. The bilge water
reached four inches below the pump engine causing it to sputter as the

pitching motion of *Tanya* raised and lowered the water level. It began to lower slowly, gaining speed as the water level neared normal.

"We are good, now, Irene. Go back to your bunk."

"I am no longer seasick. Fear must be the cure for it."

Piotr knew the patch could blow anytime, especially if the boat took another big pitch, but sharing this with Irene would change nothing. "Every man should have a wife as good as you are."

Tanya pushed on, and much to Piotr's joy the seas began to abate. They'd not sink. At least not this time.

Phil Redmond and Rick Ferranti squeezed into the CO stateroom. Redmond would have much preferred to have the discussion over dinner at the nearby Royal Marine Hotel, but he would not leave *Clamagore* with his crew restricted aboard.

Ferranti explained a fuel barge would come alongside to top off soon as the normal and fuel ballast tanks are lined up.

Redmond said, "Look, Rick, the crew doesn't know a damn thing about this Op and somebody has to coordinate with the people topside. What's the harm in that?"

"Have 'em do it via sound-powered phones. I know all this sounds stupid, skipper. Problem is ... we don't want anyone to recognize your crewmembers. You recall how Francis Gary Powers got his mug plastered all over the media when the Reds caught him?"

"Yeah. But there sure'n hell are a lot of people in the States who know these guys. What about them?"

"They don't know you're in Holy Loch. We don't want to rock the boat on the agreement we have with the Brits to base Polaris boats in Scotland. Conducting spec-ops out of here is not part of the deal."

"What about stores? We deployed for a scheduled two-week exercise and stocked only a small reserve. We ate our way through most of that just getting here."

Ferranti replied, "They're being laid topside as we speak. After dark, send your troops up and strike them below."

"Talk about cloak and dagger, Rick. How can someone on the tender not suspect something?"

"Just like in your op-order. Plausible deniability. All they can do is make conjecture that'll be officially denied. A ship was refueled and re-provisioned to proceed to the Arctic and collect hydrographic data."

Irritation obvious in his voice, Redmond asked, "Just like that?"

"I don't like this anymore than you, but it needs to be done."

"Yeah, but I don't even know enough to assess risk versus gain. Don't forget that besides you and me, seven officers and seventy-two troops are involved."

Ferranti went on, "That will be the case for any ship that undertakes this mission. You know damn well if you refuse, it will be someone else. And from what floats around about *Clamagore*'s reputation, they'd be a hell of a lot less likely to pull it off. Risking troops is hard, but you knew that when you took the job."

Redmond knew this to be true. He'd have to set faces of his crew and their families aside and get on with it.

Ferranti sensed this. "Now to important things. How pissed is your exec gonna be when he gets tossed out of his bunk for me?"

"Not half as pissed as Tim Keating is gonna be when he moves to enlisted berthing in the forward torpedo room to make room for Dave."

Terry Martin looked at the list of newly appointed officers to his Chief of Naval Operations staff, did a double take and called on the intercom, "Chief Ford."

A moment later, the admiral's writer Dorothy Ford, an attractive redhead in her early forties, entered the office. "Yes, Admiral?"

"I notice Commander Edward Moon has joined the staff. This is a real surprise. Three months ago his submarine pulled off the greatest intelligence find of the Cold War. I fully expected his next job would be mine."

"Word is, he got across the breakers with Admiral Epworth."

"If you'll pardon my French, why'n hell am I the last person to find out about this?"

"Sorry, Admiral. It floated around the gossip circle and I didn't think you wanted to hear any of that. I understand the officers in OP-31 (CNO Submarine Warfare Division) are walking on eggs. By their standards, a sharp officer of their own got out of sorts with Admiral Epworth, but no one wants to take him on."

"Get Admiral Dieter on the phone, Chief."

"Yes, Admiral."

Seconds later, the two admirals went at it.

Martin said, "Mike, why wasn't I informed of Ed Moon's sacking?"

"Sacking, Admiral? To my knowledge he got a regular transfer from command. Practically all the officers on my staff come here from command."

Martin resisted the urge to say *bullshit*. Moon had served only thirteen months of a scheduled three-year tour. If Epworth stopped suddenly, it would take a team of surgeons to remove Dieter's nose from Epworth's butt.

"Is Moon in?"

"Yes, Admiral, but he's sort of busy. Shaking down ... you know."

"Have him report to my office at ten."

"Begging the Admiral's pardon, but is this wise? There was a sort of rub between him and Admiral Epworth. Maybe this is something I should handle."

Martin thought, *Who in hell do you work for? Epworth or me?* It took restraint, but he kept anger from his voice. "Ten O'clock!"

"Then I will join him."

"No you won't. Is that clear?"

"Quite clear, Admiral. Ten a.m. it is."

At ten o'clock, Commander Ed Moon, a little overwhelmed, sat for the first time before the Chief of Naval Operations. Terry admired the officer from the beginning, five-nine, brown curly hair, blue-eyes, hefting a hundred eighty or so pounds.

"We can't get into details, but congratulations on your find. There's no need to discuss its value. We're both aware of that. But your early relief of command surprises me ... should it?"

Moon paused and looked about the well-appointed office. *How many commanders get one-on-one's with the CNO?* "I guess my CO time was up."

"Was it? Normally you'd have the job for seventeen more months. Look, Ed. I was a commander once and by then fully understood loyalty up, loyalty down. But I'm CNO now and need to know what happens in the Navy. You can see that, I'm sure."

"Yes, Admiral. I can. What is it you want me to tell you?"

"Moreover, it's what do you want to tell me? Details on your early relief would help. Word is, there was a problem with Admiral Epworth and you."

The young officer, clearly uncomfortable, remained silent.

Terry assured him, "You're not being disloyal by simply telling me what happened."

"Admiral, I don't like to complain. I believe I, and I alone, am responsible for what happens to me."

Damn, thought Martin. *Why'n hell do we instill these knightly qualities when they can so easily turn around and bite us on the ass?* "Just tell me about your last encounter with Admiral Epworth."

"Yes, Admiral. It was right after the find. You can understand why we were in lockdown at Mare Island Naval Shipyard. Security measures exceeded anything I ever saw."

"Of course. They were needed."

"Well, Admiral Epworth felt his obligation to ensure the safety of reactors aboard Navy ships exceeded any security requirements."

Martin sensed Ed's discomfort with appearing to rationalize his early relief. "Go on, Commander."

"A couple of Admiral Epworth's flunkies came aboard to inspect."

Good, he's starting to get pissed off.

Moon went on. "It didn't take long for them to trump up enough ammunition to cause a visit from the admiral."

The admiral, Martin thought. *There must be a hundred of us, but only Epworth gets his rank preceded by the word the.*

Commander Moon said, "Admiral Epworth arrived at the gate in civilian clothes as normal. The marines didn't recognize him and asked for identification. He refused in the belief he should be recognized by everyone and took off on foot for my ship with the marines in hot pursuit. That wasn't the bad part."

Martin thought, *Too bad the marines didn't shoot the bastard.* "Please continue, Commander."

"When he tried to board my ship, the topside watch carried out his instructions and demanded to see his ID. The admiral left, and when I caught up with him, all he would say is, 'Moon, you should be worried about your career'. He demanded to know what I was going to do about the men who refused him access to the ship. Three months later, I was relieved."

A pall of silence hung between the two men a moment.

"So how are you feeling about this, Ed?"

"Admiral, you better than anyone know the epitome of a submarine officer is command. I must confront the reality that I will never see that again. But I'll find something in need of doing and do it."

Martin replied, "There is no doubt in my mind that you will do that." *How do we come up with men like this? And what the hell am I going to do to get this thing straightened out?*

Phil Redmond made his ritual daily walk through the boat, common practice among diesel-electric submariners. He regarded the crew's mess as a domain of his troops and would not sit and have coffee there unless invited. However, he received an invitation every time. The crew liked him, but also had an ulterior motive. While he sat for coffee, a crewman would run through each compartment of the boat to warn of the captain's imminent visit.

This interlude provided the captain opportunity to keep in touch with his crew. Conversations centered on family, friends and plans. Most crewmen felt an obligation to appear awed in the presence of their commanding officer. They did this as a gesture, for the confines of *Clamagore* permitted no one to mask their true identity sufficiently to warrant placement atop a pedestal. Redmond liked it that way. His credo: *beware of demagogues.*

Giambri did not fall into this category. Though respectful, he spoke with the captain more as a peer.

"Guess it makes no sense to ask where we're going, Captain."

"What difference would it make if you knew?" Aware the others listened intently, Redmond continued. "You'll do what you have to do as you always have. From all that flows in, you're all pretty good at that. Sorry this comes so close on the heels of the Med deployment.

It's certainly inconvenient for me. Ever notice how often plans we make expecting to be ashore, frequently don't pan out?"

Redmond sent a subtle message that regrets over this sudden deployment did not accrue exclusively to the troops.

He went on, "Any major cancellations?"

"Nothing big, Captain," Giambri said. "Only Omensen here. He was going to be married tomorrow. That right, Ken?"

Omensen simply nodded his response.

Redmond looked at the nineteen-year-old. He thought. *I suspect he'll ultimately find he's been done a favor.* He believed Omensen had far more life to live before getting himself into a marriage.

Giambri continued. "Omensen, good thing you're not a south Philly Catholic. You'd have to pick an Italian girl or suffer wrath of the Praying Mafia."

Redmond frowned. "Praying Mafia?"

"Yes sir, Captain, pick an Italian girl, or those ladies, the Praying Mafia, would meet at church each evening and say the rosary to ask the Blessed Virgin to show this errant boy the true and correct way."

Redmond asked, "Did it work?"

"Captain, if you had to decide whether to marry an Italian girl or spend eternity in purgatory, what would be your choice?"

"A no brainer, Giambri."

"That's why I'm a bachelor, Captain. But I gotta admit when I was in Sicily, I could almost hear those beads rattling."

Finishing his coffee, Redmond said, "Well, I better get on with my walk through before everyone finds out I'm coming."

Not a word escaped sullen faces in the crew's mess.

Redmond finished his walk through, pausing in each compartment for a word or two with his troops and said nothing of various noted discrepancies. These he would enumerate with Dave Zane who an hour later would walk through the boat and insist they be corrected.

Invariably, a crewman would lament, "Why does the exec have to be such a jackass? He should be more laid back like the captain."

The sea state abated as quick as it rose, and *Tanya* plied her way east hoping to identify a navaid ashore and recover position.

Piotr wedged another blanket into the crack, this time using a sledge to seat it tightly. To attempt this in heavy seas would pose great risk of serious injury to his left hand.

Irene, completely recovered, went about preparing breakfast.

Finished below decks, Piotr went to the bridge. "Vasiliy Ivanovich, have you estimated how far the storm blew us from our track?"

"We can work that out using the heading, speed and time from our last known position. And I have a surprise. I found a sextant in the gear locker ... old and rusty, but it works."

Denisov shook his head. "A lot of good that will do us. We have no nautical almanac and if we did, have no way to know exact time."

"Ah Piotr. You're from a new Navy that has everything. I am from the old Navy where we were expected to do everything with nothing. We shall shoot the sun at noon and determine latitude."

"How will you do that without knowing the sun's declination?"

"We will know it, Piotr. The Tropic of Capricorn sits at Latitude twenty-three point sixteen south (Russians use degrees followed by a decimal, instead of commonly used degrees, minutes and seconds of arc). The sun is at Capricorn on the first day of winter and takes eighty-nine days to reach the equator for the first day of spring. It must therefore move north at the rate of point two-six degrees each day. We multiply that times the number of days passed since December twenty-one, subtract the product from twenty-three point sixteen and voila ... the sun's declination."

Norovsky folded his arms and smiled, pleased with his explanation.

"You astound me, Vasiliy."

"Do I? You should read your history, Piotr. I did not contrive this. In nineteen fourteen, Sir Ernest Shackleton, an English Antarctic explorer, sailed a converted lifeboat from Elephant Island eight hundred miles over uncharted waters to a whaling station in South Georgia. He did this with only a sextant."

"Amazing! How?"

"He sailed to the latitude of his destination and followed it to landfall. We shall do the same. We'll cheat a little and get there sooner. Bring *Tanya* to a heading of north-northeast. If we sight land, parallel it until we reach Mys Konushin. Otherwise, find latitude sixty-seven point two north with our sextant and like Shackleton, follow it to our landfall."

"Norovsky, you amaze me."

"Then you don't mind taking the watch while I go below and partake of the superb repast prepared for us by your beautiful wife."

Terry Martin arrived early for his appointment with Stanton McCord, Secretary of the Navy. An attractive lady of McCord's staff immediately ushered him into the well-appointed office.

McCord, tall, handsome in a gray pin-striped three-piece suit extended his hand and greeted Martin. "How do you and your lovely Brenda fare these days?"

"Good, thank you sir. I trust all is well among the McCords?"

"It is … thank you."

McCord peered at Martin through steel blue eyes from beneath graying hair, Terry's signal the two should get on with their agenda.

"Mr. Secretary, I wish to take as little of your time as possible. You are aware I am sure of our Admiral Epworth's ability to stir the pot."

"He is somewhat controversial, but quite effective, I'm told."

Martin knew the term effective meant different things to different folks, but did not go there.

"Agree, sir, but I find some of his methods to reinforce his message, somewhat disturbing."

McCord replied, "Oh?"

Martin related the discussion he'd had with Commander Moon.

"That is disturbing, Terry. I'm certain you are well-positioned to ensure this is not going to damage the commander's career."

"I can and will, Mr. Secretary. But Moon is a submariner, likely one of our best. And Epworth has taken something away from him that even I cannot restore … command of a submarine. Epworth is charged by the Atomic Energy Commission to certify officers for command of reactor-powered vessels. In my view, he abuses that authority."

"Well specifically, what would you have me do?"

"Nothing, Mr. Secretary. I would like your blessing to confront Epworth and have him give an accounting of his stewardship."

Pausing for a moment, McCord then rose from his desk. "Terry, you're not new to the political game. Your own appointment, whether you approve the term or not, came from a politician. Epworth, quite frankly, has us over a barrel. He is the darling of Congress and knows it would raise hackles if action of any sort be mounted by the Navy against him. I don't need to tell you that whatever we put into the budget is at the pleasure of Congress."

"I see, sir. But what are we to do if the actions of an officer are in conflict with the best interests of the service."

McCord replied, "What we can. But it is incumbent upon us to know what those limits are. I will not forbid you to talk with Rear Admiral Epworth, naval officer to naval officer. Perhaps give a view of the adverse impact he is having for which he might not be aware. But you will not initiate disciplinary action against him. Is that understood, Admiral Martin?"

"Understood. Thank you very much for your time, sir."

Clamagore rounded Norway's North Cape and proceeded eastward in the Barents Sea. Only Redmond, Rick Ferranti and Dave Zane knew where they were going and why, Zane in the loop only after twisting Ferranti's arm to its near breaking point. With no navigation aids, they desperately needed celestial observation for a departure fix, for which the ship would have to surface. No one shot stars with the ship's near antique sextant better than Denny Kolb.

Redmond first did a periscope scan of the sky to insure overcast did not obscure the navigation stars. He ordered the ECM (electronic countermeasures) raised. The report "no contacts" from the radio shack elevated his spirits. The reassuring voice of Giambri had given a similar report on results of a sonar search.

Only the captain, exec and Denny would mount the bridge, but not until Redmond could determine a horizon so Denny could measure star elevations against it.

Redmond said, "Okay, absolute minimum time on the surface. Here's the plan. Denny, the Orion constellation is bright as hell up there. You won't need a star finder. Shoot Sirius, Procyon and Castor in that order. Got that?"

"Got it, Captain."

"Then toss in Rigel for good measure." If lines of position from three stars did not intersect close to the same point, it's good practice to toss in a fourth. Redmond went on, "Dave will record the time on your mark. Pass the sextant to me and I'll read with Dave recording that too. Dave will confirm I read it right then pass it to you for the next shot. For Rigel, Dave, mark the time and we'll go below and read the sextant there. Think we can be down in three minutes?"

Denny grinned. "Didn't know I was that quick, Captain."

Zane added, "I always found cold fingers a great incentive to get the job done fast."

Ferranti stood by in the conning tower to pass steaming cups of coffee to a chain of seaman stationed on the ladder to the bridge once they were on the surface where temperature and wind chill combined to a temperature of minus thirty Fahrenheit. The sextant required barehanded operation and between observations, Denny planned to wrap his hands around the cups to warm his fingers.

Clamagore surfaced into a moderate sea state four whipped by a brisk northwest wind. The threesome mounted the bridge, Denny first with his sextant, followed by Dave Zane and Phil Redmond, both with binoculars to scan for ships and aircraft between star shots. In addition, Tim Keating in the conning tower would continue to scan with number one periscope.

They clambered onto the tiny deck slipping and sliding as cold air turned residual seawater into ice.

Denny shot Sirius. "Stand by, mark!"

They carried out the procedure ordered by Redmond, hot cups of coffee working their magic on Denny's near frozen fingers.

As Denny sighted in on Castor, concurrent with his *mark*, Redmond ordered, "Clear the bridge," and pulled the diving alarm.

The captain followed Zane, Denny and chain of coffee passers tumbling down the conning tower hatch.

Redmond asked, "Get the last one, Denny?"

"Got it, Captain."

"And I recorded the time," Zane added.

"Good. I spotted a contact to the east hull down (curvature of the earth obscuring all but the top hamper) very likely a warship."

Redmond cleared the conning tower so he and Zane could plot Denny's fix. The three lines intersected within a mile of each other.

Zane whistled. "Denny sure earned his breakfast this morning."

The ship leveled at periscope depth. Redmond searched the eastern horizon and as expected, saw nothing, the periscope optics only a few feet above the surface.

"Sonar ... Conn. Search zero-six-zero to one-two-zero true."

Giambri's voice came back, "Just picked him up, Captain. A warship. Give me a few minutes and I'll get you a classification."

A moment later, Giambri said, "A Kashin bearing zero-nine-five. Appears to be closing."

"Can you give me a guess at the range?"

Giambri replied, "Twenty-thousand, Captain."

Zane plotted it from their recently fixed position. "Looks like we got a gauntlet to run, Captain. He's sitting right smack on our planned track into the White Sea."

Chapter 23

CPO Dorothy Ford knocked then entered Terry Martin's Office. "Rear Admiral Epworth is here, sir."

Congress had selected Epworth for promotion to the grade of vice admiral and a small ceremony had been scheduled at the CNO office.

Martin planned an additional agenda but did not expect much from his controversial guest. Words of Reinhold Niebuhr's serenity prayer resonated—*Give me the serenity to accept what I cannot change, the strength to change what I can, and the wisdom to know the difference.* Martin considered the most useful of these to be the latter for his impending circumstance.

"Show him in please, Chief Ford." Martin rose and walked around his desk to greet Epworth. He extended his hand, "Good morning, Ray. Where is your good lady?"

Epworth took the CNO's hand. "Good morning, Admiral. Thanks for having me over. Much as I'd like to, I really don't have enough time to make it worth Betty's while."

"I'm sorry to hear that. Brenda and I hoped you would be our guests for lunch at the Gangplank. After all, you don't make vice admiral every day."

Epworth took a subtle jab. "I hope my next job gives me enough time for that sort of thing."

I hope the same thing, Martin thought. *Retirement. And it can't come soon enough.* Terry knew Epworth had too many congressmen in his pocket to permit that to happen. He also knew Epworth had no wish to leave. Martin rolled with Epworth's punch.

"Maybe you'll get my job, Ray. I spend most of my time looking around for things to keep me busy."

"I'm sure that's not so, Admiral. Well, I suppose we should get on with it. Do you have a photographer?"

"Waiting in the outer office swilling coffee as we speak. But could you give me a few minutes. I'd like to talk about Commander Ed

Moon. Perhaps you could give me more insight into what caused the abrupt termination of his command."

"Insight? Pretty plain if you ask me. He didn't know how to run his ship, so I fired him."

"The Bureau of Personnel is in the dark on this."

"It's not their business." Epworth's hackles began to rise. "I am responsible to the AEC (Atomic Energy Commission) to qualify officers responsible for the operation of naval reactors."

The edge came off Epworth's voice quick as it had risen. "Moon, unfortunately, had his own ideas about how that should be done. You can certainly understand why I let him go."

"Ray, I got a somewhat different story."

"Oh did you? From whom? Moon?" Epworth's body language portrayed a man struggling to maintain his composure.

His tone changed. "I'm actually disappointed. But records aboard Moon's ship were a disaster. I can't tolerate that and be consistent with my responsibilities to the AEC."

"Ray, how do you see your responsibility for combat readiness of nuclear powered ships?"

"That's not my worry. It's a TYCOM responsibility."

"True, Ray. But how many hours a day must a CO devote to nuclear power matters?"

"Let me see. Twenty-four hours less six for enough sleep. And he has to eat, so give him an hour for that. Another to look after himself. That leaves sixteen to ensure my requirements are carried out."

"How many does that leave for the TYCOM to hold up his end of the stick? Not enough, by my reckoning."

"Admiral Martin, I choose only the best and brightest. I do my best to make it easy for the TYCOM to do his job. You can't blame me if he doesn't."

Martin seldom permitted irritation to influence his words and it invariably ended in regret. "Ray, I recall you were passed over for a submarine command. I'm sure you're well over that by now."

"Of course I am," Epworth sneered. "Just like Queeg in *The Caine Mutiny*. The submariners gave me command of an insignificant tub ... a mine sweeper." Epworth grinned. "It'll sure feel good to have the

Navy's top submariner pin on my vice admiral shoulder boards. Can we call in that photographer?"

Phil Redmond did not call the ship to battle stations, but did assign top personnel at the conn, diving and maneuvering room stations as *Clamagore* approached the Kashin.

Dave Zane asked, "What do you make of her, Captain?"

"Not going any place in a hurry. No bone in her teeth."

"Likely patrolling the approaches ... maybe looking for us? Their damn spooks likely knew all about this well before we did."

"You're an incurable cynic, Dave, so you'd make a helluva CO. Too bad you're opting out. Okay, Pace, up scope for another look."

The TDC (torpedo data computer) operator called out, "Three-four-five relative," giving Pace a positioning bearing for the periscope.

"Bearing ... mark," Redmond snapped and flipped up the handles, signaling for scope to be lowered. He admired Pace, remarkably composed for a nineteen-year-old and made a mental note to discuss with him, at some future time, the prospects of NAPS (Naval Academy Prep School)—gateway to Annapolis.

Redmond declared, "He zigged left, Dave. Check with sonar. I want to know if he sounds like he's looking for anything."

Giambri's reassuring voice announced over the 21MC, "A single ping every ten minutes or so. Doesn't sound like he's onto us."

"Conn, aye, sonar. We're going to slip by him. Check the BT (bathythermograph) for best evasion depth."

Recognizing Redmond's voice, Giambri said, "Isothermal, Captain. One place is as bad as any other."

Redmond said, "We'll do it at periscope depth, Dave. As the Kashin passes, keep turning to maintain a bow-on perspective. This'll reduce our echo level if she pings."

"Once we get astern of her, Captain, then what?"

"Ever backed down submerged, Dave? The stern planes become the bow planes and vice versa. Just have to convince the helmsman to use opposite rudder for heading corrections."

Clamagore made a slow one-eighty degree turn to port, keeping bow-on to the Kashin then backed until the destroyer passed from sight.

Redmond ordered, "Sonar, search around and report all contacts." Then turning to Denny Kolb, "You got the conn. If sonar doesn't hear anything, commence snorkeling on two engines. Put everything into the batteries that they'll take and the rest into propulsion. If you need me, I'll be in the wardroom whipping the exec's ass in cribbage."

Redmond passed a compliment to his top officer ... confidence to leave him in charge of a delicate situation.

Norovsky pointed out the lights of Mys Konushin. "See, Piotr. And we're only ten miles from the rendezvous latitude. If we swing left to heading three-five-zero, we'll be there in twelve hours."

"Why don't you do it then? You have the watch," Denisov said, attempting to mask his astonishment at the old sailor's skills for determining their location.

After steadying on the new heading, Norovsky said, "We've finally come upon other fishing boats. This makes us less obvious."

"But their fishing nets are down and ours are not."

"In due time, Piotr. When we reach our favorite fishing place."

"As you say, Vasiliy."

Norovsky asked, "What are your plans after you reach America?"

"I have given it much thought, Vasiliy Ivanovich, but have no clue. We do this not for Irene and me, but for the boys. I'm told we'll find a better life for them there. I look to advice from those who rescue us."

"You're a young man, Piotr. The boys will grow up and leave the nest. Then there is only Irene and you. What then?"

"I've said already, I do not have that answer. So much in the past few days has crowded my mind. I've thought no further."

A gentle wind blew from the northwest beneath a cloudless sky, barely enough to ripple the sea as Norovsky replied, "Then you should begin. Be excited for yourselves as well as the boys. Children are happy anywhere as long as their parents are with them."

"How does an unmarried fifty-one-year-old know such things?"

"Growing older includes continuous reminders of what you should have done with your earlier life. I did have a woman who cared much for me. Katya Balenkov from right here in Severodvinsk."

"Where is she now, Vasiliy Ivanovich?"

"In America, but married."

"Why didn't you claim her when you had the chance?"

"Like you, I had far more pressing things on my mind then. The very point I wish to make, Piotr. Young men have much to learn from old men's mistakes, but they don't."

"Will I see you after we get to America, Vasiliy?"

"Probably not. They will give you new identities and a location where you will not likely be identified. This includes barring visits by people like me who could easily compromise that. And Piotr—"

"Yes, Vasiliy?"

"The Americans will expect much from you in exchange for this."

"I suspected that would be the case."

"Good. You must prepare yourself. Now get your family ready to leave on a moment's notice. A foreign submarine has no wish to linger on the surface in these waters. There is no doubt one will pick us up."

"I shall see to Irene and the boys, Vasiliy Ivanovich."

Denny Kolb, conning officer, called to the wardroom over the 21MC. "Picking up quite a few contacts, Captain. All fishing boats. We're headed into the midst of them."

"Good, Denny. Have sonar get us a few turn counts (propeller revolutions per minute). We'll put in a snorkel charge after dark. Like we did on the exercise, match sonar's input on one screw."

Sonar interrupted. "Conn, target identified. Engine running two minutes, stopped for five and run for two more."

Kolb asked, "Get that, Captain?"

"Got it, Denny. Make sure the target repeats this in an hour. Then call me and come to periscope depth to check him out. We'll have to make the rendezvous after dark, but not until we have a full can (fully charged battery)."

"Conn, aye, Captain."

Redmond, Zane and Ferranti sat alone in the wardroom to be sure everyone was on the same page as Redmond said, "If all goes well, the battery charge will be finished three hours before first light. We'll surface on the battery and approach our guy from astern."

Ferranti said, "I'm a volunteer for the boarding party, skipper."

Redmond grinned. "I think the required agility is not among your qualifications. You've been here and done that in forty-nine, I hear, but seventeen years is a long time. We need a younger man who knows his way around the superstructure in the dark. Appreciate your zeal, Rick, but we'll go with Denny."

Ferranti took no exception but like most early forties resented diminishing physical capabilities. However, this did not lessen his wish to be first to greet his old friend Norovsky.

"I'll be on the bridge in case you need a Russian speaker."

Only Rick knew it would be Norovsky who'd perform that function aboard *Tanya*.

Redmond agreed, "Actually, you'll be needed more on the bridge."

Clamagore finished her battery charge at 0300 and took station five hundred yards off *Tanya*'s port quarter.

After a report from sonar confirmed no contacts other than the fishermen, Redmond signaled Pace to raise number one periscope. A quick look around revealed only the distinctive red over white lights displayed on the fishing boats' masts per international rules of the road.

Denny Kolb and Ken Omensen stood by in the conning tower, dressed warm and with loaded forty-five pistols belted to their sides. Redmond told his boarding party they had certainly found the right boat, but just in case.

Redmond looked about his men. "Ready?"

Nods all around.

"Very well, sound the surfacing alarm."

Piotr Denisov walked from the bridge to awaken Norovsky for his watch, then heard air hissing like an angry snake as seawater ejected from *Clamagore*'s ballast tanks. He raced below and shook his friend from a sound sleep.

"Vasiliy! The submarine is here."

"You are certain?"

"Damn it man, have you forgotten I'm captain of a submarine. How could I not be certain?"

"Get yourself and family ready."

Norovsky heard the unmistakable voice of his old friend Rick Ferranti calling out in Russian.

"Stop engines and prepare to receive a boarding party. Two men."
Vasiliy yelled through cupped hands, "Stopped and standing by."
Clamagore came alongside and made up to the fishing boat.

Denny Kolb boarded *Tanya* and asked, "Do you speak English?"

The cantankerous Norovsky replied, "Better than you."

"Good! Have everyone lay topside with their gear," he said then showed surprise as the family Denisov climbed onto the main deck, dressed warmly and with all their belongings in a single canvas sack.

Denny thought, *Is that a woman or am I seeing things?*

As Omensen passed his charges to eager hands on *Clamagore*'s main deck, Denny informed Norovsky, "I am instructed to scuttle this vessel. Does it have seacocks?"

"Something better," Norovsky replied. He led Kolb below and showed him the blanket Piotr had jammed into a breach in the planking. "We used the blankets to keep the sea out. We shall remove them and let it back in."

The bilge began to flood rapidly as Kolb and Norovsky raced topside. There they found only Omensen, the Denisovs safely below decks in *Clamagore.* Kolb directed Omensen to assist Norovsky who needed no assistance at all and let it be known.

"Okay, sailor," Omensen ceded, "you next," then leapt across a widening gap between the ships with Denny following close behind.

As Omensen entered the sail door, a searchlight abruptly illuminated *Clamagore* followed by a burst of shots, likely from an AK-47 or similar small weapon.

"I'm hit," Denny yelled and fell face down on the main deck. Though firing continued sporadically, Omensen sprang from the door and hauled Lieutenant Kolb inside. There, two husky seamen dragged Denny to the conning tower hatch and lowered him through.

Redmond pulled the diving alarm and *Clamagore* settled beneath the waves.

The conning tower hatch secured, Redmond demanded, "I was told there were no warships near. What the hell?"

Ferranti answered, "Most of the fishermen carry weapons. They have to protect their catches sometimes if you catch my meaning. Some misguided nut figured he'd be a patriot."

Redmond snapped, "You got the conn, Exec. I'm going below to check on Denny. Make for the nearest international waters. Use the best speed to get us to dusk with one third battery capacity remaining."

"Aye, Captain."

Zane ordered number one scope raised and observed the last of *Tanya*, bow raised, still illuminated by the searchlight and slowly slipping beneath the waves.

The wardroom doubled as an operating room in the unlikely event it would be needed. This proved to be one of those events.

As Redmond entered the forward battery, he heard Denny yell.

"Not on my back, damn it. On my stomach."

Good. If he yells that loud, he can't be seriously hurt. Redmond entered the wardroom and found the ship's hospitalman removing Denny's clothing.

The captain asked, "Where did you get it, Denny?"

"Captain. The most inglorious wound a warrior can get. Right in the ass."

Turning to Hospital Corpsman Wilcox, Redmond asked, "What needs to be done?"

"Remove the bullet and clean out the wound. I've got to probe. It probably dragged a lot of stuff from his clothing in with it. Infection is the big worry."

"I'll leave you to it, Wilcox."

"One thing, Captain. I have no morphine and need your approval to use medicinal brandy. This is gonna hurt Mister Kolb a lot."

"As long as you save a shot for me, Doc."

Redmond went to the after battery to meet the rest of his new guests and did a double take on meeting Irene.

There goes my stateroom. He watched Ferranti and Norovsky express their relief that the mission portended success, but wondered. Sixty miles of Soviet territorial waters remained to be traversed. Redmond owed much of his success to Murphy (Murphy's law). *If something can go wrong, it will.* His planning always reflected this.

Ferranti made introductions, translating for the Denisovs. He followed protocol and introduced Irene first.

Redmond turned up the charm knob a few notches. For an instant, he considered asking her to assist Doc Wilcox, but considering the location of Denny's wound, opted against this.

Ferranti continued with introductions. "Phil, this is Captain 2nd Rank Piotr Denisov, recently of the Soviet Navy. And Vasiliy Norovsky. If I said who he is, I'd have to kill you."

The men shook hands. Neither Redmond nor Denisov would ever know how close their submarines came to mutual disaster seven months earlier in the Mediterranean. Next came the children, Pasha and Andrushka. Redmond thought they should not be permitted to hang out in the crew's mess. *It might not be the best place for them to learn English.* He'd discuss that with the COB. Bottom line, Redmond's crew, pleased with the diversion, especially Irene, liked having their guests aboard. Pasha and Andrushka had not gotten so much attention in their lives.

Later, Redmond visited Denny in the four-man bunkroom. "So how's it going, sailor?"

Feeling the effects of his medicinal brandy, he said slurring the words, "Sure wish I could've been wounded in a more dignified place."

"Denny, I'm glad it's minor. Doc tells me it cleaned out pretty good and he believes there's not much chance of infection."

Kolb said, "He gave me the bullet."

"I might have to take it back and toss it over the side. When you show it to people, they'll ask how you got it."

"Don't plan to show it around or talk about it, Captain. I don't need people knowing I got shot in the ass."

"In that case, keep it."

"Captain, if I can be serious."

"Sure."

"Worst part of what happened is how close I came to never seeing Jacqueline again. I've decided to skip your advice and not wait a year."

"It's that serious, Denny?"

"Stupid as this sounds, it is, Captain. I need her in my life."

"Denny, it's not stupid. Trust me. And what have you got to lose? Go get her, sailor."

Shifting gears again, Denny said, "Captain, I can't get a Purple Heart for this. What could I tell people when they asked how I got it? But maybe like with Giambri's missed Legion of Merit you can give me some basket leave instead ... to go to Palma?"

The next day passed happily, most of the focus on the crew's new guests. Irene came to terms with Rapinian having no wish for her to make omelets for the wardroom. She had no such problems in the crew's mess, where her pastries made a big hit.

Dusk came and after careful visual and sonar searches revealed no contacts, Redmond ordered the snorkel raised as *Clamagore* found herself thirty miles from international waters.

Redmond thought, *Nothing goes this smooth.* He called a council of war with Ferranti and Dave Zane.

"I just don't like this. I've never gotten away so clean in my life. Thoughts anyone?"

Dave asked, "Are we breaking the rules to get Denisov and Norovsky involved?"

Ferranti answered, "His bacon is every bit as much in the fire as ours. Maybe even more so with his family aboard."

Soon the Russians joined them and Redmond briefed their situation, including their inbound encounter with the Kashin. This piqued the interest of both Russians. Ferranti translated for Denisov.

Piotr described his encounter with *Proficient* a few days earlier. "She is a very capable ASW platform."

Redmond replied, "But from what we could tell, she patrols international waters, likely to prevent unknowns from entering the White. Once we're out there, she poses no problem."

"Secure snorkeling," boomed over the 1MC, bringing the discussion to an abrupt end then came the demanding voice of Benson Roman, "Captain to the Conn!"

In seconds, Redmond bounded up the ladder and into the barrel (conning tower). "What've we got, Benson?"

"Sonar picked up a single ping dead ahead and right on our track. Giambri's on the way to the shack (sonar room)."

Redmond berated himself. *How could I have been so stupid?* He reckoned the fisherman who spotted *Clamagore* radioed her position.

The Kashin skipper figured I'd head for the nearest international waters. He was right. What's done is done, and all that matters now is what happens next. Redmond focused on that.

Giambri reported on the 21MC, "A Hercules sonar, Conn. Likely the Kashin we encountered on the way in."

Redmond asked, "Any change in the BT?"

"Straight as an arrow, Captain. Couldn't be better for active sonar search."

"Was the ping strong enough to get an echo from us?"

"If we show more aspect, yes. But we're headed right at him, so he's not getting much."

Redmond said to Dave Zane who had followed him into the barrel, "Means if we turn to evade, he'll likely spot us."

"Agree, Captain."

"Get Denisov and Norovsky up here. Maybe they can shed some light that we're not getting."

The two Russians arrived and Redmond described their situation. He directed a question at Denisov who likely had exercised often with surface ships in the White Sea.

"What do you recommend, Piotr?"

"In this case, Captain, continue on this heading. I would proceed at maximum depth. His sonar doesn't look down very well."

Redmond scanned each face and read no dissent. "Benson, rig ship for deep submergence and make your depth four-zero-zero feet."

Clamagore proceeded to test depth, with ping intervals from the Kashin steady for maximum range.

Things went well and stress levels began to abate. Then Giambri's steady voice reported, "Target has shifted to short scale pinging."

Redmond had become master of not letting his voice betray inner concerns. "Benson, rig ship for depth charge."

All recognized forced steadiness in Giambri's voice, "Target increasing speed and turning right."

Denisov spoke up. "Recommend come immediately to sixty meters. He suspects you are deep and will set depth charges accordingly if he attacks."

They had not long to wait. The distinctive click-click sound of pistol activations, characteristic of U.S. depth charges (provided the Soviets on Lend-Lease during WWII) preceded two deafening explosions that shook *Clamagore* from stem to stern.

Sound powered phones had been manned throughout the ship to report damage. After each depth charge barrage, compartments simply identified themselves to assure they were still on the line. Damage would have priority and be reported immediately.

Damn, thought Redmond. *I'm proud of these guys.*

Denisov knew his family would be spared if he surrendered, for the crime against Mother Russia accrued only to him. "Captain. I beg you to surface and surrender. It's only me they want."

Redmond placed a hand on the young man's shoulder, knowing exactly where he came from. "You are mistaken, Piotr. No one knows you or Norovsky are here. It's me and my men they want. My guess is it'll be life imprisonment in the Gulag if we're caught. Getting sunk would be preferable to that. We'll try to escape by evasion, but if that fails—"

Norovsky winced. Sixteen years earlier, he too had tried to depth charge an American submarine into submission and lost his ship and crew in the process.

"I have the conn, Benson. Have sonar report target bearing every thirty seconds. We'll follow Captain Denisov's advice and make drastic depth changes on each pass."

He turned to Piotr. "I know you wish to be with your family, but the best way to protect them is for Vasiliy and you to stand by me. I'll likely need your advice."

Piotr spoke through the lump in his throat. "I understand, Captain."

As the Kashin made her second pass, Redmond dropped back down to test depth. The charges exploded above, but this time the maneuvering room reported, "Port shaft seal blown. Flooding. Pressurizing compartment."

Redmond knew this doomed his ship unless he took immediate defensive action. "Make your depth six-zero feet. Torpedo room, ready tubes one through six and open the outer doors. Set running depth ten feet, speed high. We'll shoot when she's making her turn."

Firing MK-14 torpedoes dead on provided the narrowest target and highest probability of miss, so Redmond optimized his chances by firing at the broadest possible aspect.

"I don't know how you're going to do it, Dave, but work out an optimum deflection angle for the turn."

"Aye, Captain."

On reaching periscope depth, Pace anticipated Redmond's order and had begun to raise number two scope.

Norovsky thought of the young officer from *Proficient* who boarded *Tanya.* For an instant he considered pleading with Redmond to not fire, but knew *Clamagore*'s CO must do what had to be done.

Redmond snapped the scope handles down and got a good look at the stern of his attacker. "Angle on the bow one-eight-zero and opening. Got that deflection angle for me, Dave?"

"I'll set a degree each between shots, twenty to twenty-five. Recommend fire on first indication of turn. Be sure to give me direction."

Zane knew his boss would do this automatically, but reminders are good in the heat of combat."

"You got it, Dave."

The attack party waited a minute … two minutes.

"Any indication of turn, Captain?"

"Nothing. More white water from her stern indicates greater speed. Get a confirmation from sonar."

Giambri reported, "Turn count increasing. Will get you a rate when she settles out. And conn. She's ceased echo ranging."

"What do you figure's going on, Norovsky?"

"Perhaps she knows she's backed you into a corner and your only option is to fight. They know where we are. By lengthening their runs and increasing speed, she'll be harder to hit with your torpedoes."

The commanding officer ordered depth charges in each attack to be set at various depths. "The contact is varying depth to evade. We will see to that."

A radio messenger approached and attempted to hand a clipboard to the *kapitan.*

"Not now. When we have finished off this swine."

A sense of urgency apparent in the messenger, a junior officer took the message. His eyes widened, and he said, "*Kapitan*, you must read this now."

> TO SOVIET SHIP PROFICIENT. CEASE
> ATTACK ON UNIDENTIFIED SUBMARINE AND
> WITHDRAW. US AND SOVIET TALKS TO
> REDUCE WARSHIP UNTOWARD INCIDENTS AT
> SEA COMMENCED IN MOSCOW THIS DATE.
> CONTINUING YOUR CURRENT ATTACK WILL
> JEOPARDIZE PROGRESS AND PLAY INTO
> AMERICANS HANDS.

Redmond watched until his nemesis disappeared below the horizon. "Can you believe this? He couldn't think he sunk us."

Zane replied, "Don't look to me for an answer, Captain."

"Okay, make for open water, but not directly this time. Hedge in the opposite direction of a good track for us. How's the can?"

Roman replied, "Dragged down quite a bit, Captain. Suggest secure from rig for depth charge, and we'll get some gravities (measure of battery capacity)."

"Make it so, Benson. Work us up a speed that'll get us to nightfall with half of what's now remaining."

The captain would not be cut short again.

A week later, *Clamagore* cruised on the surface in the North Atlantic on a westerly heading for home, her mission completed and successful. There would be no ceremony, nor distribution of awards, or even discussion among crew members on the amazing rabbit Redmond and his crew had pulled right out of Ivan's hat.

They'd simply be home again. To a man, they much preferred that.

Epilogue

April 1966—Doctor Jacqueline Junin looked up from her desk. Half an hour past closing the infirmary, she longed for the workday to end and return to her apartment. To Jacqueline's dismay her assistant announced another patient wished to be seen.

She heaved a sigh. "Is it important? Can it wait until tomorrow?"

"An American, Doctor. He says there's a problem with his heart only you can fix."

"*Bon Seigneur* (Good Lord)!" she gasped, "Dennis." She raced to the outer office and threw her arms about Denny's neck. Locked in their embrace, neither spoke for a full two minutes.

"Dennis, *mon* Dennis, you did come for me."

"You must have known I would."

"Yes, my heart knew, though my mind doubted ... but now you are truly here."

"This time I will not leave without you."

"I know that too, Dennis. And I will come with you."

Jacqueline apologized to her assistant and dismissed him.

A true Spaniard, he needed no apology and felt joyful over Doctor Junín's elation.

"Come ... please sit down, Dennis. There is much to tell you."

They sat on a reception room divan, hands locked each in the others. "I told Eugene of our trip to Capri."

Denny drew a quick breath, his eyebrows lowered.

"He was overjoyed that I found someone to love and who loved me."

Denny searched for words, but none came.

"Four years ago Eugene made peace with his circumstance, but knowing his accident ended our life together pained him greatly. He, again, begged me to have our marriage annulled and go to you. When I agreed, his expression of relief convinced me I did the right thing."

"My God, Jacqueline, what a loving and selfless man." *True love is letting go* came to Denny's mind and he easily saw the vast depth of Eugene's love.

"Eugene opened the door for what I want most desperately ... you to reenter my life."

Denny struggled for a response. "I want that too, more than anything. No words were exchanged, but you must have heard what my heart said to you in Capri?" Then he thought, *Wow. Did I say that?*

"I did hear your heart, Dennis. But in my letter, I said I would remain with Eugene and you wrote that you understood. How then could I hope you would come for me ... but I fervently prayed to that end. *Merci, Seigneur, de répondre à mes prières* (Thank you, Lord, for answering my prayers)."

"I had to return. To wait an entire year was impossible. My heart ached to see and hold you again." He raised a hand to her face and cupped it gently. *"Le coup de foudre (Love at first sight—thunderbolt love)?"*

Jacqueline's beautiful smile melted him. *"Le coup de foudre, mon cher* Dennis."

"The answer I longed to hear. Now, Doctor, my heart needs mending, do you think Capri could be more beautiful in April than it was in December?"

"Capri will always be beautiful to me, whatever the season."

June 1966—Piotr Denisov remained under interrogation for three months at a secret ONI facility. To his knowledge, no deal had been struck in which he would provide sensitive information in exchange for political asylum in America for his family and him. Much to the frustration of ONI questioners, Piotr told them nothing.

The Denisovs, under the witness protection program, found themselves located in the tiny town of Columbia Falls, Montana. A set of records showed them as natural born U.S. citizens, complete with social security numbers. ONI agents provided Piotr a job on the operations maintenance crew at Big Mountain ski resort where he demonstrated a superior work ethic.

Community college night classes started him toward a management degree. A burgeoning tourist industry, fueled in summer by nearby Glacier National Park and Big Mountain skiers in winter, provided opportunity for Piotr. Word of his work ethic preceded him and within three years found himself manager of a large motel in Whitefish.

Sons Pasha and Andrushka thrived on Big Mountain's ski runs—the older, Pasha, ultimately to make the American Olympic Ski Team.

Security considerations prevented Irene from meeting with Lorraine Ferranti to deliver Pasha Martinov's message to her. Irene gave it to Rick Ferranti who passed it to his wife.

Ferranti concluded, "What a nutty world. Eleven years ago, Pasha and I would eagerly have blown each other's brains out. Now I find myself delivering a tender message from him to my own wife." He wondered, *How did I ever let myself get caught up in this kind of business?*

September 1966—Rick Ferranti got himself out of *this kind of business.* With remarkably little fanfare, he came in from the cold (retired from the spook community), much to the relief of his *grandfather-in-law* Frank Gilliam. With each passing day, Frank found his chores on the farm progressively harder and thoughts of dumping them off on Rick appealed immensely.

The family Ferranti added a son and Lorraine stood at six months and counting with number two. She would exit her job at Johns Hopkins at eight point five months for maternity leave. In the meantime, babysitting chores bounced back and forth between Grandpa Frank and Daddy Rick who slowly overcame spook withdrawal pains.

In a year, Rick convinced Frank and Lorraine to reopen the bed and breakfast, his energy at an all-time high. Lorraine agreed more on the basis of Rick's desperate need for something to occupy his time, rather than belief in ultimate success. Between Rick's Navy retirement and Lorraine's substantial income at Hopkins, this could be undertaken with no financial risk.

When Frank asked who would cook, Rick had a ready answer. "A former colleague's significant other." He told of Vasiliy Norovsky's recent finding of Katya, the woman who escaped Russia with him seventeen years earlier. The passing of her husband, owner of a restaurant in the Bronx, left her widowed. Katya had no wish to remain in a big city despite help from her live-in companion, Vasiliy.

Ferranti had discussed prospects of their relocating to Maryland and both agreed, Katya driven by her strong desire to live in the country. As she had done on her arrival in America at the Wendt B&B in upstate New York, Katya brought success to Ferranti's brainchild in Maryland.

July 1967—Commander Phil Redmond left command of USS *Clamagore,* his chest adorned with four ribbons, all earned while enlisted: Expert Pistol, Expert Rifle, National Defense (called the *gedunk* medal by cynical sailors) and the Navy Good Conduct Medal (signifying he passed three years without getting caught doing anything). Despite his many unrecognized achievements, Redmond harbored no resentment. He belonged to the silent service, and in a sense relieved he'd not have to explain how he had earned any such decorations. The men he served with and cared about knew him and all he'd achieved. This by far exceeded satisfaction gained by any amount of fruit salad (decorations) spread over his chest. Camaraderie framed in those days would manifest itself in years to come, when former *Clamagore* crew would gather annually from across the nation just to pass a few days together. Though still not permitted to discuss their adventures, it would comfort them to be among shipmates who knew.

Redmond reported for duty at CNO OP-31 (Director of Submarine Warfare Office), the Pentagon. Katherine, for the eleventh time, picked up her family, moved them, and settled the children into new schools. David, now sixteen, took the move particularly hard. About to enter junior year at Ledyard High School he'd all but locked in a starting position on the football team. Now, David would have to prove himself all over again. Eleven-year-old Vera, veteran of four moves, found herself for the first time reluctant to leave friends at school. Katherine, in addition to managing logistics of yet another move, had to convince her children of the necessity for this. Theresa found it a new novelty and there can never be enough of these in the life of an eight-year-old. Wife and mother of a Navy family is a multifaceted and often not easy occupation.

Redmond found his work at CNO to contradict what he'd experienced during previous assignments, most of these at sea. Duty in Washington consisted mainly of participation in three-way squabbles among naval officers, civil servants and contractors. It didn't take long for Redmond to realize the balance of decision power resided between the latter two. *This is how it should be,* he thought. *The military must be subordinate to civil authority.* Far too many disastrous results of reversing this concept existed throughout the world.

With a strong background in tactics, Redmond decided he could best serve by focusing upon submarine combat systems requirements and requested reassignment to the Materiel Command. Here he ran into the same circumstance. Fueled by his inability to garner interest from the operational submarine community, now preoccupied with a different agenda, Redmond opted for retirement at the twenty-year mark, three of these accumulated in enlisted status.

Using his GI Bill to best advantage, Redmond prepared himself for the education field, first in evening classes while still on active duty, and then full time, ultimately earning a master's degree. Returning to the family home near New London, Commander Philip Redmond, USN (Retired) found employment as a teacher at Ledyard High School.

Dave Zane read the handwriting on the wall and followed paths taken by other competent diesel-electric submarine officers summarily booted from their chosen careers through arbitrary selection processes at Navy Nuclear Reactors.

Upon relief as executive officer of *Clamagore*, Dave said to his skipper, "Captain, it's been wonderful serving with you. Thanks seems so inadequate to express gratitude for all you've done for me."

Phil Redmond took his friend's hand. "I stopped being your captain five minutes ago. It's Phil now. Dave, the biggest debt is mine. Do you ever reflect on how much trouble you kept me out of? I could write a full-length book on that alone. Having you alongside elevated my confidence. Nothing like having an intelligent exec to keep a skipper from making mistakes. Every CO should have one good as you, Dave."

"Thank you, Captain."

"Phil."

"Sorry, Phil. Force of habit."

The family Zane uprooted from New London and made their way to Monterey, California where Dave entered U.S. Naval Post Graduate School. Upon graduation, he reported to the Commander, U.S. Naval Shipyard, Bremerton, Washington where he served until retirement.

The Zanes came to love Pacific-Northwest environs and elected to remain there.

U.S. nuclear power program officer selection criteria continued to include only top class standers. Emphasis within submarines accordingly shifted away from war fighting to propulsion related considerations, particularly reactor safety. A near perfect record validated this emphasis.

However, NATO Allies, Great Britain and France preserved the best of both worlds by dividing responsibility between war fighting and propulsion ends of the ship. This freed both factions to focus upon individual specialties with all inherent benefits. The practice is a long established one that has served the U.S. Navy well. Specialist officers of the line, engineering, supply and medical, man warships that perform efficiently in this circumstance.

Diesel-electric submariners, due to severely limited space, used line officers to perform all specialties, but always subordinated to line responsibilities. This approach disappeared mid-seventies as the Navy struck its last diesel boat from the active list.

Showdowns between U.S. and Soviet warships continued until the respective countries reached an agreement on prevention of incidents in airspace above and on the high seas, INCSEA (Incident At Sea) that has stood the test of time. It is possible Soviets regarded discussions with Americans tantamount to an achieved goal—U.S. recognition of the Russian Navy as a major naval power.

Both sides frequently used INCSEA as a political football. U.S. negotiators once announced social and informal sessions at an annual meeting would be curtailed or eliminated because of Soviet failure to apologize or pay compensation to the family of a U.S. Army officer killed by a Soviet sentry in East Germany.

However, INCSEA talks continued, likely contributing to no major untoward incidents at sea, though minor ones continued sporadically until dissolution of the Soviet Union.

July 1972—LCDR Paul Scott snapped to attention and rendered a crisp salute. "I relieve you sir," he said to the outgoing commanding officer of USS *Piratefish*, and at that moment became the first man in U.S. Naval history to command a warship he had served in as an enlisted man.

Jean Ann and the boys, Benjamin and David, now respectively thirteen and eleven, looked on proudly. Joanne, fifth member of family Scott, missed the event. Only six-months-old, the Scotts' daughter remained at home with a babysitter.

Piratefish had been upgraded to Guppy III configuration, familiar to Paul who passed a tour aboard *Clamagore*.

The event also marked the first reunion of the *Fearsome Foursome*. Denny Kolb, Benson Roman and Tim Keating, all of whom had relinquished bachelorhood, sat with their wives on the pier beside *Piratefish*. Jacqueline Kolb, just as at her first U.S. Navy event in Palma, turned every male head on the dock to follow her as though on a common swivel. Jacqueline and Denny had wasted no time. Five-year-old Eugene Kolb accompanied his parents, his dad often suggesting he rightfully deserved three citizenships having been conceived by a French mother and an American father on the Italian Island of Capri.

Mister Joe Dunn, division manager in a Massachusetts based firm that produced navigation equipment for ballistic missile submarines, also fell from the ranks of bachelorhood and attended with his wife.

That evening, the Dunns stayed over with Jean Ann and Paul per established custom. Aging had diminished the men's propensity for alcohol, but they continued long Navy related discussions well after their spouses turned in.

Paul had an experience in *Pershing* that got rehashed by the two men for easily the tenth time. His third patrol had been interrupted to conduct the first Polaris ORRT (Operational Readiness and Reliability Test). As Weapons Officer, Paul bore main responsibility for preparation and execution. He conducted himself to perfection, but the equipment did not. The ORRT involved taking an SSBN offline, replace four warheads with practice re-entry bodies, proceed to a pre-designated spot in the ocean and launch the four missiles into MILS (Missile Impact Locating System) within nineteen minutes of receiving a launch order. After twenty-four hours of system failure during separate attempts, *Pershing* made four launches, only one impacted in the MILS.

The exercise unmasked many shortfalls in a complex system that had been rushed too quickly into service, far more important than lucking out with hoped for perfect results.

System designers could generate fixes for isolated defects. However powers that be measured success with demonstration of excellent system performance. Paul stood to be the sacrificial lamb, but investigators could not uncover a single personnel error. Paul's reward: no disciplinary action would be taken.

Paul spoke of a subsequent discussion with Pete Williams, *Pershing* CO. "He told me after all was said and done, the lead investigator confided, 'Thank God we had Lieutenant Scott running the show, or this could have been a real disaster'. I believe the captain felt bad about what happened, but said it took all his effort just to keep the Type Commander from hanging me out to dry."

Joe added, "Were you surprised when he took early retirement? He was on the fast track (highly promotable) from what I could see."

Neither wished to make conjecture though both felt similarities between *Pershing*'s near sinking and *Trenchant*'s disaster haunted Williams as it did Joe and Paul.

Joe shifted subjects. "Well, old buddy, you gotta feel good about being CO, especially of the same pipe (vernacular for submarine) where you made silver dolphins (enlisted submariner badge)."

They shared a final cognac and turned in.

About Author D.M. Ulmer

 A 1954 graduate from the U.S. Naval Academy, retired Navy Captain D.M. Ulmer served thirty-two years in submarines and related assignments.

He has authored nine novels: *The Cold War Beneath, Silent Battleground* and *Shadows of Heroes*, (undersea action thrillers); *Count the Ways*, (a romance novel); *Missing Person, The Roche Harbor Caper* and *The Long Beach Caper*, (a trilogy of mysteries); and *Where or When*, (a historical novella). *The Cold War Beneath* is a sequel to *Shadows of Heroes*. Though Ulmer's submarine novels are fiction, a number of prominent submariners attest to their scenario and technical accuracies.

No surprise, Captain Ulmer continues to serve—now as a volunteer at the Seattle Museum of Flight and a local hospital. He has made many personal contacts in these capacities, some finding their way into his novels. Ulmer declares, "Everyone has a story that deserves to be told."

Captain Ulmer and his wife Carol live on Lake Sammamish in Redmond, Washington.

All of D.M. Ulmer's titles are available through patriotmediainc.com, amazon.com, and are also available as an Ebook on Kindle.

Other Books by D.M. Ulmer

Silent Battleground

The Cold War goes hot after Soviet Union attacks on U.S. Navy coastal installations and all but destroyed the American surface fleet. Ulmer moves the reader through tense combat events with skill using his 32 years of experience as a professional submariner to make this a page-turner complete with intrigue and speculation. Reviewers are touting this naval-action thriller about submarine warfare as the next Hunt for Red October.

Shadows of Heroes

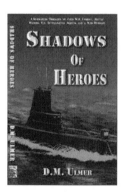

January 1949, early in the undeclared *Cold War*, the U.S. diesel-electric submarine *Kokanee* has illegally penetrated deep into Soviet Union waters of the White Sea and is detected by a pair of Russian destroyers. Depth charges fall on *Kokanee* and seem on the verge of tearing the besieged ship apart. A vindictive Russian captain is determined to eradicate the Americans.

The Cold War Beneath

The story of an event at sea off the New England coast during the post World War II years. Two submarines play a dangerous underwater game of hide and seek in this action thriller as U.S. Navy forces try to find out the Russians' true intentions for being in American waters.

Tea and *Crumpet Capers* by D.M. Ulmer

Upscale and sophisticated, light stories in the mystery/suspense genre.

Missing Person

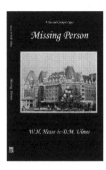

Retired Marine Corps Sgt Maj. Kincaid, turned Associate Professor of English Literature, moonlights as a writer of mystery novels. Approached by a woman *fan* who misconstrues his literary talent for bona fide detecting skills, she retains him to locate her son missing from her life for twenty years. Kincaid reluctantly accepts and finds himself in a quagmire of intrigue, greed, and murder. The drama is set in Port Angeles, near Washington State's magnificent Olympic Mountains.

The Roche Harbor Caper

In Washington State's San Juan Islands, during a weekend visit arranged by Michael Kincaid for his son to become better acquainted with the focal point of Michael's evolving romance, things go from bad to worse. Kincaid reopens a case with an official finding of accidental death many believed should have been murder. This leads to both Kincaid and his son being caught up in a wild adventure on the high seas.

The Long Beach Caper

Michael Kincaid, a retired Marine Corps Sgt. Major turned English Literature Professor, and his wife Doris, become involved in a caper while on their honeymoon in Long Beach, Washington. Their first day at Long Beach, a stranger recognizes Michael as the author of the Harry Steele detective novel series, introduces himself, then asks Michael to investigate a mundane problem within his family, keeping or disposing of their three generation legacy; the Heinrich Voelcker farm in Idaho.

Count the Ways

A grand romance in the classic sense. The love between a Naval Academy midshipman and an Iowa farm girl, a Korean War-era tragedy, and the search by a grandson for the mystery surrounding his grandparents' love story.

Where or When

An absorbing love story which spans the years set in modern-day life of the Pacific Northwest and the closing years of World War I in Europe.

Tour of USS Clamagore DVD by Brett Kneisly starring D.M. Ulmer

Filmed on location aboard USS *Clamagore*, a Guppy III diesel-electric submarine moored at Patriots Point, Mount Pleasant, SC. A former Commanding Officer of *Clamagore*, Captain Don Ulmer, USN Retired, is the tour guide. Video is presented to raise awareness of this Cold War veteran submarine's pressing need to be moved to dry land for protection and preservation for future generations.

Made in the USA
Charleston, SC
18 June 2012